# Praise for Shattered Allegiance

Shattered Allegiance is one of thos̶ ... If you enjoy historical fiction, you'll k̶ ... ...y ...eredith is an amazing author. She creates colorful characters who go through twists and turns that'll keep you guessing... It's a great book!

Christine Roseberry      November, 2020


Ms. Meredith has us following the lives of the Lexington, MacDonnogh, and MacDougal families in the early 1400s. "Shattered Allegiance" is the first installment of a trilogy that draws us into this world of intrigue on the borders of Scotland and England. Ms. Meredith explores how each side acts and reacts as the story unfolds, covering battles, spies, relationships, and death. Loved the details as to how the day-to-day living is revealed in this first book of the trilogy.

Nancy Fram      November, 2020


The characters of "Shattered Allegiance" caught my attention right away! You are instantly drawn into the world of 1400s England and Scotland.  This historical fiction book details the lives of two different families, one a wealthy English family, and the second a poor Scottish family from a clan over the border from England.

A wonderful story follows as Ms. Meredith details the love they have for their countries and families. You are also drawn into the unlikely love that develops between two of the characters, Edward and Kit, from these drastically different homes.

While reading "Shattered Allegiance" you will become invested in the lives of each character. You will not want to put the book down until the end and you see how the story concludes for these people who have become your friends.

Elayne Courts      November, 2020

# Other Books by Kay Meredith

### *Affair at Boreland Springs*  ISBN 978-1944662363

This book does everything a great book should do—grabs you at the beginning and leaves you wanting a sequel.    Debi Sutton

Let me warn the reader that once Kay has you under her spell, you will not be able to put this book down.    Linda Zang

Kay Meredith excels as a story teller. She is a master wordsmith; her use of colloquialisms entertain the reader. The reader visualizes the past…in this case, into West Virginia in the early 1900s when bootlegging moonshine provided a livelihood for families eking out an existence. Affair at Boreland Springs…out of personal tragedy comes a triumphant piece of American Literature. H. Robert Belton.

### *A Distant Whistle*  ISBN  978-1944662417

This book captures your interest from the very first page. You want to keep reading to see what adventures will happen to Nev, his family, and friends. Along the way you feel like you've been transported back in time to the early 1900s of West Virginia, and the amazing lives of the river steamboat workers.    Elayne Courts

Kay Meredith's style is similar to Danielle Steel in the way the characters are developed. Kay has followed the life of a young man from a poor family through his "growing up" years, putting as much life into his emotional journey as his physical development. This book is well done and a very enjoyable read.    Bean

Great book. Super plot that moves along rapidly. Super details without bogging down.    Sandra D.

# Shattered Allegiance

## Highlanders' Legacy Series

### Book I

# Shattered Allegiance

## Highlanders' Legacy Series

## Book I

# A Historical Novel by
# Kay Meredith

*Kay Meredith*

ISBN: 978-1-944662-56-1

Cover Design by Michael Scott, MASgraphicarts.com

# *Dedication*

This book is for Cecil Arthur Huggins and Elma Sweeney Huggins, beloved parents who were adventurers in their own right and supported me in all my efforts to prove that a child of Appalachia could follow dreams that led me all over the world competing for my country with my horses.

To Chris Roseberry, a best friend and my "adopted daughter."

To Diane Tauber, my lifelong friend and fellow traveler.

# *Acknowledgments*

There is so much appreciation in my heart for my long-suffering friends, you know who you are, who faithfully read all my books and asked for more. I will forever be in your debt.

# *Table of Contents*

**PART TWO**

# Main Characters in *Shattered Allegiance*

**MacDonnogh family...***Scottish family who had moved from the Highlands to The Borders:*

Liam ................................................father

Margaret...........................................mother

Colin.................................................son

Enid .................................................daughter

**Lexington family...***English gentry and owners of Lexington Estate:*

Lord Neville.....................................father

Lady Anne .......................................mother

Edward.............................................son

Gwen ...............................................daughter

Ned ..................................................blacksmith at Lexington Estate

Wren ................................................worker at Lexington Estate

Orville & Mildred Kingsley...........English couple who work at
Lexington Estate

Henry Asheboro .............................owner of the estate next to the
Lexington Estate

**MacDougal family.......***Scottish family who live in the Highlands.*

Hamish.............................................father & Laird of the MacDougal Clan

Malcolm...........................................son

Kit ...................................................daughter

Oliver Gordon.................................young boy who lives with the
MacDougal Clan

MacKenzie.......................................blacksmith for the MacDougal Clan

# PROLOGUE

### Borders between England and Scotland

Lexington Cove, a pimple on the route through northern England into the infamous Borders that separated Scotland and England, sounded grander than it was.

A traveler to this part of the realm was brave indeed, for life in the Borders was always perilous. Henry IV, who had seized the throne from Richard II in 1399, was by this time tired in mind and body. He lacked the power or desire to legislate order in this isolated northern region of England. Thus, the Borders was a wild and lawless place where control changed hands between the Scots and English on a regular basis and it was often difficult to distinguish friend from foe.

Lexington Cove was located in the Borders not far from Berwick, and was surrounded by a group of small estates owned by minor English landowners. Insignificant in relation to Henry's bigger problems, these estates were left to fend for themselves as best they could. Therefore, the Lexington Cove landowners had organized militias to protect their territory from anyone, Scots or English, wishing to conquer their land. The goal of the militia was to establish a reputation for ruthlessly defending their holdings.

Their easiest prey were the poor Scots who, along with a large population of English, lived in the Borders. The Lexington Cove militias raided the farms of the Scots, destroying their homes, murdering the inhabitants, and stealing or killing their livestock. The Scots, with few weapons and little cash, used wit and sabotage to exact their own brand of revenge to kill anyone who attacked them.

The fighting between the poorly equipped Scots and the powerful English gentry was brutal, unfair, and constant. This unusual mix of English and Scots in such close proximity provoked many bloody incidents and any semblance of peace was a facade to be broken at the slightest excuse.


The most popular place for the villagers of this humble community to congregate was a tavern called The Boar's Head Inn. Like Lexington Cove, the name proclaimed a loftiness sadly lacking in its physical state.

The day had begun with the consistency of porridge and only worsened with time The weather was better suited for drinking and reminiscing than working. The inn filled early with an assortment of men folk of the servant class spending their last shilling on bitter ale while offering profound political opinions.

At one table, four men, whose tongues were loosened by brew, loudly pronounced the deficiencies of the English monarchy.

They proclaimed that it was necessary for the poor English folk to take matters into their own hands because nobody in London seemed to care what happened on the fringes of the kingdom.

"God 'lone knows why anyone'd wanna help them heathen Scots," one of the revelers insisted. "Henry oughta come to the Borders 'n see what havoc they cause. Then he'd pay more attention to the welfare of 'is countrymen." The others loudly agreed.

The leader waved his mug high, splashing his companions with the sticky liquid. "If ole Henry can kidnap young James 'n hold 'im hostage, I say we need to rid ourselves of a few more Scots right here!" He thumped the goblet down hard and looked around to see if anyone was listening. Only his cronies nodded their bleary heads in an effort to prove they were as knowledgeable as the speaker. Liquid slimed unnoticed down their slack jaws.

"Aye, let's show them Scots who's in charge here," squeaked a pimply-faced cohort.

"C'mon then," yelled the self-appointed leader, his chest puffed out with importance. With that, the four men stumbled from the inn to take up their support of England. Their departure was noted by no one, and the space they left was soon filled with four more of the same ilk.

As the men went into the soggy night, they pulled their shabby over-tunics close against the whistling wind and darkening sky.

Ten-year-old Enid MacDonnogh lay sprawled across her parent's pallet sound asleep. One arm clutched her rag doll Molly while her other hand lay softly on the tail of her gray cat, Agnes. Her mother's fish stew and warm bread had nearly lulled her to sleep at the table. Finally, her father had carried her up the steps to the loft and laid her on the bed. She dreamed of butterflies that would come with spring, gliding on gentle breezes, with wings as bright as the stained-glass windows in the little chapel in Berwick. Shadows from the flickering candles bounced off the highlights of her long red hair, surrounding her face with a soft pink halo.

Enid clutched her doll tightly as the dream suddenly turned mean. The beautiful butterflies were washed away by a storm so powerful that pieces of her home collapsed in the face of such fury. The front door fell with a loud crash, permitting the wind to howl through. Her mother's precious dishes were broken and the table and chairs upended. Enid ran, trying to save what she could, but men kept getting in her way. Her mother lay across the big oak chair and her father's face was covered with blood.

"Why won't you help me?" she screamed to the men. They didn't hear her. "Brian, Arnold! Help me pick my mother up." Still they ignored her. In desperation, she yelled at the others. "Ephram, Benjamin. Papa's bleeding!"

Then all was quiet. Her lungs filled with the nippy air left by the vicious squall and she could taste salt on her lips that were brushed by the ocean spray. Once again Enid slept on the soft crest of a pillow filled with down from the farm geese as the gale, spent and impotent, slid off to the west.

"Enid! Enid!"

Someone was shaking her shoulder in a rough way that hurt. She pulled the offensive hand away and looked up. Through the edges of sleep she recognized her brother Colin. He stood above Enid, his eyebrows knitted together in a frown.

"Colin, stop hurting me!" she ordered.

"What happened?" he asked, continuing to jostle her, although a bit more gently.

"Nothing. I just fell asleep after supper and Papa brought me here while you were doing your barn chores."

Colin pulled her to the corner of the loft. "Look down there." He turned her so she could see into the kitchen below. It was a scene of total destruction.

"It's a dream, Colin," she said calmly. "It isn't real."

"It *is* real, Enid. Everything's broken and Ma and Pa are dead!"

*He's mistaken,* she thought. *I saw it all in my dream. Only a dream.*

Colin gathered her in his arms and carried her toward the steps. "You must have seen someone."

Enid nodded. "It was Ephram, Benjamin, Brian, and Arnold. They were in my dream." *Why can't he understand there's nothing to be so upset about.* "We see them every Sabbath at chapel."

Colin shook his head in her face. "It wasn't a dream, Enid!" She sniffled at his fierceness. He softened. "Come. We must go to the Kingsleys." He began to dress her in the warmest clothes he could find.

"Why?" she cried.

"Look!" He made her stand still and look at the room before her. Their mother's broken body was lying in Liam's old chair—a thin rope tied tightly around her neck. Her right hand still held the knife she'd used to defend herself. Then he forced her to look at Liam, face down beside his wife—an axe lodged in his back. "That's why," he whispered.

Enid's face wrinkled, her chin quivered, and her chest filled with sobs. "It wasn't a dream then," she said, turning her face into Colin's neck to shut away the unspeakable sight. He was careful with her then, taking her hand and leading her out of their home, where nothing would ever be the same again. As they walked toward the barn he tried once more to learn what had happened.

"Tell me again who they were, Enid."

"Brian, Arnold, Ephram, and Benjamin," she answered tonelessly.

"What did you see them do?"

"Ruin everything," she answered. "Mama, Papa, and all the house. That's all I remember."

*It's hopeless,* he thought. *She's said all she's going to.* They put the saddle on Old Jeff and prepared for the trip to the Kingsleys. "We mustn't tell anyone about your dream," Colin said.

"I won't." Enid's mind had already shut away the sight of her dead parents. To her it would always be a bad dream that had ruined her life forever.

"The Kingsleys will ask. What will we say?" asked Enid. "That it was too dark for you to recognize anyone. My being in the barn will explain why I don't know who did it."

Colin struggled to erase the sight of his parents when he'd returned from the barn that night. He tried to forget his shame at not being able to close his mother's eyes nor pull the axe from his father's back. He wanted to take back his revulsion at the thought of touching his parents, who were so badly mutilated. He knew his mind would never let him forget. It would follow him on whatever path he traveled for the remainder of his life.

"Colin, why would they do this?" Enid sniffled.

"Because we're Scots."

"But we've lived here all our lives."

"Doesn't matter. We're still Scots and they're English. And most English and Scots hate each other."

"But. . ."

"Hush, Enid. It's done. We must think of a way to survive now without allowing the English to take our home away from us. Mildred and Orville will help."

"But they're English too. Won't they hate us for being Scots?"

"They're different. They're old and they have no children of their own. They don't care that we aren't English."

"Are you certain?"

"Yes," he said, trying not to lose his patience with her. "Rest now." Colin tried to sound confident but his own heart thudded with fear, hatred, and confusion. He, too, worried about what would happen to them.

As they approached the stream that separated the MacDonnogh farm from Lexington Estate, Colin heard Enid muttering. "What are you saying?"

"That I'll never forgive them." Colin was taken aback at the strength and determination in her declaration.

Both children were silent as they continued their journey to the Kingsleys. Each was remembering the many stories their parents had told them about their MacDonnogh family home in Scotland.

*Colin, who was twelve and thought of himself as a "grownup", had never tired of hearing how, fifteen years earlier, Liam, the middle son of a minor landowner north of Edinburgh, had married his childhood sweetheart, Margaret. Over and over, he and Enid insisted on hearing how the two young lovers had pooled what money and supplies their families could spare and journeyed south to the Borders. Here the soil was better for farming and the climate made working outdoors more tolerable. Liam and Margaret had settled on eight acres of land that included a bluff overlooking the North Sea. The land was near Berwick, a small but important shipping port that frequently changed hands during the fierce warring between the English and Scots.*

*In addition to tending his own plot of ground, Liam found work as a carpenter for the Lexington family who owned an estate on the English side of the Borders. The Lexingtons, Lord Neville and Lady Anne, were English gentry who wished for peace in the Borders. Experience had taught them that all landowners profited when the peasants spent their time farming and harvesting instead of preparing for war. Since Liam was a superior carpenter, they had no qualms at allowing a Scotsman to become part of the Lexington Estate work force.*

*The MacDonnoghs were befriended by an older, childless couple, Mildred and Orville Kingsley, who also worked for the Lexingtons. In time the Kingsleys made up, in part, for the family the MacDonnoghs had left behind in Scotland. Mildred and Orville treated Colin and Enid like their own grandchildren. As brother and sister grew up in a region primarily peopled by the English, they retained only a tinge of their parent's Scottish brogue.*

Old Jeff stumbled, jostling Enid. She sighed. "Can we go to live with our relatives in Scotland?"

"No. It's out of the question," replied Colin, with a hint of irritation.

"Why?"

"Because they've never seen us. Probably don't even know we're alive."

Enid snuffled. Colin mellowed. "We're not old enough to find our way to Scotland. We've no money and no idea where the MacDonnoghs live." She cried softly against his back. "Don't worry," he continued. "I know we'll be welcomed at the Kingsleys. You'll see. We'll be there soon." She hiccupped once, then was silent.

Even in the bright moonlight nothing looked familiar. The little brook that was normally unruffled now swirled in muddy torrents around Old Jeff's legs. He slipped once or twice but then with a mighty leap he reached the other side, nearly unseating his two small passengers. The big horse stood still for a moment before plodding on, allowing Colin and Enid a chance to resettle themselves.

Wordlessly they rode on. Only the sucking sound of Old Jeff's feet as he clambered through the mud, and an occasional clap of distant thunder broke the silence. When at last the silhouette of the Kingsley cottage came into view, they could barely hold themselves on the horse's broad back. Colin slid off and went to the door. His harsh pounding brought Orville's old dog, Bowser, into full cry.

Inside the little house Orville's breath swooshed out of him when Mildred poked him in the ribs. "Orville! Git up 'n see what's got that dog in an uproar."

"Wh...wh...what on earth?" Orville stammered. "Who'd be hammerin' on our door this late at night?"

He lumbered out of bed, pulled his old robe around him, and made his way to the door. The sight of the two sodden children, illuminated by the moonlight, jarred him from all drowsiness. Enid slipped off Old Jeff and came to stand beside Colin. They were shivering and wearing clothes that were torn and muddy. Enid clutched her doll under one arm and both were so exhausted they could hardly speak.

"What's this?" Orville asked, pulling the children into the room just as Mildred arrived rearranging her nightdress.

She took one look at the children, then smothered them both into her soft bosom. "What's wrong children? Why 're ye here at this time of night without yer parents?"

"They're dead, Aunt Mildred," Colin replied quietly.

"What'd ye mean 'they're dead'?" She sounded angry. "They were fine this mornin.'"

With eyes fastened on his feet, Colin recounted the destruction he'd found upon returning to the house from his barn chores that night. He told the Kingsleys that, because the storm was so loud, Enid had slept through the entire intrusion and that neither knew who had killed their parents. Enid nodded throughout Colin's explanation. Mildred and Orville looked at one another bewildered.

"Orville, git over there." Mildred ordered. "Find out what they're talkin' 'bout. Sometimes children make mistakes."

Orville had already started making preparations to leave. He put on his heavy cloak, wrapped a wool muffler around his head, and lit a torch to show the way.

"Be careful," she warned. "We don't need any more catastrophes tonight." The door slammed shut as Orville mounted Old Jeff and rode into the night.

Mildred looked down at the children before her. *What to do,* she wondered? She took a deep breath and pushed a stray strand of hair out of her eyes. "Come," she said, as she guided them to the hearth that offered some warmth from the dying embers of the day's fire. She added more wood bringing it back to life. "Sit 'n warm yerselves here while I git somethin' to fill yer stomachs."

Mildred bustled about the kitchen fetching hot cider, bread, and butter. Then she bundled the children in goose down blankets and put them at the table. Neither made a move to eat. "Here now," she admonished. "Ye look half-starved. Eat afore ye collapse from hunger." Enid nibbled at the bread and took a few sips of the cider. Her feet dangled limply, like part of her rag doll. Colin held his head with one hand and picked at his food with the other.

"Can't either of ye remember anythin' 'bout the men who did this?"

Colin shook his head while Enid busied herself with Molly.

"They gotta be brought to justice," Mildred continued, with a slight touch to Colin's shoulder.

This time Enid answered. "Aunt Mildred, it was so dark and the thunder so loud I never heard their voices or saw a face. Only when Colin came did I know what terrible thing had happened."

Mildred dropped her shoulders in exasperation. "Can't imagine all that goin' on 'n neither of ye heard." Enid stared hard at Colin, a harsh reminder in her eyes of the pact they'd agreed to. He nodded slightly.

Being Scots, Colin and Enid knew that mentioning the names of the attackers, who were all Englishmen, could bring harm to them even though they were only children. While the Lexingtons were tolerant of all honest people and would never condone the murders of Liam and Margaret, there were many in the community who had always disapproved of Sir Neville hiring the couple to work on the estate. These people would approve of the killings, believe the children should forfeit the land Liam had purchased, and be put to work as servants.

When the two had eaten all they were going to, Mildred steered them to her bedroom. "Let's git ye to bed. Ye'll fall asleep just sittin' there if we don't do somethin' fast."

From the bottom of a trunk Mildred pulled some nightclothes worn when she and Orville were younger and smaller. She held them up for inspection. "Well, they're not purty, 'n they're nearly wore out, but they'll do. Tomorrow I'll git to Lexington Estate. There's lots of children yer size who'd be happy to share."

Colin retreated to the darkest corner of the little room, turned his back to Mildred, and put the clothes on as fast as he could. Enid sat meekly on the bed with her hands clasped in her lap. Mildred looked at the child whose eyes reflected exhaustion and fear. "Don't fret, love." She put a comforting arm around the tiny shoulders and gently changed her into sleeping clothes. "Orville 'n me'll take care of ye both."

Enid threw her arms around Mildred's neck and cried until Mildred feared her little heart would burst. When the sobs finally became sniffles Mildred carried her, followed closely by Colin, and they climbed to the loft where both were soon overtaken by the sleep they so sorely needed.

Orville rode to the MacDonnogh home as fast as he could, slid off Old Jeff, and entered the house over the fallen door as his heart thumped with dread. He held the flame high casting light throughout the room, illuminating the devastation that was everywhere. Nothing—chairs, table, or cupboard—remained whole. As he turned the flame to light all the corners, he saw Margaret and Liam. In the leaping torchlight they looked like sacrifices in an ancient Druid ceremony. Not the two people he'd seen just that morning, laughing and joking, happy to be alive. The loss of these friends he and Mildred loved as their own was beyond believing. Killed with less consideration than one would slaughter a farm animal.

After securing the torch in the wall sconce, Orville, a man for whom buttons were a task, cared for his friends with the gentleness of a mother hen. Even though he knew she couldn't feel anything, it was hard for him to use a knife to cut the rope from Margaret's neck. He forced his fingers to close her eyes, removed the knife from her hand, then laid her on the floor. Orville had not reckoned the strength it took to pull the axe from Liam's back. As he felt muscles give and heard bones grind, he tried not to think about the terrible death his friends had suffered. When finally, the mangled bodies of Margaret and Liam lay close together, Orville looked down upon them and, with head bowed, mouthed a prayer. Brushing the wetness from his face with a gnarly hand, he turned and left the home with an energy born of revulsion.

Mildred was dozing in Orville's old chair when the scraping sound of the front door roused her. Rubbing her eyes, she watched her husband shuffle into the room. His jowls sagged, etching deep wrinkles in his cheeks. His normally merry blue eyes were obscured by hooded lids. She pulled herself up and went to him. He held her shoulders close and rested his chin on her head. They remained so for a time.

"Come," she said softly. "Sit 'n I'll bring ye some ale." She guided him like a child to the chair, then went to the kitchen and returned with his mug. "Drink this. Then tell me what ye found."

Orville swigged his ale while Mildred kneaded his shoulders. When he'd finished the ale, he ran his fingers through his bushy gray hair and told her what he'd seen that night. He left nothing out; all the destruction; and the violation of Liam and Margaret.

For awhile the two were lost in thought. When they could think no more, they plodded off to bed. Mildred repositioned her sleeping hood while Orville circled the room and snuffed the candles. Thankful for a chance to escape the senseless events of that night, Orville snuggled close to his wife's amply padded body. Soon his breathing slowed and rumbled in a soft snore.

Sleep eluded Mildred. She laid her head in the crook of his shoulder. "We can't let them children loose on their own."

Orville turned away in a futile attempt to avoid the discussion he knew would bring questions better left alone.

Mildred would not be put off. "What family they've got in Scotland could probably never be found, 'n wouldn't want two more mouths to feed anyway." She leaned over his face, tickling his cheeks with her feathery breath. "Who's to say tisn't God's way to give us children?" She shook him gently. "Orville?"

Exasperated, he sat up and faced his wife, hoping to put an end to talk when sleep was what they needed. "We're too old to take on little ones."

"Fer pity's sake, Orville. No one's ever too old to take care of children. If they don't wanna stay with us, they can say so."

"They're Scots, Mildred!"

She moved even closer. "They're God's children! We've known 'em since they was in the crib. We could be parents to 'em."

"We'll see," he replied, as he lay down, giving up the struggle. "We'll see."

The following afternoon Margaret and Liam were buried under a thicket of oak trees in the meadow where they had played with their children. Few watched as the rough-hewn coffins were placed into the ground. The children held tightly to the hands of Orville and Mildred.

Colin vowed that someday he would avenge the brutal murders of his parents.

Enid cried soundlessly, and in her childlike way she asked God's forgiveness for the hate she would always carry for those who had killed her family.

# CHAPTER ONE

It had been three years since Liam and Margaret had been murdered. Colin had reluctantly immersed himself in life at Lexington Estate, Enid had held staunchly to her Scottish heritage, and Henry V had succeeded his besieged father. The citizens of England tried to achieve a modicum of normalcy in a country at odds with itself and foreign powers – not unlike the plight of Colin and Enid MacDonnogh.

Few places on earth can match the softness of an English summer. At Lexington Estate, in the charm of muted sun and lush foliage, it was time for the annual children's lawn party. Colin MacDonnogh pulled the clutched hand of Edward, heir to Lexington Estate, away from his shoulder. Sometimes the persistence with which this son of the gentry stuck to him annoyed Colin.

"You needn't hold onto me. I'd not run off from you this deep in the forest."

"Sometimes you do," came the answer from the dark-eyed lad who was two years younger than Colin.

At thirteen, Edward of Lexington was a study in contrasts. He and Colin were searching for mushrooms to take back to Mildred for the lawn party that evening at Lexington Estate. On this day Edward was serious -- concerned that no mistakes were made in the selection for such an important event. It was the summer children's gathering that Lord Neville and Lady Anne had each year for all the children of the peasants who worked for them.

Most of the time however, Edward was a fun-loving fellow always at the ready to play a joke on his companions. He took particular glee in frightening his sister, Gwen, by jumping out at her from behind the hedgerows when she was engrossed in selecting flowers for a special occasion. He took a care though not to provoke Colin, whom he had idolized since Colin and his sister Enid had come to be educated by the Lexington tutor three years earlier. It had been after drunken English peasants from the Lexington Cove area had massacred their parents.

Edward wished Colin were more enthusiastic about being his best friend. "Why don't you like me?" he asked, with the forthrightness that always unnerved Colin.

"I like you alright, Edward. Why would you ask such a ridiculous question?"

"You often seem unfriendly towards Gwen and me."

"It's just your imagination," Colin answered brusquely.

"Do you blame us for your parents being gone?"

"You mean murdered, don't you?" Colin looked up at him from his crouched position. "Of course, I don't blame you. How could children like you be responsible for that?"

"Who do you blame then?"

"All Englishmen, both high and low born, who feel the Scots have no right to live in their own land."

"Oh," Edward said and looked at the ground.

Colin was chagrined. He actually liked this young heir to the big estate. Edward never passed anyone, regardless of status, without friendly words of greeting. "Oh, come now Edward. I was teasing," Colin relented. "The only time I'm upset is when your reading outshines mine."

Colin clapped Edward on the back and laughed enthusiastically, returning the lad to his affable self. No one could resist Edward's nearly black eyes and ebony hair that constantly fell over his forehead giving one the impression they were speaking to someone behind a delicate face mask. "We'd best get these mushrooms to Mildred before she has both our hides," Colin said with a laugh. Edward nodded in agreement.

The two comrades walked back to the mansion, skipping stones and cuffing shoulders along the way. When Mildred finally received the long-awaited mushrooms, a specialty normally reserved for wealthy adults, she blistered their ears unmercifully for the tardiness.

Enid sat sullenly under a mulberry tree, shielded by its branches from the festivities taking place on the Lexington lawn. Her bright red hair cascaded down her back stubbornly escaping the yellow ribbon Mildred had worked on so painstakingly. Enid didn't care. "No matter how many parties they invite us to it will never make up for what they did to us," she muttered to Rex, who was always at her side. "Regardless of how often Colin says we should take advantage of the education we're getting I shall never teach English children!" Rex cocked an ear and licked her hand.

In the three years since she'd watched her parents die, Enid had remained locked in the pain of that night. Colin insisted she be polite and that she was. However, she never showed any appreciation for the privileges the Lexingtons showered on her and Colin. Secretly she admitted it wasn't Lord Neville and Lady Anne's fault. And truth to tell it was difficult to ignore Gwen's overtures of friendliness. Gwen, with her delicate coloring and awkward body, was so opposite from her brother Edward. Enid knew Gwen envied *her* glistening red hair and compact stature. But Enid had made a vow to avoid all the English. There would be no exceptions.

Gwen was dancing with several of the children. Soon they would play blind man's bluff. Everyone loved it when Gwen was blindfolded, because with her long legs she often stumbled and landed in a heap -- waiting for one of the peasant children to help her up. While she laughed with them, in truth, she despised her height and loose-jointedness. Now at age eleven, she prayed every night that her long platinum hair would be transformed into a heavy mass of curls like Enid's.

Lord Neville and Lady Anne watched the frolicking young people from the circular veranda that formed the main entrance to their spacious home.

"Seems like Colin is becoming more tolerant of Edward," Lord Neville observed.

"Yes, my love. I actually overheard the two of them laughing uproariously at some joke they'd pulled on Gwen last week."

"That would be when they put a frog in her flower basket," Neville harrumphed. Anne looked at him with eyes full of mischief. "I see you're not upset with that little episode," he continued with an indulgent tone.

"No, dear. Anything that brings them closer won't hurt Gwen in the long term. I just wish we could break through the shell Enid lives within. She must be so unhappy. What can we do?"

"Nothing other than what we're doing now. Just continue to love her and overlook her air of dislike." He stroked his bearded chin. "Perhaps I shall try to bring her back something special when next I travel to London."

With that the two of them walked down to mingle through the happy crowd and enjoy the robust laughter.

# CHAPTER TWO

It was 1416, a year since Henry V had defeated the French at Agincourt establishing England's status as a European power. Colin had become a part of the Lexington Estate's armed fighters; Enid's resentment of her life among the English was deeper than ever; and Scotland was torn between those in the north who were loyal to the Scottish king and the Border dwellers who often sympathized with England.

At Lexington Estate, Edward choked back the laughter that bubbled for release as he put a hand down to help Colin to an upright position. It wasn't often the magnificent young Scotsman was unhorsed by a jouster two years his junior and four inches shorter.

"Just luck," Colin squeaked, from lungs that were short on breath. "Your run started before the command was given leaving me little time to raise my lance."

"Don't be such a spoil sport, Colin. You've knocked my arse into the dirt ten times to every one time I get you. Can't you admit that everyone has bad timing now and then?"

Colin chuckled in spite of himself. "Aye, Edward. That was a good and honest thrust. Before long both of us will be ready for a real battle." Peace restored, they trudged off the practice field and home to a hearty meal.

Colin still couldn't recollect how Edward had stopped being a nuisance and become his closest companion instead. He supposed it was probably because everyone else was older and laboring at all the jobs required on an estate that provided most of the staples for all its residents, man and beast alike. And there were no other Scots at Lexington Estate for him to befriend.

Therein lay the crux of Colin's dilemma. Those many years ago both he and Enid had vowed to avenge the deaths of their parents by the English. But being so young they didn't know how to bring this about -- just that they would never become sympathizers with the English. Enid had maintained that declaration, remaining aloof from the Lexingtons and refusing to express appreciation for their efforts on the behalf of the MacDonnogh orphans.

"I, on the other hand, have become a part of the English community," Colin whispered to himself, while he watched Edward enter the back entrance to Lexington Estate. As he let his horse meander the familiar distance from the estate to the tiny MacDonnogh home called Windcrest, he searched through all the twists and turns of his life trying to understand how he'd come to this point. It was a raw spot which caused ill will between Enid and himself that had worsened with each year.

He pondered for some time. It was difficult for him to accept his reason for capitulating, (for that's how he perceived it). Colin knew in his heart that he'd had no other choice. While Enid could harbor her hate and keep her distance, it had been up to him to provide the best life he could for the two of them. Had he been as truculent as she, it would never have behooved Lord Neville and Lady Anne to take in the two orphans to educate and include in the Lexington activities. Were it not for the intervention of Lord Neville, Windcrest would have been confiscated by other landowners without so much as an eye blink after the deaths of Margaret and Liam. Acquisition of land belonging to Scots was heartily applauded by most Englishmen.

When the single chimney of Windcrest came into view, Colin gave up the impossible task of winning Enid over to his strategy. *She's sure to flatten my ears when she comes home this evening,* he mused. *Why does she refuse to believe that cooperating with the English is the easiest journey through our lives? I know of no other means to survive in an area where nobody trusts anyone and everybody is judged by which side of the Borders commands one's allegiance.* He sighed and headed to the barn to milk the cow.

Enid had watched through the Lexington mansion's kitchen window as Edward and Colin rode in together from their day at the practice field. She ignored Edward's hearty "hello" as he ran past her into the formal part of the house. *They laugh together with their private jokes as though they were blood brothers,* she thought bitterly. *I know Colin needs the friendship of another young man but why does it have to be an Englishman? We should have gone to Scotland to grow up with other Scots. We may not have had the advantages the Lexingtons have given us but we'd have found our family and lived with others of our kind.*

She turned petulantly and went into the pantry for the dried herbs Mildred had requested. She couldn't wait to get back to Windcrest among her own things and her beloved pigeons. Her hand stopped halfway to the cluster of rosemary hanging just above her head. The pigeons that *Lord Neville* had brought her from London. She loved them so. Their cooing and scratching lulled her to sleep at night. Enid tossed her guilt aside however, reasoning that were it not for the loss of her parents, she'd have no need of pigeons to help her fall sleep.

That evening, Colin and Enid stretched their weary legs and sat in companionable silence, a rarity for brother and sister whose opposing ways of dealing with the English had driven a wedge between them. Nothing would ever change the love they had for one another, but that did not alter the fact that neither understood the other's position.

"It's so peaceful here. My happiness would be complete if I never had to leave Windcrest," Enid said, looking toward Colin whose fingers idly sorted through Rex's heavy coat.

"Aye," he answered quietly. "It's a part of the day I look forward to as well."

"Then why must we ever return to Lexington Estate? You could set up your own carpentry shop. People would be willing to bring their small jobs here for the superior work you do."

Colin looked at Enid with such sadness in his eyes that she stopped abruptly and waited for him to speak. "I'm a warrior, Enid, like it or not. I can't set up a shop for that."

She watched as he readjusted his angular body to an erect position, slowly scrutinized the house they lived in, then faced her squarely. "These past six years I've watched and hoped for you to accept our lot in this life," he said. He let a few seconds slide by.

"Think about how much you love Windcrest," he said, with a sweep of his head that included the entire cottage. Enid cocked her head with a question on the edge of her lips. He interrupted before she could give voice to the thought. "Do you think we would have been permitted to live here without the influence of Lord Neville? Do you really believe this place would have been held for us while we got old enough to live by ourselves without Lord Neville's constant protection from the other landowners?"

Colin watched as confusion, resignation, and anger skittered across her face. He raised his hand as a shield against her words. "Say nothing. I can no longer listen to your distaste for my cooperation with the Lexingtons. I've done the best I could to preserve for you all there is left of what you remember. Yet you become more resentful with each year."

Enid's blazing eyes and stiffened neck relaxed. Was this the first time he'd offered a different perspective from her own. Or was it just the first time she'd really listened?

"Which would you have, Enid? The life of a peasant or one with more independence at the cost of cooperating with the English?" He waited for her answer. None came.

"For you the life of a peasant would mean working in a tavern and accepting advances from mean, filthy men who would leave you with nothing, except maybe a babe in your belly." Enid's eyes flew wide with the idea.

"Do you think I've always enjoyed being a part of the Englishmans community?" Colin leaned toward Enid, scaring her with his vehemence. "Well, now I *do* like the place I've carved from the total destruction laid on us six years ago, and I don't want to spend my life hanging back. One day I'd like to marry and have a family and the only people I know are *English*, Enid. Am I supposed to forsake living just because the Scottish family we may or may not have reside somewhere in the Highlands?" Only the sound of the crackling embers broke the silence left by Colin's outburst.

Enid was dumbstruck. She'd had no idea of the controversy that raged in Colin's heart. Her shoulders slumped. She rose and hugged his neck, stretching her cheek to his ear. "Forgive me," she murmured. "I never meant to cause you so much pain." She turned then and trod up the steps to her bedroom in the loft. He watched her go, knowing the rift would never be healed but perhaps now a bit more understanding would make his role easier.

# CHAPTER THREE

Lexington Cove had changed very little during the ten years since Liam and Margaret MacDonnogh were slain by English peasants from Lexington Cove. In a climate unfriendly to lumber and metal, keeping the normal decay at bay was difficult for even the most serious proprietors. The little fishing vessels suffered from seaweed, wood rot, and barnacles. It also took a good eye to decipher the words on the signs above the storefronts.

At Windcrest, Colin MacDonnogh faced a quandary. Today he would take part in a meeting of the Lexington Cove landowners to formulate plans to defeat the Scots. For the past two years they had ambushed and pillaged English livestock and military supplies at an alarming rate. This was a situation Colin hoped would never come to pass. That was not to be, however. Fate had thrust him into the unenviable position of having to join with the English, enemies who had killed his family, in a campaign against Colin's Scottish homeland. He was smothered by a feeling of hypocrisy that went to the very soul of who he was. All his years of justifying to Enid his reasons for being absorbed into the English world now felt like hollow excuses for his cowardice.

It wasn't as though Colin wanted to fight for the English. Rather it was the result of the circumstances of his childhood. In the years since his parents had been murdered, the English community was all he had known. As their forces had been depleted in the past two years, the English had gladly accepted Colin's courage in battles defending against the Scottish Highlanders. There were those who loathed having a Scotsman within their midst but the majority swallowed their pride, preferring that he fight for them rather than against them.

He was not fond of all English people – only those with whom he'd grown up. He'd felt no remorse when Arnold had died a few days after the murder of his parents. Arnold's widow claimed it happened when her unfortunate husband stumbled over a broken fence rail and impaled himself on the scythe he'd been carrying. Colin however, knew it was a result of the knife locked in Margaret's hand as she'd died. Nor was he among the mourners when a few years later, a drunken Benjamin drowned in a ditch. Only Ephram and Brian remained as a constant reminder of their terrible crime. Loyalty to the English cause bore little resemblance to his care for the Lexingtons who had nurtured him for the past ten years. How could he live in peace with himself when his allegiance was shattered and torn between his Scottish heritage and his English benefactors?

A hearty, "Hello in there" led Colin away from the feeling of melancholy that filled his chest. Edward was in the barnyard swinging his hat to deflect the ravens flying at him, angry at being interrupted in their search for grain. Edward made up for all the mean-spirited gentry who'd ever cast a spiteful glance or made an unkind remark to him. Colin grabbed his greatcoat and left the house.

From her window in the loft, Enid watched and allowed her distaste for Colin's friendship with the young English lord to fill her heart with sadness. Since he'd revealed to her that he'd only done what would allow them to keep their home, she had ceased her efforts to persuade Colin to renounce his ties with the English. It had created a more peaceful existence for the two. Beneath her agreeable manner however, her sentiments toward the English had never changed. But her love for her brother was so great that she would not permit her loyalties to cause him grief.

As Edward and Colin grasped each other's elbows in greeting, Enid had to admit that their association had been a healthy one. Colin's normally shy demeanor had expanded to one of affability through Edward's gregarious influence. In turn, Colin had taught Edward to change his tendency to be slipshod into that of methodical workmanship. Together the two had wooed many a maid, but never the same maid.

Even their physical differences complimented one another. Edward was two years younger and of a slighter build than Colin. His raven-colored hair and wide black eyebrows that arched over sparkling dark eyes had wiggled the two out of many a tight spot. Colin, with piercing blue eyes, a mane of fiery red hair, and shoulders that filled most doors had saved them from countless tavern brawls. In a way they had become equal in their abilities. One quick and the other strong. It was a friendship that rarely encountered a bumpy patch.

Edward watched in admiration as Colin put the tack on Thor, the massive chestnut stallion given to him as a colt by Lord Neville.

"When are you going to let me breed that little mare of mine to Thor? The offspring could be breathtaking."

"When I get him completely trained. If I put him to breed this young I doubt I'd ever make a reliable warhorse of him. At the first sniff of a mare in heat, I'd be unhorsed and left to the mercy of the enemy."

Edward laughed loudly. "You're probably right. Thor's just like you when a pretty barmaid catches your eye."

"You're one to talk," came Colin's sardonic reply. "At Amber Morris's soiree last Saturday you were so knotted up in the hedgerows with Clarice Nottingham that I left without you."

They were still trading jibes as they rode into the village of Lexington Cove. The aging sign of the Boar's Head Inn hung slightly askew and waggled in the breeze like a tree limb ready to drop. The two men handed their horses to the lackey and shoved through the double doors. The atmosphere was already smoky, smelly, and rife with vulgar comments to the barmaids, interspersed with denigrating remarks about the Scots. Colin ignored the remarks and looked about for Lord Neville. Within seconds he heard Neville's shout accompanied by a sedate waving of his hat. Neville was seated in a shadowy corner along with Jeremy Hawkins and his father, Rufus.

Lord Neville watched as Edward and Colin approached him. Neville had been criticized by his peers for taking Colin and Enid into his home, but he had never regretted the decision. To Neville's way of thinking he'd provided an education and family for the two MacDonnogh orphans. While this in no way made up for their loss, they had not been left to fend for themselves at an age when they would surely have perished. Colin was like a brother to Edward, for after producing a daughter Lady Anne had never again conceived.

Lord Neville's biggest disappointment was that Enid had never become close to any of the Lexington family. She kept to herself and even though Gwen never ceased trying to bring a smile to Enid's face, the girl remained aloof. But Neville spent little time considering these things, allowing that short of having the power to return their parents to them he'd done his best for the MacDonnogh children.

A gust of sharp air as the last of the landowners entered through the tavern door roused Neville from his reminiscing. He rapped his whip handle hard on the scarred table bringing the gathering of wealthy landowners to order.

"Hear now!" he thundered. "We're here to make plans to fight the Scots, not to drink ourselves into oblivion." Heads snapped to attention and all talking ceased. The only sounds came from the many dogs lying under the tables as they reshuffled their bony bodies into more comfortable positions.

Neville continued. "I don't need to remind you that for the past two years the Highlanders have made a mockery of our English fighters." He looked out into the crowd of red-faced, overfed aristocrats and understood why.

"Our resources are seriously depleted and we can expect no help from King Henry who cares little for our small estates." Heads nodded. "We must make plans and develop strategies on our own behalf. We must not fail! Otherwise, I fear we are certain to lose our lands to Scotsmen who will be happy to kill us all to acquire our holdings." He allowed time for this frightening prediction to sink into the stubborn heads of his gentry friends who had refused to believe such a circumstance could come to pass.

A collective sigh rose from the group of pampered men. They were dressed in long silk tunics over full sleeved linen shirts, tight hose, and high leather boots. They had a strong reluctance to don armor and prepare to fight. They also were loath to relinquish their trips to London where whoring and gaming could be enjoyed at a prudent distance from wives and children.

"I'll brook no excuses," Neville admonished. "We must cooperate and our determination to win must be the overriding force behind our objectives. Is that clear?"

A reluctant, "Yes," rumbled through the assemblage.

"Is there anyone present unwilling to give their full measure to this end?" Neville scrutinized the men through eyes accustomed to sorting out the 'doers' from the 'dawdlers.' He noted their grudging agreement.

"So be it. With our combined forces I calculate we can field approximately one hundred men comprised of fifty archers, thirty-five foot soldiers, and fifteen knights. We will march on June 16th to Potter's Crossing for the attack. The Scots will be grazing their sheep there at that time. I expect trained fighters with battle-worthy equipment!" Neville gave a curt nod indicating the meeting was over.

It was a solemn, thoughtful group who left the Boar's Head Inn and made their way to their respective estates. Every man among them was aware of the seriousness of the situation. They had little stomach for an all-out attack against the brutal Scots who had no amenities to keep them home and at peace. However, the English had no choice but to fight if they were to preserve their lavish lifestyles.

Among the Lexington staff, Wren looked like all the other nondescript servants dressed in drab colors. He quietly worked in and around the manor performing various duties and brought no attention to himself. In fact, it was doubtful if anyone working in the stables even knew Wren. Today he was sorely agitated. He had an urgent message to deliver to Malcolm and he needed to accomplish it without his comings and goings being noticed. He scanned the peasants working in the gardens and lawns of Lexington Estate and was upset that they had not yet gone to their huts for a mid-day meal. "Don't they know the work'll be waitin' when they return?" he muttered under his breath. "That soon as one task's finished 'nother'll be assigned."

Outrage clogged his throat. He began the coughing he could not control when he was provoked. He knew the others laughed behind his back. No matter. None of them were important. *Why don't they leave,* he wondered, with renewed hatred in his heart? *I gotta get this information off to the Highlands.*

Thirty minutes later the manicured lawns were empty of workers. Wren surreptitiously perused the carriage sweep and front windows of the mansion before darting through an opening in the hedge to send word to Clan MacDougal.


In the Highlands north of Edinburgh the air was crystal clear. It was easy to breathe. Heavy clothing felt comfortable. The forests were swathed in mist that curled around the trees like clouds come to earth. It was a landscape at odds with itself. There were soft velvety valleys flanked by stony crags rising into the heavens, and bubbling mountain streams interrupted by raging waterfalls.

Hamish MacDougal and his son, Malcolm, sat with their backs warmed by the muted sunlight while mending equipment. Hamish was fifty and his deeply lined face revealed the effects of decades of squinting through the mountain haze. His skin was cracked and dry like neglected leather, the result of a lifetime of working in the merciless wind. He moved stiffly from years of sitting on cold ground with only a wool tartan between him and the frigid earth

It seemed like a lifetime ago when Hamish's wife, Collette, and their youngest son had been killed in an English attack into the Highlands. Hamish bore a hatred for the English that had torn his soul apart as surely as a sword in battle. It gnawed at him constantly. Now, after two years of besting the English, using the Scottish tactics of marauding and ambushing, the Scots felt the time for a final campaign was fast approaching.

Hamish knew Malcolm had received information from Wren concerning the latest plans of the English. "What've ye heard?" Hamish asked, as he hammered out a support for one of the kitchen cauldrons.

Malcolm looked up from the fishnet he was mending. "They're plannin' their attack fer June 16th - high noon at Potter's Crossing; 'bout fifty archers, thirty-five foot soldiers, 'n fifteen knights. Only way they can do that's to form one column wide through Narrow Gage, 'n then be ready to fan out into three companies fer the final formation."

Hamish hit his thumb with the mallet. "Damnation!" He sucked on the bruised appendage, then looked again at his son. "Go on."

"Plantin' the rumor that we'd be north of Berwick grazin' sheep at Potter's Crossing got 'em all fired up. They think we'll be easy pickin'. They're collectin' money 'n fighters faster'n bees makin' honey."

"It'll be the first time them miserable fools stopped gamin' long 'nough to work together," Hamish observed. He frowned as he looked at his thumb that was already turning blue. "Can ye be sure of Wren? Can't have no foul-up what with all that's at stake."

"Put yer mind to rest, Pa. He's always been dependable."

"Aye, that he has." His words were less a statement and more an introduction into another idea that wanted to be heard.

"What else 're ye thinkin', Pa? I know that tone."

Hamish chuckled. "Can't hide anythin' from ye nowadays. That's a good sign ye're nearly ready to take over my job."

"Git on with it then, Pa." Malcolm stopped his repairing and turned his complete attention on his father.

"Things 're comin' to a head, Malcolm. Tis time to establish contacts on the Borders with Scots we can rely on fer help if need be."

"Ye're right, son," Hamish continued. "Wren's done 'is part well but he's in no position to organize a network of Scottish sympathizers."

Malcolm looked with respect at his father. Although the MacDougals were a small and impoverished clan, Hamish, with shrewdness and forethought had managed to maintain their independence through all the misfortunes they had suffered. "After Potter's Crossing we'll study how to set up such a system, Malcolm. There's always last-minute snarls in complicated schemes that need an organized group of native folks to help smooth the way."

Hamish studied his son as Malcolm got back to the job of fixing the fishnet. Those fingers so gentle with the thread could as easily tear the throat from an attacking enemy. His slightly arched nose and intense green eyes reminded Hamish of the hawks who soared on the strong mountain air streams ready to swoop with deadly accuracy on unsuspecting prey below. His face was framed by a thick mass of red hair which fell to his shoulders in wavy cascades, softening an otherwise cold and uncompromising countenance. Hamish believed beyond doubt that a heart as fierce as William Wallace himself beat within Malcolm's chest.

Hamish could remember every stage of his son's life. By the time Malcolm was four he could ride his pony wildly over the hills and valleys of the Highlands. By eight he could kill a rabbit at twenty paces with a bow and arrow. Before he was twelve Malcolm could fight with shield and sword from a horse running at breakneck speed over rough terrain. Large and sometimes a bit clumsy, his strength and stamina had become legendary. There had never been a need to teach Malcolm about women. They vied for his attention and while he took one now and then, for the most part he was oblivious to his charm. He spent most of his time planning and implementing attacks on the English. Strong and fearless at twenty-two, Malcolm had become a man that other men followed.

Kit, four years younger than Malcolm, reminded Hamish of his wife, Colette, especially now that she was a young woman of eighteen. Hamish had tried to be both mother and father to his children but it had been hard for him to understand the needs of a girl. They were so much more complicated than boys. In her mountain world without a mother, Kit grew up as brave as any boy, climbing trees and challenging Malcolm to race with her.

Remembering his own mother's ways of healing, Hamish had been able to clean her skinned knees and cut fingers. He'd taught her how to cook, sew, and clean. However, from the time she'd begun her monthly flux, she was a puzzle to him. Sometimes she would be moody and other times she became a bossy little woman. In the end, he encouraged her to follow her desire to heal. Hamish sent her to Brigit, a neighbor, for instruction in nursing and the use of herbs for medicinal purposes.

Kit and Malcolm made Hamish thankful for what he had. But his heart still ached for Colette with a need that had nothing to do with raising children.

# CHAPTER FOUR

It was a moonless, courage-corroding night. Edward crept carefully along the hedgerow, constantly looking over his shoulder to make certain no one followed him. Shame shot through his body as he went about his cowardly plan. Once away from the mansion, he slipped into the forest and hurried along the route he'd known about all his life. Edward had been seized with such foreboding that only this secret trip to Emiline, the crone who lived deep in the woods of Lexington Estate, could assuage his fears. It was said she could cast a spell potent enough to overcome even the strongest evil power.

In a knapsack strapped on his back, he carried a fresh loaf of bread, a round of butter, and a sharpened carving knife, as he'd been instructed to do by one of the housemaids. Only humble offerings such as these could entice the old witch to offer up spells ensuring success. It was well known that these creatures could be capricious and the spell could go either way. Thus, it was important to maintain a demeanor of respect and humility.

Edward tapped hesitantly on the door of the ancient hut. He heard a chair scrape along the dirt floor, followed by the shrill meow of a cat. The door opened reluctantly, as though unwilling to allow outsiders to look within. From the black depths a pair of milky eyes studied him. Edward tried in vain to speak. The moments dragged on.

"Well," came an irritated voice from within. "Why've ye disturbed me?"

Edward stared intently at his feet. "I've brought things," he muttered, "in hopes that you could advise me about the battle on the morrow." He pulled the sack out and thrust it in the old woman's hands, nearly knocking her over.

"Tis a good thing I know everything without dependin' on fools like ye to explain yerselves." She disappeared into the hovel with the offerings, returning shortly with a long stick in one hand and the other clutching things Edward couldn't quite see. A spotted dog of nondescript lineage trotted jauntily behind, his scraggly tail wagging confidently to and fro. Come Wags," Emiline said, motioning to the dog. "We've work to do." Before Edward could run off, she took his hand in her own bony fingers and led him to a fire that burned quietly in a clearing adjacent to her little hut. She forced him to kneel, with his hands clasped at his navel and eyes staring into the bright flame. Wags sat on his haunches nearby with his busy tail clearing the area behind him of twigs. The dog's nose twitched at the smoky air as he calmly waited for the ceremony to begin.

Without warning Emiline raised both hands over her head and threw bits of parchment into the fire while pointing to the heavens with the stick. The flames leapt and crackled like a frenzied chicken caught in the jaws of a wolf. Burning fragments rose like malevolent, misshapen fingers before fizzling and dropping to the earth. All the while she droned a mysterious chant.

Edward wanted to run, fearing he was about to be offered up in sacrifice. But he was frozen on the spot, his knees digging into the pebbly dirt. When he thought he would die of suffocation, the fire returned to a peaceful glow, Emiline came out of her trance, and Edward could breathe again. He remained motionless as she dipped her fingers into a battered brass pot, then smeared his face with a greasy mixture smelling of herbs and fish. She clasped his hands once again, looked deep into his eyes, and nodded her head. "All will be well," she croaked, then stepped back and waved her hand toward the forest, indicating he was dismissed.

When Edward had gained the protection of the forest he shot a parting glance over his shoulder. Emiline was stooping beside her faithful companion. Wags was greedily licking the contents of the brass pot. As Edward hurried back to Lexington Estate, he felt as beaten as the old pot and to his dismay his confidence had plummeted. An uneasy knot in his stomach told him that another crone like Emiline was probably performing a similar ritual for the Scots.

The following morning Edward awoke in a cold sweat. The tips of his fingers tingled. His mouth was dry and his tongue felt big enough for two people. His chest had that clutch of fear brought on when he came face to face with a wild boar. Through the haze of nether-sleep he tried to remember why he was so upset. Somewhere in the distance he heard a horse neigh. The clang of hammer to anvil pounded through the morning silence.

As though touched by hot metal Edward leapt from his bed. Today, the years of practice that had produced broken bones, sprained joints, and bloody wounds would be tested. The enemy would not stop the fight to allow a young lord time to catch his breath or remount his horse. Today the battle would be real!

He hit the floor at a run and headed for the window that overlooked the stable yard. From this vantage point Edward gazed down at a regiment in apparent chaos. Grooms were leading horses to impatient riders, fighters were inspecting their equipment, Ned, the blacksmith, was yelling that there were too many horses in his shop - someone was bound to be kicked! The Lexington Estate militia could ill-afford the loss of any man before the battle had even begun. Edward spun on his heel and yelled for his page to assist him in getting into the complicated quilted undergarments.

The booming commands of Lord Neville reminded Edward that he was late. By Neville's side was Colin, methodically soothing frayed nerves and directing all the men to their proper places. In a matter of minutes, the entire force began to shape into the disciplined fighters they were trained to be. Edward ran down the staircase to the stables where his groom, Thomas, waited quietly to assist him in putting on his suit of armor. "Hurry, Thomas," Edward ordered impatiently.

"Best take time to git it on proper, m'lord. Ye'll be needin' all the metal ye can carry today. Lark's got 'is on good 'n snug 'n he's awaitin' fer ye, none too patient."

Thomas fastened the last binder as Edward hurried to his horse. He threw a hasty 'thank-you' over his shoulder and mounted Lark as quickly as the cumbersome armor would allow. Thomas shook his head and prayed silently that his master would return safe by twilight.

As the rows of warriors marched off, Edward took his place between Lord Neville and Colin at the head of the company. It was comforting to ride between the two men he admired most. The measured steps of a fighting force on the move, coupled with warm sun on armor, erased the memory of his unsettling visit to Emiline

The road widened and the sun stood higher in the heavens. Sounds of men and horses from other estates floated toward them on the slight breeze. With them came the realization that the fight ahead left no place for complacence. Tension settled heavily on the shoulders of all the warriors from the many Lexington Cove estates. Looking around, Edward saw fear written in the dusty creases on the faces of his comrades. Colin and Lord Neville constantly surveyed the area as though expecting an ambush from every thicket and hillock. To a man they were facing death and the highborn knight was as susceptible as the lowly foot soldier. Emiline's toothless visage rose in front of him like a specter from the grave, stealing away the tiny spark of confidence he'd felt earlier. Edward longed for the wooden swords and mock battles of his childhood.

The forces of Lord Asheboro and Lord Stanford were the last to join the militias of the other estates. Throughout the groups the mood was the same: fear of the dangers ahead and apprehension as to who would not return. Not a heart among them was soothed by the knowledge that *this* time the English would be the aggressors.

The road was dry and rough. Noses and eyes soon crusted with the dirt disturbed by so many horses and men. The armored knights got the worst of it. Unlike the foot soldiers who could wipe a face or clean a nose, the men entombed in metal were forced to endure the abrasive particles. They filtered through the armor and combined with their sweat causing itching which could not be appeased.

The fresh vines and colorful flowers that had greeted the front marchers were soon obliterated by a heavy layer of grime which filtered skyward and blocked the sun's rays. Men and horses alike gave in to the suffering. They plodded stoically forward resembling ancient marchers depicted in stained-glass windows of cathedrals.

Within two hours they were in sight of Narrow Gage. It was a lovely valley of soft grasses, not quite a mile in length and kept green and damp by the springs that flowed even when the rains were sparse. It was well named, being barely wide enough for twenty men to walk abreast. The sides of Narrow Gage rose at an angle of about twenty degrees, to a height of fifty feet and were lined with scrub pines and tall oaks. All of this made it difficult to spot anything above or beside the marchers.

Normally, entering a confined space such as this went against prudent military practices. However, this valley was the only access to Potter's Crossing. Aware of the tactics of the wily Scots, Lord Neville signaled the troops to halt at the entrance to the valley. Outriders preceded the main force to ensure no enemy lay in wait. Shortly, Mindus, one of the men from Lord Asheboro's estate, rode back with his lance held high signaling that none had been detected. Neville raised his arm and the English moved forward toward Potter's Crossing to attack the Scots as they drove their sheep to pasture.

Sounds of warriors on the move rustled through the valley; armor clanged with each step, arrows whispered as they rubbed feather to feather, foot soldiers' pikes occasionally banged against each other. A mood of anticipation, laced with dread, enveloped the fighters.

Edward's courage began draining from his body along with the sweat that ran down to the bottom of his feet, soaking his undergarments. His eyes were blinded by salty perspiration from his forehead. His armor was like a prison that he feared would also become his burial vault. The horse behind him stumbled. He shortened Lark's reins lest he falter as well. Edward looked toward his father, wondering if Neville was ever fearful of dying. Colin appeared fearless and aggressive with an abundance of strength that seemed unending. Edward wondered how a man acquired such self-assurance.

The terrain made a slight descent. Edward thought he saw a glint of sunlight on metal. The company moved slowly, hampered by the close quarters. Edward heard the muffled sound of a horse nickering. His head jerked up. *These Scots are all cowards,* he thought. *They ambush from behind trees and fight without armor. An honorable fighter has little chance against such heathens.* His body was soaked in its own fluids. Once again, the taunting face of Emiline rose in front of Edward like a barrier between him and the courage he desperately needed. "Damn her," he muttered.

As the Lexington force neared the end of the valley which opened into Potter's Crossing, the wind changed. A horse stamped an impatient foot and neighed. Lord Neville realized they were in a trap. He rose in his saddle ordering a full gallop forward, hoping to save at least part of his men. The command was lost in the yells of the wild riders who descended upon them from the sides of the valley. They had hidden there with their hands loosely covering their horse's nostrils to discourage any neighing. The faces of the Scots were painted bright blue and their hair was stiffened with tallow. They wore coarsely woven tartans and animal skins. The English felt as though they were being attacked by Druids who would offer their prisoners as live sacrifices to their gods. Whether the English tried to advance or retreat, they were blocked by the Scots at both ends of the valley.

Soon the English were in complete disarray. They were trapped in the moist footing where the horses lost their balance, leaving men in armor floundering on their backs in the muck. Foot soldiers and archers were unable to use their weapons either, as they too, fell into the worsening sea of mud. The forces that had entered the valley last had little choice but to trample on the men in front of them.

The Scots were everywhere. Darting in and out with battle axes sharpened and a will to let as much enemy blood as possible. The English could do little to save themselves. Many dropped to the ground feigning death in hopes of surviving. Others ran into the pines only to be felled by Scots awaiting just such a ploy.

Before Neville, Colin, and Edward could regroup for attack, the ground soldiers behind them were shoved into their horses separating the three men. Edward made the dangerous mistake of turning in his saddle to see what had happened to his father. Suddenly, his breath was knocked from his body by a solid blow to his back, leaving him stunned and gasping for air. In an effort to remain mounted he threw his shield to the ground and grabbed his horse's mane. The man opposite him looked to be only a teenager with just a mace and sword - no armor. Edward knew however, that this youth was deadly. With all of his strength he made a rush with his lance. It hit the young man in the shoulder knocking him into the sludge. As Lark was jostled in the melee Edward saw the man stand up, shake the hair from his eyes, and scramble back onto his waiting horse.

Lord Neville was fighting for his life. His opponent had many advantages. The Scotsman was young, much stronger, and he fought with the fanaticism of one who had little to lose. Neville had no room to wield his long lance. He tried to maneuver but the Scotsman wheeled to the right, rammed Neville's horse with his own horse's shoulder, then hit Neville with a mace in the abdomen. The pain paralyzed him -- the reflexes of his years of fighting failed. His only thought was to escape the armor that was now cutting hard into his stomach. As if from a distance, Neville saw his horse's head lower and with a frantic whinny fall to his knees. Lord Neville hit the ground with such force that he could feel his ribs crack. He sank into a swirling pool of shadows and dispassionately watched the knife descend upon him. The pain melted into the mists. . .then it was quiet.

After unhorsing his first adversary, Edward tried to locate Neville and Colin. To his left he saw Colin fending off two Scots. With a mighty heave Colin's horse leapt forward out of reach of the Scots' deadly maces and into the thicket where other Scots were attacking the retreating English foot soldiers. Knowing Colin was in command of his situation, Edward searched the chaos for his father. Amid several downed English, he saw his father defending himself against a Scotsman whose face was demonic in its expression. Edward struggled to go to his father's assistance but was blocked by the body of a horse that had fallen on its rider. He floundered in a sea of men and horses and watched helplessly as the Highlander knocked Neville to the ground. In an instant, the warrior leapt off his horse, pinned Neville to the ground, and without hesitation slit his throat.

It had happened in mere seconds. Before Edward could even react, the Scotsman had remounted and returned to the battle. Edward spurred Lark through the pandemonium toward his father. It was only a few yards but might as well have been miles. For every three steps forward, Lark slipped back two in the treacherous footing. Through all the turmoil a question raced through Edward's mind. *How did this happen? How was it possible for the Scots to put the English in such a compromising position once again?*

Just as Edward was close enough to see Neville's blood darkening the polished chest plate, he was hit hard from the side. The blow knocked Lark forward and Edward once again grabbed mane to stay mounted. With a violent pull on the reins, Edward wheeled to face his enemy. For an instant their eyes met. The hate Edward beheld in the cold eyes of the man facing him left no doubt that this would be a battle to the death.

With a fury that represented all his ancestors, a bloodcurdling oath issued from Edward's mouth. He recognized this man as the one who had just killed his father, Lord Neville.

But Edward was no match for Malcolm. Malcolm had nurtured his hatred since childhood, when the English had killed his brother and mother. Edward fought from rage that had just this day enveloped him. Malcolm's years of hatred enabled him to kill instantly and without emotion. It mattered not to Malcolm how many lives he intruded upon when it was possible to kill an Englishman.

Edward and Malcolm darted and parried the way they had practiced from the time they each were strong enough to pick up the instruments of war. But Edward, for all his fury and determination, was not equal to this Highland warrior dedicated to freeing Scotland from the tyranny of England. Malcolm hit the already dazed Edward with his mace, knocking him off his horse and into the mud. He jumped off Magnet and aimed his sword at the struggling knight's throat. Suddenly a riderless horse charged between the two men, hitting Malcolm and hurling him into the mire with a force that brought tears to his eyes and setting his head buzzing with pain. Both fighters lay in the blood-smeared slime, Edward unconscious and Malcolm too groggy to move. Lark and Magnet, exhausted from the struggle, stood patiently beside their riders.

Colin had long ago lost sight of Edward and Neville. He had killed one Scotsman but the scuffle of the battle had shoved him into a thicket on one of the steep sides of Narrow Gage. The sounds of the battle diminished as Colin concentrated on eluding a small band of Scots who had seen him enter the trees and were now tracking him. He watched from behind a huge oak tree as they stalked him with weapons raised and eyes scanning the forest.

A low-pitched horn broke the deadly quiet that occurs when the killing is nearly done and it's time for each side to assess its losses.

"MacDougals! Prepare to depart."

Without hesitation the Scots turned and ran to the horses that were standing at the edge of the trees. Colin let his long-held breath expel from his chest. As the sounds of the enemy died into the distance, he cautiously retraced his steps to find his men.

The devastation before him was beyond anything Colin had imagined could happen. Looking toward Potter's Crossing, he saw the Scots preparing their dead and wounded for the return trip to the Highlands. They had confiscated as many English horses as was possible to lead. In front of him the English lay scattered about the ravaged valley. Knowing there was nothing he could do to either stop the Scots or regain the horses, he found his fallen English comrades and began to organize a way to get them back home.

He had not gone far when he found Lord Neville lying on the ground with his faithful horse, Sparticus, standing beside him. He scanned the battlefield for Edward but saw no sign of him anywhere. Surprised at Edward's absence, Colin attended Lord Neville. Later he would search for Edward. He removed his armor and knelt beside Neville - the man who had diluted Colin's soul by making him not quite Scots and not quite English. A man Colin had at times hated and at other times respected and admired. As he removed Neville's armor he made no attempt to stop his tears.

Malcolm regained consciousness. His eyes focused enough to see that the English lay defeated and the Scots were preparing to leave for the Highlands. He glanced down at his fallen opponent, motionless in a heap of armor, but still alive. With all his desire to kill, it was not within Malcolm to slay a disarmed and unconscious man. He stooped for a closer look and recognized the Lexington crest. This man could be worth a good ransom. Money the Scots needed to continue their resistance. Malcolm removed the warrior's helmet and leaned forward. The knight's right arm lay at an angle indicating a broken bone or dislocated shoulder but his heartbeat and breathing were strong.

Working as quickly as his own injuries would allow, Malcolm removed the armor from both horse and knight. As he was lifting the chest plate from the horse Hamish rode up, his brow furrowed with concern.

"Malcolm, 're ye hurt bad?"

"Just dazed. Got knocked down by a loose horse," Malcolm answered, taking time to catch his breath.

Relief smoothed Hamish's face. "What bit of rubbish ye got there?" He leaned forward and squinted. "He's no kin to us that I recognize. Leave 'im there 'n bring the horse. If there's somethin' them English *can* do tis breed good horses. MacKenzie can turn that metal armor of 'is into weapons fer us."

"He's one of the Lexingtons," Malcolm answered. "I recognize the crest. They'll pay well to git this dandy back. Help me git 'im strapped on."

"Tisn't worth the effort son." Nonetheless he dismounted to assist Malcolm. "He'll not make the trip to the Highlands. When captured the English have little spirit to live."

"He's not wounded bad. We can always kill 'im, but first let's see if we can turn 'is sorry hide into funds fer more battle supplies. We're in need of money."

"Aye," Hamish answered grudgingly. "But I doubt he'll be worth the bother." In short order the two men strapped Edward onto his horse. Hamish remounted and looked at his fighters. "Ready, men?"

A collective "Aye," rumbled through the group.

The battle had lasted little more than an hour. The MacDougal clan, wounded in tow, began the arduous trip to the Highlands leaving the stench of death behind.

As the trail ascended the rocky terrain became more forbidding. Night was fast approaching as they rode into their campsite at Morris Glen which had been their reconnoitering spot for years. The battle-weary men and horses settled in for the night to gather strength for the final climb the next day.

The English plodded home in defeat. Both man and beast were half dead from thirst and injuries. With heads bowed and hearts heavy, each fighter contemplated his losses.

The Lexingtons had suffered much. The unimaginable had happened -- Lord Neville was dead. His fighting men had always understood that their own lives were at stake in defense of their master. But the possibility of losing their leader had never been considered. It was a crushing realization that had them wondering what the future held. Adding to their misery was the fact that Neville's son, Edward, was missing. No one knew if he still lived.

Colin rode beside Ned, the blacksmith at Lexington Estate. In his late twenties, Ned was all muscle and possessed tremendous strength from a life of forming iron into whatever was needed: armor, horseshoes, or household items.

Colin looked at his friend of many years. "How can a band of ill-equipped men defeat us time after time?"

Without hesitation Ned replied. "They're faster'n us, 'n they always git us in places where there's no room to maneuver."

Before the discussion could continue, a rider approached from behind. Colin and Ned turned in their saddles as Lord Henry Asheboro, whose estate bordered Lexington, fell into step beside them. Henry was a pompous man, proud of his connections with the nobility and unused to defeat. He leaned toward Colin. "I've had plenty of time to think about why they've been able to make us look foolish these past two years."

Colin's eyebrows arched as he looked at the man few respected. "Oh? Have you come to a conclusion?" Colin wore a guarded expression, never having had complete trust in this man who thought himself superior to the other landowners.

"Matter of fact I have," answered Henry, looking down his nose at Colin and ignoring Ned completely. "We've a spy in our midst. I told Neville that last year but couldn't convince him that one of our own would sell out. Neville and his high-minded morality. What a fool he was."

Colin's clenched jaw was the only sign of the outrage he felt at this insult toward Lord Neville. Ned kept his fisted hands around his reins. Neither spoke, knowing this was not a man to rile.

Hugh Averil and Reginald Holms joined them as Henry continued. "Yes, we've a spy among us and now that Neville is dead, I say we go after the traitor."

Hugh responded. "I've thought about that myself, Henry. I figure it has to be someone close enough to learn our strategies without arousing suspicion. Got any ideas who it might be?"

"Probably one of the Border Scots," replied Henry. "And I've got an idea how to sniff him out." Colin ignored the slight to his heritage.

"How's that?" Reginald asked.

Puffed with pride at being the one now in command, Henry answered. "Simple. We set a trap to expose his identity"

"I'll call a meeting of the oldest landowners, the time and place known only to them. We'll plan dates and strategies. When everything is in place we'll inform the others."

All eyes were on Henry, who was ready to fill in more of the details.

"Every militia must be ready to ride within six hours notice." Henry overlooked the raised eyebrows. "The most important point of all is to change the method of fighting for all our militias.

It's imperative to match the 'ambush and run' maneuvers of the Scots. We must abandon armor, straight formations, and heavy horses if we're to beat the enemy at their own game."

"Impossible!" growled Reginald.

"If you want to keep the Scots from taking our homes and lands, you'll make it possible," Henry answered, then looked at Hugh. "What do you think?"

"I'm in favor of whatever it takes to put these Scots down once and for all."

"I'll begin setting the plan in motion straightaway," Henry replied, then broke from the group and rode toward his own estate.

Colin and Ned had been quiet throughout the discourse, being underlings and thus not expected to offer any opinion. When Reginald and Hugh also rode off in separate directions the two men looked at one another. Ned was the first to speak.

"What do ye make of that?"

"We'll wait and see, Ned. We just follow the orders from our superiors. That way we're not responsible for the success, or failure, of whatever plan these old men come up with."

For a time, the two rode in silence, engrossed in their own thoughts. Finally, Colin spoke so quietly that Ned had to lean toward him to hear. "Telling Lady Anne that her husband is dead and her son is missing will be one of the hardest things I've ever had to do in my life. I wish I could just leave and let someone else do it."

"Twon't be easy, Colin, but ye're the only man they've got left to turn to. Like family, I mean. Someone's gotta keep the estate goin'. Hopefully Edward'll return soon. Lady Anne 'n

Gwen'll be too distracted over Neville's death 'n Edward's welfare to be thinkin' of the day to day things."

It was a long speech for Ned but Colin knew what he said was true. Horses had to be shod, cows milked, workers fed, and crops cared for regardless of who died. Colin was so exhausted, both in mind and body, that the thought of more responsibility was beyond pondering. Still, he'd have to find the strength to help the family that had made his life bearable after the loss of his own parents.

Colin looked over his shoulder to make sure Neville's body was secure on the horse's back. Neville's ankles were tied to his wrists with a rope that looped under the belly of his horse. *Seems so sad to carry Lord Neville in such a disrespectful way. But dying in battle more often than not brings with it a loss of dignity,* he thought.

"Things'll never be the same, Colin."

"No. Things never are when families are torn apart," Colin answered.

Ned was embarrassed. "I'm sorry. I fergot 'bout yer folks. Ye've been at Lexington Estate so long ye seem like one of 'em."

"Don't be sorry. So much has happened since their murders it seems like that was another life in another place. I've never met any of my family in Scotland. Except for the odd insult from Englishmen who don't count, I feel as much English as I do Scot."

"'Course ye do. Some say ye're as much a Lexington as Edward." Ned hesitated. "I don't understand Enid though. She ignores us, only speaks when she has to, 'n never smiles. Wonder why that is?"

"She blames all English people for the killing of our parents. Enid wants nothing to do with them and feels I'm untrue to my own ancestry," Colin answered without emotion. "It seems as if Enid wills herself to hang onto the hate," he continued. "She's most content at Windcrest with her pigeons. I thought it would help when Lord Neville brought back those two birds from London for her. At the time, she acted like it was small payment for the grief she lived with. But now, those pigeons are the most important creatures in her life."

They entered the forest that surrounded Lexington Estate. It wouldn't be long before they would have to face Lady Anne and Gwen. Behind them broken equipment clanked and scraped back from whence it had come that morning. An occasional moan rose from the group of men as an injured leg was forced to walk. Those more seriously injured were pulled in litters by the few horses that hadn't been stolen by the Scots.

As the remnants of a grand force made its way home, Colin mulled over the circumstances confronting the Lexingtons. *Who will take over leadership in the family on a permanent basis? Lady Anne and Gwen are ill prepared for the duties of managing a large estate. Unscrupulous overseers are more apt to take advantage of women than men - usually because the women are not knowledgeable about field management, breeding farm animals, maintenance of land and buildings, or dealing with peasant workers.*

*Lord Neville's brothers and their families are scattered about England and have their own interests to look after. It's not my place to solve these problems,* he thought. *At the end of the day I'm only a Scotsman the Lexingtons felt sorry for.* Colin was comforted by Ned's presence as they approached the gatehouse and he made his way to the sad task ahead.

# CHAPTER FIVE

The kitchen at Lexington Estate was separated from the main house by a covered walkway. It was a large, high-ceilinged room with a stone floor. An enormous worktable stood in the middle, close to the ovens and fireplaces. The pantry, situated in one corner of the room, smelled of dried herbs, smoked meats, and fresh vegetables. Along the back wall were basins for cleaning utensils and produce. Behind each basin was an opening in the wall where garbage was thrown out to be picked up each morning and fed to the pigs. Nothing went to waste in the Lexington kitchen. Mildred Kingsley, who had worked for the family since childhood, was responsible for the smooth running of the kitchen. This was a position of great authority due to the many guests who visited there.

It was here beside Mildred that Enid had spent most of her childhood. Mildred had patiently taught her what she needed to know in order to manage her own home someday. On this day it was Enid's turn to wash the large baking pans used for the breads, cakes, and pies. She stood on a stool which made her tall enough to reach the unwieldy utensils and was humming

'The Maypole Jig', a tune she'd overheard Dora, the scullery maid, singing.

Mildred and Lady Anne lamented the fact that Enid refused to use her education to find a position as a tutor in one of the wealthy homes in the area. Both women had tried to convince Enid she was too small for the heavy work in the kitchen, especially when she had the knowledge to be a teacher. But Enid had insisted on working with Mildred, since any contact with the English seemed to her an insult to the memory of her parents. To Enid's way of thinking the English aristocrats smelled badly, talked loudly, and belittled the Scots. She wanted no part of them.

It was late afternoon and preparations were being made for supper. Foot soldiers and knights alike would be fed from the Lexington kitchen upon their return, ensuring plenty of nourishment for the exhausted fighters.

Enid's wrists hurt when she lifted the big pans, causing her to stop and rub them now and then. She hoped the pain wouldn't get so bad that Mildred would have to find a bigger person to take her place. She studied her tiny hands as they gripped the large baking pan and wondered why she was so small. Especially when her brother was so large. Thinking of Colin sent her into a flight of daydreaming.

He had taken care of Enid since the death of their parents. He always bundled her up in her heaviest wool clothing when the weather was cold. Thinking she should be taller, Colin constantly urged her to eat more. As youngsters they had frolicked and laughed together when they swam in the ocean. The two were always ready to play a joke on one another. She smiled faintly, remembering how he would tie her long hair to a chair without her knowing until she tried to rise. Colin, however, was a fair man. Now, he would not tolerate her making disparaging remarks about the Lexingtons and he encouraged her to be friendlier to the family that had been so good to them.

"Enid!" a voice jolted her. The heavy pan slipped from her grasp, splashing water over her apron and the floor around her. "Come girl, finish up," Mildred chided. "The men'll be home soon wantin' food 'n drink. Bring me some parsley from the garden to brighten up the fish."

Enid would feel better when Colin was home safe and sound. She always worried when he was on a campaign. When he'd left that morning his eyes were as dark as stormy weather. He'd been thinking about the conflict ahead and had no appetite for breakfast. As she ran to pull the parsley she untied her apron and threw it carelessly toward the hook. It missed the mark, making her return to hang it up.

When she pulled the last sprig of parsley from the soft earth a distant clanking sound brought her head up. Far down the carriage sweep she could see a group of men making their way slowly toward the mansion. Her heart tripped like a woodpecker and with a loud scream, she dropped the parsley and ran.

Lady Anne was in the drawing room embroidering a runner for one of the formal tables when she heard the commotion. The needlework fell to the floor as Anne raced for the front entrance.

In the library, Gwen was trying to understand her father's estate management notes. The noise brought the cat in her lap to instant flight, digging its claws into her gown and slashing a hole in the delicate silk fabric. Gwen jumped at the rude interruption and scanned the front garden for what might have caused such a reaction. Seeing the disheveled marchers making their way up the drive she hoisted her skirts to her knees and made a headlong run for the lawn.

Outside she found herself in a pandemonium of shouting workers, squawking chickens, and baying dogs. In an instant she had overtaken them, mindless of the spectacle she must present. As the wind whistled past her ears, Gwen heard the high-pitched wail of Alice, one of the upstairs maids whose brother Alfred was a foot soldier in the Lexington militia.

Ned was mounted alongside Colin, who held the rope of another horse. When the two men saw her, they dismounted. Her eyes were riveted on the horse behind Colin. She saw her mother standing beside the horse he led. Lady Anne was crying. There was no need for anyone to tell Gwen that the dead man strapped to the horse was her father. In the blurred background she saw Enid standing quietly, her eyes never losing sight of Colin.

Ned and Colin untied Lord Neville from his horse and laid him gently on the ground. Lady Anne knelt beside her husband's body, cradled his head in her lap, stroked his face, and pushed the hair from his closed eyes. With a handkerchief meant only for decoration, she wiped the dried blood and crusted dirt from his forehead. The cadre of defeated and wounded men respectfully splayed around Lady Anne, like water divided by a tiny island. She remained there supporting her husband's body with her own until there was no one left to pass.

As the sound of the stumbling men and horses retreated into the distance, Lady Anne looked up at the family around her. Her voice faltered and her chin quivered but she valiantly kept the tears locked within her eyes. She did not want to lose her composure in front of the servants. "We must prepare him for burial."

Ned, Orville, and some of the uninjured fighters carried Neville to the underground crypt. In the evening mists, the shadowy figures looked like a tableau from an ancient burial rite. Lady Anne, distraught at the death of her husband, had not yet realized that her son Edward was not among the returning men.

Gwen searched through the procession for Edward. She saw Silas, the son of one of the gardeners, shuffling with his head down and his left arm dangling by his side. There was Montrose, Mary's betrothed, lying on a litter with blood staining his tunic and just the faintest sign of breath. Edward was nowhere to be seen. Panic pumped through her veins so hard she feared her entire body would explode. "Colin! Where's Edward?" she shouted.

He looked at her bleakly. "He isn't with us."

"What do you mean? Is he dead too?" Her voice was frantic.

"I searched the battlefield for him. He wasn't there. I think the Scots took him prisoner and will want a ransom." Colin's words were barely a whisper. It was as if he tried to soften the blow with a quiet voice.

"How could this happen? I thought the Scots were pasturing sheep and we were to surprise them with an ambush!" Her voice was very shrill.

Colin looked up then, annoyed that he seemed to be the target of her fury. "Somehow they knew our plans. We were ambushed as we entered the valley. With no room to maneuver, they had us trussed up like a Christmas goose." His shoulders sagged and he started to walk wearily away.

But Gwen was not to be ignored. She followed on his heels. "How did they know? Was Edward alive when they took him away?"

Colin turned slowly and spoke deliberately. "Some think there's a traitor relaying information to the Scots. I don't know what Edward's condition was when he was taken captive." Then he turned and walked resolutely toward the manor.

Gwen was ashamed. It was unfair to launch such an attack on Colin. In her heart, she knew he grieved for Lord Neville as surely as she did. She ran after him. "Colin, I apologize for being so rude. Please forgive me."

He was undone by her contrition. She was overwhelmed at such a great loss to her family. Colin knew how that felt. He turned and held her to his chest. "I know you didn't mean your words and I'm certain Edward is alive. Otherwise the Scots wouldn't bother taking him into the Highlands." He stroked her hair as he had when they were children, when the hurts were scrapes and cuts from running wild in fields full of thorns and ditches. "We'll wait for their instructions." Colin rested his cheek against hers before continuing. "And yes, I forgive you."

His coarse tunic scratched her face. He smelled of sweat, blood, and death. She clung tighter around his middle. "What will we do? What will we do?"

He had no answer. "Come," he said. "Your mother needs us."

Together they walked to the mansion. Enid followed quietly behind. Mildred met them at the entrance, her face lined with worry wrinkles. She motioned the two toward the parlor. "She's just learned Edward's missin'. Tis nearly more'n she can bear."

Anne lay on a chaise lounge, motionless except for her fingers which constantly combed through the lace on her handkerchief. She stared at the ceiling but Colin knew she saw nothing. Candlelight flickered over her face cruelly exaggerating the fine lines and puffy eyes. Gwen was stunned. It occurred to her that Lady Anne might literally die of a broken heart. She ran and knelt beside her mother, taking Anne's hands into her own to stop the incessant motion.

"Mother, speak to me."

Anne continued to stare into nothingness, then mumbled something.

"I can't hear you. Please speak louder."

Lady Anne faced Colin and asked the question that had plagued her since seeing Neville strapped on his horse. "Do you think he suffered long?"

"No, Lady Anne. He did not."

"How can you be so sure?"

"I've seen such injuries before. Lord Neville would have been immediately unconscious, thus unaware of any pain."

She seemed relieved. Colin would forever keep to himself the agony leading up to the blow that caused Neville's death -- knowing that no battle is defined by just one thrust. It begins with that first sight of the enemy charging and ends when one side vanquishes the other. In between, a warrior never stops jabbing, lunging, retreating and advancing - doing whatever it takes to remain alive. The result is always the same: a man either lives or dies. So simple. So unalterable.

"What of Edward? Do you think he lives?"

"I'm certain of it, Lady Anne. They wouldn't carry him back into the mountains otherwise. It's their usual way."

Minutes drifted by with the only sound coming from the great emerald drapes as they whispered in the evening breeze. Finally, Lady Anne spoke again. "How did they know our plans?" Her voice was faint -- as though talking to herself.

"Lord Asheboro thinks there's an informer among us."

"I can't fathom such a thing," she said, faded and defeated by the day.

Gwen rested her forehead on her mother's now quiet hands. "What do we do, Colin?" Her voice quivered as she fought the tears that threatened to destroy what composure she had left. She looked at Colin. "You must be tired of me asking that question over and over."

"Not at all, Gwen." His words were calm. . .full of concern. "We can make a plan later when we receive the ransom message with instructions. I'm sure it'll be along shortly. They need money for supplies."

Mildred whisked into the room, followed by Anita, one of the servants. "I need to take 'er to 'er bedroom now."

Colin and Gwen, aware that this was a gentle dismissal, rose and retired to the library. They sat opposite one another, like two islands nearly touching, but isolated by separate thoughts and worries. Colin stared into the black void of the fireplace. Gwen studied her father's portrait above the mantle. Both ignored the wine brought by Allison Ann.

Colin was the first to speak. "I know it's nearly beyond thinking about, Gwen." She looked up expectantly. "But with

Lord Neville dead and Edward taken prisoner it will be up to you and your mother to manage this estate." He could think of no way to make the subject easier to broach. "Furthermore, the troops must be immediately introduced to the 'hit and run' tactics called for now."

"We've not yet buried Father and you expect us to supervise this estate *and* plan for another battle!" Gwen's voice shook with emotion and she faced him with a frown that marred her perfect skin.

He ignored her anger. "I know it's unreasonable but we can afford very little time to mourn. The Scots will not be resting on their laurels."

Gwen sighed. "I know you're right, Colin. I'm ready to assume my part in preserving this estate as well as our heritage. But determination and dedication to a cause are worthless without expertise." Her voice steadied as she expressed her concerns. "Mother will be indisposed for awhile. That leaves me - and I've not the slightest idea how to manage an estate." Her eyes were as hard as the anvil in Ned's shed. "It's up to you to lead us. At least until Edward returns."

Colin studied her carefully. In less than a day, Gwen had become a woman unwilling to be a victim of her losses. She looked at him calmly and with purpose. "You know Lexington Estate and its business far better even than Edward. I'm willing to learn how to handle the daily affairs of the estate, if you promise to train our men." Her voice was steady. "We must bring these murderers to justice."

Somewhere in the cobwebs of his mind Colin remembered his own vow of revenge so many years ago. Now he looked into

Gwen's eyes, full of resolve to right a wrong committed to *her* family. He wondered, *does she realize that throughout the Borders this night there are other women, both English and Scots, who feel as she does?* He wondered, too, *will she be any more successful than I have been in my own quest to avenge my family.*

His shoulders slumped as exhaustion took its toll. He had no inclination to resist. "Very well. I'll assist until Edward returns." He stood up slowly. "Now I must go to Windcrest before I can no longer move."

She bowed slightly. "I bid you good night then." With each step up the staircase, her heart ached so that she thought it surely must be bleeding.

Enid had waited patiently on the terrace, hugging her knees to her chest. That day she had watched Lady Anne and Gwen face the loss of Lord Neville. She was surprised to realize that the gentry suffered no less than the peasants who served them. Their eyes were red and swollen from crying and their silk handkerchiefs could not stem the flow from their noses any more than her old muslin handkerchief had when she'd lost *her* family. The sorrowful homecoming enlightened Enid to the fact that no one was immune to tragedy. It gave her a strange feeling of connection and, in an odd way, a feeling of completion. To her it was only fitting that at last the mighty Lexingtons knew what it felt like to have their family torn asunder.

She was chilled and sleepy when Colin finally appeared. Daniel brought Old Jeff around and she rode silently beside Colin back to Windcrest. Both were numbed into a cheerless limbo by the day's debacle.

Gwen parted the curtains in her room and watched as Enid and Colin walked their horses, side by side down the carriage sweep littered with the broken remains of a defeated force. Their knees touched in family companionship. In sorrow, their bond was strengthened - a bulwark against adversity. Gwen envied this closeness. How she wished her life was as simple as theirs.

She bowed her head and sighed. The future seemed fraught with insurmountable obstacles and changes to be made. Gwen wanted to sleep her worries away, like those petty childhood problems that were always put to right in the morning by a smiling mother or father. She let the curtain drop, turned, and went to bed—too discouraged to even change her clothes.

# CHAPTER SIX

Today Lady Anne would allow the grief to overwhelm her. For now, she would postpone her concerns over Edward's whereabouts and leave to others the planning of battle strategies. She sat on a stool near the bed she had shared with her husband for nearly twenty-five years. Neville's portrait on the opposite wall was a haunting reminder that from this day forward he would be only an image in her mind. The sadness that drained the energy from her body was bittersweet. After today, grieving would be a luxury for the nights when she reached for his familiar chest - only to find an empty space.

She could not expect less from herself than from the others whose sacrifices equaled her own. Therefore, today she would mourn. Tomorrow she would begin her search for what the future held for the estate that she must protect for her children and grandchildren. Neville had loved her for her devotion to the family. She could not let him down.

"Come, Lady Anne," Mildred coaxed. "Ye must rouse yerself else ye'll be missin' Lord Neville's funeral."

Anne obediently put on the clothes Mildred handed her. Her gown, of black silk interwoven with white threads and small side panels of dark gray, emphasized her tiny waist and thin shoulders. Behind the black veil that fell gracefully from her three-cornered headdress, her eyes swam in liquid pools that reflected sorrow and confusion. She held tightly to Gwen's hand as they descended the staircase and began the short journey to the family burial ground.

Colin and Enid walked behind Lady Anne and Gwen to the cemetery that was situated on a hill overlooking the sprawling estate. Ancient oaks stood, like impassive sentries, protecting the hallowed spot. Close to thirty mourners followed their mistress to pay their final respects to a beloved overlord. Many of these workers and friends grieved over deaths and injuries in their own families. Lady Anne hugged them all and thanked them for their faithfulness. She had made certain that none would go hungry or without help while the injured recovered.

Gwen had grown up with these folks. She'd played with their children - some of whom had died at Potter's Crossing. Today they cried together during a time of shared grief and care for one another. Somehow it knitted them back together, like the frayed seam of an old tunic.

Father Henson, in his first year of serving the Lord, nervously fingered his robe and hoped he wouldn't forget the sermon he'd prepared for this occasion. When everyone was in place he began: "Children of God," he droned. "Today, we. . ."

Anne's eyes misted as memories whisked her into the past. In that wooden box poised over the cruel hole in the ground lay the man who had spirited her away one afternoon long ago. He'd led her to a formal black carriage with the Lexington crest emblazoned in gold on the sides. She could still smell the wild roses in bloom and feel her soft silk gown slide over her legs as he handed her into the chaise. Neville had promised her a view of the sparkling sea and eternal love. Now the story was over. Only the dream remained.

Colin also allowed his thoughts to wander as his eyes scanned the peaceful setting that could not camouflage the sorrow. He thought about the coming weeks of drastic changes that must be accomplished in the Lexington Estate militia. It took his mind away from this respectful ceremony for the departed that only reminded him of the unholy way his parents had died. He planned to put proper headstones at their graves. How he wished there really was a God who enforced the doctrine of love that every religious man in the world spouted.

Enid stood as though carved in stone, staring straight ahead with expressionless eyes. This was the first funeral she'd attended since her parents had been murdered. She made no move to join in the communal grieving, allowing that it was yet another sign of outrageous English emotion. *Insincere - the lot of them*, she thought with contempt. *They act as though only the English should be mourned - that the Scots are unworthy of such feelings.* Enid would rather have been at Windcrest among her pigeons and childhood memories.

"So, dear ones. Let us not mourn the loss of our beloved Lord Neville but rather rejoice in his victory in the Lord," Father Henson advised, with a wisdom only the young espouse. When his prayer of benediction was over, the sorrowful gathering slowly returned to their homes and the uncertain future that faced them all.

The next morning Colin rode Thor over the well-worn path for his first day as leader of the Lexington Estate fighting force. He knew better than most how much work was involved in the ambitious plans of the English to match the Scots in battle tactics. He was aware too, that the other landowners would pay him little mind since to them he was only an adopted Scotsman and not to be trusted. It was an unreasonable mission facing him but in honor of Lord Neville, Colin intended to have the Lexington men ready by the time Edward returned.

Thor effortlessly leapt the little brook and within minutes the chimneys of the Lexington mansion broke above the tree line. The stately manor never failed to impress him, however much he tried to remain objective. It was a large rectangular residence framed in timber, with walls of stone and mortar. The rock wall that had completely surrounded the house in earlier times had been partially eliminated, allowing the addition of a carriage sweep that made a graceful curve in front of the formidable structure. This drive encircled a manicured garden that provided most of the arrangements of fresh flowers throughout the manor. The curved veranda that formed the main entrance was flanked by dormers lifting to the second and third stories. Directly behind the home was a small pond, once part of a moat, that was now home to ducks, geese, and a pair of black swans.

As Colin stepped into the large stone foyer and walked across a colorful woven rug, he glanced at the tapestries hanging on the walls picturing Lexingtons of the past in heroic deeds of battle. Sunlight sliced through the arrow slits - a subtle reminder that at one time this peaceful home had provided for its own defense. Colin prayed it would not be necessary for the present dwellers to protect themselves in similar fashion since he was certain the Scots would make quick work of this luxurious estate.

He walked into the library where Gwen and her mother waited. Allison Ann had just arrived with scones and milk and was arranging them on the hand-carved oak sideboard. To the left of the sideboard was a large fireplace, from which the odor of charred wood from winters past puckered his nose. A light summer breeze did little to alleviate the staleness that permeated the furnishings. Allison Ann opened the heavy damask drapes allowing shafts of light to soften the harsh shadows that cast a pallor of defeat throughout the room. Then she bowed to Lady Anne and slipped out without a sound, closing the massive doors behind her.

Lady Anne sat impassively on a severe upright chair. She was unaware of the activity around her, yet immersed in the ambience of this room where she'd spent so many hours with her husband. It was an invisible barrier of a past which Colin and Gwen could not penetrate. They were left to begin the deliberations on their own. Gwen looked at him expectantly. Her fingers toyed with the lace on her silk handkerchief.

Colin did not know how to begin. He was more at home in the rough and foul-speaking world of men than discussing estate matters with women. His confidence had faded like the aged tapestries in the foyer. He cleared his throat. His chest itched from his linen shirt. He poured a glass of wine then sat down and concentrated on the Lexington family portrait hanging above the mantle.

When his throat had relaxed he spoke quickly. "Lady Anne, Gwen has asked me to assist you in the operation of the estate until Edward returns. Does this meet with your approval?"

She nodded. "Yes, Colin. There is no one else to trust. Gwen was right to ask for your help." Her lackluster voice was weak and after those few words she stared through the windows into the lawn beyond.

Colin was surprised at Lady Anne's dismissal of matters so important to her own welfare. His eyebrows arched as he looked at Gwen expecting some sort of explanation. She shook her head slightly. *Don't these women realize it's their fortune at stake?* Colin wondered. *That my contribution is purely one of returning the favor they did for Enid and me. Why can't they understand how important it is to prepare themselves to run this estate?*

Colin turned his gaze once more to Gwen. Gone was the skinny child with bruised knees and mischievous laugh. Vanished was the belligerent young woman blaming him because the Scots had killed her father and captured her brother. Her hair, that was forever flying in her face, was today captured with combs - no tendrils falling out of place. Her mourning gown of dove gray trimmed in white accentuated her slim, angular body. *She must be about eighteen now*, he thought. He cleared his scratchy throat again.

"Do you think Mildred will be able to supervise all the activities of the house and gardens until your mother is stronger?" He noted her nod of approval. "That will allow you time to ride the estate and tend to the management of forests and hunting areas, welfare of the tenants, and seeing to the crops. You can expect help from Townsend. He worked closely with your father in these matters and will be more than happy to instruct and serve as your teacher." Colin dried his moist neck with a linen handkerchief. "That will leave me time to prepare our forces in the method of 'hit and run' fighting. I fear it will take patience to convince our men that this new way has merit."

Gwen astonished him with a voice full of enthusiasm. "I'll ride over to Townsend's straightaway. I used to cuff his son, Will, when he'd pull my hair during church. It will be good to see both of them again." She turned her head thoughtfully in the direction of Lady Anne. "I shall also make a point to visit all our wounded fighters to make certain they are healing properly and their families have plenty of food.

Relieved at Gwen's improved spirits Colin stood up. "I leave you to make your plans while I go to Orville and Ned to begin the changes in our militia. The road ahead will be long and filled with tempers stretched beyond their limits." He clasped Lady Anne's hands in his, bowed to Gwen, and quickly left the room.

"Mother, shall I help you to your room?" Gwen gently touched her mother's elbow.

"No, dear. I want to walk in the gardens a bit. By myself."

Gwen watched Anne's halting steps as she left the library. It was the walk of a woman old before her time. Gwen asked herself, *will she ever recover? Will there ever be a smile on her lovely face again?*

As her mother disappeared from view, Gwen's thoughts returned to Colin. *Why was he so tense? Perhaps he feels out of place among all the English. Some will probably suspect him of having a part in these treacheries. I'd forgotten long ago that Colin was not English. To me, he's part of the family.* She chewed her lower lip as she ascended the staircase to change into her riding habit. She hoped she was capable of performing the responsibilities Colin had outlined for her.


Colin strode to the stable yard to find Ned and Orville. He was eager to put distance between him and feminine sights, sounds, and smells. The odor of horses being shod, sweaty men, and the sound of Orville yelling at a luckless apprentice was more to his liking.

"Orville! Ned! Spare me some time," he bellowed.

Ned put down his hammer and Orville beckoned for Earl to take over the grooming. They approached the large table under an oak tree where Colin waited. Orville's old knees creaked as he settled himself onto the bench. Ned nodded to Colin and sat down with the smoothness of joints not yet abused by work.

Without preamble, Colin announced: "Orville, Ned. I need your help."

Orville's bushy eyebrows climbed into his forehead like two hairy caterpillars. "How could ye be needin' any help from an old man like me?"

Colin briefly explained to Orville how Lord Asheboro and the others believed there was a spy in the midst of the English community. The oldest landowners were to meet in secret to plan attack dates. When prudent, this information would be sent by trusted couriers to the remainder of the community.

"What's that got to do with me?" Orville queried.

"Everything," Colin answered. "The plan Henry Asheboro has proposed is that we refit our knights so they wear lighter clothing and ride smaller, faster horses. They must learn to fight without armor, using tight maneuvers, and with weapons that are easier to handle. And while I'm not fond of Asheboro, I agree that our present tactics put us at a disadvantage."

Orville interrupted. "Still can't figure where I fit in this plan."

Colin put a hand on Orville's shoulder. "Our blacksmiths have never fashioned anything other than heavy armor. We need your expertise in reworking our present weapons into smaller shields and shorter lances."

Orville sputtered. "I've not worked an anvil fer nigh on eight years now. Old Harvey, over at Lord Asheboro's, hasn't worked one fer nigh on ten years!"

"I know," replied Colin. "But you'd only have to instruct the younger smiths, like Ned here, how to work with metals unfamiliar to them - not build the weapons yourself." Ned nodded vigorously as Colin continued. "We need the advice of men who've spent a lifetime working with all sorts of metal. Lord Neville always said you were the best of your day." Colin let the silence settle over them, then asked. "What do you say, Orville?"

Orville eyed the man he'd guided into adulthood. "I can't say 'no' to ye, Colin. But I'm not promisin' anythin'. The idea of changin' a whole army from bein' knights to bein' whatever the Scots 're like in three months or so goes beyond anythin' reasonable."

Colin remained silent allowing Orville time to think. Minutes crept by. Ned and Colin clasped their hands and waited. Orville chewed on a dried twig and his eyebrows now furrowed in the middle of his forehead. Finally, he looked up. "How'd ye intend to replace the horses? Them Scots took most of our quickest ones.

Light weapons 're good fer nothin' if ye can't run fast."

Taking this as Orville's agreement to help, Colin let go of the chest full of breath he'd been holding. "Asheboro will take our big horses to London and trade for what we need. He's got connections there and will provide the men to make the trip."

Orville wiped the sweat from his face with an old rag pulled from somewhere inside his battered tunic. "Looks like ye've put a mite of thinkin' on this. Least I can do's help teach them young smiths." He looked at the two young men. Then with a hint of warning in his voice, Orville said, "Just remember, I'm makin' no promises."

# CHAPTER SEVEN

Timmy Cameron had picked the best of all the trees to perch himself. He'd been up since daybreak, even though his ma said the men wouldn't reach Clan MacDougal much before afternoon. He wanted to be the first to see them so he could run and announce it to the others. Timmy was only five and, although small for his age, none of the other children could run or climb trees as fast as he could. His father, Fennell, was one of the bravest fighters of the clan. Timmy had heard the other men go on about how courageous Fennell Cameron was.

Timmy was napping in a crook of the big oak when the sound of horses brought him wide awake. Through the leaves he spotted the ears of Hamish's big chestnut warhorse. They were coming! He climbed down and ran as fast as his short legs could carry him, his red hair flying behind like a pennant in a stiff wind. Cupping his hands around his mouth, he yelled. "Ma, Ma! They're here. I heard 'em. Then I saw 'em!" With that he turned and raced back, leaving the families to follow when they could. His breath was coming in short gasps when he reached the first of the men. Sure enough there was his pa.

"Pa!" he yelled, running to his father who was leading a lame horse. "What happened? Did we win? Did ye kill them English bastards?" He grabbed his pa's leg.

"Hush, Timmy. Don't let yer ma hear ye sayin' such words. She'll have both our hides." Fennell lifted his son into one arm and struggled on toward home. "Aye, we won, son. But I feel like I was horsewhipped in the process. Old Prince got cut purty bad."

Aggie Cameron had heard Timmy's yell. She hurried to the big bell outside her door and pulled the lever hard. Within minutes women and children came running from whatever chore they were performing and headed down the trail to the oncoming men. They carried canes and litters for the wounded. Each woman prayed that *her* husband or son had not been injured or killed.

"Clem. Over here!" shouted Irene Duplin, pulling her husband to her and supporting him with her shoulders. "Where's Magpie?"

"Her leg got broke. I had to put 'er out of 'er misery," he answered in a broken voice. Irene pretended not to notice the tears captured within her husband's eyes. She knew it wasn't physical pain but rather the loss of his faithful horse that brought him such anguish.

Inez Thigpen ran frantically through the tired and shabby fighters. "Where's Isaac?" she cried. "Where's my husband?" Jeb Lyons nodded toward the back. Inez hurried toward the men being transported on litters. She recognized his tartan, one that she had woven. It lay over his body, a once proud pattern now dragging in the dust. Inez fell to her knees and clutched the stiffened body of her husband to her bosom. How would she explain his absence to their two young sons? How could she describe him to the one now growing in her belly? A low keening sound came from her chest. She lifted her face to the heavens. "Why Isaac?" she cried. "Why'd ye not take one of them barbaric English?"

When she was quieter Ruby Tillot gently pulled her up, saying the others would prepare Isaac for burial. Inez resisted, clinging to her husband. "Think of the little ones, Inez," Ruby reminded her. Reluctantly Inez gave up her hold and allowed Ruby to lead her to her cabin. Inez wiped away her tears, lifted her shoulders, and went through the doorway tucking away her own sorrow so she could care for her children who were now fatherless.

Hamish watched as each man was met by his family. "Mind them open wounds, Brigit," he said. "We did the best we could but we've never got the proper mixtures with us when we're on a march."

Brigit nodded. Her practiced eyes had noted all of the wounded and she had already decided who needed her attention first.

Losing even one man to the English struck a hole in Hamish's heart. Now that the heat of battle was over and he saw the toll in heartbreak and suffering it made on his people, he doubted if the success was worth the losses. There was little satisfaction in knowing the English had lost much more since they seemed to have an unending supply of men and equipment. Each Scottish clan was small and closely knit, usually blood relatives combined with men who had sworn fealty to a particular laird due to common interests. After a battle, even with minimal losses, Hamish always felt personally responsible and unfit to be their leader.

Malcolm noticed the sadness that had visibly weakened his father. "Pa," he said, as he pointed to Edward. "Ye can kill this'n if ye want."

"'Twon't bring Isaac back. Killin' one man, fer revenge on an entire race, won't make me feel better." He handed his horse to Eli then turned toward his own home. Malcolm followed, vowing that the fighting would only end when Scotland was free of the English yoke.

Clan MacDougal was located north of the village of Edinburgh. It was in a part of Scotland where the forests were so thick and the trees so tall, that there were places where sunlight barely reached the ground. The mountaintops were clothed in mists that released disembodied shapes which seemed to blur the edges of reality. It was a landscape of contrasts, with peaceful valleys amid rocky crags that soared to the sky where only hawks dared to live. Life in such wilderness was unforgiving - like the swords that had cut into their men and altered lives forever.

By English standards, Clan MacDougal was humble even when one considered the fact that it was home to a powerful laird. However, the MacDougals enjoyed a better life than clans further north where the land was not as suitable for farming and the weather was severe throughout much of the year. Wattle and daub dwellings, framed in lumber, and covered with thatched roofs were scattered about in a loosely knit community. Sheep, cattle, pigs and chickens roamed at will while the horses were kept in rough-cut enclosures. A crystal-clear lake fed by a mountain stream lay in the valley, like a magnificent gem.

A fire, needed for cooking and warmth, burned constantly in the middle of each home. With few windows and poor ventilation, the interiors were dark and smoke-filled. It was not uncommon to lose several of the oldest and youngest each winter to lung problems. As Malcolm and Hamish passed the MacBride home, they heard Liza coughing. "I doubt she'll live to be ten," Malcolm said, shaking his head sadly. Hamish's shoulders drooped even lower.

The MacDougal cottage was slightly apart from the rest, indicating Hamish's importance as head of the clan. His home had two rooms on the ground floor with a loft above where the two men slept. Below the loft was a kitchen area and Kit's small bedroom. In the middle of the kitchen was a raised hearth equipped with a cooking spit, a pine table with three stools, and Hamish's heavy oak chair. It was his prized possession and favorite place to doze with his feet propped up on a footstool. Malcolm had built a funnel to channel smoke through a hole in the roof making the air cleaner and easier to breathe. A small cupboard and worktable gave Kit space to prepare meals for her small family. On either side of the door was a window covered with oilcloth, a luxury that greatly enhanced the light given off by the candles.

"A bowl of Kit's stew'll taste good 'bout now," Hamish commented, as he took a healthy sniff of the savory aroma wafting from his home. Too exhausted to argue further about the burden of caring for a worthless piece of humanity, Hamish helped Malcolm remove the Englishman from his horse.

"Aye," answered Malcolm. "I could smell it soon as we topped the last hill." He grunted when the weight of the semi-conscious man came to rest on his shoulders. "Tis good to be home."


Kit MacDougal, ruler of the MacDougal home, (notwithstanding the importance of her father and brother), knew the two would be out-of-sorts and hungry after a campaign in the Borders. Since early morning one of her famous fish stews, seasoned with herbs and scallions, had bubbled in the cauldron hanging on a spit over the fire.

Years ago her mother and younger brother had been killed during an English raid. She had fought her sorrow by taking over the chores her mother had taught her, running Hamish's home efficiently and frugally. By the time Kit was in her early teens, the kitchen was her domain. She expected Malcolm and Hamish to honor her schedule just as Hamish tolerated no disobedience from his men. A separate cupboard was stocked with bandages, herb mixtures, and splints since the clansmen could ill-afford misplacing these precious supplies. Being prepared often meant the difference between saving or losing a life.

At the sound of hooves crunching on the stone path, Kit brought out the pitcher of ale that had been cooling in the well, set it on the table, and picked up the loaf of dark bread that was warming on the hearth. The thin scar that ran across the top of her left hand brought a faint smile to her face. It had happened when she was twelve and still a novice at slicing bread.

Kit might have been considered plain in some circles but to her looking pretty had never been as important as being practical. She didn't own a mirror and each morning her long auburn hair was pulled into a bun at the nape of her neck to keep it out of the way while she worked. Malcolm teased her about the freckles that sprinkled over her nose and spilled onto her cheeks. Once, years ago, Kevin MacNally had said her green-flecked eyes reminded him of a beautiful cat he'd once owned. She'd boxed his ears good and chased him from the cottage with her broom.

She was molding the butter, admiring the perfectly round shape and rich yellow color, when Hamish and Malcolm came through the door. A loud groan brought a clutch of fear to her chest. She dropped the wooden paddles and turned toward the sound. The sight facing her was confusing. A wounded stranger, his arms draped over the shoulders of Malcolm and Hamish, moaned once more before slumping into semiconsciousness.

"Who's this man? Why didn't he go to 'is home clan? How bad's he hurt?" She shot the questions at them like arrows from an archer's bow.

Too out of breath to answer, Malcolm and Hamish dragged their cumbersome load toward a stool.

"Don't put 'im there!" Kit commanded. "Take 'im to my bed. Can't ye see he's barely conscious? Ye don't need to haul 'im all over the Highlands. Lay 'im down." She ordered them about like they were fools with no knowledge of caring for the wounded. Ignoring their mean looks, she hurried ahead and turned the coverlet back. She supported the man's head, while Hamish held his mid-section, and Malcolm lifted his legs onto the bed. As soon as the injured stranger was settled, Kit began to remove his tunic and undergarments.

"Now, tell me 'is name 'n why ye've brought 'im here?" she asked, already engrossed in her nursing.

"He's the young Lord Lexington," Malcolm replied. "He's. . ."

"He's an Englishman!" Kit yelled, causing the patient's eyelids to flutter. "Ye mean to say ye've brought one of them wretched murderers into our home? Fer me to heal?" She ceased her ministrations and advanced toward Malcolm with hands fisted.

"Ye allowed this, Pa?" She turned an accusing look in Hamish's direction.

Hamish put up his hands as though to ward off the devil. "Ye'll have to ask Malcolm 'bout that. I'm too tired to explain 'is ridiculous scheme." Hamish let out a great breath then plopped his exhausted body into his old chair.

Kit turned with hands on her hips and fire in her eyes, "Malcolm. Explain!"

Malcolm had never been able to intimidate Kit. In fact, he was the one usually retreating from her territory. The words tumbled from his mouth so fast that Kit had to listen carefully not to miss the meaning. "He's the only son of Lord Neville of Lexington Estate, who was killed in the battle. His family'll pay well to git their only son 'n heir returned." He wiped the sweat from his brow and sat down wearily on a stool near the bed. "We need money to restock 'n repair our weapons if we're to press our advantage afore the English regroup. I need ye to nurse 'im to where he's healthy 'nough to make the journey back to the Borders." Malcolm looked at his sister with what he hoped resembled the imploring eyes of a puppy.

The prisoner began thrashing his arms and rolling his head back and forth. Kit hurried to his side, momentarily forgetting the argument with Malcolm. He seized the opportunity to escape and join Hamish in the kitchen.

While it was not her way to ignore humans in pain, Kit resented having to nurse one of the enemy fighters. *I hate Malcolm for putting me in this position,* she thought, as she began examining the man who now occupied her bed. "His right shoulder's the worst," she mumbled, then flexed his wrist and elbow. He didn't flinch but the slightest pressure on his shoulder brought forth a quick intake of breath. His pulse was strong but both eyes were swollen nearly shut. The right cheekbone was discolored and there was a small wound on his chin.

"Malcolm!" Kit yelled. "Git some water heatin'." Malcolm pulled his sore body up and went forth to do his sister's bidding. He was already beginning to feel that he would have a more active role in the nursing of this prisoner than he had counted on.

Kit pushed her irritation to the back of her mind and began a methodical assessment of Edward's injuries. She cut the shirt on his left side so she could then pull the clothing under his body to the right side. He was a big man and difficult for her to maneuver without causing more damage to his shoulder. When the job was finally accomplished she sat on the side of the bed for a few minutes, catching her breath and rubbing her shoulders.

Not hearing any sound from the bedroom, Hamish called. "Kit! Ye alright 'n there?"

"Aye, just outta breath. He's a big oaf 'n can't do anythin' fer 'imself."

Malcolm entered the room just as Kit had pulled off the prisoner's pants and was preparing to relieve him of his undergarments. "Kit! Let me do that."

"What'd ye expect, Malcolm? That I could minister to someone without disrobin' 'em to determine their injuries? Ye 'n Pa certainly aren't qualified to handle a wounded man."

Malcolm stood speechless, still holding the pail of warm water.

"Give me that 'n git out while I go to work! And don't be so pious. Ye brought 'im here fer me to heal. I'll try to do that but I'll tolerate no advice from ye."

Malcolm put the water beside Kit and headed out of the room, acutely aware that he had not considered all the ramifications of bringing a wounded Englishman into their home for Kit to nurse. She twisted her head and watched him go. He'll be the first to know that his irresponsible decision will cause hardships for many before this ordeal is over. She turned her attention once more to her patient and with professional expertise continued her evaluation of the severity of his wounds.

While many young ladies had lusted for Edward, Kit took little notice of his broad shoulders and muscular chest that tapered into narrow hips and legs. He looked strong enough to squeeze the life out of a half-grown buck. She'd cared for many men shaped such as this and had long since grown accustomed to their anatomy. Now and then, however, Kit had wondered how these male parts looked when the men were healthy. When these thoughts intruded into her nursing concentration she blushed and hurried off for more supplies, leaving Clare or Brigit to work on the patient. But a hated Englishman did not evoke such interest. *This is just a pampered aristocrat who will probably die the first time he sleeps outside on a Highland winter night*, she thought maliciously, then cared for his wounds with the same dispassionate efficiency she would summon for an injured sheep.

"Malcolm," she bellowed. In the kitchen Malcolm covered his ears. "Bring some clothes fer this man. Yers'll probably fit better'n Pa's."

*All I have are tattered shirts and tartans*, Malcolm thought peevishly, as he trudged up to his pallet. *I doubt that will be acceptable to an Englishman.* Prudently he kept his thoughts to himself and followed Kit's orders.

By the time Malcolm returned, Kit had finished bandaging her patient's shoulder and he now lay with the rest of his body stark naked on the bed. Malcolm's cheeks reddened. Kit looked at him. "Don't just stand there. Put them clothes on 'im while I git a meal on the table. Pa's within an hour of starvation." She got up and headed for the kitchen.

"We'll all be in a better mood with a belly full of food. Later I'll put a sling on 'im to keep the arm 'n shoulder quiet while it heals."

Malcolm looked dubiously at Edward. He hadn't bargained on having to help with the care of an injured prisoner. A naked one at that. He was reluctant to be put in such an intimate situation with any man, Scottish or English.

As he hesitated, trying to decide how to begin, Kit yelled from the kitchen. "Malcolm, care fer that man afore he dies of the chills."

With the care one would take with a leper, Malcolm began to clothe the patient, who was only partly conscious. Malcolm could dress, saddle up, and be on the attack within minutes but putting clothes on one naked man took him longer than milking two cows. When Edward was finally dressed Malcolm was sore, exhausted, hungry, and furious. "Why'd I ever think this was a good idea?" he snarled.

In the kitchen, Kit had brought out the heavy earthenware bowls she loved. She'd traded one of her tartans for them in the street markets of Edinburgh. She traced her finger over the rough surface and admired the subtle coloring and impression of a rainbow. Hamish snuffled abruptly as his chin dropped to his chest. Kit left her daydreaming and ladled out two helpings of stew, poured the ale, and sliced the bread.

"Smells good," Hamish said, as he situated himself at the table. "Where's Malcolm?"

"In the bedroom dressin' 'is English captive in Scottish clothes."

Hamish chuckled. He knew that money was desperately needed for the Scots to continue their assaults and he agreed that Edward would bring a large ransom. However, it went against the grain having an enemy in his own home being tended to by his daughter. At least he could laugh over the fact that the English prisoner would be dressed as a Scot.

Malcolm arrived for the stew just as Hamish and Kit were getting up from the table.

"I suppose everythin's cold now," he grumbled.

"The kettle's still over the fire. Help yerself," Kit said, and offered a further warning. "This is just a samplin' of how much time that man'll require. So don't be expectun' the laundry 'n cookin' to be as punctual as normal." She carried her bowl to the basin then gathered scraps for the dogs.

"I'll leave fer the Borders within a week," Malcolm mumbled. "The way Kit feels she'll kill 'im afore I can git any money fer 'im." He ate in silence while Hamish went off to visit the homes of his clansmen and see to the well being of his men.

Through snatches of dreams filled with noise and confusion, Edward's brain began to ascend from an abyss. The more awake he became the more he desired a return to senselessness. There was not an inch of his body that did not suffer. His eyes had shrunk to slits that allowed only a glimmer of light into his head, which itself, ached as though he'd been attacked by a blacksmith's hammer. Somewhere in the fringes of light and darkness he heard the rustle of a person close by.

"Where am I? How did I get here?" Edward struggled to form the words from lips now doubled in size.

"Ye're in the Highlands at Clan MacDougal," a woman's voice answered. She sounded resentful. "Ye were dragged here by my brother, Malcolm. I've brought ye some soup 'n ale. Should be easy on yer swollen mouth." He felt a wooden spoon begin to separate his sore lips. He tried to turn his face away.

"Who are you? Why am I here?" he asked in a raspy whisper.

Kit was already in a foul humor and now she was greatly irritated. "I've no time to answer all yer questions. Talk to Malcolm. He's responsible fer ye bein' here." She moved the spoon again toward his mouth. "Either eat or ye can wait 'til tomorrow. I've other work to do."

Edward was not so senseless that he didn't notice the rancor in the words of the speaker. "I'll feed myself," he mumbled, and reached in the direction of the disgruntled voice. The scream that came from his mouth brought the dogs to baying and caused Kit to put the food down and attend to her patient. He shook uncontrollably at the horrific pain. Her firm hand steadied his shoulder and she applied a cool cloth to his forehead.

"Have it yer way," the voice said, with a bit more compassion. "But ye'll have to use yer left hand. As ye've just learned yer right shoulder's been injured." The woman placed the spoon in his left hand and continued talking. "A Highlander'd never make such a commotion over such an insignificant wound."

Edward gritted his teeth and vowed not to let another sound of pain slip from his swollen lips. He glimpsed the outline of what he thought was the bowl and thrust the spoon into it. Halfway to his mouth the utensil slipped from his grasp and soup spilled down his front.

"Now I've gotta change yer clothes 'gain." Her voice was indignant. "That fish'll smell all the way to Edinburgh when it's laid on yer chest awhile." Kit retrieved the spoon and fed Edward the remainder of the soup, interspersed with swigs of ale. Too hungry and sore to object, he humbly cooperated.

After the meal, she returned with another ragged shirt. "I'll need yer help to remove the dirty one. Pull yer left arm out first." Edward did as he was told. "Now try to raise yerself up while I drag it out from under ye, then I'll slide it down yer right arm." Edward slowly followed her directions. When the right sleeve came off he clinched his jaws to keep from crying out.

They reversed the process to get the clean one on. "This is Malcolm's last clean shirt. Try not to soil it til I git the laundry done tomorrow."

As Kit struggled to get Edward into the dry shirt she studied the patient she resented so much. Her best assessment was that he was almost as tall as Malcolm and had a mane of hair as black as a raven's wing. His forehead was accented with heavily arched brows. With the dark facial bruises, the overall effect left him looking like Satan. When the man once more lay quiet and flat she felt his body begin to slide once more into sleep.

Taking care not to disturb his slumber Kit smoothed the wrinkles in the coverlet and fluffed the goose down pillow. *This is a good time to put splints on that shoulder,* she thought. *Perhaps he won't notice the pain so much.*

Kit brought out splints made of thin oak slabs and placed one on either side of his upper right arm, securing them with strips of coarse linen. After wrapping the arm and shoulder with a piece of cloth about six feet long and six inches wide, she supported the entire side with a sling that tied at the nape of his neck. As she worked her patient occasionally released a muffled snatch in his breath to indicate he'd noticed a disturbance to his sleep. Eventually she straightened up and massaged her aching lower back. Her patient was snoring lightly and regularly, obviously more comfortable than at any time since his injury had occurred. Kit harrumphed at the unfairness of it all and left to clean up the kitchen.

Kitchen pots clanging, dogs barking, and alien accents being spoken forced Edward's brain to struggle up from the dark canyon where he slept. He fought through crusted eyelids into the twilight of his surroundings trying to evaluate the quarters he inhabited. The walls of the primitive dwelling were made of rough-cut notched logs, caulked with mud that in places had chinked out leaving tiny openings to the outside. The window to the left of his bed was covered with oilcloth offering only a blurred view of sky and stars. To his right he peered through a doorway into what appeared to be a tiny kitchen. The rough-hewn floor boards protected the dwellers from living on the sod but allowed the musty odor of dirt and mold to filter through the spaces.

The bed pallet was covered in a soft linen shell, with a light goose down coverlet and pillows of the same filling. Taken all around Edward was as comfortable as anyone with the wounds he suffered could be whether he lay in one of his richly accessorized beds at Lexington Estate or this humble cottage in the Highlands.

As his eyes wandered through the meager furnishings of the room the need to relieve himself became an overpowering sensation. Remembering his belligerent nurse made him determined to care for himself.

"Miss!" he called as he tried to sit up.

Kit came to the bedroom, lit the candle on the chest next to the bed, and turned to face him. She knew full well what her patient's problem was. Edward nodded toward the door. "I must attend to my personal needs. Could you ask your brother to assist me outside please?"

"The men have more to do than play nursemaid to a wounded Englishman. Them who aren't injured have earned a rest." Kit pulled a chamber pot from beneath the bed, placed it beside him, and extended her arm to support him to the side of the bed. "If ye think I'm goin' to drag ye outside, think again. Not only 're ye too heavy but it would ruin the bandages I've just put on yer shoulder. Here, take my hand."

With a look of horror, Edward shrank back as if to escape the attack of a vicious wolf. This was followed by a grunt of pain.

"Too proud to accept help from a woman? Or just a Scots woman?" She turned to leave. "Let me know when ye're ready to come off yer high horse."

"Wait!" he gasped. "Please."

Kit returned to the bedside. "Why ye English think the world turns on yer every whim is a mystery to me. The sooner ye learn ye're no different'n anyone else, the better ye'll fare."

Edward's full bladder far outweighed his pride, leaving him no choice but to take hold of her hand and let her position his legs over the side. She supported him with her shoulder while he lowered himself onto the offensive chamber pot.

"I'll be in the kitchen," Kit said. "Yell when ye're finished."

Edward was mortified! He'd never been so disabled as to need assistance with such a personal situation. Years ago, when he'd sprained an ankle jumping off a horse he'd needed help for a few days. But it was his manservant, Giles, not a maid, who had performed the disagreeable task!

Clumsiness, pain, and cumbersome bandages robbed him of any modesty. The process seemed to take forever, leaving him dizzy, sweaty, and exhausted.

"I'm finished if you have time to help me," he muttered feebly, to the voice in the shadows of his new existence.

Kit returned and assisted Edward back into bed. He leaned on her heavily, keeping silent as the pain shot prisms of light through his bloodshot eyes. He felt defeated and humiliated as he watched her leave with the chamber pot.

"Malcolm oughta be doin' this!" Kit declared angrily to a nearby goose as she threw the smelly contents over the hill.

# CHAPTER EIGHT

The back door squawked on its rusty hinges as Kit threw it open with a vengeance and tossed breakfast scraps into a yard full of waiting animals. She plopped the milk pail onto the table causing a shower of tiny white droplets to fly into the air like snowflakes through an open door. Stripes, the house cat, leapt from the kitchen stool and greedily licked away all traces of Kit's outrage.

"Malcolm'll pay fer this if I have to track 'im all the way to the Borders 'n beat 'is thoughtless hide!" Kit sputtered, as she threw some tin cups on the table. "The coward! To leave on 'nother one of 'is trips to who knows where." She grabbed the egg basket and headed out the door. "Expectin' me to nurse that English bastard back to health. I oughta feed 'im to the wolves instead." She shoved a defiant hen off her nest. "*Malcolm*'ll need healin' when next I see 'im." An old rooster scurried off as fast as his useless wings would allow, feathers floating in his wake. Pride, a yearling colt, turned and ran from the commotion with knees high, tail arched stiffly above his back, and snorting loudly.

Hamish ran into the yard throwing his tartan around him on the way, his white legs exposed like the belly of a turtle knocked upside-down. "What'n the name of God's happened?" he yelled, stumbling over one of the cats hunkered in the path. "Why're the animals in an uproar? Have we been attacked by a wolf?" With one hand holding the tartan in place and the other pushing straggles of hair from his eyes, Hamish looked left and right for an assailant.

"No, Pa. The livestock 're in fine fettle."

Hamish rubbed the sleep from his eyes. "Why 're they all so agitated then?"

Tendrils of Kit's hair had escaped from her bun, the bottom of her dress was muddy from dragging in the dew, and traces of yolk marred her apron bib. Hamish glanced into her basket and, seeing several cracked eggs, decided it would be best to wait for her to explain.

"Malcolm left afore dawn this mornin' on 'nother of 'is wild goose chases. My ill- placed temper caused the animals some distress." She walked toward the cottage. "Why couldn't he've waited 'nother day or two? Til that wretched man in there doesn't need to be helped everywhere?"

"Ahh well, Kit. I could help ye this mornin," he offered, thankful that no blood had been shed.

"Fat lotta good that'll do. Then ye'll be off 'til dark, 'n gone 'gain tomorrow while I'm still here caterin' to 'is needs." Kit glared toward the room where Edward lay. She turned and brandished a knife in Hamish's direction. "Mind ye, I won't let 'im die. I'm not a heathen. But I'll not play wet nurse to a spoiled aristocratic dandy."

Hamish rued his decision to let Malcolm bring the injured Englishman into the village. This was just the sort of situation he'd feared. "No one expects that, Kit." He tried to soothe her with a voice he normally used for a frightened colt. "I didn't want the man brought into our home either. But Malcolm's hell-bent on gettin' 'nough money to replenish our weaponry."

"I know, Pa," Kit replied, with an air of resignation. "T'isn't yer fault I'm mad. I know we need the money." She laid the knife on the table and continued. "Still, it goes 'gainst the grain to nurse an enemy back to health so's he can lead troops to fight us 'gain later." She wiped a smear of honey off the table and sat down.

"Well then," Hamish replied, in a brighter tone of voice. "While ye fix breakfast, I'll go to MacKenzie's shed 'n git an idea how low he is on iron." He hurried off, happy to be out of range of Kit's fury and pleased to be excluded from helping with the patient's daily care.

Kit watched him go, sorry for her unreasonable outburst. *I know Malcolm was only doing what he believes is best for our people and Hamish is trying to tolerate the captive for the same reason. The least I can do is not be so resentful and get him healthy as quickly as I can,* she mused. With a dispirited drooping of her shoulders, she started fixing breakfast. Not being an overly repentant person however, Kit gloated over the knowledge that for the next several days Malcolm would be sleeping on the cold ground and eating stale bread and hard cheese. "I hope he breaks a tooth," she said to Stripes, who blinked an eye before going back to sleep.

Hamish was thoughtful as he returned from talking with MacKenzie. He had not realized how little material was left for making horseshoes and repairing the weapons and equipment necessary for any fighting force. He had to admit that it was a rare piece of luck for Malcolm to bring home a prisoner who would command a large ransom. Money they could use to replenish their iron reserves. *I'll have to persuade Kit to accept the importance of this endeavor and not go so hard on Malcolm,* he thought, as he approached his home.

The smell of meat frying convinced Hamish that Kit had returned to a better humor and it was now safe to enter her domain. The past few days had nearly used up all his energy and optimism. He was in need of a good meal. His steps quickened at the thought and as he walked through the door, Kit turned with a pleasant expression on her face. "Ye're right, Pa. We need to make a profit off that creature. I'll give 'im the best care I can so's we can take 'is sorry arse back 'n exchange it fer lots of money." Hamish wondered why she was now so amenable, but when it came to the moods of women, he asked no questions. Instead, he attacked his breakfast with the gusto of a suckling calf.

She bustled about bringing him more bread and butter. "I'm sorry I've been so difficult. Malcolm's right. We *do* need money fer our cause 'n I'll try harder to be civil to the beast while he recovers."

Hamish was so surprised at Kit's willingness to cooperate this quickly after threatening to take Malcolm's life, that he ceased eating and closed his mouth tightly. A piece of bacon dangled from one side, like a loose twig in a bird's nest.

"I'll need help with the man, what with ye 'n Malcolm 'way. He's heavy 'n it takes so long to tend to 'is needs that my normal chores 're well behind." She handed Hamish some honey to break the trance he seemed to be in. "As he improves he'll bear watchin' so's he can't escape. Then all our efforts'd be fer naught."

The last remark brought Hamish back to the business of eating. He swallowed the bacon, broke off a piece of bread, washed it down with ale and answered. "I'll talk to Ben Gordon today - see if he'll let Oliver come over. The boy can be depended on 'n heaven knows he's got energy 'nough fer two grown men."

"Oliver's a good choice. He won't let the man git outta 'is sight. By the way Pa, what's the prisoner's name? I gotta call 'im somethin' other'n 'cowardly English bastard,'" Kit replied.

Hamish let out a loud guffaw, spewing breakfast leavings across the table. "Ye mustn't be so vindictive Kit, although I won't deny havin' a laugh at an English gentleman bein' at the mercy of a Scottish lass." Kit smiled at Hamish's admission of his own questionable motives. "Malcolm says 'is name's Edward. That sounds better'n 'cowardly bastard.' I'll go talk to Ben now." With that Hamish left, a chuckle still bubbling in his throat.

Kit went to the well, drew some water in a large earthen basin, and resolved to do her best to be a compassionate nurse to a patient who represented everything she hated most.


The commotion of the morning had filtered slowly into Edward's brain. Hearing the strong words between the man and woman in the adjoining room reminded him that he was living in circumstances over which he had no control. The pain that wracked every part of his body made it impossible for him to think further than the next moment.

While his vision still permitted only blurs and shadows his ears informed him that his tormentor, who claimed to be a nurse, was on her way to his bedside. He hated to admit his need for her help. The dreaded chamber pot ritual had torn away all vestiges of self-esteem he'd ever possessed. He doubted if his body would ever function properly again.

He tried to envision what this woman looked like. She sounded young but even when she was angry and her words harsh, she cared for him with an obvious amount of experience and sensitivity to his pain. *Why does she go to so much bother*, he wondered? *The Scots are heathens who will probably kill me and bury my body under a pile of rocks. They'll collect the ransom and claim I was killed by wolves on my return to Lexington Estate.*

Then her shadowy figure approached and Edward shuddered inwardly as she unceremoniously helped him on and off the despised pot. When he was once again settled in the bed, she sat down beside him. He looked away. Her cool fingers took hold of his jaw and turned his face back again. "Won't do ye any good to turn 'way," she said. "Furthermore, ye oughta be glad I'm willin' to nurse yer wretched body. Without care ye could lose the sight in one of yer eyes. Must've hit a rock when ye fell." She cleansed his face carefully then placed a cloth over his eyes. It felt good.

"What did you say about my eye?" he asked, with a hint of panic coloring his words.

"Tis a thin film coverin' yer right eye," she answered. "And slight seepage." She wiped the eye with a soft cloth trying to bring the film off the surface. Then she covered his left eye. "Can ye see anythin' at all?"

He blinked hard several times. "A little, I think. Are you wearing a blue tunic?"

"Aye," she answered. "How many fingers am I holdin' up?"

He tried hard to see through the haze. "I can only see your hand, not how many fingers." Edward was panting with the effort to see.

As she watched fear take over this arrogant young man lying in her bed, Kit saw him not as an Englishman but as a patient devastated at the thought of losing an eye.

"Try to relax," she said quietly. "'Tis a good sign ye can see a little. I'm goin' to leave a cloth on the right eye to keep out light 'n any dust that might further aggravate it." She fixed an eye patch with soft bandaging then checked to make sure the sling and splint on his shoulder were still secure. "I reckon ye're ready fer breakfast by now."

Her soothing words gave Edward hope and he appreciated the fact that, for now, she was no longer bullying him. Nonetheless, he was suspicious. In his short time at the MacDougal home, Edward had learned that Kit's moods came and went as capriciously as spring showers. It was wise to remain aloof while within range of her voice.

She fed him the usual fare of fried pork, eggs, hard bread, and ale that he considered to be very bitter. He missed the fruit and cake selection always in abundance on the tables at Lexington Estate and he longed for the smell of freshly cut flowers and newly laundered bedding. How good it would feel to wear silk again instead of rough linen or scratchy wool. Even so, with all its primitive furnishings, the home was clean and the food substantial.

"Ye're gettin' better with that left hand," Kit remarked, breaking into his reverie.

He looked at her with his good eye. "Does that mean you'll let me use the chamber pot alone?"

"Not 'n a hare's heartbeat," she answered, without a flinch. "Til I'm sure ye won't lose yer balance I'll be helpin' ye, 'n that's that!" She picked up the remains of breakfast and left the room without another word, back stiff and eyes blazing. Edward knew he'd made her angry again. He sighed and wished he was dead.

In less than ten minutes she was back, carrying a basin full of water with steam roiling off the surface hot enough to cook a chicken. *My God*, he thought. *She's going to burn me alive.*

"From the smell of things, yer whole body needs a scrubbin'. Sit up 'n help me git yer clothes off."

"You'll scald me with that!" he yelled, pushing to the far side of the bed, which still left him within arm's reach of Kit. "Don't come any closer with that hot water," he ordered, with what he hoped had the ring of authority.

"Ye're in *my* bed 'n ye smell like ye've been sleepin' with pigs. By the time ye're undressed, the water'll be the proper temperature. Now cooperate or I'll call Brigit to help."

Knowing she would be true to her threats and unwilling to be exposed to yet another woman, Edward complied grudgingly. Forgetting any earlier appreciation, Edward now wished he'd never met this willful woman. However, he kept his silence and helped her remove the shabby, smelly clothes.

She inspected his shoulder. "The bruise is spreadin' down into yer chest." Instantly concerned, Edward tried to read the expression in her eyes. "That's to be expected though," she continued. "Ye're gonna look a lot worse afore ye git better." He thought she sounded gleeful.

"Lie flat while I clean yer lower half," Kit said, as she wrung water out of the cloth.

"Not in a hare's heartbeat," he mimicked her earlier words. "I'll die first."

"I'm sure there's many women here who'd be glad to thrust a knife through yer soft belly. However, we need money more'n we need yer blood right now. So, hold still!"

She removed the coverlet and began tugging at his undergarments. Edward struggled to pull her hands away then stiffened as pain shot through his shoulder. Kit ignored his actions and methodically continued to pull off his clothing.

"Ye look no different'n countless other men I've nursed but ye certainly smell worse. I thought ye pampered English were a fastidious lot."

Edward could not abide her taunting voice. "We are! But at home men servants would do this. Our ladies are too refined to be subjected to such sights. They're..."

"I know," Kit interrupted loudly. "They're delicate. They live in a society that enslaves others to do their dirty work." She shook her finger in his face. "Ye English 're a lazy lot who steal our livestock, burn our crops 'n homes, 'n kill our people. Ye call that civilized, Edward?" She wondered what had happened to her resolve to treat Edward with more respect.

It was the first time she'd called Edward by his given name. It knocked him off guard for a moment but the feel of her angry breath blowing in his face and calling him names brought a similar fury within his own heart. He hoisted himself up on one elbow, ignoring the pain.

"We provide homes, food, and land for our tenants. They want for nothing. Moreover, the Scots raid the English so don't harangue me about your oppression. You don't live close to the Borders. You're unaware of what the situation really is." Edward sank back onto his pillow that was now damp with sweat. He was so still that only his chest, which rose and fell with his labored breathing, indicated he was still alive.

"Don't talk to me 'bout providin' fer yer tenants. What choice do they have? Ye strip 'em of their pride 'n ability to provide fer themselves then expect 'em to appreciate their 'benevolent enslavement.'"

"Isn't that better than living the way you Scots do?" Edward returned in a strained voice. "In squalor, disease, and deprivation. Barely able to survive much less experience life's finer aspects." They were face to face trying to out shout each other.

"What 'finer aspects' of life do yer peasants experience? Disregardin' the few annual holidays when the gentry give 'em a wee glance at splendor afore sendin' 'em back to their hovels." Her scrubbing became more vigorous. Edward's skin began to burn.

"Ouch!" he shouted. "I'm not one of your sheep to be shorn. I suppose this invasion of my privacy is to be expected in this primitive place."

"Ye deserve the treatment ye so easily hand out to others," she retaliated. "This is nothin' compared to how ye English treat the souls of so many people." She threw the coverlet over him and stood to leave the room in a huff. "If I had my way ye'd be turned out 'n left to find yer own way through the mountains while ye're still barely able to move. Ye'd be a good meal fer the wolves."

"I welcome the chance to leave this heathen place on any terms," he shouted at her departing back.

Kit felt defeated. She had once again allowed her hatred to destroy her ability to nurse properly, regardless of who the patient was. Summer loomed long and bitter to these two antagonists forced to endure it together.

Few words passed between them during their ensuing morning rituals. Throughout his first two weeks Kit helped Edward on and off the pot then assisted him with his bath. By the time she'd fed him breakfast, she was already worn out. Yet her duties of cooking, cleaning, milking, and feeding the livestock had not even begun.

Their resentment increased as the days pressed on. Edward felt better and wanted to perform his morning cleansing in private. Kit wanted to be rid of him, but feared he would reinjure himself. Additionally, his right eye had not yet returned to normal. There were times she was so tired of the added work, not to mention the affront to her idea of fairness, that she wished she could leave Edward in the wild to die and let the ransom go to the devil.

One morning Edward awakened before Kit arrived with her ungracious remarks and condescending manner. He could see shafts of sunlight filtering through cracks in the wall. He was able to turn his head in the direction of sounds coming from the kitchen. His chest no longer felt like a tree lay across it and he could move his legs without causing pain in other parts of his body. A quiet chuckle was the closest to a laugh he could get but the happiness in his heart was tumultuous. He was getting better!

He heard Kit assembling her equipment. Soon her solemn face would be coming through the door. He wondered how much longer he could tolerate her animosity.

Oliver yelled something unintelligible from the barnyard. "Can't hear ye, Oliver. I'm busy takin' care of Edward." Her tone was conciliatory. He was furious to be looked on with such lack of regard.

She set the bandages and water down with a thud. The water splashed in his face. He shielded himself with his good arm and cursed silently. She removed the supports from his shoulder and manipulated his arm to assess the improvement. Edward hid his grimace behind a face as hard as granite. Concealing his pain was not necessary since Kit was more absorbed in the progress of her patient than noticing the feelings that might be sketched on his face. He was amazed. One minute she was surly and the next instant she treated him with pride because of her ability to nurse, as if it didn't matter that he was English.

"Better," she said with satisfaction. "Ye don't need them splints any longer. But ye'll have to be careful with yer movements." She took hold of his right hand. "Squeeze," she ordered. "Let's see how much ye can grip afore tis painful."

He squeezed.

"Ouch!" Kit sputtered, pulling her hand from his. "Ye've recovered better'n I'd hoped." She massaged her hand.

"I didn't mean to hurt you, Kit, but you did say for me to squeeze." Edward wanted to clarify that point before she condemned him for it. "Are you hurt?" he inquired insincerely.

"Nay," she replied, holding her face tight, determined not to let her temper get the best of her once again. "Next time I'll let ye practice on a piece of wood. Let me see if yer eye's better." She began removing the patch. Her breath felt like dandelion down skimming his face. It tickled. Edward chewed his lip to keep from laughing.

Her fingers gently dislodged the bandage and his eye gradually came into her view. He saw a look of concern flicker across her face.

"What's wrong?" he asked, trying to sound unconcerned.

"I wish it twasn't still seepin'," she sighed.

Terror jolted through his chest. The fear of even one blind eye made him forget he was lucky just to be alive.

Kit felt his body tense and his breath come in ragged spurts. She realized she'd been thoughtless in letting her concerns be known to the patient. Brigit had always cautioned her against such action. "Here now, tis better'n yesterday. Let's try this." she said, hoping to calm him. "Can ye see anythin' when I cover yer other eye?"

"A little," he replied cautiously.

"What can ye see?"

Edward stared hard into her face. "Your eyes. They're green! Yes. They've got green flecks in them. Right?" He was proud to be able to distinguish something so minute.

"How'd I know if they're green?" she answered, flustered at such a remark. "I'm lookin' out of 'em, not into 'em." She settled her expression again to one that was austere and noncommittal. "What color's the bow I've got tied in my hair?" She turned her head toward him.

"It's blue, I think. Or maybe dark green," he said. He felt like he had when Mr. Moffitt, his tutor, questioned him during his studies. "Is that right?"

Watching Edward, helpless and worried, Kit thought he looked less like a formidable knight and more like a child in need of comfort. She felt old. She had nursed so many of her clansmen who had left the mountains with the courage of lions and returned with their boldness and dignity in shreds. Once healed, they went off to battle again. When would the cycle end?

"Well," Edward spoke loudly. "Am I right?"

His abruptness jarred her from her thoughts. "Almost. Tis purple. But it'd be easy to make that mistake in this poor light," she said, trying not to discourage him. "We'll keep the patch on fer 'nother day or two just to be sure."

She resented feeling like his mother. *I don't need another soul for whom I'm responsible,* she thought sadly. Her heart was heavy with the despair of knowing hers would always be a life destined for hardship and loss.

As Edward helped her remove his sling and undershirt, he was confused at why Kit had become so pensive. Normally she was more than willing to scold him for being English, being wounded, and being her prisoner. He was silent as she studied his upper body in a dispassionate manner. "Most of the bruisin's gone. Ye look a sight better'n ye did when they dragged ye into these mountains." His sigh of relief fanned Kit's hair away from her face.

She frowned while she restored her hair to order. "Ye can git yerself on 'n off the pot now. God knows tis not a chore I'm sorry to give up." She picked up her nursing equipment and left. *I didn't ask to be here,* Edward thought angrily. *I'll be glad to leave this black hole of poverty.*

Edward couldn't wait to take care of his own needs. As soon as the back door slammed proclaiming Kit's departure, he reached down to pull the chamber pot from under the bed. It might as well have been on the moon. He'd had no idea how difficult it would be to make his sore, stiff body get out of the bed, bend over to pull the offensive vessel out, then sit down on it! Still harder was getting back up, straining his back and leg muscles while pulling with one good shoulder. He grunted, groaned, and struggled until he was almost upright. He took a great gulp of air into his burning lungs. The effort cost him his balance. He slipped -- and the pot, with its smelly contents, teetered on one edge. Determined not to let it spill he let loose of the bed, grabbed the pot, and set it straight just before he fell backward onto the rough floor.

He lay there a few minutes, gasping like the bellows in Ned's blacksmith shop. Finally, he pushed himself up into a crawling position. With one arm and two knees, Edward dragged his unwilling body to the bed, pulled himself up by its frame, and fell onto the mattress with his last bit of strength. He seriously doubted if he'd be able to feed himself that day, much less get on and off the pot again.

From the kitchen, he heard the banging of dishes accompanied by Kit's fishmonger voice. "Stripes, git 'way from that butter afore I skin ye alive." This was followed by hasty footsteps as she chased the hapless cat from the house.

"Hell will freeze over before that despicable woman knows how bad off I am," Edward vowed, as he began to pull on his tattered Scottish clothes.

The next morning he emerged from his pain-slogged sleep to the sound of voices just outside the window. By now, he was interested in the comings and goings in his surroundings since the thought of escape was a possibility upon which he'd begun to dwell. He pushed himself off the bed and shuffled to the window to have a look, positioning himself in the shadows so as not to disclose his presence. Kit was speaking to a short, dark-haired girl, obviously in her last days of pregnancy.

"Are ye feelin' well, Melanie?" she asked, as she massaged the woman's shoulders and back. This was a Kit whom Edward did not recognize. *Why doesn't she show me that sort of consideration? Why must she always treat me like someone who doesn't matter?* he asked himself. "Tis my third one Kit. Feelin' well's not a consideration. Tis the discomfort of not bein' able to see my feet that's the problem." Both women laughed, hugged one another, then Melanie headed for her own cottage.

"Send Angus over when the time comes," Kit reminded her friend.

"Aye. Ye know my deliveries better'n I do by now."

Kit waved, then turned to face the irksome task of caring for her prisoner. When she eventually entered the bedroom, she saw a smiling and friendly Edward. "Good morning, Kit. Looks like a lovely day today."

Kit's eyes flashed with suspicion. "Ye hungry?" she asked curtly.

"Yes, I am," he answered enthusiastically, hoping she'd notice his good spirits.

"Good. Hoist yerself to the kitchen. Tis time fer ye to eat at the table with the rest of us." After a perfunctory glance at his eye, she left the room.

Edward was once again reminded of his childhood schooling and the tutor who was never satisfied with his efforts. It seemed he was destined to spend his time in the Highlands with another person who would never admit he had any redeeming qualities.

After much huffing and puffing in the process of the chamber pot and dressing, Edward arrived at the table just in time to see Kit and Hamish finish breakfast and go on to their morning chores. He was glad to eat without his belligerent jailers watching his every move but his pride smarted mightily that they thought him too feeble to escape.

He hauled the old basin to the well and painfully drew water for his wash. Kit was humming a nondescript tune while she laid the laundry on the bushes to dry. It riled him that she never acknowledged his presence in her vicinity. He'd never been treated with such indifference. At home Giles always heated his bath since washing in cold water was beyond believing. "One would think she'd be worried I'd try to escape," he muttered sullenly.

While Edward thought he'd gone unnoticed Kit had, in fact, observed him from beneath lowered lashes. *It's time to enlist Oliver's help,* she thought. *I'll speak to him this forenoon.*

Later in the day Edward sat on a stump, chewing a sprig of grass and contemplating his plan of escape. *I'll need to know all the trails and where they lead,* he thought. *I must also get my body strong enough to make the trek back to Lexington Estate.* He pulled himself up with the rough cane he'd fashioned from a fallen limb. He was nearly knocked off his feet when he bumped into a young boy standing behind him.

"Good grief! Who the devil are you, and why are you lurking behind me?"

Edward was staring into a pair of mischievous blue eyes, accompanied by a crooked smile that was decorated with an abundance of bright freckles. He was about as tall as a cow's hip and spindly as a weanling colt.

"What's your name?" demanded Edward. "You shouldn't sneak up on a body like that. Didn't your mother teach you better?"

Undaunted, the young stranger sidled close as if to support Edward. "My name's Oliver. I don't have a mother 'cause she died from the fever when I was five. Haven't got brothers or sisters neither. Just my pa, 'n he's always workin' with the other men."

"Why are you here, young man?"

"Hamish said if I don't let ye escape I can have a colt of my own this fall. And my name's Oliver, not young man."

"Just how do you propose to ensure my remaining here as a prisoner, Oliver?" Edward asked pompously

"When Kit's busy I'm to keep ye in my sight 'n if I see anythin' untoward I'm to yell real loud to MacKenzie He'll come catch ye right away. What does 'untoward' mean, Edward?" His words tumbled out on top of one another, making it difficult for Edward to keep up.

"It means suspicious. . .oh, for God's sake, why the devil am I explaining vocabulary to some little heathen of the Highlands?" Edward said, holding his head in his hands.

Oliver's face fell, nearly crumpling into tears.

"Tis not a very nice thing to call somebody. Didn't *yer* mother teach ye better?"

Immediately contrite at his thoughtlessness Edward took hold of Oliver's shoulders. "I'm sorry, Oliver," he said gruffly. "You're right. That was an impolite thing to say. Do you think we can forget it and start over?"

Oliver's smile broke through like sunrays on a misty morning. "Aye, Edward. How'll we start over?"

"I'd like to see your village. Meet some of the people. Think we could do that?"

"Let's git goin' then," replied the lad, nearly bowling Edward over. "I know everyone."

"I'm sure you do, Oliver," Edward answered, as he tried to keep up with the gregarious little Scot.

*This is perfect*, Edward thought. *I can learn the land and strengthen myself at the same time while being with someone pleasant.* He grinned, feeling better than he had since his arrival.

# CHAPTER NINE

Edward dug his heels into Lark's heaving sides. He looked over his shoulder into the blackness and heard the sound of hooves hitting clay and stone in their effort to overtake him. If I can just make it around the next turn, I'll be within sight of Lexington Estate. Lark's strides shortened and his breathing came in labored gasps. Edward's thoughts were not for Lark's welfare but rather his need to escape the Scots pursuing him and getting to his family home. He urged the exhausted horse forward in one last effort galloping headlong toward the end of the carriage sweep that led to safety.

Edward leapt out of the saddle not waiting for the lackey to take his horse. Within seconds he was pounding on the massive front door. No one came. He yelled loud enough to bring the dogs to howling. Where are the servants? He could hear them speaking in muffled tones in the foyer. Edward pressed his shoulder into the big door. He groaned from the pain and opened his eyes.

He was in a bed! He hadn't been on Lark at all - riding to Lexington Estate and freedom. He shook his head and tried to focus his eyes on something familiar. Moonlight filtered through the window illuminating a blue and white washbasin sitting on the table next to him. Then Edward remembered. He was in the Highlands - a prisoner of the Scots! The disappointment so completely possessed him that only gradually did he become aware of someone pounding on the door of the little cottage. The pounding was punctuated by yelling.

"Pa!" Kit yelled. "Sounds like Angus. Melanie's time must've come. Git that door open quick while I gather my things." Hamish mumbled something unintelligible as he fought his way to consciousness. His bare feet sounded like leaves rustling as he scurried across the floor in search of a candle. The bolt to the front door slid back allowing the shouts to drown out all other sound.

"Kit! Melanie's in labor!"

"I'm comin', Angus. Calm down afore ye wake the entire clan." Kit filled her bag with medicines and instruments as she spoke. "Pa. Git Oliver over here to guard Edward. Angus, ye stay with Edward 'til Pa comes back with Oliver." She snapped the orders so fast that Hamish had trouble keeping up with who was to go where and with whom. She shut her pack and hurried out the door. Hamish left, then returned within five minutes dragging Oliver who was struggling to pull a tunic over his night shirt.

"What's wrong?" Edward shouted into the melee, hoping someone rushing by would enlighten him.

Hamish stopped to let Angus pass before coming into the dimly lit room. Now fully awake he took charge, treating the situation like a field commander shouting orders to his men.

"Oliver, come here 'n stand by Edward." When the two were side by side Hamish took a piece of soft rope and secured Oliver's left leg to Edward's right one. He left enough rope to loop around

Edward's neck. He handed Oliver a large cowbell, waggled his finger in the boy's face, and issued a dire warning. "Kit 'n I'll be busy all the night. If this man tries to go anywhere, grab hold of somethin' 'n ring this cowbell." Oliver nodded obediently. Then Hamish picked up a heavy cauldron and followed Angus.

Edward was mortified to be tied to a child. He could drag Oliver to London and back if he was healthy. But his body was weak and the sight in his right eye still very unclear. He was bound to the boy and there was nothing he could do about it. He was humiliated that it took so little to stop him from escaping.

Sometime during the night Oliver and Edward fell asleep on the hearth amid an assortment of dogs and cats. From time to time each elbowed the other in the ribs, bringing exclamations of outrage depending on who got jabbed. Finally, the clamor of early birds and shuffling feet on the rocky path outside brought them into wakefulness.

"'Nother healthy girl fer Angus 'n Melanie," Kit announced, as she placed her supplies back in the cupboard. "Maybe one of these times they'll have that boy they're tryin' so hard to git."

"Aye," Hamish chuckled, while he untied Edward and Oliver. "But many more 'tries' 'n they'll need 'nother house." Edward disappeared into the bedroom and the much-needed chamber pot. Hamish pushed a groggy Oliver off in the direction of his own home.

Kit sighed and sat down at the table with a heavy plop while Hamish dropped into his chair by the hearth. "Seems like babies only come in the middle of the night," he observed, as he stretched his legs out to relieve the cramps that plagued him after long stints on his feet.

"That's so's we'll have time fer mornin' chores," Kit mumbled.

Hamish nodded, then got up and trudged off toward MacKenzie's. She watched him go, wishing he could sleep awhile.

"I'd best git started afore I fall into a sleep so deep that the devil 'imself couldn't wake me," she whispered to herself. Her steps were slow and her movements automatic. These were chores she could perform without thinking. She threw grain to the chickens and fed the orphan lambs. With a body that cried for rest, she headed to the barn, milk pail in hand.

Edward watched in disbelief as father and daughter went about their daily work although they had been up all night. Their stamina and strength amazed and shamed him at the same time. He decided to help even though he was their prisoner. Had he sorted through his motives Edward might have admitted it was not totally from compassion that his help would be offered. Rather it was to prove he was as good as any Scot when it came to working a body that was exhausted or injured.

Once Edward had decided to be helpful, he faced the question of *how* to help. His choices were very limited. He didn't know how to milk a cow, was too weak to chop wood, and didn't have the inclination to tackle the washing of worn-out Scottish clothes. In due course, he decided to fix the morning meal. He'd watched Kit do it many times and knew it wasn't a difficult task. Besides, his stomach was growling so it seemed the logical thing to do. He smiled at the idea of proving that the gentry could be just as thoughtful as those born on lower rungs of the social ladder.

When the blaze in the hearth had settled down to hot embers Edward placed the heavy cooking flat on the iron stool that straddled the fire. His trip to the smokehouse took several minutes of careful maneuvering but eventually the smell of pork frying had all the dogs following the scent to the kitchen door.

"What's next?" he mumbled, as he looked around for a reminder. He spied the empty egg basket, grabbed it, and went outside in search of nests. One of the big red hens was sitting on her clutch located under a bunch of heather. Edward stooped to ground level, shoved her off the nest, and made a grab for an egg. His hand was but an inch or two from the treasure when he was hit with flapping wings, vicious talons, and a beak that could have put holes through pig skin. Edward's retreat from under the bush would have done justice to a man running from a pack of hounds.

"I had no idea hens were so protective," he muttered. As he sat beside the egg basket, chicken feathers floated past his eyes and an infuriated hen stared him in the face. Suddenly his nose twitched in response to a frightening odor.

"Jesu!" he yelled, scrambling to rise and running as fast as his sore body would carry him to the cottage. He clambered into the kitchen just as the burnt meat began to ignite. Grabbing a jacket off the wall to protect his hands he lifted the flat from the fire and headed outside. After hurling the smoking mess into the yard, he dropped to the ground in a sweat-drenched heap, thankful that a fiery catastrophe had been averted.

By the time Hamish and Kit returned, Edward had carefully retrieved some eggs, started a new pan of meat frying, and was slicing bread. Exhausted, the two hadn't noticed the cats and dogs feasting on the burnt meat and grease in the yard.

Hamish was surprised that Edward had taken the initiative to fix the meal. To be sure, the bacon was limp and the bread stale, but the eggs were tolerable. This was no time to be mean-spirited. "Thank ye, Edward." His tone was one of grudging approval. Edward nodded, glad that someone had noticed his effort to be helpful.

Only the sound of teeth chewing tough bacon and hard bread broke the silence. When their jaws could do no more all three pushed away from the table and stared into the hearth. Edward took the breakfast leavings away and threw the scraps to Stripes, who played with the leftover piece of bacon like it was a mouse.

Kit's body refused to move, so exhausted was she from a night of delivering Melanie's baby. Too tired to get up, she laid her head and arms on the table and closed her eyes. Edward took away the mugs, being careful not to disturb Kit's position. Hamish sat down in his old chair by the hearth.

"You should take her to her own bed, Hamish," Edward nodded in Kit's direction. "It's time she had her room back and I'm strong enough to negotiate the ladder up to the loft now." Edward threw the dirty dishwater into the yard, not at all pleased with his role as a servant.

When he returned he realized that Hamish had made no move to assist Kit to her bed. Thinking the sight of an Englishman helping his daughter to her bed would spur Hamish into action, Edward roused Kit enough to stand and walk toward her room. But Hamish was already sound asleep, snoring softly in rhythm to his breathing and oblivious to his daughter's plight.

Edward shook his head in disgust at Hamish. He gently roused Kit and guided her toward the bed. He sat her down, laid her head on the pillow, then pulled her legs up off the floor. She covered her brow with one hand and pulled the coverlet up with the other. Soon she too was sound asleep, with legs askew and one arm hanging over the edge of the bed.

Edward gathered his meager belongings, began taking them to the loft, and looked at Hamish who had roused from his slumber and was staring into the fireplace. On his second trip to the loft Edward decided to jar the old man into action.

"Kit's back in her bed and could do with a sponge to her face and some loose clothes to sleep in." Edward struggled up the ladder, which was not accommodating to people without total use of their limbs. It was then that he heard the door slam as Hamish left the house, muttering that he'd had enough of females and their needs for one day.

A loud thump from the bedroom followed by some unintelligible language, sent Edward hurrying in to Kit. She had tried to turn over but was too close to the edge of the bed. She'd lost her balance, rolled off the bed, and landed in a heap on the floor tangled in clothes, blankets, and pillows.

Edward looked down at her - terrified. Kit struggled, unable in her half-awake state to escape all the restraining material that bound her to the floor. Edward looked out the window in search of help. He saw instead the back of Hamish's hat as he topped the hill heading for one of the pastures.

With the look and sigh of the downtrodden, he leaned over the woman who was the bane of his existence to see what was to be done. She'd fallen asleep again in the soft goose-down coverlet. Kit snuffled contentedly, as though it was normal to slumber on the floor in daytime wearing clothes still blood-stained from delivering a baby. Edward's first task was to lift her back onto the bed. He discarded his cane and began the daunting job of lifting Kit with his weakened arms into a bed that seemed unduly high. It had been a long time since Edward had picked up a shield, let alone a full-grown woman who squirmed as he disturbed her dreams. He grunted and swore but finally got her and all the bedding back into place.

Her clothing was a confusing mass of material entrapping her body. Edward tried to release the tunic that had twisted around her waist. His large fingers had difficulty unfastening it at the neck - the button seemed to be larger than the thong that secured it. Pieces of her apparel gradually gave way and Edward reddened from forehead to chest at the sight of her soft, unblemished skin protected only by a scanty undergarment. Her long legs and firm, rounded hips left an indelible imprint under the thin material. He felt as if he were robbing a bird's nest while the mother was away.

*Enough,* he thought. *She can finish the job herself.* Whereupon he replaced the coverlet over her entire body and quietly left the room.

# CHAPTER TEN

Kit's dreamless slumber was rudely interrupted when Stripes jumped on her chest and began making a nest on her stomach. She pushed the cat to the floor, rubbed her gritty eyes, and wondered why she was still in bed while the sun's rays filtered through the window. "Must be mid-afternoon," she mumbled, trying to remember why a vague recollection of Edward standing by her bed skittered through her head.

She sat up slowly, sore and groggy, with legs throbbing as though MacKenzie had pounded them to a pulp on his anvil. Her hair was so tangled that her fingers wouldn't go through it and her mouth tasted like she'd been chewing leather. She plodded to the kitchen basin and splashed water in her face. When she glanced down at her feet her eyes widened in shock.

"God's teeth!" she roared. "I'm not dressed." Forgetting the fatigue that had stiffened her body, she ran to her trunk, grabbed a gown, and pulled it over her head. The earlier impression of Edward beside her bed once again assailed her—this time with much more clarity.

"Edward did this," she howled, trying to get a comb through her hair. "Where is he? I'll have 'is hide on a stick!" Kit, usually modest and unwilling to display much of her skin, stormed out in search of the hapless Edward and completely forgot her shoes. Stripes took refuge under the bed leaving her kittens to bear the brunt of Kit's tirade.

"Oliver!" Kit yelled, as she ran out the door in the direction of the blacksmith shed. "If ye've let that scoundrel Englishman escape, ye'd better git yer own sorry self 'long with 'im." She was barely into the yard when Edward hobbled around the corner of the house. He was looking as crestfallen as he could to hide his enjoyment over having finally gotten the best of Miss High and Mighty Kit.

She came toward him at a run, one hand on her hip, the other poking into his good shoulder. "What kinda gentleman'd remove my clothes without my knowledge 'n consent? Eh? And ye call yerself enlightened!" She'd shoved him into the rough wall, having no care for any injury she might inflict. Edward groaned, hoping to distract her. "Ye could've fetched Brigit," she continued, ignoring his plaintive expression.

"Ye're a cowardly, irresponsible, lazy, 'n untrustworthy wretch of a man with no morals. If I didn't have to nurse ye back to where ye're worth a thousand pounds, ye'd be fed to the wolves!"

"A thousand pounds!" he sputtered. "Is that the ransom?"

"Aye. Why anyone'd think ye're worth more'n twenty is beyond me," Kit answered, as she tried to smooth her hair.

Edward shook his head in despair. The caring person who'd just spent a night of back-breaking work to deliver her friend's baby had just turned into an unreasonable shrew with the voice

130

and vocabulary of a fishmonger. If he lived to be ninety-five he'd never understand women. It was easier to be a warrior and face death instantly and with honor. He turned to leave.

"Where 're ye goin'?" Her voice shook with anger.

"As far from you as possible. First, I'd like to mention that Brigit was busy caring for her own family. Second, your father wanted no part of making you comfortable. He sent Oliver home and left soon after muttering something about checking the pasture down by the lake." Edward stopped for breath. "Can't say I blame him for wanting to escape any problems concerning you or any other woman for that matter. That left *me* as the only one here to get you from the kitchen to your bedroom."

Kit opened her mouth to answer but before she could utter one word Edward shoved his face into hers and continued his own diatribe. "Believe it or not Kit, you look no different than all the other women I've seen wearing no clothes. Why you think you're different than all the rest of the women in the world I'll never know!"

She picked up the broom and aimed it at his chest. He deflected it with his good arm.

"You looked exhausted and cramped so I did the best I could to make you feel better. You're the most ungrateful, loud, spiteful nag I've ever had the misfortune of meeting!" He turned away.

"Furthermore, you'd be that way whether you were Scot or English," he shot over his shoulder then hurried off as fast as he could with his cane. "I'll leave this godforsaken place before anyone can collect a ransom on my behalf," he whispered, as he scanned MacKenzie's shed for Oliver.

She shook her fist at his departing back. "That's it. Run—like all English cowards." She spun on her heel and headed into the kitchen to prepare the evening meal. Nonplused and red-faced, she swept the hearth then cut carrots and cabbage for a venison stew. Kit was too stubborn to admit she might have been hasty in her judgment of Edward. As an afterthought she looked to see if her chemise was clean and without worn spots.

The entire clan had heard the loud disagreement in the MacDougal household. While Kit was normally even-tempered and reasonable, she could flatten ears if a point of fairness needed to be defended. In this case, however, more than a few sympathies lay with the crippled Edward. He was considered by most to be an object of pity and therefore should be treated with the forbearance needed when caring for the elderly or slow-witted.

"Edward!" It was the welcome voice of Oliver, calming Edward and bringing him back to good humor.

"Oliver, have you time for a walk with me to stretch my cramped legs?"

"Aye," Oliver answered, saying nothing about the harsh words that had passed between Edward and Kit. "And a beautiful evenin' it is fer a stroll."

Oliver supported Edward's injured side as the two ambled through the poor communty. Edward had never before been this close to poverty—where the houses were so small and dark. The smell of stale air drifted from the cracks of the wattle and daub dwellings making his eyes water.

"Hello Edward," yelled some of children playing in the dirt. He noticed none wore shoes, many had coughs, and their clothing was shabby and ill fitting. He could not help feeling desolate over the hopelessness of their situation. Still there was an air of pride about these people. An attitude that they were not to be judged by their meager possessions but rather by their determination to never be subjects of the English.

This stubborn resolve of the Scots instilled Edward with a need to be away at the earliest possible moment. He felt guilty that his own persistence paled in comparison to the single-minded purpose of these Highlander men and women. *It was true,* he admitted to himself. *A life of privilege and luxury killed the ability to suffer pain and indignity while pursuing even the most improbable ambitions.* He chatted nonchalantly with Oliver, greeted all he met with a friendly face, and began to formulate a plan to escape. His only hope of surviving once he did leave was to know the territory and learn the trails that would lead him south to the Borders. He would have to gain the confidence of the clanswomen so as not to appear suspicious in his wanderings throughout the area. He was so deep in thought that he lost track of what Oliver was saying.

"Edward!" Oliver spoke loudly and shook his arm. He turned a guilty glance in Oliver's direction.

"I'm sorry Oliver. What did you say?"

"I asked do ye like honey? Twill be ready soon."

Edward stopped in his tracks. *That's it,* he thought. *That's the answer.* Looking at Oliver, he nodded that, yes, he liked honey.

"Then let's go see the hive."

As they crossed the field to an ancient oak that was home to a thriving beehive, Edward remembered the fables his mother had recited to him as a child. Especially the one about "making more friends with honey than vinegar." Now I understand its meaning!

*Treating people graciously and with consideration will, more often than not, elicit respect and courtesy in return. I must get to know the clansmen, offer to help where possible, and become like the other working members of their community. I want my wanderings and offers of assistance to be normal to the MacDougals. In other words, my actions must make them forget I'm English.*

The most distasteful part would be getting on better terms with Kit. Perhaps one way to go about that would be to help make her workload easier, he mused. *She's always complaining about the extra drudgery I cause her. I'll offer to learn how to milk the cow, gather the eggs, and fetch vegetables and herbs. Instead of responding to her sniping, I'll 'turn the other cheek.'* That was good advice he'd heard from the pulpit as a child. The more he thought about it the more eager he was to begin.

Edward subtly guided Oliver on a different return path to the MacDougal home. As they approached, Kit came toward them carrying a basket of clothes to the bushes where she would spread them to dry. Edward walked up to her as steadily as he could. "Let me help you with that," he offered. Even to his own ears his voice lacked the ring of sincerity -- something he'd have to work on.

Kit looked at him askance then handed him the basket with a thrust to the abdomen that nearly knocked him down. He barely held on to it while trying not to fall. *This hell-cat will be the undoing of me yet*, he thought angrily, while covering his face with a broad smile.

"Thank ye, Edward," she said sweetly.

Struggling to regain his balance, Edward continued. "I'd like to learn to milk, too."

"We'll see," she answered.

Edward was propelled into a new day by the loud crowing of a rooster just outside his window. Sunlight streamed through a small hole in the wall stinging his eyes. He turned on his belly trying to avoid the harsh noises but peace was not to be his.

"Edward!" Kit yelled above the din of the chickens. She picked up the milk pail and banged it on the table. "Git dressed. Cows git spiteful when they don't git milked on time."

He dragged himself out of bed and began the tedious job of dressing. He figured cows would probably be just as happy to get milked later in the day if they had a choice. "My mind must have been elsewhere when I agreed to help with a chore that is performed at such an ungodly hour of the morning," he muttered.

When Oliver arrived to report for his job of guarding Edward, Kit gave him new orders. "Go help MacKenzie. Edward'll be with me. He's gonna learn how to milk," she said, with a wicked wink.

Oliver backed out the door, head down to hide his surprise at this turn of events. "Aye, Kit. But holler if ye need me 'cause tis loud in MacKenzie's shed." He left on the run leaving Edward at the mercy of Kit.

"I'd like to see that lesson," MacKenzie said, when informed of the change of plans.

As Edward followed Kit down the hill, he couldn't help but notice the athletic and supple body she had developed through a lifetime of vigorous activity. She was unfettered by the outlandish styles and stilted movements of English women. Her motions were natural and fluid. He dragged his eyes away from her and studied a hawk circling above them instead.

The barn, which clung tenuously to the hill on which it was built, was full of cobwebs -- complete with dried insects trapped within them. Edward turned up his nose at the stale smell of last year's hay. Just outside two horses stood head to tail swishing flies off one another while Mazie's latest litter of pups chased through the flimsy structure. Behind him a loud snort blew into a feed bucket, sending clouds of dust into the air. Startled, he turned and looked into the placid face of a brownish-colored cow quietly chewing her cud.

Edward had grown up with farm animals. Except for the horses and dogs, however, he'd always viewed the less glamorous cows, sheep, chickens, and pigs from a distance. He'd never been up close to a cow - not since childhood anyway. Her tail constantly swished flies off her back, her breath was hot and smelled of clover, and her tongue kept coming out and reaching up into her nostrils. Disgusting habit to Edward's way of thinking.

Kit observed him from beneath her bonnet and smiled at his look of distaste at Nell's tongue.

"She's bigger than I expected," he said. "And she really smells bad." He was beginning to have some doubts about his grand plan to get on good terms with Kit.

Kit gave him a short demonstration in milking then said, "Come over here to Nell's left side, put the pail under the teats, 'n begin."

Edward's face reddened at handling such an intimate part of a female's anatomy, even if she was just a cow. It was made all the more embarrassing to have Kit looking over his shoulder with a smirk on her face. Reluctantly, he positioned himself with his head leaning into Nell's left flank, like Kit had done. Then he held the pail between his knees under Nell's udder and forced his hands to take hold of two teats, like Kit had done. Finally, he squeezed, like Kit had done. Here the similarities ended.

Nell would not let her milk flow - a feat Edward had not known a cow could do. He squeezed harder. His fingernails dug into her tender skin. She let out a bellow, kicking viciously with her left hind leg. Edward landed on the floor, spitting dirt and looking eyeball to eyeball with a stray hen.

He sat dazed between the overturned stool and empty bucket. Shaking his head to dislodge a piece of straw he gingerly examined himself to be sure that he had not acquired yet another injury. When it was apparent that only his pride had been injured, the future heir of Lexington Estate slowly picked himself up.

Kit looked at him, laughing so hard that her bosom shook. "It'll take some time afore she fergives ye fer such rough handlin'. Guess the English aren't quite as genteel as we've been led to believe." She retrieved the bucket, patted the cow on her forehead, and sat down to finish the job.

Edward was astonished by the way Kit's face softened when she laughed. She looked young. Playful. Vulnerable. He turned abruptly and limped outside to wait.

It wasn't long before Kit appeared through the barn door with a smile still tugging at her cheeks. Looking pointedly at the stingy amount of milk in the pail, she stated, in a tone more than a little derisive, "Let's git back up the hill 'n see what else ye can muddle up afore noon."

As they trudged back to the little house Edward mulled over the unfairness of it all. How would it ever be possible for him to get on the good side of a woman who obviously had no inclination to be on friendly terms with an Englishman?

During the ensuing days, Edward and Nell arrived at a compromise. He didn't squeeze too hard and she allowed her milk to flow, albeit slowly. He began to relax during this time of mindless activity and now enjoyed the smell of hay and the sound of the milk as it streamed into the bucket. The first spurts made a splashing noise on the bottom of the pail but as the bucket filled it became a soft murmur that brought foam to the top like tufts of wool. The feel of Nell's soft, warm side with her regular breathing lulled him into a state of well-being. He could forget plans of escaping, duties facing him upon his return home, and even the death of his father.

A loud clang followed by a yelp from old Lance, forced Edward abruptly back to the day at hand. He grabbed his clothes and dressed as fast as he could. "Hell's bells. Can't that woman ever do anything without making such a racket?"

He crashed down the ladder, dropping his boots with a thud. Kit's head jerked up at the commotion. "If all Englishmen 're as clumsy as this one, I don't know how they ever conquered anythin," she mumbled. "What's goin' on?" she yelled, running and wiping flour off her hands onto her apron as she followed the noise to its source.

"Nothing," replied Edward, as he dusted himself off and tried to look unperturbed.

"Well, slow down," she ordered. "At this rate ye'll break somethin' else I'll have to fix."

Edward set the table while Kit tended the meat. Both went about the routine they had established during the weeks of his recovery. It had become a quiet time, both lost in their own thoughts.

Looking up as Edward went to collect the eggs, Kit grudgingly admitted that she'd gotten used to having him around. "Course he's as awkward as Oliver most times," she muttered. "But he's someone other'n the dogs to talk to."

But Edward had made a positive impression on the other women of the clan. Brigit, Clare, and even Inez were taken by his charm and sense of humor. They would come up with the most trivial jobs just to have him around.

As he made his rounds of the hen's nests, Edward evaluated the past weeks. He'd been fanatical about getting his body strong enough to travel. He was a familiar sight in the community, shadowed by the ever-present Oliver. Easy-going by nature, Edward enjoyed getting to know the clansmen on a first-name basis. In England he'd never mingled with the laborers and servants. He'd been surprised at how intelligent and clever they were.

The women of the clan truly enjoyed his company. He played with the children, serving as referee when necessary. They had ceased thinking of him as an enemy and accepted him as Oliver's charge. The children considered him one of them – not an adult.

Gradually even the men, with the exception of Hamish and Malcolm, were willing to include Edward in social activities as long as Oliver was in attendance. With his unquenchable enthusiasm, Oliver had brought both the Scots and the Englishman to the point where all accepted the situation with indifference rather than hostility.

Edward's body was nearly back to normal. The soreness in his shoulder was gone. He could reach the middle of his back to scratch a flea bite and he thought he could run the length of the settlement without losing his breath. Lifting was still very painful. He was unable to carry the pail of milk all the way from the barn with his injured shoulder. To remedy this, every day after milking Nell, he exercised by lifting a saddle up and down. Eight, and sometimes ten times, were all he could manage.

"Edward!" Kit yelled from the kitchen. "What's takin' ye so long? We just need the eggs - not the hens!"

He still resented her authority over him and her constant orders to perform mundane odd jobs. *Doesn't she know I'm a landowner?* He thought angrily. *That one day I will inherit all the Lexington Estate lands? Can't she treat me with dignity?* Nevertheless, he picked up the basket of eggs and made a hasty retreat to the kitchen.

"Why 're ye lookin' at me?" Kit asked, after they'd finished eating. "Have I got honey on my cheek? Are the eggs hard?"

Edward hadn't realized he'd been staring. "No," he said quietly. "Everything tastes good. The eggs aren't hard and you don't have honey on your cheek."

With a quiet sigh he stood up and took the dirty dishes to the basin. Kit followed his pensive movements with her eyes, wondering why he was so subdued on this beautiful morning. She hadn't realized how much she expected him to always be cheerful, even after a disagreement full of loud words and exaggerated body motion.

Edward went out the door just as Oliver came into the yard. "Mornin' Edward. What 're ye doin' today?"

He looked at the boy affectionately. "After we finish milking, I thought I'd test how good my shoulder is. Maybe chop some wood for Kit."

"I'll help." Oliver grabbed the milk pail and ran toward the barn. His bare feet left deep prints in the moist ground.

The milking was done by the time Kit came outside wearing her sun hat. Oliver made a production of giving her the pail, bowing as he handed it to her. Edward crossed his arms over his chest and smiled at the two, unable to curb his cheerful nature for long.

"Thank ye, kind sir," Kit said, laughing at Oliver as she bobbed a curtsy in return. "What a wonderful surprise on this fine day."

Then the antics were over and it was time for work. Kit returned to the house while Oliver and Edward headed for the chopping block.

Edward picked up the axe and looked at Oliver. "When I looked yesterday Kit had only about three days worth of wood. We'd best replenish that, don't you think?"

"Aye," Oliver answered. "I'll bring them slabs. Ye split."

"Aren't they too heavy for you to carry?"

"Nay. I carry heavier stuff fer MacKenzie. 'Course he has to help me with them anvils. They're heavy even fer him."

The two worked in contented unison throughout the morning. They heard Kit banging about in the kitchen putting away cookware, sweeping the floor, and chasing Lance out when she found him under a chair or table. Edward's shoulder began to throb. He stopped and sat on the chopping block rubbing the injured area that promised to be a painful reminder for years to come.

"Oliver, how about getting us some water. My throat's dry. How about yours?"

"I'd not say 'no' to a sip 'bout now," he answered, trying not to let Edward see how tired his arms were. "I'll go git some from Kit."

Edward watched him go. *I'll miss the little bugger*, he thought. *He's got more energy than five youngsters back home.*

Kit and Oliver came toward him together. She carried a rag in one hand and a bucket in the other. "Thought ye could use this, what with all the sweatin' ye're doin'," she said, handing him the rag.

"Thanks." He watched her as she walked to the spring to fill the bucket. He found it hard to believe she was the same age as his sister, Gwen. Life was not so kind to Kit as to her contemporaries in England, yet her shoulders never drooped regardless of how heavy the load. Even though he resented her forthrightness Edward knew that stubbornness was why her spirits never sagged for long, even under the most trying of circumstances. She carried it all with an effortlessness that a young woman in England would find difficult to muster.

"Why 're ye starin' at Kit, Edward?" asked Oliver.

"I'm not "staring" at Kit, Oliver," Edward said huffily. "I was just wondering where Malcolm is?" He wanted to change the subject. "I haven't seen him lately."

"He's gone off on 'nother one of 'is trips," Oliver replied, inspecting a scab on his knee.

"Oh? Where does he go?" Edward asked nonchalantly.

"Don't know," Oliver threw over his shoulder, as he followed Kit.

*I'll wager I know where he is*, Edward thought. *He's gone to Lexington Estate for the ransom and I plan to stop that.*

After the evening meal, Edward helped Kit clean the table, carefully slipping away a chunk of cheese and some bread to add to the provisions for his escape. Every morsel of food he could sneak out would be imperative for his survival. Edward's thoughts were consumed with retrieving the ransom from Malcolm as he was returning back from Lexington Estate to the Highlands. Since there seemed to be only one main way in and out of Clan MacDougal, Edward thought it wouldn't be too difficult to ambush Malcolm along that route. "The Scots have advantage enough without money garnered on my account," he whispered to himself.

He clambered into the loft and quietly checked all his provisions, making certain everything was stowed safely in the sack hidden under a pile of dirty clothing. His body tingled with anticipation of tomorrow night when, finally, he would leave this miserable piece of land and the people who dwelt in it.

# CHAPTER ELEVEN

Edward awakened as the edges of night were just beginning to be fringed with light. Unable to dress and begin his chores so early without bringing suspicion upon himself, he had time to sort out his endless thoughts. *Has it been a month ago that Kit worked through the night to deliver Melanie's baby? Is Malcolm already close to returning to Clan MacDougal with the ransom? Am I prepared physically to make such an arduous trek back to Lexington Estate? Can I even find my way? With my escape, will Oliver be denied the colt he's been promised? Have I chopped enough wood for Kit?*

He tried to conquer his confusion by mulling over the joys that awaited him upon his return home. He would be reunited with his mother and sister, as well as Colin and Ned. How Edward missed the sounds and smells of Ned's blacksmith shed. All his friends would come to see him and they'd go hunting, riding wildly without a care in the world. There would be parties with lots of lovely young *English* ladies vying for his attention. How wonderful it would be to return to his pampered life again! Edward's excitement at his impending escape once more captured his soul. This time his homecoming would be real - not a tortured dream. He couldn't wait to get to the end of the day.

When he thought morning would never come, shafts of sunlight filtered through the cracks in the cottage wall. He heard the farm animals stirring in anticipation of their morning meal. Before long the world clamored with sounds of birds feeding their noisy offspring, frogs belching as they plopped into the lake, and mournful calls of distant owls. Close by, a couple of cats were fighting, seemingly to the death. Edward hoped Stripes was not involved.

Below, he heard Kit's bare feet pad outside for a pail of water for her morning toilette, giving Edward the cue that he could begin his own cleansing. He slung on his threadbare Scottish clothes and carefully descended the ladder, making certain no clumsiness would bring attention to the fact that today he was quicker than usual. But his happiness made it impossible for him to slow his steps through the little cabin to the well outside for water.

In less than fifteen minutes Edward reentered the little home, his face glistening with the rough scrubbing he'd just given himself with a tattered linen cloth. He stood at Kit's elbow peering over her shoulder as she prepared the morning meal, sniffing heartily as the smells of bacon titillated his nose and made his mouth water. She chuckled at his enthusiasm. When the bacon was tender and the eggs nearly ready to flip, he poured the ale and fetched the butter and milk from out of the bucket that hung in the cool well hole. As Edward moved faster, Kit moved slower. He wolfed his food down, eating twice what he normally would, then waited impatiently for Kit to finish.

"Ye're beginnin' to eat like a man 'bout to work in the fields all day, Edward," she said. "And yer skin looks less sallow." *Hopefully Malcolm will return before Edward is strong enough to escape*, she thought, as she poured him more ale.

Edward coughed nervously. "Just the cool air. And you know how Nell's bag hardens if she isn't milked promptly." Edward felt traitorous, knowing he'd never given a tinker's damn about how Nell's bag felt. All of his friendliness and helpful overtures covered an ulterior motive that now made him feel dirtier than when he'd first been dragged into Kit's home, broken in body and spirit.

"The cat'll make a mess of my kitchen if we don't clean up first. And that'll make me madder'n a little hardenin' of Nell's bag," Kit answered.

Her meaning was not lost on Edward. He was ahead of her as he stood up, ready to help clean the kitchen. In his haste to clear the table he chipped one of the earthen mugs. *Thank God it's not one of her special ones*, he thought.

Even so, she was displeased. "Have a care, Edward! Them mugs 're precious 'n can't be repaired like metal."

Eventually, the kitchen met with Kit's approval. Edward grabbed his cane while Kit picked up the milk pail. They walked down the rocky path in silence, enjoying the sounds and smells of the day. Dandelions paraded along the path. Robins, chickadees, and magpies provided a symphony for the morning rituals. Edward made his way with care, fearful of slipping on the loose stones. Kit pushed ahead of him, sailing forth like a monarch in full regalia. She sucked in the fresh air that was accented by the pungent smell of newly scythed hay.

Edward looked at her scornfully. *There she goes. Acting like she's the queen of this pathetic country*, he thought, shaking his head in wonderment at these penniless Scots who carried themselves with such pride. *Thank heaven I have only one more day of this primitive life.* He sighed and prayed for the time when he would be on his way to Lexington Estate and people he understood. He concentrated on crossing a small ditch that had been chiseled into the hill by summer rains.

The sound of scrabbling pebbles and an exclamation of surprise brought Edward's head up instantly. Helpless to change the outcome of an accident rushing to its finale, he watched in horror as the scene in front of him concluded with the speed of summer lightning. Kit's feet shot out in front of her. The bucket she carried flew over her shoulder as she landed on her backside, then rolled to a motionless heap at the bottom of the hill.

"Kit! I'm coming!" he rasped, and scrambled awkwardly down the steep incline after her, no longer mindful of his own safety. Her head had landed on a large flat rock and already a wound just behind her right temple had begun to swell and redden. Edward placed his hand underneath her head and his face over her nose, trying to feel her breath. Just then she moaned.

"Thank God," he said, and lifted his head to look around. No one was in sight.

"Oliver!" he shouted, then returned his attention to Kit. Her hands moved feebly toward the wound on her head.

"Kit!" Edward whispered. "Can you hear me?"

She nodded weakly. Once again Edward called for Oliver— no answer—leaving him little choice but to get her back to the cottage by himself.

"Hold onto my shoulders," he instructed.

She tried to reach around his neck but hadn't the strength to hold on. Edward, more frightened than when he'd faced Malcolm's fury in battle, grabbed her under her armpits, gave a mighty heave, and tried to stand up. Kit's legs buckled and she fell back against his chest, bringing Edward to his knees. Pain ripped through his injured shoulder as though someone had shorn it from his body with a broad sword.

"Help! Help!" he shouted as loudly as he could. Still no one answered.

Knowing it was useless to waste more breath yelling, he braced one leg and pushed up with the other in a second attempt to stand. The muscles in his thighs burned as though a hot dagger had been shoved into his leg. For a moment, his own discomfort was greater than his concern for Kit. Her body shifted as Edward tried to lift her off the ground. She wasn't heavy but Edward was tiring fast. What would normally have been an easy task became a frustratingly painful endeavor. He summoned every ounce of energy to his weakening body, grunted, strained, and swore until finally he was standing up! With feet wide apart, he rested as best he could before beginning the laborious trip up the hill. His feet kept slipping as his ungainly load dragged him backward. Edward was fast approaching his own collapse.

"Help! Anyone, help!" he shouted, as loud as his heaving lungs permitted. But the noise from MacKenzie's shop made it impossible for anyone to hear him.

Edward was desperate. Straining to keep both of them upright, he clawed and pulled them both to the top of the hill. No time to rest - his breath was coming in short, ragged spurts. The swelling behind Kit's ear was worsening and her breathing was barely noticeable. Finally reaching the cottage, Edward dragged her backward through the door and into her bedroom. He collapsed upon her trunk -- too exhausted to do more. Kit lay with her head against his chest, vulnerable and unaware of the effort Edward still faced.

With a power he didn't know he had, Edward cupped her body within his own then walked slowly backward to the bed and sat down. He twisted himself until they were longways, then gradually raised her lower body with his legs. With both of them now on the bed, he lay down flat and scooted from under her and off the other side.

Edward rested an elbow on the bed and watched her for a few minutes, as if to convince himself she would live. He examined the nasty bruise on her head, which continued to swell. Still breathless, he forced himself to get a clean cloth from Kit's supply. He soaked it in cool water and then placed it over the wound.

Next came the touchy question regarding her clothes. "She can rave all she wants. I'm going to get these clothes off of her." His words were aimed at Stripes, who watched placidly from a corner of the room. "I won't have to listen to her anyway. I'll be gone soon."

As the clothing came off, her breathing became more regular and she mumbled. Edward hastily put a light coverlet over her body. "Kit, can you hear me?" he asked, his head just a few inches from her face.

She looked at him through slitted eyes. "My head hurts."

"I know," he answered. "You hit it when you fell." The breath he expelled fanned the hair out of her eyes. "Can you take a sip of water?"

He leaned to where his ear nearly touched her mouth in order to hear her. "Aye," she whispered. He brought the water and held her head while she drank. Her helplessness confused Edward. He'd always thought of Kit as someone even Fate would hesitate to disable.

"I'll go for help," he said, and started to leave.

She fumbled for his hand. "There's no one to come," she whispered. "Oliver doesn't know what to do 'n the others 're workin'." She lapsed into silence, rested a bit, then continued. "Give me a little more water then go milk Nell afore 'er bag hardens."

Edward threw his hands up in exasperation. "Kit, you're barely conscious and all you can think of is that damned cow."

"Edward, please," she begged. "Twon't take long."

"Very well. But if you get delirious don't expect any sympathy from me." With a parting look of disbelief, he hurried off to the barn.

Nell shook her head ominously in objection to Edward's rough hands. Nevertheless, he hurried through this bothersome task, spilling and sloshing the milk. He threw grain to the chickens and pulled Nell rudely into her pasture. Truthfully, Edward had believed himself to be above these duties, knowing this was only a temporary situation. Kit's accident had done nothing to change that view. His insulated life at Lexington Estate had never prepared him for the daily work of a peasant.

In about half an hour, he once again entered Kit's room to find her incoherent. The wound was discolored and more swollen. It was the breaking point for Edward. He didn't care how mad Kit might be later. *He* was going for help.

He put another cool cloth on her head then left for MacKenzie's shed, where he knew Oliver was working. As Edward broke into a trot, he realized he'd regained energy and his painful shoulder had eased to a dull ache. Vaguely, he noted that this was a good omen for his escape.

"Oliver!" Edward bellowed, as he entered the shed. "Kit's hurt. I've got her in bed. Bring Brigit quick." Then he turned and headed back to the MacDougal cottage. Oliver dropped the hammer he was holding and sped off, leaving a trail of dust in his wake.

Edward was replacing the cloths on Kit's wound when Brigit hurried into the house. She entered the little bedroom with the authority of a field general and nudged Edward with her elbow. "Move, Edward. I can't care fer 'er with ye underfoot."

Edward reluctantly went to the foot of the bed. Brigit lay her ear on Kit's chest, listened to her heart, and felt the rise and fall of her breathing. She gently pushed Kit's eyelids up to see if the pupils were dilated then carefully manipulated the rest of her body to make certain no bones were broken. Edward was impressed with Brigit's efficiency and thoroughness.

"Well, nothin' injured that rest won't cure," Brigit announced, as she straightened up. She sponged the dirt off Kit's arms and began to remove her underclothes.

Edward discreetly took himself to the kitchen and sat down. Out of the corner of his eye he saw the hem of Kit's shift float to the floor as Brigit wasted no time getting her patient more comfortable. He heard water being wrung out of the cloth and a few unintelligible comments from Kit, followed by strong words from Brigit.

"How on earth could ye be so clumsy, Kit? Ye coulda been hurt bad." There were loud plops as Kit's shoes were dropped to the floor. "And ye always goin' on 'bout Edward havin' three left feet! Well, from now on, young lady, ye'd best keep yer criticism to yerself."

Edward's head flew up at the mention of Kit making spiteful remarks about him behind his back! His mouth was open to rant out loud just as Brigit came into the kitchen and proceeded to give him his orders.

"Well, she's not in any real danger as long as she follows orders." Brigit looked at Edward with raised eyebrows, emphasizing the necessity of Edward's enforcing those orders! "She's to lie flat in bed, only raisin' 'er head when ye help 'er to eat – nothin' but broth." Brigit paused to wipe her forehead. "No sun. No work. Keep them cool cloths on 'er head til the fever's gone. I'll have 'nother look in a few days." With that, she gathered her skirts about her and left, shooing an errant chicken out the door on her way.

Edward felt like he'd just been hit in the chest by an angry bull. What was that she'd said? A few days! He'd planned to leave tonight! Furthermore, taking care of an ailing Kit would be somewhat akin to fighting a wounded badger without a weapon. He shoved the image from his mind.

*This is not my mess!* he thought. He stood up and took the morning scraps to the chickens pecking just outside the door. *Hamish will be home this evening and I'll stay for another day to help get the situation in hand.* He felt it was the least he could do after all the nursing Kit had done for him, undoubtedly saving the sight in his eye.

By noon, Kit was feeling better. The rest, cool cloths, and darkened room gave her the illusion that things weren't as bad as she had thought. From the kitchen, where he was gathering up the soiled cloths Brigit had used on her head, Edward heard Kit call.

"Edward, can ye come here, please?"

Edward's compassion for Kit's predicament had evaporated once he was assured of her recovery. *Now* he wanted to get even with her for all those times she'd made him feel helpless and embarrassed. He wanted her to feel the humiliation of being cared for by someone who had little regard for the sensibilities of the patient.

"I'll be there as soon as I finish the morning chores," he yelled back.

Edward glanced into the yard and noticed steam rising off the water he was heating. After dragging the basket of soiled dressings and dirty clothing to the fire, he dumped the whole mess, along with a bar of lye soap, into the boiling water. He kicked the burning wood from under the cauldron so it would cool then pulled the scrub board from its perch in a tree. This was a slab of oak with parallel ridges carved into it, designed to help remove stains that collected in the clothes of people whose lives were spent working in dirt-laden conditions.

Edward had watched Kit dip the laundry in the hot water, lay the pieces across the board, then slather on more lye soap. He'd noticed that, after she first scrubbed them, she rinsed them in a pot of cool lake water. Thus, Edward began a job which seemed to him to be fairly simple.

"Damnation!" he swore, as the hot water burned his skin. He jerked his hands free and thrust them into the pail of cool lake water. After more colorful oaths, he fished a tartan out of the water with a small tree limb, laid it on the board, and applied the soap. "Hells bells!" he roared, as lye seeped into the hay scratches on his hands. Edward dropped the material, doused his fists again in the cool water, and looked around for someone to take over this job. There was no one.

When his throbbing hands had cooled somewhat, he spread chicken grease on them and again tackled the pile of dirty clothes. An hour later, with raw knuckles and stiff shoulders, he finally laid the last of the clothes on bushes to dry. To be sure, some of the garments scrubbed toward the end of the session still had signs of stains. Others had even been relegated to another day. Wearily he dragged the basket back to the kitchen and went to see how Kit was faring. Edward was as exhausted as if he'd spent a full day in battle. And he was bruised and bloody to boot!

As he entered her room Kit was fumbling with the coverlet, trying to free her legs from the tangled mass which had wound around her hips and feet. She swore feebly, panting with the exertion. Looking up, she saw Edward leaning against the door frame with his arms crossed over his chest.

"Well, don't just stand there," she ordered. "Help me git my feet on the floor." He shuffled slowly toward the bed. She saw that his hands were wrinkled and red.

"What do you want?" he asked wearily. "Brigit *did* help you with the pot, didn't she?"

"I'm hungry, Edward," she answered. "Help me to the kitchen."

"Not while I draw breath!" Edward roared. "I'll not have the entire village at my throat for not taking proper care of you after you've nursed me!" He strode toward her menacingly. "Now cooperate or I'll tie you to the bed." As he retreated to the kitchen he threw a parting remark into the air behind him. "I'll bring your meal shortly." Kit watched him go, speechless.

Edward returned with the broth, propped her head up with a pillow, then held the bowl with one hand while handling the spoon with the other. It was awkward. His fingers hit her chin, the spoon hit the bowl, and the soup spilled onto the bed—

reminiscent of Edward's first meal in the Highlands. By the time he'd cleaned up the mess and fed Kit, the ordeal had taken nearly an hour and both were too exhausted to make disparaging comments to one another.

Kit dozed while Edward cleaned the kitchen. In the late afternoon, Oliver ambled in, grabbed a heel of bread, and stuffed it into his mouth. "How's Kit doin', Edward?"

"She'll be alright, Oliver. But she sure is hard to take care of."

"Aye, Edward. But she's so purty."

Edward's jaw dropped. He had no idea Oliver even noticed things like that. "Oliver! Sweep the hearth while I go milk Nell."

When Hamish returned home that evening, he was disheartened to learn of Kit's accident. He'd thought her too agile to allow such a thing to happen. He grumbled to himself. "First, Malcolm puts the household in a muddle by bringin' an Englishman into the clan. Now, Kit's injured 'n unable to nurse the prisoner. Oliver's not qualified to do more'n watch Edward, 'n Malcolm's off to the Borders collectin' a ransom that isn't worth the havoc the whole episode has caused." Hamish worried what else could go wrong. He also wondered if Edward had played any part in Kit's fall. Did he trip her? Push her? Tired beyond belief, Hamish plodded into Kit's bedroom to assess this *latest* calamity.

She lay flat on her back, eyes closed, and skin pale except for the bruising that had spread onto the right side of her face. The sight of his invincible daughter in such a state shook Hamish to the core. Edward stood quietly beside her, fear and worry scribbled in the solemn lines of his young face.

Hamish was rarely caught without a plan of action but this was one of those times. He looked first at Edward, who obviously expected Hamish to take charge. Then he studied Kit, who was unable to move. Hamish's head ached. But years of fighting had given him the ability to plan even under duress. He cleared his throat and aimed an icy stare at Edward, who was now sitting on the trunk at the end of Kit's bed.

"What happened?" Hamish asked.

Edward related the entire episode—how the accident occurred, the care already given to Kit, and Brigit's instructions for the coming days. Hamish listened, nodding from time to time. When Edward had finished Hamish had made up his mind.

"Thank 'ye Edward. I'll take over now. Brigit has 'er own family to care fer 'n Oliver's got no nursin' trainin'. MacKenzie 'n Campbell can handle my work til Kit's up 'n 'bout."

"Yes sir," Edward answered, unable to hide the relief in his voice. "Do you want me to show you where I've put the supplies?"

Hamish nodded and followed Edward out of the room, his chest puffed slightly at having a child who still needed his help. It made him feel younger somehow.

However, as fate would have it, nursing was not one of Hamish's strong suits. He was all thumbs, frowns, wrinkles, and worry. As he soothed her swollen head, he dropped the cloth onto her face. In his haste to retrieve it, he knocked the bowl of cool water on her chest leaving her gasping for breath.

"Saints be damned, Hamish," Edward yelled. "You're doing more damage than the rock she fell on. At this rate she'll be in bed for a month recovering from your clumsiness."

If the comment hadn't held an element of truth, Hamish would have flattened Edward with one swipe of his powerful right hand. Instead, he threw the cloth on the floor, shot Edward a hateful glare, and yelled. "Well then, ye take care of 'er! God knows she's cared fer ye long 'nough." He paused to catch his breath. "I leave in the mornin'. Have 'er healed by the time I git back!" With that, Hamish whirled and was gone from the cottage, leaving the ominous threat hanging heavily in the air behind him.

Edward slumped between the bedridden Kit and the departing Hamish. How could he escape now? He ran after Hamish as fast as his recovering body would allow. As Edward blasted the door open in an all-out effort to catch Hamish, Oliver, who'd been standing guard for just such an attempt, jumped in front of Edward and stopped the escape with his own body. The two fell in a heap, spluttering oaths and sorting out their various limbs.

"Good grief, Oliver," Edward shouted. "I'm trying to catch Hamish. Get out of my way."

But it was too late. Hamish was gone from view. Edward turned to look at Oliver's crestfallen face. It was impossible to be mad at the boy for long. He enjoyed having the gregarious little Scot at his heels and he knew how serious Oliver was about not letting his prisoner escape. Skimming Oliver's hair out of his eyes, Edward consoled him.

"Never mind, Oliver. It wasn't your fault. Come, let's see to Kit." Side by side, the two went into the little house. Remembering his own awkwardness at caring for Kit, Edward decided to try a new approach. Pulling Oliver aside, he whispered. "Go to Brigit's and see if she can come. I think Kit would be more at ease under her care, at least for tonight."

"On my way, Edward," he answered, and left running.

Next morning Edward was up early and down in the barn, exercising his arms before he faced his newly acquired household duties. The ritual was always the same. He tied the colt to one of the support poles and lifted the saddle from the floor up onto the horse's back. It was a system that got the colt used to being saddled and strengthened Edward's shoulder at the same time. After three times he stopped, sweat pouring from his forehead and chin. Then he began again.

"Whatcha' doin' Edward?" Oliver asked, as he stood in the doorway. He was chewing on a piece of straw with one leg crossed in front of the other.

Edward whirled at the sound. He hadn't heard Oliver come down the hill. With the light behind him, Oliver looked like a ghostly vision standing at the mouth of a black cave.

"I looked fer ye up yonder," Oliver continued, with a nod toward the house. "How come ye didn't wait fer me like ye always do?" Oliver scanned the barn with a quick sweep of his eyes, as though trying to find something amiss. "What's the sense of puttin' the saddle on then takin' it off?"

"Thought I'd get the colt used to being saddled. Figured I might as well do something until Hamish returns. Think he'd appreciate that, Oliver?"

"Probably," Oliver replied. His voice seemed troubled. He ambled over to the young horse and scratched him between the ears.

Edward noticed Oliver's suspicious words and stiffened frame. He tried to alleviate the situation with conversation. "Has Malcolm sent any word?" he asked, watching Oliver continue to search the barn with his eyes.

159

"Nay. He don't have no way to send word," came the guarded reply. "He'll be back when 'is business is done.'"

Edward regretted Oliver's wary attitude. He went about his barn chores while Oliver leaned on the fence just outside. The feel of Nell's warm flank didn't soothe Edward as it usually did. He was sorrier than he thought he'd be at the possible loss of Oliver's trust. When the milking was finished and the two walked back up the hill, Edward tried again.

"Oliver, Brigit said Kit is to have well-cooked vegetables tonight. She said you'd be able to help with fixing them. How long does it take? Should I put them in the kettle now?"

"Don't ye English know anythin'?" Oliver said scornfully. "Vegetables don't take long to cook," he continued, with a sideways glance at Edward. "And be sure to throw a slab of pork rind in else Kit won't eat 'em."

They entered the house with a measure of companionship restored. Kit called to them in a pleasant voice. Edward and Oliver looked at each other in disbelief, all tension gone between them. Oliver was first to speak. "Edward, I'll go git them vegetables while ye take care of Kit." He left hastily, basket in hand and thankful to be doing something that did not include being near Kit in case she got out of sorts.

Edward wished Oliver had not gone. Kit was pleasant when the lad was about. He cocked his head toward Kit's bedroom.

"Edward, could ye help me a minute, please," she asked sweetly.

He was puzzled by her graciousness. Then he was wary. He peeked cautiously through her door. "What do you want, Kit?"

"Will ye help me outta bed so I can tend to some personal needs," she said matter-of-factly, as she pulled the coverlet off her long, slim legs.

"No, but I'll be happy to bring you the pot," he answered, with the same polite tone Kit had used. "As I recall it has been well established that all of us have the same *personal* needs and we all look alike. Therefore, you have nothing to be ashamed of."

She was incensed at his insincerity, not to mention his disrespect. Before she could turn her sputtering into foul language, Edward continued innocently. "Brigit has gone to the fields. Her instructions were for me to fix your vegetables, continue with the cool cloths, and make certain you do not leave your bedroom." To emphasize his adherence to the sacred orders, Edward took Kit's arm and settled her feet on the floor.

She turned her head away, rationalizing that if she couldn't see him then he wouldn't see her. She tried to ignore the degradation of sharing such a personal experience with a stranger - even if he left the room during the ordeal.

While Kit was indisposed, Edward sat in the kitchen to contemplate his possibilities. There didn't seem to be many. He decided to help Kit until she could manage on her own before he left. He needed more food anyway for the trip down the mountains. Hopefully, two more days would still give him time to escape before Malcolm returned.

Edward roused from his thoughts when he heard Kit say she was finished. He helped her back into bed, her unyielding body a symbol of her fury at being handled by a man. It was impossible not to notice the offensive contents of the hated chamber pot.

Edward almost softened as he remembered his own humiliation in the same circumstances. However, all compassion disappeared when he emptied the smelly mess into the latrine. He held his breath and tried to think of happier times.

*I should be going to a party tonight,* he thought. *Deciding which tunic to wear with my new boots. I'm soon to be the Lord of Lexington, an estate most of my peers envy.* He recalled how much fun it was when the prettiest young ladies vied for his attention. He was an extremely eligible bachelor, which gave him a feeling of power he thoroughly enjoyed.

*Only two more nights of this,* he thought, as he returned the revolting pot to its resting place under Kit's bed. *Then by God, Hamish will have to take care of his daughter!*

For the next two days they worked out a routine that gave Kit maximum privacy but still allowed Edward to care for her properly. Oliver was forever in the background, offering advice to Edward and endless chatter to Kit. Edward and Kit displayed a quietness heretofore not a part of their relationship. Both were preoccupied with their own concerns.

It wasn't like Kit didn't have her own goals. But she always used Malcolm and Hamish as her reason not to acknowledge them. She was a pillar of strength to her family and clan. Kith and kin demanded all of her time, providing a legitimate reason to ignore her own future. But now bedridden, the role she had always felt to be her life's work had been snatched away in the few seconds it had taken for her to fall from the top of that wretched hill to the bottom. To make matters worse, she was being tended to by an Englishman who, although slow and clumsy, seemed capable of performing her daily chores almost as well as she did. Not only was she in pain but she was disheartened as well.

For Edward, caring for a sick person and doing degrading chores, which he considered to be women's work, was not the responsibility of an heir to an estate. Yet here he was, a titled member of the English nobility and soon to be envied landowner, working as a servant for these Highlanders, who he reckoned to be little better than cave dwellers. Thinking beyond the next hunting expedition or soiree was the most taxing thought Edward normally had to face. He'd had little experience communicating with anyone except others of his own elite class, especially women who seemed to think their ideas were pertinent. In England, one simply did what everybody else did and took for granted it was the right thing to do.

But as the time approached for Edward to leave, doubts began to assail him. By nature, he was not a devious sort. And truth to tell, he was loath to dupe these people who had brought him back to health. Edward had come to admire the Scots' courage in resisting the efforts of the English to overcome them and confiscate their lands. He didn't understand nor did he know how to handle his ambivalent thoughts. He was anxious to be away from a situation that made him feel guilty over his loss of confidence in the English morals he'd been taught to believe.

Finally, his last day in the Highlands faded into an evening decorated by a full moon and cloudless sky. Now that the time was close at hand, Edward was surprised that the idea of leaving no longer brought him joy. His time in captivity had allowed him to consider how he felt about the English treatment of the Scots over the years. With his escape, he was making a choice between two sides wherein dwelt both good and evil. Whichever choice he made offered an imperfect solution. *Why did Father never explain to me that adulthood meant making hard compromises?* he mused, as he plodded through his chores. He refused to allow his thoughts to run forward into the night when he would leave.

After Edward had fed Kit her evening meal, he and Oliver leaned against the trunk of an old oak, chatting like two friends who'd grown up in the Highlands together. Oliver showed Edward the scar on his arm where one of MacKenzie's hot tongs had slipped. Edward reminded Oliver of the cracks in Kit's walls that should be re-caulked before fall. Edward would miss Oliver. It was one of his compromises that was hardest for him to swallow. He sat for awhile after the lad had gone to his own home, considering the irony of his affinity for this young lad.

Later, a light mist cleansed the village of dirt from a day of working in fields and pastures. Dry throats were soothed by a mug of cool ale and weary bodies settled their bones onto goose down pillows or a soft nest of grass. Above the sounds of squawking geese and baying dogs, Edward heard children laughing and parents talking over events of the day. The aroma of stews bubbling in heavy cauldrons made his mouth water. With all the hardships these people endured, none of it had erased the contentment they found in one another. He sighed, confused at the lonely feeling that claimed his heart.

"I'll soon be back with my own family," he whispered. "How will my life be changed?" He gazed into the star-filled sky, rejoicing that his eye had healed completely and his shoulder no longer hurt when he carried water to Kit for her nightly wash.

Though he tried, Edward could not shove away the feeling of admiration he had for the lass who had nursed him as well as any of the English doctors with all their disgusting leeches and potions.

Edward's large body filled Kit's bedroom door when he came to help her with her bath the next evening. Kit noticed his expressionless face. During their time together, Kit had reveled in the fact that she could read his moods as clearly as constellations in the sky. Edward's mouth was always the giveaway -- a tiny upward curve if he was amused or downward slant if he was trying to hide anger or pain. But tonight, she saw nothing except skin as smooth as the lake on a windless day. She breathed deeply as he came close to fluff her pillow. He smelled as fresh as newly cut hay.

Edward turned his thoughts away from her mouth, where a smile usually lurked when she thought he wasn't looking. He stared past her green-flecked eyes that brimmed with fire when she was furious at his clumsiness but softened when she cared for his wounds.

As he pulled Kit's shoulders forward, she grasped his arms to raise her body up. A lump in his throat that seemed the size of an apple nearly choked him. Kit instinctively tapped his back to dislodge whatever had brought on the sudden fit of coughing. She brushed his chest with her bosom as she surrounded his large body with her arms. He felt her heart beat, smelled her scent of primrose, and rubbed his roughened fingers over her cheek.

Leaving Kit would make a hole in his heart that could never be filled - a reminder of the brief time in his life, when pain and humiliation were the catalyst that enlightened him to the fact that no one 'side' ever contained all the right answers or truths.

"Kit, we should finish your bath," he whispered into the soft depression of her throat. She released him then and he felt a chill go through his body. Neither spoke as he handed her the wet cloths to sponge with. When she was finished, he helped dry her shoulders where she couldn't reach, taking care not to let his fingers touch her skin. When he pulled the coverlet over her upper body, Kit's eyelids fluttered in a vain attempt to stay awake. He bent and kissed her forehead then left quietly, carefully closing the door as he went.

Knowing he could ill-afford such care for a Scottish lass, and that once back at Lexington Estate all would be as it was before, Edward quickly prepared to leave. He went to his pallet and pulled the food he'd been storing from under an old tartan that Oliver had given him. Like many a secret, the evidence that he was planning an escape had lain within reaching distance of Hamish but gone unnoticed since it was covered by a familiar Scottish plaid. Edward felt good that one of the wiliest of the Scots had not given a young Englishman credit for being clever enough to use one of the oldest of ruses - hiding one's plans under the nose of the enemy.

When he heard Kit's soft, regular breathing he climbed stealthily down the ladder and out of the house. Stripes raised her head out of her belly, then promptly re-curled and got back to sleep. He made his way slowly down the hill to the barn, careful not to slip on the stones but at the same time turning his head around often to make sure he was alone. He'd used goose grease that day to lubricate the rusty hinge on the barn door so as not to cause a noise and alert the many dogs that lived with the families.

Once his eyes adjusted to the dark, Edward found the saddle and set about tacking up with as little fuss as possible. Before leading the young horse, now named Rory, out of the barn, Edward stuck his head out and spent several minutes perusing the area. Once assured that all was as it should be, he led Rory up the hill and onto the path that would take him to the Borders and Lexington Estate. He mounted and began his long trek home.

A tree branch falling onto the roof aroused Kit. She felt a slight breeze that rustled in the tall grass just outside her window, then turned her head slowly to a more comfortable position. The unmistakable sound of a hoof on stony ground brought her fully awake. Ignoring her throbbing head Kit got out of bed, grabbed her shawl from atop her trunk, and wrapped it around her body as she hurried outside. As she looked into the horizon, fully clarified by moonlight, Edward's lean, young frame was silhouetted against the sky for one brief moment before he crested the hill and dropped from her vision. The horse he rode was a strong colt not long in training. Oddly, she hoped the young horse wasn't more than Edward could handle with his wounds just barely healed.

Kit stared thoughtfully into the space Edward left behind as he journeyed back to the privileged culture and home where he'd been born. She then turned and walked slowly into the simple cottage that was *her* home. For the first time in her life, Kit questioned the birth bonds that tied her to these Highlands. She knew she'd think differently when the sun rose. The soft life of the gentry didn't appeal to her and the smell of the mountains and lakes of Scotland overshadowed the stifling aristocratic life in the Borders. She knew the clothes worn by those privileged ladies would snuff the life out of her.

But this was not a time for common sense! Kit was angry with herself for letting Edward escape. She had known he would go. Why had she permitted it? She could easily have raised her voice and Edward would have been recaptured in minutes. And why did his leaving bother her so much?

As Edward began his descent back to his home, he stopped Rory and looked back once. Something clawed at his insides, like a rat tearing at a corn husk. Why did his long-awaited escape leave a taste of loss in his soul?

# CHAPTER TWELVE

*Between the Highlands and the Borders*

Malcolm stared down the steep bank and watched loose stones slide forward, gathering momentum as they careened into the valley below. He'd been bitten by horseflies, bees, and fleas. He looked like someone in the last throes of a case of pox. His food supply was stale and nearly gone. To make matters worse, it had taken him three hours longer than normal to complete the trip from Clan MacDougal to his meeting place with Wren.

Hamish and Kit had been less than supportive of Malcolm's effort to bring funds into the clan. Their fighting successes against the English would be wasted effort without money to repair and replace their old unreliable weapons and equipment. Hamish continued to think Edward was more trouble than any amount of money he'd garner. Kit practically refused to care for a patient she felt would simply fight them again as soon as he was healthy.

Malcolm knew he'd have to get Edward back to Lexington Estate with all possible haste before Kit allowed him to die from lack of attention!

Wren would be waiting in the sheep meadow near Potter's Crossing as usual. The image of Wren brought a smile to Malcolm's face. His thoughts meandered back to the first time he'd met the little fellow. The Scots owed everything to the enigmatic little gnome of a man who had come into their lives and made their rebellion a success. Without revealing his source, Wren had accurately provided them with all the dates and places where the English could be ambushed. The steady motion of Magnet lulled Malcolm back to that first meeting. He remembered the entire incident.

> *It had been a little more than two years ago when he and some of the other MacDougal men had herded their sheep to pasture near the village of Berwick. It was about noon and while the dogs kept watch, the men shared bread, cheese, and ale. They were leaning against some half-grown trees.*
>
> *"Malcolm, how long ye think we can stay here afore we're noticed?" Rafe Campbell asked, picking a piece of grain from his teeth with a twig.*
>
> *"Not more'n two days, way I'm thinkin'," Malcolm replied. "Somebody's bound to be travelin' near here, see our camp, 'n git suspicious."*
>
> *"I sure don't like leavin' such good grass so soon," interrupted Clem Duplin.*
>
> *"'Bout the time we git some weight on these sheep we go on the move 'gain – afore they've had*

*time to git fat," he continued, wagging his head in discouragement.*

*"Aye, Clem," answered Malcolm. "But one day we'll be free of the English yoke. Then grazin' our sheep on good pasture won't have to be done on the sly."*

*Morse Thigpen took a bite of his bread, chewed awhile with the few teeth he had left, then had his say.*

*"Ye're always sayin' that, Malcolm. But ye've not mentioned how that'll come 'bout."*

*Before Malcolm could answer, Rafe interrupted. "Would ye look at that mess comin' toward us."*

*The other men lifted their heads and trained their eyes on the emaciated figure approaching them. With mouths half open, they studied the creature in silence.*

*Finally, Clem asked, "Ye figure that's a man or a woman?"*

*"Cain't tell," replied Rafe. "Looks like a man that never got 'nough to eat when he needed it."*

*By now the stranger was close enough for them to hear him wheezing. They could see that it was, in fact, a small man of indeterminate age.*

*About that time, the fellow was beset by a fit of coughing that bent his wizened body in half and lifted one of his tiny feet off the ground.*

"My God, man! Here. Have a drink of ale," said Malcolm, rushing to his rescue.

"Thank ye sir," the little fellow gasped, taking a big swallow and immediately choking and sputtering the ale onto the ground.

Malcolm slapped him between the shoulder blades, nearly knocking him down.

"Stop!" the fellow exclaimed weakly. "Just let me stand still fer a minute."

He stood stock still, arms slack at his sides, head bowed. The MacDougal men stared in disbelief. None of them uttered a word.

After the newcomer passed a few minutes without coughing, Malcolm continued the conversation. "Here, sit down. We've got extra bread. Looks like ye could use a meal." Malcolm pulled a section off his own loaf and handed it to the stranger. "Why don't ye sit a spell. Tell us why ye're here."

The MacDougals watched the little fellow in fascination as he slid down the tree trunk and pulled the legs of his worn-out trousers down over his shoes. He bent his knees, using them to support the hand holding his ale. When he'd finally come to a full squat, Clem broke the silence. "What's yer name, boy? We cain't eat with ye if ye don't have a name." Malcolm looked at Clem quizzically, wondering what having a name had to do with sharing food.

"Wren," the boy replied. "Call me Wren."

"What're ye doin' hereabouts," Morse asked suspiciously.

"I'm lookin' fer folks who might've come from the north," Wren answered, looking across the pasture toward the sheep. "Would ye folks be them by any chance?"

"We might," Malcolm replied, with a slight turn of his head, indicating to his men to head toward the sheep. "Why'd ye be lookin' fer northerners?"

"Are ye the. . ."

"Speak up, boy. What with all that coughin' 'n wheezin', I can barely understand a word ye're sayin'."

Wren cleared his throat, spat, and spoke again. "I asked, 're ye the leader? And my name's Wren, not boy."

"Aye. I'm the leader. What do ye want?"

Wren's oversized cap drooped down his forehead obscuring his face. Malcolm couldn't see his eyes since they were hidden behind the sprigs of dirty red hair that enveloped his beardless face like a spider web. Malcolm reckoned it would be a long time before this frail boy developed a beard.

"How old 're ye, Wren?" Malcolm asked.

"Old 'nough."

Malcolm chuckled at the forcefulness of Wren's words. He liked the boy's enthusiasm and decided *to let the matter be.   Wren scooted closer to Malcolm and the pungent odor of fish assaulted Malcolm's nose. He forced himself not to turn his head away, for fear of offending him.*

*Cupping one hand to the side of his mouth, Wren talked to Malcolm. "I've a grievance with the English. They've killed some of my relatives 'n I wanna git even with 'em." Wren peeked out from under the cap just enough to see Malcolm's eyes.*

*"Go on," Malcolm ordered.*

*"Would ye know anybody from the north who might be havin' a complaint toward the English too?"*

*"I might," Malcolm replied. "Just what'd ye want to say to any northerners who aren't too fond of the English?"*

*"How'd I know ye're not English?" Wren asked.*

*"How'd I know ye're not English yerself, sent to spy on anyone grazin' sheep hereabouts?" Malcolm answered in kind.*

*Wren slowly searched one of the pockets of his voluminous coat and pulled out a ragged, yellowed handkerchief. Very carefully he unfolded it and laid a ring in Malcolm's palm. Malcolm turned it over and studied the crest carefully.*

*Looks like the ring of a Scottish clan," he said, then handed it back to Wren.*

"Aye." *Wren replied as he replaced the ring in its flimsy sheath.*

"MacLendon? Or maybe, MacDonough?" *Malcolm asked.*

"Maybe," *Wren exhaled heartily with breath that matched the smell of his clothing.*

*Malcolm held his breath and turned his head slightly.* "Git on with it, man. I've not got all day."

"I can tell ye the movements of the militias 'round Lexington Cove: dates, forces – everythin' ye'd need to know fer a surprise ambush."

"Why'd ye do that fer people ye don't know?" *Malcolm asked, scanning Wren from lowered lids.*

"I told ye!" *Wren's words were agitated.* "I wanna help stop the English from killin' us Scots. I've got the way to do it. Do ye want my information or not?"

"I'll make a deal with ye," *Malcolm said, hoping this little fellow was honest. If Wren was what he claimed to be, the Scots could become a real threat to the English, rather than just a nuisance easily put aside. It was a long shot, but he was ready to try anything that had a thread of hope to bring freedom from the English.*

"Git me the date 'n place of their next planned attack. We'll be there, under cover, just to make certain ye're not tryin' to git us caught."

*Wren stood up on stiff legs. "I'll send ye word when ye return to the Highlands. Here's how to git the message.*

*Rafe, Morse, and Clem had been watching the two talk. As Wren stood up, he pulled Malcolm's head close to his own. The three men watched in amazement while Wren whispered in Malcolm's ear.*

*"Can ye beat that," sniggered Clem. "That mite thinks we'd listen in."*

*"Don't think I ever had ears so good I could hear that far, even if they wuz talkin' real loud," laughed Rafe.*

*As they joked, Malcolm and Wren shook hands and Wren retreated from whence he had come.*

The bite of a deer fly stopped Malcolm's recollecting. He swatted the insect and laughed at the memory. In the past two years, Wren had more than lived up to his promise. Time and time again he'd supplied the Scots with information that made it possible for the rag-tag Scots to bring the English to the point where *they* were now the hunted - running short of men and supplies. All because of a diminutive man with a score to settle against the English. Malcolm hurried forward, anxious to see his unlikely collaborator again.

By early evening, Malcolm sat under a tree in the sheep pasture waiting for Wren. The little man's presence was announced by his coughing long before he came into sight. Even after two years it was still difficult for Malcolm to understand his fast speech, which was often interrupted by nose-blowing, coughing, and spitting.

Wren approached wearing his usual garb, an oversized coat which billowed in the breeze, allowing a glimpse underneath of shabby clothes like those worn by fishermen. Wren kept one hand holding onto his enormous hat that threatened to blow away in the wind, while the other fist clutched a knobby oak walking stick. Upon seeing Malcolm, Wren waved with the hand holding his hat, then quickly retrieved it just as it floated from his head. It was the first time Malcolm had seen more than the tendrils of hair that normally straggled down Wren's forehead from under the hat. His hair was the color of a dirty pumpkin. It lay flat, oily, and lifeless against his head.

Regardless of his bizarre appearance, Malcolm felt a kinship to this little man who took such dangerous chances on behalf of the Scots. Malcolm couldn't even speculate what had caused so much hatred that Wren was willing to put his own life at risk to bring bloodshed to the English. However, Wren was not unusual in that respect. The Borders were filled with Scots more than ready to spill their own blood for the opportunity to do damage to the hated English.

Malcolm and Wren met at the edge of the meadow and grasped each others' shoulders with a familiarity that had evolved during their mutual project of defeating the English. Malcolm had to stoop quite a bit to be on Wren's level but he did it as inconspicuously as possible.

"Wren, tis good to see ye 'gain."

"Aye, Malcolm," Wren wheezed. "Were ye happy with the outcome at Potter's Crossing?"

"Aye. Our gains far outweighed my hopes. Not only did we capture some good horses 'n armor but we bagged ourselves an Englishman who oughta bring us 'nough money to supply our needs fer a large campaign."

"I know that, Malcolm. Remember, I work at Lexington Estate. Whole place's been in an uproar since Neville was killed 'n Edward taken prisoner." Wren had always refused to use the titles these two men carried with them. "What brings ye down here?"

Malcolm didn't mince words. "I need yer help deliverin' the ransom note 'n retrievin' the money."

Wren's wheezing and coughing ceased altogether as the little man looked at Malcolm with eyes full of disbelief. Malcolm was surprised. Wren had taken so many chances in the past without question. Why did this request agitate him so?

"Tisn't there 'nother way?"

"I'm 'fraid not. Ye know yer way 'round the place, 'n obviously nobody suspects ye of spyin'. Besides, ye're small 'n tis easier fer ye to hide in places I couldn't, even if I did know where to go." For the first time in their acquaintance, Malcolm could see a large part of Wren's face. He watched as fragments of emotions played across his face like clouds teasing a full moon. Fear, confusion, and in the end, acceptance of the job ahead of him.

Wren's chin dropped to his chest. Malcolm could barely hear the words he spoke. "I'll have to work closer to the enemy than ever afore. Don't know if I've got the heart fer it." Wren's voice quivered.

Malcolm clasped Wren's bony shoulders. "Course ye have. Ye've duped them English time 'n 'gain. They've still got no idea who ye 're. This oughta be the last time ye have to put yerself in such jeopardy."

"Give me the note. Might as well git it over with." Wren held out his hand to receive the distasteful letter.

The resignation in Wren's voice seemed to cause his tiny frame to shrink even more. Malcolm felt pity for this little creature who carried a heavy secret. "Thank ye, Wren. I'll wait til I git the message that the money's in yer hands. Then we'll meet here 'gain at dusk two days hence."

"Aye." Wren tried too hard to sound confident – like he thought Malcolm wanted him to be. "With luck, this'll provide 'nough money to buy the weapons we need to gain our freedom." Then he turned and walked away.

Malcolm was struck by the loyalty of this little person who seemed so lonely. Not for the first time did he wonder what his story really was. Wren crossed the meadow and passed from sight into the shadows of the forest. The moon rose higher in the heavens, bringing out a multitude of night creatures who scurried about foraging for food. With Magnet hobbled and peacefully grazing, Malcolm laid his head on his saddle, pulled his tartan over his body, and fell into a troubled sleep.

While Wren set off to procure the ransom money, Malcolm scoured the local countryside with a much more critical eye than on previous trips. This section of land, the Borders, separated England and Scotland and its boundaries were questionable in the best of times. They changed constantly, according to which side was in control of the most strategic area at the time. Malcolm wanted to set in place a network of loyal Scotsmen willing to fight with their northern kinsmen for freedom. It was what Hamish had suggested before the ambush at Potter's Crossing. The Highlanders would need a system of support from Scots living here in the Borders in order to make the campaign successful.

Malcolm made a crude diagram of Lexington Cove. It was a quiet village which surrounded a small inlet. It was lined with fishing boats, secured to large timbers driven into a cobblestone pier. Rimming the landing were a smithy shop, an inn/ pub in bad need of repair, a stable, and a few dilapidated hovels which housed fishmongers and tavern workers. Most of the shutters were slightly askew on the pub, and its sign proclaiming the White Whale Inn hung from salt eaten chains and threatened to blow away in the gusty wind. The stench of rotting fish permeated everything within sight of the village. Pieces of partly eaten carcasses lapped against the fishing boats as they rocked softly in the gentle waves. On the hill behind the bay, the remainder of Lexington Cove presented a slightly better picture and aroma. The Boar's Head Inn was located here -- somewhat better lodgings for gentry forced to lower their standards when traveling in these primitive hinterlands.

Later Malcolm traveled the countryside along rutted roads. His face was shielded under the brim of a large, shapeless hat while he observed the comings and goings of three farms. He picked the poorest looking one and walked slowly up the lane that led to the simple cottage. A husband and wife were working in the barnyard feeding livestock and milking a cow. Two young boys were helping. The smallest of the two gathered eggs while the older one, assisted by a dog of mixed breeding, separated lambs from their mothers.

Malcolm ambled slowly, using a crooked cane so as not to pose a threat. He listened carefully, hearing the unmistakable hint of a Scottish brogue. The four looked up as he approached. The man leaned on his pitchfork and the woman peered from under the cow she was milking. Neither offered to speak. With a slight nod of her head, the wife signaled the boys to go into the barn. Without a backward glance the children followed her orders. The farmer came to stand between his wife and Malcolm.

"Ye lost?" he asked, casually glancing toward the barn.

"Nay. Just tired 'n thirsty," Malcolm answered. "Mind if I rest awhile?"

"Suit yerself. Where're ye headed?"

"North."

The farmer continued talking to Malcolm. "Where're ye comin' from?"

"London," Malcolm replied. "I'm a tinker. Been there earnin' money fer my family back home." He looked around the barnyard. "Yer wife got anythin' she needs repaired? I'd do it fer a good meal to git me on my way."

He looked at his wife. She shook her head. "Guess we don't have anythin' broken that I can't fix."

Malcolm went on, emphasizing his heavy Scottish brogue. "Could ye spare me a drink of water then?"

The man's eyebrows raised. "Don't hear that accent much 'round here," he said quietly. "What's yer name? Where'n the north 're ye goin'?"

"Name's Malcolm MacDougal. On my way back to the Highlands." He could see the older boy peeking out from behind one of the barn doors. The boy saw Malcolm's glance and shrank from sight. "What's yer name?" he asked the farmer.

"Calvin Lucas."

"I know a family by that name. They live near Leith. Ye any kin to 'em?"

"Nay. Been livin' here more'n fifteen years," Calvin moved toward the well, carrying the fork with him. His wife got up from the cow and carried the bucket toward the house. "Say, ye want a drink?" Calvin asked.

"Aye," Malcolm replied. "And I'd pay ye fer some bread 'n cheese since ye've nothin' fer me to fix."

The woman hesitated, waiting to hear her husband's answer.

"Evelyn, bring the man a drink 'n some food." Calvin faced Malcolm. "We don't take money from hungry travelers. Sit on that stump 'n she'll bring somethin' out." Calvin pointed toward the chopping block then he leaned against a tree.

Malcolm sat, pulled out a filthy rag, and wiped his dirt-encrusted face. Silence hung between them, like a ripe apple soon to drop from the tree. Both picked at calluses on their hands while they waited for Evelyn to return. Malcolm searched for a way to get on friendlier terms with this family. "Yer older boy looks like a lad in my village."

"That so?" Calvin responded. "Red hair 'n freckles 're common in the north. Are ye Scots?"

"Aye."

Calvin took a deep breath. "What're ye really doin' here in the Borders, Malcolm? I've known many a tinker, 'n ye're not one." Malcolm nodded.

The two boys ambled over from the barn. "These 're my sons, Angus 'n Neil." Calvin motioned for everyone to go into the house. Evelyn shot him a sour glance.

They sat on small stools on a dirt floor. Calvin spoke to his wife. "Mum, this's Malcolm MacDougal. He's on 'is way back to the Highlands."

Evelyn looked at Malcolm with undisguised mistrust. Without a word she turned and began stoking the fire. Angus and Neil sat near the hearth holding tight to their mugs of cider.

The three adults continued exchanging information regarding mutual Scottish origins. Finally, Calvin wanted more than just hints. "Do ye know anythin' 'bout the Scottish attacks in these parts?"

"Aye," Malcolm answered. " Fact is, I know many of the Scots who fought in them skirmishes."

Calvin coughed nervously. "I've never been acquainted with any of 'em personally but I've not minded that the English've had to lick their own wounds fer a change."

Malcolm grabbed his courage and jumped headlong into what he hoped would not mean he'd have to run for safety. "Like I said, I'm from the Highlands. My father's Hamish MacDougal, laird of Clan MacDougal. In the comin' months we plan to lead a group of men on a final ambush 'gainst the English."

Calvin looked up sharply. Evelyn's face tensed and she looked even more grim.

"I've prowled the village disguised as a fisherman. I know the layout 'n names of the surroundin' communities."

Calvin stretched, then looked hard at Malcolm. "Ye still haven't said what ye want from us."

"I'm hopin' fer yer help. If I can worm my way into the community by workin' as a tinker, I can learn attack dates 'n numbers of fighters." Seeing no resentment in Calvin's eyes, Malcolm continued. "Then we'd need volunteers to git to the Highlands with the information. 'Cause if I disappear from the community, the English'll know I'm a spy, 'n launch an attack straightaway." Malcolm took a drink of his ale then went on. "That'd ruin any hope of takin' our country back from the English."

Angus and Neil had joined their father and listened to this conversation -- their eyes bright with excitement.

"Ye're sayin' ye need an underground group of Scots here to serve as messengers to the north?"

Malcolm nodded.

"I think I can find 'nough men willin' to take the chance," Calvin offered.

The remainder of the day was spent making plans. Calvin offered to be the courier to the Highlands and suggested Douglas MacClure as the man to organize other willing fighters in the area. Though elated, Malcolm felt like a fly caught in a spider web. He realized that all of these complex plans would come to naught if Wren didn't return with the ransom money.

The morning after Wren had met with Malcolm, he approached Lexington Estate. His breath came in short, shallow gasps and he could barely swallow. His face was covered with bright red splotches which he tried to cover with the brim of his floppy hat. The carriage sweep had never seemed so long or the portico pillars so tall and imposing. He tried to stifle his sneezing as he mingled with the countless other workers in the gardens and lawns.

Getting so close to family members could spoil everything. For the moment, he forgot the grand scheme of defeating the English and gave in to his despair at being put in such a dangerous position. It was something he'd never bargained for.

Wren carried the folded ransom note in a packet deep in his large pocket. He had to get it out and lay it beside the front door while no one was looking. When the workers took their mid-day meal, Wren moved quietly to the large front entrance of the mansion. He slid his hand into his pocket and grabbed the packet. Footsteps! For an instant, Wren's feet were fixed to the spot like the roots of a tree. Then fear goaded him into action. He dropped the bundle and let it fall near the entryway. Like a fox going to ground, Wren scurried to the side of the mansion and slipped through a tiny opening in the hedge. He collapsed on a garden bench as beads of perspiration burned his eyes and he struggled desperately to breathe without wheezing.

Allison Ann admired the lovely bouquet of roses mixed with iris as she walked toward the main entrance to the Lexington mansion. *They'll look lovely on the sideboard in the library,* she thought, as she buried her face in the fragrant bunch of flowers. "Lord in heaven" she squealed, falling to her knees while still managing to hold the bouquet together. She looked around sheepishly, happy to see that no one had seen her clumsiness. In front of her and the cause for the near accident, was an oily package, tied with strips of leather. "What on earth?" she muttered. Holding the flowers in one hand, she picked up the pouch and noticed writing on the front of it. Without further ado she carried it directly to the library where she knew Gwen was and handed it to her. "Here, M'aam. I nearly lost me knees 'n me flowers over this piece of drivel. Since there's writin' on it I 'llowed as how ye'd best have a look." She curtsied, and left to find a vase for the bouquet.

Gwen fingered the packet, reading the name of Lady Anne on the front. With trembling fingers, she opened it and watched as a crudely written note floated to the floor. Its block letters announced that the ransom note had finally arrived.

LEAVE 1000 POUNDS
IN THIS PACKET IN THE
GUARDHOUSE BY 8 O'CLOCK
TONIGHT. NO ONE IS TO GO
NEAR AFTER THAT. FOLLOW
THESE INSTRUCTIONS AND
EDWARD WILL BE RETURNED
UNHARMED. IF WE DO NOT
RECEIVE THE MONEY HE WILL
BE KILLED.

She rubbed her palms carefully over the parchment as though any rough treatment might put Edward's return in jeopardy. A shadow fell over her hand.

"What's that you have, Gwen?" her mother asked.

"It's the ransom note for Edward," Gwen whispered. "They want one thousand pounds."

Lady Anne took the paper, scanned its words, then clasped it to her breast. For the first time since the death of Lord Neville, Gwen saw a flicker of life in her mother's eyes. Gwen embraced Lady Anne to discreetly mask the quiet sobbing the older woman could not withhold. Mother and daughter rejoiced for a few moments before Anne shook herself and took command.

"Say nothing of this to anyone until Colin sees it." Gwen nodded.

Colin had barely dismounted that evening when Gwen ran to him with the news. He was dumbfounded. The traitor who had confounded the English for the past two years must live or work at Lexington Estate! Colin knew without a doubt that *he* would be the prime suspect.

"Where's your mother, Gwen?"

"In the library. She wants your opinion on how to handle this."

"Well done," he said, and strode toward the library. He hastily bowed to Lady Anne. "This note is not without its ramifications. We must proceed carefully."

She nodded.

He continued, looking from one to the other. "*No one*, including our own people, is to know of this note. I would be the first suspect. That could put this entire estate in jeopardy. Later, through our own observations here, we will strive to root out the traitor." Colin raked his sweaty fingers through his hair, leaving spaces like garden rows ready for planting.

"You're right, Colin." Anne turned thoughtfully and faced him squarely. "We must handle this discreetly."

Colin smiled. It seemed that the arrival of this note had brought Lady Anne out of the melancholy she'd suffered since her husband's death. Colin was as thankful for that as he was over the knowledge that Edward would be returned.

Anne continued. "For the welfare of Lexington Estate, we shall keep this between the three of us. The other landowners are too angry now not to take their spite out on the closest Scotsman they can get their hands on. Colin, can you place the money in the required spot?" He nodded. "Gwen, bring the little trunk your father kept in the large locked drawer of the desk in the library. Here's the key." She slipped a ribbon holding a gold key from her neck and handed it to Gwen. "Neville would want us to do whatever we must to facilitate the return of Edward, preserve the strength of Lexington Estate, and maintain *your* integrity as well, Colin," Lady Anne said, looking at him with the same compassion that had prompted her to bring Colin and Enid into her home those many years ago. In that moment, Colin knew the love and respect he felt for this woman was not wrongly placed.

When Gwen returned and Lady Anne had placed the required money in the packet, the conspirators held hands, allowing their single strengths to flow to one another.

It was midnight. As Wren once again approached the Lexington mansion, he tried to keep his wheezing as quiet as possible. A loose stone caused him to fall to his knees, becoming entangled in his bulky clothes. He swore, extricated his legs, and walked on fighting his body that wanted so badly to turn and run.

In the shadows that constantly changed as moonlight sliced erratically through the clouds, the guardhouse to the Lexington mansion rose like a ghoul emerging from the depths of an evil swamp. Wren fancied he could see devilish night creatures hiding behind every tree and hedge. The thorns of prickly bushes grabbed his clothing, pulling him into a near frenzy. The air was so heavy he felt as though he was struggling through an endless sea of mud.

With a furtive look around, Wren dropped to a crouch and crawled across the last few feet, imagining that an armed militia awaited him behind the fence. Just outside the building he bent forward and slid his hand along the side of the opening at the base of the door frame. The floor was slimy with mud. He stretched his arm as far as it would go, then leaned a little further into the opening. He grabbed desperately and got hold of a small snake! Stifling a scream by stuffing his hand in his mouth, he jerked backward and fell on his haunches, trembling.

With the last bit of courage in his soul, Wren forced his hand back into the black void. Slowly. Slowly. This time he searched along the other side of the door frame and felt the edge of something rough. He seized it. Then holding it tightly to his chest with both hands, Wren ran as fast as his cumbersome costume would permit into the protection of the mist-shrouded forest.

The next day, Wren and Malcolm met once again in the meadow. Wren thrust the valuable packet at Malcolm. "This has cost me more'n ye'll ever know," he said, offering no further explanation as to the enormity of his effort.

"I know, old friend," Malcolm answered. "No one's given more'n ye to this mission. We'll not ask more."

The two conspirators, campaigners of different sorts, looked at one another with a respect that came from their hearts. They clasped shoulders and parted company with the understanding that Wren would send word to Malcolm as soon as the English plans became known. Both felt like they had hold of the tail of a boar hog - afraid to hold on and scared to let go.

# CHAPTER THIRTEEN

### *Edward's trek to Lexington Estate*

While Edward's departure from Clan MacDougal had been bittersweet, once on the way his chest filled to bursting with confidence and excitement. All thoughts of respect and sentiment he'd gained for the Scots during his imprisonment left with the speed of a summer squall. They were replaced with impatience to see Lexington Estate and his family again. He chuckled with anticipation, a feeling he'd thought never to experience again. Life in the Highlands offered little opportunity for merriment. And when one did laugh, it was with fingers crossed to ward off the sadness which always lurked in the unforgiving circumstances in which the Scots lived.

Even though he'd been mostly unconscious when the Scots had dragged him into the wilderness, Edward was confident his years of hunting and tracking with his father would be his source of guidance as he made his way back to his beloved home. Edward wanted to see the look of shock on Malcolm's face as the ransom money and his pride were lost when he was ambushed by the very Englishman Malcolm had treated with such arrogance. As Rory shuffled his way down the hills, Edward's hopes flew ahead of them like arrows winging their way to a target. A peace as comforting as his mother's arms settled over him, protecting him from any discomfort the elements might brew. Rory's soft motion rocked him like a babe, lulling him into a half-sleep.

When the horse stopped with a lurch Edward was rudely shaken from his slumber. He blinked his eyes trying to focus on why Rory was standing still, waiting for a signal from Edward. In a terrifying moment, the reason became obvious. Edward was staring into thin air! Rory had stopped at the edge of a cliff. It dropped into a gorge so deep Edward could not see the water that he could hear roaring at the bottom! The trees and wild underbrush obscured any actual view of the river or a path down to it.

With deadly clarity, Edward realized he was lost in a place where a stranger could be swallowed up by the wilderness and die with no one being the wiser! In his youthful pride at achieving a successful escape, he had relived his cleverness, while paying little mind to his surroundings or the direction Rory had traveled. In the length of a short breath, Edward's emotions plunged from elation to despair.

The most pressing issue at hand, however, was that in addition to being lost, Edward faced the real possibility of being launched into the nothingness in front of him. Backing up is not a natural movement for a horse, especially a newly trained one. At any time Rory might rear and bolt forward into the abyss. Sweat trickled down Edward's neck and back, burning and tickling at the same time. He froze, fearing that any movement might encourage Rory to take another step toward the edge of the cliff. His breathing became very shallow since he feared any excessive chest movement might knock Rory off balance.

In the end, Edward dismounted as carefully as if he was handling one of his mother's prize Ming vases. He guided Rory backwards by steadily pushing on his chest. The horse was reluctant to back up into something he could not see. His steps were stiff and painstakingly slow. When they had made enough progress backward, Edward carefully turned the colt around and walked ahead - a catastrophe barely averted.

The ordeal had cost Edward every ounce of strength and confidence he'd had. He was exhausted and sore and wondered now what had ever made him think he could find his way out of these miserable mountains alone. His plan to intercept Malcolm, retrieve the ransom, then continue to Lexington Estate was that of an impudent fool! Edward's heart sank with the realization that he'd be lucky to live long enough to find his way to *any* civilization.

Somewhere in the cobwebs of his mind he heard his father's voice. "Think, Edward!"

He snapped to attention as surely as though Lord Neville was in front of him. He looked into the heavens. Between the clouds that scudded across the moon he saw streaks of light breaking through the darkness. Dawn was but two hours away. He studied the land around him. Above, the Highlands rose into endless mists. Below was the bottomless chasm. In the distance, he heard the waterfall that fed the river. Nothing in all his youthful training had prepared him to survive in such conditions.

Then he remembered hearing an infuriating remark from Hamish. "When captured, the English have little will to live."

"I'll prove the old man wrong," he vowed loudly. He sat on the trunk of an upended tree while Rory munched leaves off the nearest branch. Somewhere in his addled brain there must be a solution born of common sense. He rethought lessons his father had taught him that had to do with finding one's way. But Lord Neville had never placed Edward in a situation where the foliage was so thick and the landscape was nothing but mountains and rock. He could see nothing familiar to use as a landmark.

But as Edward looked up through the branches that formed a leafy canopy over the forest floor, he was reminded of the time, years ago, when he and Colin had been lost. Edward was in a panic. But Colin had used this as a chance to prove his bravery and superiority.

Edward could hear him still. "Not to worry, Edward," Colin had said, stretching to his full height and shading his eyes with one hand. "It's easy to find our way home."

"I'm not worried," Edward had answered, in a tone he hoped hid the fear that fluttered in his stomach. "But, *how* do we get back?"

"Like this." Colin turned slowly, pretending he was scouring the horizon with an experienced eye. "At the bottom of every hill is a little brook which continues down until it joins the next stream." Colin sounded like a schoolmaster teaching geography. "All these streams run into rivers which lead to the sea." He'd looked at Edward as though Edward should understand perfectly.

"What's that got to do with us being lost?" Edward replied angrily.

"Everything!" answered Colin. "We simply follow the brooks until they become large streams, which eventually flow into a river. Somewhere along that river bank, we'll come to a village where we can ask directions to Lexington Estate." Colin's confidence made Edward think the scheme might actually work. Side by side, the two boys had followed the maze of streams that would lead to a river and people.

By late afternoon, they were safely back home. Neither ever told a soul of their adventure and from that time forward, Edward had worshipped Colin. To his youthful eyes, Colin had saved them from starvation and wolves.

"That's it then," Edward mumbled, as he took Rory's reins and settled himself again in the saddle. "It worked once. It could work again." Thus, Edward renewed his long journey home the way he'd followed Colin those many years ago.

It wasn't easy. In some places, the loose stones caused Rory to slide and where it was muddy his feet sank in over his fetlocks. Branches snagged and tore at the horse's skin and Edward's tartan. Clothes and horse hair were soggy from the heavy dew. Fearful of coming to the edge of another drop in the early morning shadows, Edward kept Rory moving slowly.

They had negotiated several levels of descent when tongues of light began to filter through the trees. "Thank God," Edward breathed, as they reached the bank of a small stream. His shoulder throbbed from the constant jostling and the deer flies had bitten through his clothing, sucking his blood and leaving angry red welts. As the sun rose higher Edwards clothes began to dry, sticking to the tiny spots of blood left by the deer flies. Finally he dismounted, disrobed, and jumped into the cold water, cleansing his body and refreshing his spirits. While Rory ate the abundant grass and lowered his muzzle into the sparkling stream for his own refreshment, Edward ate a portion of his cheese and bread, which was made tastier by some wild berries he'd found. Both needed all the nourishment they could get since it would be another day of hacking through more underbrush and hostile footing. Within thirty minutes, they were on their way again.

The warm sun on his back and the distant sound of the forest animals had taken Edward into a nether-world, obliterating all concerns of primitive Scots, the perilous journey, or ransom money forfeited. Suddenly the motion of Rory scrambling down a bank into water for a drink, returned Edward to the venture at hand. Before him stretched the calm surface of a small river. He knew it would lead him home. Silently he thanked Colin for once more showing him the way. Edward sighed, quenched his own thirst, and urged Rory forward along the bank.

By early evening, neither man nor beast could go further. Edward hobbled Rory and set about making camp. He ate the final pieces of his cheese and bread, washed it down with the dregs of bitter ale, and vowed this would be the last tasteless Scottish food he would ever eat. He rested his head on his saddle and let the soft sounds of the gurgling river ease him to sleep.

The next morning, when the first tinges of dawn shafted through the trees, Edward was facing the banks of a full-fledged river. The terrain was flatter, the underbrush not so thick, and the familiar smell of wood smoke tickled the tiny hairs inside his nose. He pushed Rory into a gentle canter on the narrow trail, squinting his eyes to see what lay ahead. Finally, in the distance, Edward recognized the little village of Lexington Cove. He was nearly home! He slowed Rory to a walk.

Edward clattered onto the cobblestone wharf wearing a haggard expression, long beard and hair, and ragged Scots clothing. The villagers picked up their forks and hoes and surrounded him. They stood sullenly, with faces full of distrust and ready to use their makeshift weapons on the stranger in their midst.

Edward was astonished. Forgetting that he looked more like a highwayman down on his luck than the prestigious Lord of Lexington Estate, his eyes flashed with indignation. He yelled at the man closest to him. "You there! Clear the way so that I may continue my journey to Lexington Estate."

Looking at him with the respect one would have for a captured thief, the man laughed. "Hear ye," he bellowed to the group. "This ragamuffin's on 'is way to the great mansion of Lexington Estate."

The villagers who encircled Edward dissolved into fits of laughter. Some of the women made obnoxious bows, throwing their skirts up in exaggerated curtsies.

Edward was incensed. He'd never been treated with such disrespect, even in the Highlands. He vaulted off Rory, thrust his right hand forward, and displayed his signet ring with the family crest. "See for yourselves," he said, in a voice filled with anger. "All your heads will be hanging from trees if this crowd doesn't disperse immediately."

Instantly fearing for their lives, the crowd slid away from Edward like oil spilled on water. He remounted and walked sedately through the opening in all his tattered splendor. The men and women of Lexington Cove hung their heads and prayed the young master would forget their vulgar behavior in his joy of returning home.

At last, Edward sighted the woods and chimneys of Lexington Estate in the distance. His chest puffed with pride at the scene of privileged life in England. Briefly, he wondered if Kit was relieved at no longer having to bear the existence of an Englishman in her home.

## *The Highlands*

As Edward was dragging his insect-bitten body down the lush carriage sweep of Lexington Estate, Malcolm was arriving at Clan MacDougal, both exhausted and elated. As usual, Timmy Campbell had been perched in his tree and upon seeing Malcolm had announced loudly that the English prisoner had escaped two nights past. Malcolm was actually relieved when he learned of Edward's departure. It saved him the job of making a return trip to the Borders with his hated prisoner.

After all, the Scots had the money in hand for him and Malcolm was certain that if the wolves didn't get him, the wilderness would. Edward had been nothing but trouble from the time Malcolm had dragged him into the Highlands. With his princely ways he had enthralled the women to where they were willing to defend anything he did! They'd begun wearing more hair ribbons than they did for their own husbands, for pity sake. *Wonder how they feel now*, Malcolm thought viciously, *with their hero gone and making them all look like fools.*

Hamish was stacking hay when he saw Malcolm ride into the village. He dropped his pitchfork, met Malcolm at the barn, and the two talked while they cared for the horse together.

"S'pose ye heard 'bout Edward's leavin," Hamish said, as he pulled the saddle off Magnet's sweaty back.

"Aye. Musta passed 'im in the night," Malcolm replied.

"I just hope the idiot survived the trip down the mountains," replied Hamish. "Don't know what made 'im do such a damn fool thing."

"He probably hoped to intercept me 'n git the ransom money back," Malcolm said. "Tisn't our fault if he dies on the way."

"His family won't see it that way, Malcolm," Hamish pointed out. "They'll think we sent 'im into the wilderness on purpose. Or that we killed 'im once we got the money. They might suspect he was never alive in the first place. If he's not returned, we're in fer more trouble'n we can likely handle. They might even ask fer assistance from the king."

Malcolm stopped in the act of brushing Magnet. "Hadn't thought 'bout that," he said, feeling foolish.

Hamish propped a leg on the fence. "Well, ye'd best start thinkin' 'bout it,"

*That Englishman will plague me for the rest of my life,* Malcolm ranted to himself, as the consequence of the entire debacle with Edward filtered through his mind.

Hamish studied his son as Malcolm's eyes spewed anger, frustration, and finally acceptance of yet one more wrinkle in his plans. Then, in a voice filled with deadly determination, Malcolm spoke. "I've made contacts with some Border Scots like ye suggested. In two days, I'll travel back to the Borders. MacKenzie needs iron 'n leather fer repairs anyway. I'll snoop 'round 'n find out the whereabouts of Edward. If he's safely home, we'll go on as scheduled. If not, we'll hasten our plan to attack."

"So be it," Hamish said, then turned and walked back to the house.

"Regardless, twas still worth gettin' the ransom," Malcolm mumbled, when Hamish was out of earshot. "Now we've 'nough money to rearm and reoutfit our fighters." Malcolm turned

Magnet out to pasture then followed Hamish up the hill to the cottage. He was thoroughly disheartened since no matter what he did for the advancement of the Scots, something always went wrong to make him look unfit as a leader.

When Malcolm entered the kitchen the remains of a stale breakfast stared him in the face. Even Stripes ignored the leavings. He climbed to the loft and laid down on his pallet, resolved to sleep in a reasonably comfortable spot to regain strength for whatever Fate decided to throw at him next.

Sometime later, early evening Malcolm supposed by the muted light, he was awakened by the clattering of cooking utensils from the kitchen. This was interspersed by an occasional 'yip' from the dog, indicating a well-aimed broom to remove the animal from under the feet of the woman of the house. "Sounds like Kit's in a real snit 'bout somethin'," Malcolm mumbled. "And that somethin's probably me."

Malcolm descended the ladder to face his sister and be done with it. She was adding leeks and carrots to a cauldron of venison. Kit gave no indication that she realized Malcolm was in her vicinity. Malcolm sighed. "Kit, where's Pa?"

"I don't know," she answered, without looking up.

"Fer God's sake. We've got a serious problem with the English if Edward dies in 'is foolish escape. I need to talk with Pa…"

Before he could finish, she threw her hands in the air sending the bowl of vegetables and peelings careening to the floor. "I'm not the imbecile who brought the wretch here in the first place!" she shouted. "Takin' care of 'im was never my idea, remember!

So, the problem's yers to solve. Go find Pa yerself." She advanced menacingly with one hand on her hip. The other hand poked him in the chest pushing him into the table. Malcolm grabbed a chair for support as his feet slipped on the peelings. "Just cause yer grand plan's put all of us in jeopardy, don't look to me fer help," she continued. "I'm tired of it all. Do what ye want, but leave me out of it!" She turned and left the cottage, leaving Malcolm to restore order to the kitchen.

He regained his balance then looked around wondering where to begin. He wasn't even sure where Kit kept her rags to clean up such a mess. *What on earth could have brought about such rage? Malcolm wondered. After all, the man she complained about nursing is gone -- one would think that would make her happy!* Malcolm had the broom in his hand, trying to capture the scattered carrots and leeks, when Hamish returned.

"What on earth happened in here?" Hamish exclaimed, when he walked into the kitchen. "Did one of them pigs run through the kitchen?"

"No, Pa. Tis Kit," Malcolm answered. "Don't know what's got into 'er. First, she wouldn't say anythin'. Then all hell broke loose 'n she actually attacked me." He gave the table a final swipe. "Talk some sense into 'er, Pa."

"Where is she?" Hamish asked.

"Don't know. Maybe down at the lake. That's where she goes when she's in a bad mood." Malcolm found a knife and began preparing new vegetables for the cauldron.

Hamish shook his head and left the cabin. "Seems like all I do nowadays is run back 'n forth among these two rapscallions of mine, tryin' to make peace 'tween 'em," he muttered. "They make the English look tame in comparison." His weary legs trod the familiar path down to the lake, where meals were caught and tempers cooled.

Kit was sitting on a rock, her knees tucked under her chin and jaw muscles clenched. She didn't acknowledge Hamish's presence. Instead, she looked across the water and into the distant mountains. Hamish remembered how much easier it had been to soothe skinned legs and scratched arms. Now the wounds were inside her soul somewhere and hard for him to define. He was at a loss as to how to begin.

With joints creaking, he sat down beside her, rubbed his gnarled hands, and pulled at a blister on his palm. An owl sent out a lonely call from a distant tree. Frogs plunked into the water. Pink streaked the horizon, proclaiming good weather on the morrow. A salmon slipped its silver belly out of the water. The hum of locusts lulled the cattle into a trance.

Hamish's sense of harmony was usually nurtured by the smell of wood fires, the aroma of supper stews, and the pungent odor of new-mown hay. He understood the rhythm of the seasons and man's tenuous hold on his place in nature's scheme of things. But he could not fathom a young woman's heart. He glanced at his daughter. "What's wrong 'tween ye 'n Malcolm?" he asked quietly.

"Nothin', Pa. I'm just tired." She rubbed her eyelids gently.

When she offered no further explanation, Hamish pressed on. "Kit, I'm yer Pa. I've growed ye up since yer Ma died. Patched yer cuts, rescued yer dogs, 'n taught ye to cook. I even told ye what was happenin' when ye had yer first blood." His face reddened but he resolutely continued. "Twas easy to fix them problems. But now, I need ye to tell me what I can do to help."

*Such a long speech for Pa*, Kit thought, as she looked into his face. It was wreathed in wrinkles and his eyes were full of confusion. She turned her head away.

"Everythin' changed when Malcolm brought Edward here fer ye to nurse," Hamish continued. "Did he force 'imself on ye?"

Kit's head shot up. Her eyes fired with anger. "Course not, Pa! Like I said, I'm just tired from all this work 'n worry 'bout battlin' the English. Go on back to the house. I'll be 'long shortly."

Hamish sighed and stretched his legs to relieve the cramping. He thought back over the past weeks when Edward and Kit had been together so much. They'd seen a lot of strife in a short time but toward the end they'd begun to tolerate one another fairly well.

"Did he make fun of us Highlanders?"

Kit shook her head and pulled a blade of grass.

"Ye wouldn't be missin' 'im would ye, girl?"

She turned on him with lightening flashing from her eyes and the voice of a fishmonger spewing from her mouth. "Why'd I be missin' a despicable Englishman, who caused me so much work, never even had the manners to thank me fer healin' 'is shoulder, or savin' 'is eyesight?"

Then ye're not angry he left?"

"I'm mad at Malcolm fer bringin' 'im here in the first place," she answered, in a quieter tone. "Makin' sport of our homes, our clothes, 'n our honest ways."

Hamish hoped the evening sounds and smells would calm her further. He waited patiently. After a minute or two, she turned and looked at him with the love in her eyes searing into his soul.

"I just resent 'im, I suppose. The fact that Edward, like all the English, sees no good in us Scots grates my soul. They consider us to be poor people put here to serve their needs." She looked at her hands, red and swollen from lye soap and daily chores. "I'd hoped he'd see us as strong, intelligent, 'n independent people." She took his weathered hands in hers. "It hurts." She brought his fingers to her lips and kissed them lightly.

Hamish took Kit in his arms as he had when she'd skinned her knees and elbows as a child. "Ah, lass. 'Tisn't proper to mingle with the gentry 'n expect 'em to see any good in us." He stroked her face and cradled her head against his chest.

They stood up together, looking across the smooth lake gleaming in the early moonlight.

"I'll stay here awhile," Kit said.

"Aye," he answered, turning to go.

"And Pa?"

Hamish turned to look at her.

"I love ye," she said, with a melancholy grin.

Hamish grinned in return then trudged back up the hill—every bone that had been broken, every torn muscle, and all the scars on his battle-weary body forgotten in the trace of her smile.

# PART TWO

# CHAPTER FOURTEEN

*Lexington Estate*

It had been a week since Edward had dragged his half-dead carcass down the manicured carriageway and into the bosom of his family. He lay delirious with infected insect bites and bruises over his entire body—a result of his head-long flight from the Highlands. Even his horse, whose name no one knew yet, stood disconsolately in the stall, loath to move his joints even to walk to pastures full of juicy clover. While Edward's return was cause for great rejoicing, Lady Anne and Gwen rarely left his bedside, worried for fear he might yet die from the ordeal.

There was so much to tell him but they weren't even certain Edward recognized them through the fog of his exhaustion. His fever broke after a few days and he began to rest more peacefully. Lady Anne got him to sip the broth Mildred had brewed and strained so that no solid material remained that could choke him. Finally, there was reason to hope he would recover.

When she was certain Edward would survive, Gwen returned to the work she'd assumed during the many weeks of his absence. She was surveying the eastern portion of Lexington Estate, noting which pastures should be rotated and which fields were ready for harvest. In the process, she planned to visit the peasant families living in that area.

The morning had arrived with no soft filtering of the heat through mist. From the onset, the sun beat relentlessly onto the earth as though intent on turning everything into a wilted heap. It was mid-morning and Gwen was so hot she felt nauseous. There was still one more tenant to visit. She halted Cleopatra under a tree and pulled a small white handkerchief from under her sleeve to dab at the moisture on her face and neck. She loosened her tunic and pushed damp tendrils of hair from her neck and cheeks.

The normally restless mare was more than happy to stand awhile. It had taken most of the morning to travel over the territory Gwen had designated for herself that day. No air moved in the forest and the insects were voracious, leaving tiny droplets of blood on Cleopatra's neck where she'd been bitten. From time to time she stamped a foot and shook her head to dislodge the nasty creatures.

Gwen wiped her forehead with the back of a gloved hand. She sat very tall and inhaled deeply before shifting her seat to a more comfortable position in the saddle. Since childhood she'd insisted on riding in a man's saddle, much to the distress of her mother. No one had ever given her a logical reason why women should ride side-saddle. It was poppycock as far as she was concerned.

Lady Anne had tried to convince her that young girls could be injured by straddling a wide horse. Gwen, however, had never seen the sense of it. Not only did it make the horse off-balance but riding for long periods in a side-saddle caused her back to ache.

For the past few weeks, Gwen had spent more time on the back of a horse than in the manor. Lady Anne had implored her to take a companion along. Otherwise, she had pointed out, Gwen could expect to be the object of gossip among the very proper English ladies. But Gwen had been determined. She wanted to get to know the Lexington Estate families personally and show them that she was approachable and truly interested in their welfare.

Cleopatra lifted her head at a clanging noise in the distance. Gwen could hear the sound of horses galloping, men yelling, and the clash of metal to metal. She picked up the reins and prepared to run. Cleopatra's nostrils flared and she pranced on the spot. Gwen tilted precariously in the saddle and shortened the reins as fast as she could, pulling the nervous horse in a circle.

"Damn these ridiculous clothes," she muttered. She tried desperately to sort herself out of her long sleeves that interfered with the reins as she attempted to get control of the frantic horse.

The noise that had upset the mare drifted off into the distance, giving Gwen time to pat the horse's neck and talk in a soothing voice. Cleopatra snorted once more then settled a bit. But with her head up and ears pointed in the direction of the meadow, she was still poised for instant flight. Gwen had to see what all the commotion was about. She walked Cleopatra toward an opening she could see through the trees, but before she could get into the field beyond the gap the uproar commenced again. This time Gwen recognized the loudest voice. It was Colin.

The mare let out a mighty snort, stiffened her neck, whirled, and ran back from whence she'd come. Gwen grabbed hold of both reins and pulled as hard as she could while bracing with all her might in the stirrups. *Thank God I'm not in a side-saddle*, she thought, as she did her best to regain control of the runaway horse. She finally pulled Cleopatra down to a slow trot. Gwen's shoulders were aching, her hair was flying about, and her breath was coming in great heaves. Sweat marks from under her arms and across her shoulders made for an altogether unattractive picture.

With much backtracking, coaxing, and petting, Gwen eventually guided Cleopatra to the edge of the clearing. She kept herself just behind the tree line so as not to be observed. Her eyes and attention were glued to the scene before her. She had never observed horsemen fighting without full armor.

"Hugh!" Colin roared. "Get your arse back on that horse! A twelve-year-old girl could do better."

Colin was everywhere, darting and shifting through the mass of men who were barely able to stay mounted while fighting at such speed. With a thud, Colin's horse was hit broadside by a loose horse of yet one more unseated fighter.

He bellowed so loud that Cleopatra flattened her ears. "The next man to hit the ground gets to help Mildred in the kitchen! And when I looked this morning, she had a mountain of cabbage to wash and even more fish to clean."

The men went at each other with increased fury. Colin was relentless. "You're too slow! The Scots will make fast work of you then roast you for an evening meal!"

Colin raced toward two men who had fallen off their horses and were resorting to fist-fighting. He vaulted off his horse, grabbed the two by their shoulders, and shook them until they dropped their arms to their sides.

"Howard. . . Denver. You're supposed to fight the Scots, not each other. Remount!" The men stooped to pick up their weapons. Colin continued, "The Scots will get a good laugh just before they lop your heads off and throw them to the crows. Unmounted men are the easiest targets of all." He watched as the two disgruntled fighters ran toward their horses that were wandering at the far end of the field.

Gwen couldn't take her eyes off the men and their leader. Gone was her concern over the heat and her own discomfort. Cleopatra had edged out from under the protection of the trees. So engrossed was Gwen that before she realized her proximity to the mock battle, she was nearly hit by Colin as he raced by.

Colin wheeled his mount digging furrows in the sod, then with sword drawn he headed back toward the trees at full speed to investigate the intruder. He realized at the last instant that his sword was aimed directly at Gwen's heart. He sat Thor down on his hocks nearly upending the two of them.

"Good God, Gwen. What are you doing here?" Colin shouted, unable to keep the impatience out of his voice. He flinched at the thought of the men's vile language. The fighting had stopped, shields and swords were at rest, and the men stood quietly looking at Gwen.

"How long have you been here?" Colin asked, before she could speak.

"Only a few moments," she answered. "I was on my way to Bernard Smythe's place when Cleopatra got excited at the loud noises." She rebuttoned her tunic as she talked. "I apologize for any problem I may have caused." She nodded toward the group of men to include them in her apology, then turned her horse back toward the woods.

Colin was ashamed of his harshness. "Never mind, Gwen. We've had enough for today." Grunts of agreement rustled through the group as Colin dismissed them. "Spend the rest of the day having Ned inspect your horses and equipment for any injuries or repairs that need attention." They rode off, glad to be on their way home after a day in such miserable heat.

"Come Gwen, I'll ride home with you. Tomorrow will be soon enough to visit the Smythe's."

Gwen was embarrassed at interrupting the work of the warriors and observing Colin in his role as their commander. He'd always been her childhood nemesis - not a man that other men respected and obeyed. Colin and Edward had spent their growing up years amusing themselves at her expense. She'd fought back with her own practical jokes, treating the boys with disdain, or reporting their pranks to her parents. But now Colin was a military leader. He would probably resent the presence of a woman who had placed herself in the sanctity of fighting men at practice.

"Truly, Colin. It isn't necessary to accompany me. You should return with your men."

"They know the way home, Gwen. And they've had enough of me to last them for a month of Sundays. Come." He placed his horse beside hers and in doing so encouraged Cleopatra to walk beside Thor. They rode for some time in awkward silence. Finally, when they could see the smoke from the Lexington kitchen curling lazily into the sky, Colin spoke.

"What do you think of our fighting men?" He was after all, no different than any other man who needed the approval of the women he protected.

She turned slightly in her saddle, studying his stern profile out of the corner of her eye. "I'm no expert, Colin, but they look very fierce to me." Gwen was ashamed at how uneducated and dry her words sounded. She had meant to convey the tremendous enthusiasm and pride she had for Colin's willingness to develop Lexington Estate's militia.

Colin interrupted her thoughts. "They must get a lot better before they'll pose a threat to the Scots. They just don't like riding without armor, on small, fast horses." He rubbed his right elbow which had suffered a hard blow during the drills. "You'd think the past two years of defeat would prove to them that we must fight the enemy on their terms."

Gwen leaned toward him and rested her hand on his arm. "You'll get them turned around, Colin. I'm sure of it. And when Edward has sufficiently recuperated, he can help you."

He looked at her and smiled. Through the years they'd lived as brother and sister, and Gwen had always reassured him of his capabilities. It helped him now when he'd been left to preserve an English estate, while deep in his heart, there still lurked a Scotsman who wondered how his loyalty had run so far afield.

The evening meal at the Lexington mansion had taken on a much brighter atmosphere now that Edward was home. Hopefully, he would be able to join them soon. Colin, Lady Anne, and Gwen walked into the dining room in comradely fashion chatting about the day's events.

"How are things going in the practice field, Colin?" Lady Anne asked.

"Getting our men ready for battle without armor would test the patience of the Archbishop of Canterbury," he answered, with a rueful smile. Gwen walked quietly behind, hoping Colin would omit the fact that she had observed their practice that afternoon.

The aroma of spicy venison and roasted vegetables titillated their noses as Giles seated the ladies. All talk of the workings of Lexington Estate ceased and a feeling of contentment descended over them, like a soft mist at twilight. Colin sipped his wine and let his mind drift off to a place where all his responsibilities lifted from his shoulders and his body felt light. He hadn't realized how Edward's return had raised his spirits. Their years together at Lexington had brought Colin to care for Edward like a blood brother. In some ways, he was closer to Edward than he was to his sister, Enid.

Colin heard snatches of sentences as the two women discussed the house staff. He was glad Lady Anne had overcome her sorrow enough to manage the household, while Gwen handled the imposing farming schedule of the estate. Colin could remember when Gwen's biggest concern was planning her next soiree and agonizing over a new ball gown. Now, she was more interested in controlling the loss of lambs to roving wolves.

"Don't you, Colin?" Lady Anne was asking.

"Don't I what, Lady Anne? I'm afraid I was wool-gathering."

"I was saying how much I wish Enid would join us. Why do you think she keeps herself at such a distance?"

"She'd rather be with her pigeons, Lady Anne," Colin replied, knowing that Enid's distaste for the English was a subject best left untouched. "I've given up trying to bring her into our circle."

Lady Anne recounted that day years ago, when Lord Neville had brought a pair of pigeons from London for the shy Enid. He'd hoped they would bring her out of her shell. However, the opposite had happened. Enid had accepted the birds, to the exclusion of all else.

"And now there's a flock of them," Colin said, with a vague swipe of his hand. "Sometimes, in warm weather, she sleeps beside their cages."

Giles and Celia came in with apple tarts and wedges of cheese. When the dessert was a delicious memory, Colin rose and offered his arm to Lady Anne. "Ladies, this has been a lovely evening. But if we're to survive this schedule of madness, we must all get as much rest as possible."

"You're right, of course, Colin," answered Lady Anne, as she took his arm. "Gwen and I must say our 'good nights' to Edward as well. He seems to look forward to our visits now. It's such a relief to know that soon he'll be able to relieve you of at least a part of your work."

Anne and Gwen walked with Colin to the foyer. He turned, bowed to them both, then left, dreading the coming weeks of battle practice fraught with sore muscles and testy tempers.

Morning arrived with a humid stillness that caused everyone to move as though they were hitched to a wagon. Enid left her beloved pigeons and rode Old Jeff to the kitchen at Lexington Estate. The old horse plodded along slowly, the years having caught up with his body. She was glad to prolong the journey as much as possible, not wanting to spend any more time than she had to among the English workers in the Lexington kitchen. Today was the day Mildred had said Enid must take some kettles to the tinker for repair. This was a chore she fought against doing every time but was never able to convince Mildred to assign it to someone else.

When Enid arrived she saw the hated kettles waiting outside the door to be strapped to the back of Old Jeff's saddle for the trip. She dismounted and entered the kitchen for one more attempt. "Please, Aunt Mildred, let Hilary go. She loves to flirt with Alfred and he'd much rather see her than me."

"Now, young miss, just don't waste yer words. Ye need to git 'way from this kitchen 'n see folks yer own age. Hurry up, so ye can be back by the noon meal." Mildred wiped flour off her hands with her apron and turned her attention to the new scullery maid, who was making a mess of preparing the stew vegetables.

Enid frowned. Her back stiffened with anger as she walked out the door. Colin, along with Mildred and Orville Kingsley, were the only people on earth she cared a whit about. Still, it angered her when Mildred joined with Lady Anne, trying to coax her into associating with English acquaintances in an attempt to make Enid more sociable. Today she cringed at the thought of getting close to Alfred, another Englishman, who in Enid's opinion, was too talkative and smelled like soot.

Soon the dreaded tinker's shed came into view and she could delay the inevitable no longer. After removing the kettles from behind Old Jeff's saddle, she entered the shed and handed Alfred the items.

Alfred looked them over: two pans (one missing a handle and the other with a small hole in its side) and a cauldron with a large hole in the bottom. As he held them at arm's length, sizing up the repair, he smiled at her. "Mornin', Enid. How 're ye today?" He always thought of her as such a queer little bird, unfriendly and uppity. *Nothing like her brother,* Alfred thought. *It's hard to believe they're related.*

Enid stared intently at the wall behind Alfred's right shoulder as she answered. "I'm well thank you, Alfred," she said, then turned and walked out the door. "I'll wait outside."

Alfred nodded and began gathering up his tools.

Enid sat on the bench under a tree to wait while the kettles were fixed. Her hands fumbled with the pockets of her apron. Heat crept up her neck and her face glistened with perspiration. She hunched her shoulders over, trying to make her body as obscure as she could, and prayed it wouldn't take Alfred long to fix Mildred's kitchenware.

The sound of scuffling, accompanied by youthful laughter, caused Enid to raise her head slightly. Through the branches, she saw two young men who worked as gardeners for Lady Anne. The taller one was wearing a shabby yellow tunic, so faded and thin that in places the material barely remained intact. His knees poked through holes in his long, droopy hose, that were also in dire need of repair. The shorter boy wore the same uniform, with the exception that it appeared his tunic had been red at one time. Both wore pieces of roughly cut leather around their waists, which belted the tunics. They smelled strongly of barnyard animals as they stumbled toward Alfred's shed, cuffing one another in youthful good humor. Then they spied Enid.

Enid's chest constricted in fear and disgust as she watched the two youths heading toward her. Her head sank lower into her chest and she closed her eyes, pretending that an invisible fog protected her from the intruders.

"What's yer name?" the taller one asked, while the other hitched up his drooping hose and sat down beside her. "I've seen ye in the Lexington kitchen."

Enid screeched like a piglet caught in a hawk's talons. She jumped up from the bench as her eyes searched wildly for a way to escape. Old Jeff raised his head from the clover he was munching, to see what the fuss was about. Inside the shed, Alfred dropped his tongs with a clatter and ran toward the unearthly scream. The two boys were so startled by the outburst that they turned and ran— right into the path of the oncoming Alfred. All three fell in a tangle of arms and legs while Enid dissolved into tears, mortified at the commotion she had caused.

As the dust settled, Alfred stood up slowly then gave a hand to the other two. He picked their caps up from under a bush and, taking each by a shoulder, quietly guided them on their way. Neither looked back as they made a dash for the woods.

Then he approached Enid, but stopped before getting too close. "Now lass, they didn't mean no harm. Just wanted to pass the time of day." He looked at her with eyes full of sympathy and continued. "If ye're alright, I'll finish them kettles in no time. But ye'll have to leave the cauldron. It'll take a couple of days to finish."

Enid was too ashamed to look Alfred in the eyes. "Yes, I'm alright, sir. I'll wait here until you're through with them."

Within half an hour, Alfred brought out the repaired kettles and fixed them to Old Jeff's saddle. He offered to help Enid on, but she shook her head and mounted from the bench. Alfred watched her disappear down the path, scratching his beard in wonderment. Enid reminded him of a chick lost from its clutch.

Enid was devastated by her behavior and embarrassed at having to speak to Alfred. *Hilary will have to come back for that cauldron*, she thought. *I'll never do this again!*

For once, the sight of Lexington Estate was a joy to Enid's eyes. She breathed easier when Mildred looked out the door and said, "Yer're back sooner'n I expected."

"Alfred wasn't busy so he got right to work on the kettles. Hilary will have to go back for the cauldron in two days though. Alfred said it takes a longer time to fix a cauldron that large."

Mildred's eyebrows arched at the mention of Hilary, but she took the kettles from Enid's outstretched hands and changed the subject. "Child, yer face is too white. Ye need to git out in the sun more." She brushed a stray hair from Enid's face. "Ye spend too much time cooped up with them pigeons." Mildred bustled about, setting Enid down at the big table then passing her a bowl of porridge and bread still warm from the oven. "Don't know why ye insist on stayin' in the kitchen with me. The Lexingtons didn't spend all them years educatin' ye to read 'n write so's ye could be a scullery maid!" She took a huge dollop of butter and spread it on Enid's bread. "And ye need more meat on them bones of yers. Tis just not right fer a young woman to be so thin. Won't catch a husband with such a flat chest," she muttered.

# CHAPTER FIFTEEN

Lexington Estate was in an uproar. Tonight was the gala ball celebrating Edward's safe return to his home and family. Huge candles beamed from every window, while harp and lute music wafted through the corridors of the mansion and formal gardens. Every door was manned by elaborately dressed servants, offering the guests drinks from silver trays decorated with fresh roses. Fiery torches rimmed the lake like a lady's jeweled necklace. An enormous table had been set on the lawn offering sweets, savory fish dishes, sides of venison, pork, beef, and mutton, along with beautifully layered nests of jellied fruits. The long white damask tablecloths dragged the ground, hiding dogs that waited beneath the sumptuous fare for any morsel that might drop from a clumsy hand.

Gwen ran into her mother's bedroom with the enthusiasm of a fourteen-year-old girl. "Mother! How do I look?" she asked, whirling about on tiptoes. Her platinum hair had been swept up into curls and secured by a lavender ribbon. She had never accepted the restrictive head dresses coveted by her friends. Her silk gown was woven in shades of lavender, and designed with a panel of gold brocade in front allowing her delicately pointed shoes to peek from beneath the elegant dress. Her flowing robe was affixed just under the bodice with a gold braided cord, emphasizing her regal silhouette. Gwen's only regret was her sparse bosom which, although well-padded, still looked flat when compared to the other young ladies.

"I can't wait for Edward to get reacquainted with everyone," she said, stopping in front of the mirror with a critical look at her reflection. "Do you think I should have worn black? I don't think Father would want such a celebration to be done in drab colors, though," she said, turning slowly and not waiting for Lady Anne's answer.

Lady Anne's gown was in the same style as Gwen's, except it was black with a dove gray inset. Her headdress was moderately tall, with a dark gray fall of the finest silk. She looked at her daughter fondly. "Well, Gwen, perhaps you should have worn gray or black this soon after your father's death but it's too late to change now. And I agree that Neville would want you to wear a bright gown in honor of such an auspicious occasion."

Gwen ran to her mother and hugged her. Lady Anne laughed. "You're acting like a child again, Gwen. Not like the capable young woman who has been so worried about lost lambs, barren cows, and crops lost to bad weather." She stroked her daughter's cheek softly. "It's so good to have both my children at home with me."

Her eyes got a faraway look. Gwen suspected her mother was remembering how much Neville had enjoyed the parties at Lexington Estate. He had always made sure all the children of the servants could peek in at the adults and snatch a sweet from the big tables. And he had always set aside a special spot on the vast lawn for games and prizes.

"Come Mother," Gwen said, tugging at Lady Anne's elbow. "Our guests will be arriving soon." Anne let out a little sigh and walked beside Gwen into the foyer to receive their guests.

As Colin and Enid approached Lexington Estate that evening Colin was captivated by its magnificence. At night, the simple but elegant architecture was highlighted by countless sconces inside and out. "I never appreciate the beauty of this place more than when we have parties," he remarked to himself, not expecting Enid to respond.

"Why shouldn't it be beautiful?" she answered sullenly. "The Lexingtons have money to hire whatever it takes to make this the grandest estate in the area. Under those circumstances the most thoughtless of landowners can produce a scene of loveliness."

He was surprised at her vindictiveness since she had not voiced her disapproval of the Lexington family for some time now. Colin stopped Thor, causing Old Jeff to stop as well. "Enid, why do you resent the Lexingtons so much? They've done more than society ever required to make up to us for the loss of our parents."

"The point is, Colin," she replied, her eyes burning with hate, "We never would have needed their help if our parents hadn't been killed in the first place. Where's the honor in trying to make up for such an atrocity? Answer me true!"

Colin saw the bitterness that had robbed Enid's face of all youthfulness. He knew it was hopeless to try to convince her that life was a matter of letting go of the hate that bound her to the past. That survival was more than harboring hopes that the conquerors would one day be the downtrodden. It was a fact he had accepted grudgingly, that Enid would never understand why he chose to live at peace with his losses, while she remained tied to a reality that had faded with the years.

"We've discussed this already, Enid. I only know that nothing can change what's gone before. And living for those long ago departed offers no hope for the future." He sighed. "Come. Try to be pleasant. The Lexingtons still mourn the loss of Lord Neville and . . ."

"At least they have Edward back. And they haven't lost their lands or money. I've never understood how you allow yourself to forget what happened to our parents."

"I haven't forgotten, Enid. I've just learned to survive," he said, with more anger than he'd intended. He urged both horses forward as they made their way toward the splendid home, whose sorrows and animosities were cleverly hidden behind its brightly lit facade.

Edward was elated! He stood at the top of the graceful winding staircase looking down at the ballroom abuzz with happy voices. Everyone in the surrounding estates had come to let him know how happy they were to have him once again in their midst. Never had he appreciated his heritage so much as now, with the memory of the barbarous Highlanders still fresh in his head and the scars still visible on his body.

From his position, he could see the long, graveled carriage sweep lined with ornate carriages on their way to the Lexington mansion. Brass, leather, and wood fittings had been buffed to a high gloss. High-stepping horses pranced in the evening air, seemingly aware of the specialness of this night. Drivers and footmen were dressed in their finest livery.

The young ladies from other estates had tried to out-do one another. Most had ordered their finely woven silk and rich colored attire from the best tailors in London. Every frock showed just the right amount of cleavage while still maintaining the ladies' dedication to decorum. The ornate head dresses often required the wearers to turn sideways to negotiate a tight turn. And every young woman with any sense of style permitted a glimpse of an ankle now and then. Discreetly, of course!

Nor did the young men lose this opportunity to show themselves to their best advantage. Mid-length tunics in bright hues fit over silk shirts with full, flowing sleeves. Tight silk hose accentuated well-muscled thighs while their calves were enclosed in soft leather boots. Few occasions offered men and women the chance to impress one another as did these large parties. And in remote areas of the kingdom, any reason was an excuse for a celebration.

As the rest of the Lexington household gaily partied the night away, Enid steadfastly refused to join, insisting instead on helping Mildred in the kitchen.

"Come child," Mildred chided. "Go enjoy yerself with the others." She gave Enid a gentle shove.

"No," came the terse reply. "I want to get this night over and go home to Windcrest." She retrieved her apron and tied it tightly around her waist once again.

Mildred sighed. Saddened by the knowledge that Enid was determined to nurture her resentment as long as she lived.


Edward walked slowly down the curved staircase with one hand on the banister supporting his still aching body. Generations of Lexingtons regarded him from their musty portraits which marched beside him down the steps, like so many soldiers. He studied them curiously. He'd never learned their names - just their expressions. Most were sour old men, either sitting in an uncomfortable chair or standing in front of a freshly killed stag. Only one, somewhere in the middle, had a smile on his face as he sat on an elaborate chair surrounded by his lovely wife and numerous children. Edward hesitated before this ancestor, who apparently enjoyed just being alive. *What made him smile,* Edward wondered. *Was he happy because he loved his wife and delighted in the prospect of raising their children? Or did he enjoy the privilege of siring such a family, attesting to his virility, while never giving up his mistresses or gaming tables?* Edward would never know the answer. He shrugged and continued down the marble steps into a sea of "perfect people" who understood the value of elegance and proper deportment.

Sounds of a robust jig accompanied by shouts of encouragement, mingled with the smells of food and flowers. Exquisite bouquet arrangements softened the sharp cooking smells. Edward took a great gulp of the air and ambiance into his lungs. Never again would he take his good fortune for granted.

He nodded enthusiastically to all his friends and neighbors as he made his way to the ballroom, which looked like a fleet of colored jewels whirling in the shimmering candlelight. His compatriots had arrived en masse to welcome him home. Dressed in their finest clothing, they implored Edward to tell them all about his stay with the crude, uneducated Scots.

"Say Edward," Cranston Hewitt yelled. "Did you have fun with those Scottish lassies? I've heard they're very generous with their favors!" He grabbed his crotch and danced around while the other laughed raucously.

Edward joined in the laughter. He'd spent many a merry night at pubs and parties with these men, making fun of whatever or whoever came to mind.

As he danced with first one young lady and then another, Edward's gaze wandered through the scene before him, like a pickpocket looking for a victim. He'd been approached by so many eligible women that he'd lost track of who they were and where they came from. He knew the air of shyness was a thin veneer, hiding the fact that they had all been thoroughly coached by their mothers to insure they projected the proper demeanor.

Once a young English lady married, she concentrated on producing heirs and running her husband's household efficiently. She was expected to turn a blind eye to the dalliances he would have throughout the marriage. In his wildest dreams Edward could not imagine Kit harnessing her feelings, much less pretending ignorance of a husband's indiscretion! *Thank heaven English wives understand duty and propriety*, he thought, as he nearly lifted Grace Monroe off her feet in a rather wild reel.

"Say old man, come join us for a glass of wine and tell us about your life among the heathens." It was Reginald Turnbull, eldest son and heir to the title of an adjoining estate. Before Colin had come into Edward's life, Reginald had been Edward's companion in childhood pranks. They had waded the streams together, skimming stones along the glassy surfaces. They'd caught toads and turned them loose in church, barely surviving the wrath of their parents when identified as the culprits. Nothing was secret between them. Edward smiled, remembering those years that seemed like distant traces of fog whisked away by the winds of Scotland.

As the two childhood chums walked into the dining room, Reggie placed a hand on Edward's back. "They didn't rob you of all memory of our fine, decent life, did they?"

"I'd have to be dead to forget how precious living in England is," he answered quietly. The two young aristocrats immersed themselves in the sanctity of their society, assured of their prestige and position. "It does feel good to be back," Edward said firmly.

Edward maneuvered across the fairy tale room, exchanging greetings along the way with folks he'd known since he was no taller than the bird baths in the formal gardens. He was enveloped in the wonderful feeling of belonging. His chest expanded, straining his tunic to near bursting.

He was chatting with Lady Pierpont, who was bringing him up to date on, *had he noticed her lovely granddaughter Penelope* and *wouldn't she be a catch for some lucky young man*. Out of the corner of his eye he saw Lady Cordelia Staunton on a collision course toward him, looking like a pirate ship in full sail. Her enormous bosom bobbed nearly out of the low-cut gown. She held her lorgnette close to her eyes, so as not to lose sight of her prey.

"Ah, there you are you naughty boy!" she exclaimed. "I've been looking for you everywhere!" Edward could feel a hot rash creeping up his neck and into his hair.

Taking her elbow, he guided her away from the group, bending his head low in an effort to direct the discussion to a quieter level. However, since she was a bit deaf anyway, the only benefit he received was an overhead view of those gyrating globes, leaving him with a tarnished vision of feminine charm.

With the lorgnette nearly touching Edward's nose, Lady Staunton continued. "My niece, Lucinda, will be arriving from Bath next Sunday. Harold and I are having a lawn party to introduce her to the young people here. You simply must promise to come," she implored, through faded blue eyes. He took a step backward trying to escape her garlic-laden breath.

"Of course, Lady Staunton," Edward replied, with a discreet nod to Hugh Radcliffe for rescue. "I'd be happy to attend." He bowed over her puffy, brown-spotted hand then deftly extricated himself from her clutches.

"There you are, Hugh!" Edward said, trying to mask the relief in his voice. "I've just assured Lady Staunton of our presence at Staunton Estate next Sunday to welcome their niece Lucinda to this part of England. What do you say?"

Hugh had little recourse but to nod his assent as the two men backed away, then turned in the direction of the beguiling Eloise Thompson.

With a low "harrumph", Lady Staunton charged off in search of new victims.

"There's Eloise," Edward said enthusiastically, as he dragged Hugh toward the young woman. Eloise was as beautiful as Edward remembered. She was a petite blond with a well-developed bosom. Her mouth was full and red, which more than made up for the fact that her nose had a slight hook to it and her eyes were a bit close. She batted her accented eyelashes and, with a voice attempting to be sultry, said, "Why Edward! Hugh! Have you boys come to fill a spot on my dance card? You're just in time. I have only two dances that haven't been spoken for." Edward and Hugh quickly put their names in the open spaces. Hugh had the first dance. Much later in the evening it would be Edward's turn to claim the popular Eloise.

When he thought the wait would drive him to madness, it was finally Edward's turn on Eloise's card. He could feel every move of her sensuous body as they danced a lively jig. The tops of her breasts shook invitingly, barely staying inside the confines of her gown. She moved energetically to the tempo, allowing the shape of hips and thighs to be outlined in the delicate silk dress. Edward's throat thickened and his hands went clammy when he felt her muscles work beneath the seductive material. He wanted the dance to go on forever!

But eventually, the music stopped and the musicians lay down their instruments and made their way to the tables for refreshment.

"Eloise, would you like to take a stroll in the gardens?" Edward asked. "They've been pruned especially for this night."

She looked up at him with eyes half lidded. "I'd love to, Edward. But won't Gwen and Lady Anne be needing your attention?"

He cleared his throat and looked around the room. "Gwen is thoroughly engaged by Reginald and Mother is overseeing the placement of more food."

"Well then. Shall we?" she said, taking his arm.

Edward guided her into the seclusion of the garden. As the sounds of gaiety became muffled, Eloise sidled close to Edward and slipped her arm around his waist. He looked down into her eyes. A few specks of eyelash coloring had fallen onto her cheek

"What was it you wanted to show me, Edward?" she asked, as she wet her lips with her tongue.

Edward ignored the space between her two front teeth as he guided her to a bench. "Sit here with me awhile, Eloise. Catch me up on all that's happened in my absence."

They sat close. She turned to face him, took hold of both his hands, then pulled him so close he could feel her breath on his face. "Nothing's happened," she said petulantly. "All anyone can think of is fighting those dreadful Scots. There hasn't been a party since Lord Neville was killed." Her mouth was nearly touching his. Was it his imagination or did she, too, smell like garlic? "It's so boring. I'll be happy when the Scots have been vanquished and we can get back to our normal life." Her tongue touched his mouth. Edward jumped in surprise.

"I believe the music has started!" he exclaimed. "We must return so your next partner won't come looking for you."

Edward placed her hand on his arm, ignored her look of dismay, and walked Eloise back to the ballroom where he handed her to Anthony Lewis with an elegant bow. As Edward hurried off he heard her saying, "Anthony, I hear the Lexington gardens are superb. Would you like to walk with me through them?"

Edward closeted himself in the library and nursed a glass of wine. He longed for an informal atmosphere, where one could breathe fresh air and never have to suffer the stilted attitudes and behaviors of the gentry. He thought about the simple celebrations he'd watched in Scotland that honored birthdays and anniversaries of special occasions. No one wore silk and most of the children had no shoes. There were torch lights instead of expensive candles, crude oak tables in place of polished mahogany, and hearty ale rather than smooth wine. But their laughter and dancing were robust and sincere. And there were no predatory mothers trying to make the best match for their daughters. It was a shock for Edward to realize that he missed the independent Scottish villagers and his quiet time milking Nell. Above all, he longed for freedom from the expectations of his structured English society.

Sometime after midnight, when the musicians were tired and the food had gone cold, the party came to a sodden conclusion. Guests who'd arrived so beautifully turned out were assisted to their patiently waiting coachmen and coaches. Many stumbled as they went and countless slurred sentences escaped their slack mouths. Their expensive garments revealed stains and wrinkles garnered from an evening of too many indiscreet actions. Edward watched in disillusionment as they trundled off. He gladly retired to his own room with only a perfunctory good-night to his mother and sister, who blamed his lackluster attitude on exhaustion brought on by too much frivolity.

He dismissed Giles, peeled off his finery, and climbed into bed. He felt a discouragement that went beyond lascivious maidens and boisterous friends. He tried to erase the tawdry behavior of many of his people, but he could not. The conscience that had come to live within him while he was in the Scottish Highlands now reminded him that he, too, possessed flaws as serious as any of his companions. He wanted to be independent, yet could not dress himself without the aid of a manservant. He wanted to be a good steward of Lexington Estate, but had no idea how to manage pastures and forests. He hoped to best utilize the specialties of his vassals, but didn't know their names, much less where they lived. He dreamed of becoming a great warrior, yet had little desire to kill and maim men who were defending principles of their own. Sleep was slow in coming—only a maddening acceptance that when all was said and done, Edward, Lord of Lexington, was just one more inept, arrogant Englishman!

The sound of a horse neighing brought him out of his taunting nether-sleep. It was time to get to the practice field to assist Colin. With a determination to become better than his indolent English comrades, Edward performed his morning ablutions without the aid of Giles. After much cursing, in the process of fetching water and locating his wardrobe, he was ready to take his place at the helm of Lexington Estate's militia. As he urged Rory into a slow trot he was reminded that, today, he would help set into motion a plan that could well mean the death of Scots who had, sometime when his back was turned, captured an important place in his heart.

He would be expected to assist in perfecting fighting tactics he'd never experienced and didn't understand. Edward was mesmerized by the sight of seasoned warriors being thrown off small, quick moving horses. The speed with which the mock-battle proceeded was beyond his ability to follow. *How can I ever fit into this new way of fighting,* he wondered fearfully? *I'll probably be the first casualty.*

# CHAPTER SIXTEEN

*Windcrest*

Enid felt lonely—left to fend for herself while Colin spent his energies on the problems of the Lexington family. This morning it seemed to her that he was little concerned with furthering any interest in their own MacDonnogh family. While they were growing up, she had looked forward to the time when their education with the Lexingtons would be over. She had assumed that Colin would find and marry a Scottish lass and produce offspring so that once again Windcrest would be filled with the sounds of a happy family. Enid had given up her own hopes of marrying. She had been content with the thought of being the spinster aunt who would love and cherish her brother's children.

But it seemed that her dream would never come to pass. Colin worked long hours at Lexington Estate researching methods of ancient warfare, then experimenting with them in mock fighting conditions with the militia. She didn't understand why he was so intent on bringing destruction to the Scots. It saddened her to think that Colin had forgotten *he* was a Scotsman. Hadn't he heard the whispers among the Lexington servants, wondering why it was that Colin had never received anything more than a scratch from all the battles during the past two years? Wasn't he aware that the mighty English lords who professed to be his friends secretly believed *Colin* was the traitor? *How I wish I could find a place to exist where there was no one but my family,* she thought.

Her stomach growled. Outside she could hear her pigeons as they joined the chickens scratching for corn. She put on a heavier over gown and hurried down the steps to rekindle last night's fire which was now only a faint glow deep within the ashes. Her feet were cold on the floor making her toes curl up.

How she wanted to see her mother in the kitchen again, slicing bread and setting out the butter and honey. Her mouth watered at the thought of bacon frying. A smile brightened her face. In those long-ago winters when she was tucked in her bed, Enid fancied she could actually *see* the smell that wafted to her tiny pallet from the hearth below. She sighed and laid a log on the fire that was slowly lumbering to life.

She heated a mug of apple cider and warmed her hands around its smooth sides. Steam from the hot drink swirled about her face. Childhood memories seeped out of the vapor and claimed her mind. The memory of Pa coming in the back door with a pail of warm milk was as fresh now as it had been those many years ago. Enid imagined the sound of chairs being pulled to the table and Pa's prayer of thanks before anyone could take a bite. She remembered Ma bustling about the house mending and cleaning.

Puss jumped up on Enid's lap, dragging her abruptly from her haunting memories. Rex twitched an ear at the commotion as he lay by the fire which was now in full blaze. She sat motionless while Puss pushed against her cheek and looked expectantly at the bread and butter which lay within reach of a well-stretched paw. Enid roused, patted Puss from head to tail, then offered the heel of the loaf to the hungry cat. Rex stretched, yawned, then came close for his share.

She exhaled a chest full of heavy breath then rose slowly to perform the morning chores that came to her automatically, regardless of the sadness in her heart. Her feet made a scuffling sound as she padded about the house setting it right. After washing the mug Colin had left near the chair that morning, she picked up her apron from under a stool and swept out the mud tracked in by the cats.

Tears burned the backs of her lids as she made her bed, meticulously smoothing the threadbare coverlet that had once lain on her parents' pallet. When she fluffed the goose down pillows she noticed they would soon have to be restuffed. The threads in the lace doilie under the candle holder were worn and thin. Her mother had tatted it when Enid was learning to walk. She fingered it as softly as she would the feathery fluff on a baby bird.

The smell of leather in Colin's room reminded her again of their father. Liam had begun to teach his son how to hunt and fish when the boy was only seven. Who would have thought that by twelve, Colin would be the man of the family? How she hated the English! They had destroyed her life before it had barely begun

The morning sunlight revealed a cobweb in the corner beside the fireplace. Enid destroyed the offensive network with a vicious swat of her broom, wishing it was Ephram instead. She had no pity for the old man who now sat helpless in a chair, maimed by an enraged bull who'd hit him from behind as he'd walked through the animal's pasture in a drunken stupor. She remembered then how vicious those men had been the night they had killed her parents. "My only wish on this Earth would be to see them burning in Hell," she whispered.

Enid took a final turn to assure herself that the kitchen was spotless, then headed out the door to care for the farm animals. She forked hay into Bessie's manger, threw grain to the chickens and her beloved pigeons, then went to the pasture to check on the sheep and Old Jeff. As she approached the fence, her attention was claimed by smoke curling from the many chimneys of the Lexington mansion.

Enid turned her head and looked at the single chimney of Windcrest with its thin wisp of smoke barely visible. To her, the chimneys of the two vastly different homes represented the disdain with which the English held those beneath them. The smoke from Lexington was robust—moving briskly into the sky. But then, there are many more souls to warm there she realized. Here at Windcrest there really isn't a family, thus little need for warmth.

Enid's shoulders sagged with a sense of desolation. Her skin was cold. She felt defeated. *Why do I strive so hard to make Windcrest a home,* she wondered, *when Colin spends most of his time with the Lexingtons? He has lost his connection to our childhood home and the memory of our parents. He doesn't care about the home he has with me.*

Overhead the screech of a gull announced the coming of a squall. Instinctively Enid's feet turned toward the bluffs she loved so much—to watch the turbulent weather as it approached the shore and controlled the creatures within its sphere. The brisk wind gave her a feeling of exhilaration that made her buoyant and confident.

The thick grass tugged at her ankles. Rex raced joyfully through the meadow. He, too, was energized by the commotion brought on by swooping gulls. Lightening sliced the clouds in the distance, revealing a black sky beyond. The storm was coming fast. Enid was scarcely away from the barnyard when the wind descended in a vortex that grabbed her hair, blowing it around her face, then fast away in strands that became a part of the whirling melee. It was sound, motion, and a fury that awakened her senses.

Through the sun's rays, which tried valiantly to pierce the black heavens, Enid saw vestiges of her father's smiling face. Or was it just shadows that played with her imagination? She felt her mother kiss her lightly on the cheek and brush the hair from her eyes. Perhaps that was only spray from the ocean. She heard her childhood friend, Claudine, laugh gleefully as she had when they had last skipped through the clover on May Day. Could that be the squawk of a gull near to hand? She could smell holly, pine, heather, and wet wool. Or maybe it was the wind bringing those familiar scents to tantalize her nose.

Enid struggled into the storm, trying to reach the cliff. She needed to experience the tempest from her favorite vantage point, partway between earth and sky - her connection to a power that went far beyond all things earthly. She finally reached the edge of the bluff and lay belly-down to breathe in the renewing spirits which nature sent in the height of a squall. Rex's barks had changed to a more frantic note but they were swept into the gale the instant they left his mouth. The wind lipped up over the tufted edge of the cliff and cleansed her face with its fury. She laughed into the storm, secure in her perch far above the crashing waves that washed the sandy shore below. Enid felt powerful. Invincible. She wanted to join those raw forces that would carry her into the sky—to fly with all the winged creatures who'd been endowed by

God with the ability to escape the earth and all its surliness. She'd had enough of this world.

Enid stood, spread her arms wide, and leaned over the edge. The powerful currents billowed her skirts and lifted her into space—a tiny speck that hesitated for an instant before plummeting to the rocky beach below. Her body fell soundlessly and rested quietly among the flotsam carried in by the angry waves. With a mighty sigh, Enid's soul ceased its tortured travail on Earth and joined the childhood which had waited for her all these years, carefully tucked between the edges of sun, storm, and memory. Rex howled mournfully.

It was late afternoon when Colin returned to Windcrest. He looked for Rex, who normally met him well before he reached the barn. He thought he could hear his bark somewhere in the distance. He stopped and looked around, noting several sights that were not proper for Windcrest at this time of day.

The pasture animals were hanging their heads over the fence and Bessie's bell was clanging in her stall - an indication she was past her time to be milked. Enid's pigeons had not been caged for the evening to be fed. "That's odd," Colin mumbled, as he went around the side of the house to herd the birds into their cages. They ignored him and continued their foraging.

"Enid!" he yelled. "Come help me coax these wretched birds in. They never pay any attention to me." The arrogant birds flew out of his reach then landed in the middle of the chickens. "I give up," he said, throwing his hands up in disgust. "Enid can cage them when she gets back from wherever she is." He went through the back door, pulled his dirty boots off, and laid them under the coat pegs. He straightened his frame slowly to its full height, rubbing his neck with one hand and massaging his lower back with the other to work out some of the stiffness.

*"I don't know if I have the energy to get the bath water and wait for it to heat,"* he said to himself. "Where in the devil is Enid!" he muttered angrily. He peered into the kitchen. Puss was licking the butter dish, after which she sat on her haunches and proceeded to clean her paws.

"You'd better get off that table before Enid catches you," he warned, as he shoved the cat to the floor. "What could possibly be so important to keep her away so late in the day?"

Colin was exhausted. Riding with the Lexington Estate's fighting men had worn him to the place where he thought his seat bones must be ready to poke through his skin. He had not a thought left for anything except rest. He poured a mug of ale and sat down to enjoy the silence. No clanging of metal. No vile swearing when men were thrown ignominiously off their horses. No dust clogging his eyes, throat, and nose. Just quiet.

His peace was rudely broken by the long mournful howl of a dog that Colin recognized immediately as Rex. He jumped up from the table, overturning the ale in his haste. Not stopping to put on his boots, he ran into the meadow that bridged the distance between the MacDonnogh house and the bluffs of Windcrest.

The howling got louder the closer Colin got to the cliff. He ran faster. He could hardly breathe. His chest had closed onto his lungs with a dread he didn't understand. He slowed to a walk the last few steps which brought him to the edge of the cliff. In the darkening sky he could see Rex sitting on his haunches baying at the moon which was just a trace in the early evening sky. Beside the dog Colin recognized the lifeless form of Enid.

Later Colin could not recall running down the treacherous path to the shore. He was unaware of the pain in his bloody feet as he ran the final strides to where Enid lay. His only thought was to reach her before her life ebbed into the sands to be carried to the sea by the never-ending tides. But her ashen face told him that the last breath she had taken was when her body collided with the shore. He realized that Enid had chosen to leave this world rather than try to go on living among the English, who had destroyed her life so many years ago.

Rex began to whine. Colin could see by the sand that covered Rex's jaws and underbody that the dog had spent the afternoon fretting by the side of his beloved mistress. Colin gently stroked the dog's head. Rex hunkered beside Enid, nudging her face with his nose then looking at Colin as if to ask why she refused to rise. He could almost bear his own anguish easier than he could watch Rex mourn a loss he didn't understand. *At least I know why she did this*, Colin thought as he knelt beside her. *Her death is my fault!*

It was not Enid whom Colin held in his arms on this stony beach. It was the hollow shell which had housed the sorrow and hatred that remained after her ten-year-old mind was driven beyond its limit. She had never been able to understand a world that could snatch her parents from her in such a cruel manner. Her loving and trusting soul had been buried with them in those plain boxes ten years ago.

Colin wished he could reverse time and go back to this morning when Enid was still alive. He'd do something to stop her. If he could just relive this day, he'd never leave her again feeling deserted and with no reason to live. But in his heart, Colin knew he'd ignored Enid long before today. He'd occupied the years in his own quest to find some direction and meaning within the English society. He'd disregarded her resentment at being forced to live among the very people who'd caused her heartbreak.

It was Enid who had been the honest one. She had refused to overlook the injustice done to them, never faltering in her belief that the guilty should be punished—not collaborated with. She had stood alone against a group of people, including Colin, who had expected her to put in a reasonable length of mourning time then accept her new life with serenity and gratitude.

Colin reached for Rex's furry neck. The dog whined again. Colin held onto Rex with both hands and buried his face in the dog's soggy fur. Time stood still for the two forlorn creatures.

When the muscles in his legs were hardened with cramps, Colin lifted Enid from her sandy bed and carried her up the rutted path to Windcrest. There he cleansed her body, dressed her in her favorite green gown, and left her to lay in repose while he built her pine burial box. The flames from the torch devoured the darkness where Colin stood working throughout the night. As the sky streaked pink and a muggy haze settled over the summer morning, the last peg was placed in Enid's coffin.

The final task was digging the cavity where her resting place would be. Colin chose a plot in the meadow near the graves of their parents. He dragged the coffin to it. Sweat was pouring from his body when the digging reached a depth where the earth turned to particles of rock.

Colin was determined that in her last contact with humankind Enid would not be subjected to the English who had brought her such sorrow. He alone, a Scotsman, and her brother, would perform the service. He dressed in his finest clothing, with a feeling of purpose that allowed him, for the moment, to shed the awful guilt that had enveloped him since he'd first seen Enid lying in the sand.

He gathered her once again in his arms. With Rex following behind, tail between his legs, they made their way to the meadow. The sun was high in the sky, shooting spikes of light through the heavens. Before he closed the coffin lid, he kissed Enid on both cheeks and arranged her beautiful hair lovingly around her face. A single tear slid from his eyes and dropped onto her lips.

Enid was so tiny that the box, even with her in it, weighed well under what Colin was capable of handling. However, because he wanted nothing to disturb her position, it still took a bit of heaving as he placed the box into the black void. By the time he stood over her casket preparing to offer a prayer, his fine clothes were soaked with sweat and torn in several spots.

Colin looked heavenward where, it was said, an all-powerful Being resided. He had long ago forsaken any connection with the church. He believed instead that one's destiny dwelt within the individual's ability to cope with the often mean elements of the world. He put no stock in "good conquering evil." With Enid's death, he was certain that in the end, good things only happened to the people strong and wealthy enough to make it so. However, on this occasion, Colin prayed. He asked the Supreme Ruler that Enid had believed in for benevolence on behalf of her tortured soul.

The sound of the dirt covering her coffin echoed out of the past, when as a child of twelve he'd watched the same ceremony obliterate his parents forever. With each shovelful, Colin prayed that Enid was already reunited with Margaret and Liam, living where life had stopped for her ten years ago. His own mortality and aloneness overcame him. He was driven by a need to know for certain that the beliefs of everlasting life, taught to him as a child, actually did offer the solace of seeing his family somewhere again in the future

Colin and Rex walked slowly back to Windcrest, connected by their grief. He wandered aimlessly through the house thinking of his sister. He was ashamed to admit that, in truth, he hadn't known her very well at all. He'd learned to ignore her hatred, overlook her moodiness, and disregard her need to remain true to her Scottish roots. He'd thought that in time she would accept their fate of being a part of an English community. That had never happened. What was it that had made her so resolute in her decision? What had convinced her that death was better than capitulation?

Colin climbed the steps to her little room that overlooked the cages where her pigeons lived. He walked among her belongings, hoping somehow they would help him know her better. He opened the chest where she kept her special things. On top was the little wood carving that their father had made for her when she was just learning to talk. It was a rather crudely made pony which she had petted so much that the ears were nearly worn smooth. Underneath lay the lace mats Margaret had tatted as they sat around the fire in the evening. There were the mittens Enid had outgrown. And even little booties that both children had worn as infants. Colin fingered them tenderly.

As he went through the chest, it was a chronicle of their family life until the deaths of Margaret and Liam. Dried flowers, a shell necklace, christening bonnets. All the mementos a family accumulates through its rituals.

At the bottom, Colin found an old sack which seemed out of place beside the rest of the treasures. It was rough burlap, stained and tied at the top with a string. Curious, he pulled it out and untied the top. What he saw brought a sad smile.

Inside were Liam's clothes he'd worn when he was fishing. Colin had no idea that Enid had kept their pa's smelly old clothing. It surprised him that she had been willing to allow their "fishy" odor in her precious trunk. Rex cocked his head and thumped his tail at the familiar smells. Colin remembered Pa in that old hat and the stained tunic and hose. Margaret had often tried to burn them but Liam always rescued them at the last moment. Colin chuckled at the memory.

As he closed the lid, the image of Enid's final moments of life invaded his mind. Did her fall seem to her to take minutes or just seconds? Was there a final moment of searing pain? Was she aware of that instant when her body expelled its last remnant of life? Or did a feeling of peace envelope her and shield her from the indignity of leaving this world? Did she see the white light that always surrounded angels in paintings?

Colin lay back on Enid's bed and tried to sleep. But his mind was too full of shock and sadness. Thoughts crept around the edges of his consciousness. Fragments of words from long ago flitted toward him, then capriciously danced away. Frantically he forced his brain to remember what his heart had buried. The faces of his parents on cold winter nights, sitting in front of a snapping fire and telling Enid and himself about the family they'd left behind in Scotland.

He rubbed his eyes trying to clear the fog from his memory. His mother had spoken of her own parents. They had lived in Glasgow, as he recalled. One summer Margaret had gone to visit an aunt near Edinburgh, where she'd become friends with Liam's cousin, Elise. Colin remembered his mother's shy laughter when she recounted Liam plucking her from a large tree she and Elise had been climbing. They had ventured too high and were afraid to come down. Liam's strong arms had carried them both to safety.

Throughout his childhood, Colin's father had been plagued with congestion in his lungs. When he and Margaret had made their troth, they decided that after the marriage they would travel to the southern part of Scotland where perhaps his coughing would be relieved by better weather. To the distress of his father, Thomas MacDonnogh, and the outrage of his mother, Vanessa, the newly-weds had taken their modest inheritances and traveled to the Borders to build their own family in a climate more suited to their needs.

*How ironic,* Colin thought bitterly, *that the journey to a land they had thought auspicious would eventually tear their little family apart.* As it all came back through bits and pieces of his frazzled mind, Colin wondered if his grandparents still lived. What his aunts and uncles were like. If his cousins still farmed in the place of their birth. Deep within his soul, a longing to see and know his heritage emerged.

# CHAPTER SEVENTEEN

Soft morning sunlight filtered through the wavy panes of glass. Colin blinked and turned his head away from the brightness. His mouth tasted like it was full of wool. Eventually the shrill-mouthed ravens outside his window left him no alternative but to get up. He had no idea what time it was or even what day it was. Why was he lying on Enid's bed and how long had he been there? In a daze, he made his way to the window and looked down on the tranquil scene below. Why did it seem at odds with the heaviness in his chest? He massaged his temples trying to push away the fogginess that clouded his mind.

In the barnyard, the chickens were sorting through the dirt in their endless search for grain. The barn cat was teasing a mouse she'd caught and Bessie was stretching her neck under the fence for clover that was just beyond her reach. Before long, her bag would harden if she wasn't milked. A few of Enid's pigeons flew to the ground to join the chickens.

Enid! She was dead! Colin's mind refused to believe she would never be a part of his life again. Mildred and Orville would wonder where she was. And the Lexingtons would be sending someone to see if he was ill. Colin forced his reluctant body to move. It was a shock when he realized that regardless of how devastated he was by Enid's death, the farm animals still needed to be cared for. This realization brought a semblance of priorities to Colin—and a sense of stability as well.

Within minutes, he was in the barn milking Bessie and even though Enid had been performing this chore for years, Colin was gratified to find he hadn't lost his touch. Soon the other animals had been fed as well and Colin returned to the house where he faced Rex and Puss, both of whom were ravenous. Rex sat patiently beside the hearth, knowing Colin would feed him soon, but Puss had already jumped on the table and was helping herself to the butter.

"Off with you," he ordered, as he swept Puss to the floor. She huffed herself off on stilted legs to Rex's side where she set about cleaning herself as though she had been soiled by a heathen. Colin ignored her indignation, stowed the milk in the well, then ate his own breakfast of bread and honey washed down with ale. Nothing tasted as it should, but Colin knew he needed nourishment for the day ahead. He was anxious to have the terrible chores that loomed ahead of him out of the way. He fed Rex the scraps, put a saucer of milk in front of Puss, then headed for Enid's pigeons. While performing the morning chores he'd decided the only proper thing to do with Enid's birds was to turn them loose to be free, as she now was.

As he walked toward their cages, his attention was taken by one of the birds who seemed to have something white caught on its leg. While Colin had never had any feeling for these animals, in honor of Enid he was compelled to relieve the creature of something that might be uncomfortable. Grabbing some grain, he laid it on the floor to entice the bird toward him. Unable to resist such a treat, the bird was soon eating the grain while Colin picked up the leg and inspected it. "Looks like a tiny piece of linen," he mumbled. As the bird continued to feast, Colin carefully removed the encumbrance from the delicate appendage.

Colin studied the curious piece of material in his hand. Something was written on it. He looked closer. To his astonishment he saw the date, 16 June, noon, P.Cross. He read it over and over before the full meaning of the message became clear to him. It was the date of the battle at Potter's Crossing where Lord Neville had been killed!

Colin stared at the pigeons in their cages. Slowly, the meaning of the past two years became clear to him. In his research he'd read how homing pigeons had been used since biblical times to carry messages. It had never occurred to him that Enid's pet birds might be used for this very purpose! He'd never given Enid credit for knowing how to train them or to make the contacts necessary to set up a receiving base for them in the Highlands. She'd always seemed too withdrawn and shy to take such aggressive steps. He shook his head in wonderment at her resourcefulness.

Obviously, several birds had been sent off with the same message and this one returned with the linen still affixed to its leg. Enid had somehow overlooked it or not seen the necessity for its removal. Colin sat down on the mounting stump, feeling as though he'd been hit broadside with a battle axe. He couldn't take his eyes off the insignificant looking piece of linen.

He inspected the remaining cages for further evidence. It had been a day since they had been cleaned. Perhaps there were more of the little missives that had fallen into the crevices of the coops. He opened one of the doors. There, peeking from under the edge of a hinge, he spotted a sliver of white. With the end of his knife, he pried it carefully from where it had fallen. With a suspicion that was fast becoming a certainty, Colin deciphered the weathered date of a Scottish ambush that had occurred a few weeks before Potter's Crossing.

He could no longer deny what was almost impossible to believe. For more than two years, Enid had collaborated with the Highlanders, informing them of all the English plans to attack the Scots. Enid was the traitor! And he, Colin, had been the unwitting carrier of the information. Brother and sister had regularly shared their daily activities each evening after both had spent a hard day at work. It was the only time Enid had ever shown any interest in the comings and goings at Lexington Estate. With absolute clarity, Colin now understood why.

Now, in addition to feeling responsible for Enid's death, Colin knew he'd provided the information that had led to *all* the losses the English had incurred since the conflicts had become so deadly. Many were friends his own age, some with families to provide for. He knew them all on a personal basis and felt their losses as though they were his own. *She must have arranged that I would always be spared any injury,* he mused. *That explains why I've remained unscathed!*

It took Colin little time to decide that Enid's secret would never be revealed by him and all evidence burned after he cleaned the cages. She deserves to be remembered as a good, albeit aloof person, he decided. It was one small atonement he could offer in return for her having had to live years with the English she loathed so much. It was still beyond his comprehension that one so small and shy could be the key person in such a treacherous plot. Strangely, he felt a sense of respect and pride for her courage, even though her actions had cost the life of Lord Neville, one of the finest men Colin had ever known.

As he ruminated over the boldness of Enid's plan and her ability to implement it, Colin poked into the crevices of his own life since his parents had been murdered. The facts he faced were not easy to accept. While Enid had never questioned her belief that the English should be considered their enemy, *he* had forgotten his own vow to avenge their deaths. Instead, he had traded his hate for security and acceptance from the English, refusing to believe that beneath their facade of civility they hated him for the Scotsman he was.

Colin had put all his energies into proving to the English that he could, in fact, be trusted and depended on to lead them into battle against his own people. What more could the English ask of him? However, deep within his soul, he had always known his efforts were in vain. In the end, he, Colin, was not of English blood. The information he now carried with him could put a noose around his neck. In her death, however, Enid had transferred to Colin a new determination to sever his ties to the English and never allow his heritage as a Scotsman to be undermined again. *No one* would ever learn from him that the lowly kitchen helper, Enid, had brought the mighty English to their knees. Colin smiled and shook his head at the implausibility of it.

He wrote letters to both the Kingsleys and Lexingtons, explaining Enid's death from the storm and his decision to travel into the Highlands in search of his blood relatives. He wished them all well and gave the farm animals to Orville and Mildred, except the pigeons (who had by now all flown away) and Rex, who would travel with him. He planned to ride Thor and use Old Jeff as a pack horse for what supplies he could take along.

As the sun broke in the eastern sky the next morning, Colin left the home he'd known all his life. He looked back once, then turned his face into the horizon. Even with all the grief he carried in his heart, Colin had no regrets about his actions. He silently mouthed a prayer that this was the path that would lead him beyond his anguish to whatever his destiny held.

# CHAPTER EIGHTEEN

## *The Highlands*

Malcolm stopped in the middle of stacking hay to wipe his brow. He leaned against the scythe and gazed into the sullen sky. He was thankful to whatever gods there might be, that at least the sun's rays were covered by clouds today. Maybe it would rain by evening.

It had been four days since his return from the Borders. Kit remained distant and Hamish continued to avoid him, tending to the clan's endless needs which claimed most of his time. Malcolm had never felt so alone. He'd always been at the center of his people who expected him to be their next leader. Now, it seemed as though everyone was too busy with their own affairs to pay him any mind. They had little time to discuss with him a strategy to defeat the English, which to Malcolm's way of thinking would benefit all Scots. Instead, they were taken up with the business of harvesting and preparing for winter. The Scots wanted the question of their freedom to rest for a while after the successes they'd had in battle. Malcolm knew this was a deadly path to follow. The English elite, who didn't have to worry about doing their own harvesting, would be more determined than ever to launch a heavy campaign before winter set in.

To make matters worse, there had been no word from Wren. Every day he'd hoped for a message concerning whether or not Edward had made it safely back to Lexington Estate. Such information would save him another trip to the Borders – he'd barely been home long enough to get rested up for harvesting! However, if Edward *had* been successful in returning home, he could apprise his fellow landowners of the location of the MacDougal clan and assist them in planning an attack before the Scots could prepare. *I can't let that happen,* Malcolm thought. *We have to plan another surprise attack before the English beat us to the punch. Wren must know how desperate I am for word from his side of the Borders!*

He watched a hawk swoop to the ground and, with deadly accuracy, pluck a half-grown rabbit for her young. Everywhere tiny creatures of field and forest were gathering and storing food for the coming winter. A splash in the lake reminded him that Kit expected him to bring fish home for supper. He leaned the scythe against a tree and was on his way to the lake when a speck on the horizon caught his attention. He shielded his eyes with his hand and squinted into the muted sun to watch its approach. A bird glided to the ground, landing not too far from where he stood.

Malcolm could barely suppress a shout of joy! He had the pigeon in hand within seconds. He searched for a message but found nothing. Thinking the bird had escaped by mistake, he took it to the cages in a pine thicket where they were housed. Just as he closed the cage door, another bird landed by his side. Then another. And another. Within an hour, the cages were full —and not one carried a message. Malcolm was dumbfounded. Something must have gone terribly wrong. Wren would never allow his pigeons to leave all at once with no explanation to Malcolm.

He was worried. *I must get to the Borders and learn what's happened,* he thought. *Perhaps Wren is ill. Or injured. Or worse – captured!* His mind buzzed with all the possibilities. *Whatever the case may be, I have to get to the Borders and find out. We've made too much progress to lose our fight now.*

During the afternoon, Malcolm devised a plan to gather the information without Wren's messages if necessary. While he waited for Hamish to return he collected food and clothing, then took Magnet and his pack horse, Loppy, to be reshod.

Near sundown Malcolm spotted Hamish coming into the settlement. He hurried toward his father slightly out of breath.

"Malcolm! What's got ye in such a knot?" It had been a long day and the old laird walked with stiff strides and aching shoulders.

"Somethin's amiss at the Borders. All the pigeons arrived today without messages. I've gotta leave immediately 'n find out firsthand what's happened." Malcolm's words stumbled from his mouth like a drunken sailor trying to tell a tale.

"Calm yerself, Malcolm. Ye're makin' no sense." Hamish motioned Malcolm to sit, as he poured a mug of ale for both of them. After Malcolm had taken a long swig of the bitter liquid, Hamish encouraged him to speak slower and explain just what the problem was.

Malcolm told him how Wren's pigeons had all arrived that day with no messages attached. He was beside himself at the thought of losing the system of communication that had been so successful. It had been an ingenious idea—instigated by Wren, the funny little man only four Scots had ever met. By using the pigeons, messages had been exchanged between the Borders and the Highlands within a few hours. A man on horseback might take nearly three days and would run the risk of being discovered as well. Wren's disappearance could mean the end of the Scots advantage unless a new strategy could be worked out.

"I'll leave now. We gotta know what's happened to Wren."

Hamish looked thoughtfully at the floor. "Aye, I s'pose ye must. Have ye a plan?"

"Aye. First, I'll alert our supporters in the area that there's a hitch in the plan, 'n that they're to hold tight til I learn what's up. Then, I'll go to Lexington Cove in disguise. Maybe I can learn some news of Wren since he works fer the Lexingtons. That's also where the English forces 're outfitted fer campaigns. The details we need'll be found in Lexington Cove."

Malcolm drew a diagram of the fishing community on the table. "If Wren's outta the picture, I'll git a job in town 'n send the information with our Scottish volunteers."

"How'll ye be disguised?" Hamish asked, as they got up and headed toward the barn.

"As a tinker. I've worked with MacKenzie 'n can repair anythin' needed in kitchens 'n stables." Malcolm smiled at the thought of working for the English. "If need be, I'll dress as a fisherman come from down river 'n thinkin' to relocate. From all my trips to graze sheep, I know the people in the area a little. Twill be easy to become a part of that poor community."

Hamish's brow furrowed. "Tis risky, Malcolm. Ye could be taken prisoner. Then where'd we be?"

"I know the danger Pa but tis the only hope we have. I've gotta take the chance."

Hamish advised his son further. "Ye'll have to tread lightly."

Malcolm nodded.

"Will ye be campin' at Morris Glen as usual?"

"Aye. I'd like to draw them English there fer a battle. It'd be easy to catch 'em up in all the tight spots 'n heavy underbrush."

"I'll start gatherin' the clans in that area, 'n wait there til I hear from ye," Hamish said. He was satisfied with Malcolm's plan but knew his son would soon learn that an idea is easier mouthed than put to action.


Years before, Morris Glen had been one of the locations where travelers stopped and restocked for the arduous journey into the more remote northern Highlands. A large wattle and daub structure was designed for the needs of men on the move and had been maintained in minimal repair. There were small rooms for sleeping and a rough kitchen. Behind that house was a stable and blacksmith shed. Adjacent to the house was a well, capable of supplying a substantial number of men and horses for all their water requirements. The grass was lush for the horses to forage and the hunting abundant to feed the men. It had served as a launching site for many of the successful Scottish forays into the Borders.

"While I'm gone, be sure to stock Morris Glen with food 'n medical supplies so we won't be caught lackin' on that score," Malcolm instructed. "I'll send one of the Border Scots with attack information. He'll use the code word 'Oliver' so ye'll know he's authentic."

Hamish nodded, then loaded Loppy while Malcolm readied Magnet. "Are ye certain ye can pull off this disguise as a tinker?" Hamish tried not to let the worry show in his voice.

"I'll just look destitute, like peasants everywhere, Pa," Malcolm answered, with a trace of bitterness.

Hamish smiled then patted his son on the back. "Spoken like a true tinker. Now go 'n ply yer trade." He made a silent plea for his son to return alive and unharmed. His own body was fast needing someone to take over the rigorous duties that had aged him before his time.

### The Borders

On the morning of the third day, Malcolm arrived in Lexington Cove. He'd had to leave Magnet at the Lucas farm to avoid raising suspicion by riding in on a magnificent war horse. Instead, he entered the small town, leading Loppy, his old pack horse. He immediately started his tinker's spiel to the villagers, who laughed and welcomed another peasant into their midst. Itinerant travelers were a common sight and strangers trying to eke out a livelihood were a welcome addition to all the local grumblers.

Malcolm planned to lodge himself in a tiny rented cubicle over the stable and spend his evenings in the taverns, carousing and getting to know folks. It was the perfect place to acquire a feel for the comings and goings of the community. The most sacred secrets were often divulged from a pub stool by men under the influence of ale and the feeling of comradeship.

However, following through with a plan that had seemed logical back in the Highlands, now caused even Malcolm's sturdy heart to thump nearly out of his chest. He had never been so close to the enemy before without weapons. He thought he knew how Jonah must have felt in the belly of that whale.

By mid-morning, Malcolm had rented a small room and convinced the stable master to loan him a broken cart to carry his tools. He made small conversation as he watched the waggoner repair the wheel. "I used to know a fella from hereabouts. Name was Wren. Worked fer the Lexingtons, I think. Ye ever hear of 'im?"

The bewhiskered old man shook his head and went on with his job.

Once the wheel was repaired, Malcolm was ready to begin his career as a tinker. He slouched on the flimsy cart and goaded the recalcitrant Loppy into a slow walk. In Loppy's equine mind she was a pack horse - not a driving horse. Therefore, it was an unwilling partner Malcolm had to work with.

When he reached the wharf, Malcolm made his pitch to repair anything broken in kitchens, on fishing vessels, or in a blacksmith shed. His voice was full of enthusiasm and unbelievable promises. He presented such a rakish figure that a few of the men stopped their work and listened. Eventually, one of them approached him.

"Can ye make horse shoes?" asked a short, muscular man wearing a leather blacksmiths apron.

"Aye. Any size 'n faster'n them dawdlers in London," Malcolm bragged.

"I need 'em strong as well as fast." returned the smith dryly.

"Ye supply the iron 'n I'll forge the best shoes ye've ever seen," replied Malcolm more boastful than before.

"Then be here at daybreak tomorrow." With that the man turned and hurried back to the horses lined up in front of his nearby blacksmiths barn.

Tired of calling out in a strained voice and assured of work in the best possible location for collecting information, Malcolm went to the pub, ordered an ale, and sweet-talked the barmaid into inviting him into the kitchen. There he spotted several knives and hatchets that needed sharpened. It took a bit of talking to separate the old cook from money to repair his utensils but in the end Malcolm prevailed.

Malcolm was comfortable with these people. They were hard-working laborers who, in their own way, were also held down by the English gentry. As he looked around the dark, foul-smelling pub at men aged and bent while still relatively young, Malcolm felt a kinship. They earned very little for long hours of back-breaking labor in revolting conditions, working for overlords who expected nothing less than total subservience. Who could blame them for heavy drinking and reveling into the wee hours whenever they had a chance?

The big-busted barmaid, Tilly, approached. "Where're ye from?" she asked as she sidled up to the group of men and leaned over the table. Her bodice was barely able to contain a bosom that would have done justice to a heifer. She smiled big, revealing a few missing teeth. As she stooped to refill his mug, the odor from under her arms and her breath nearly knocked him to the floor.

"Well, m'lady," Malcolm replied, taking a big swig from his mug, "I've been in London fer too long. A man needs fresh air." He winked at her. "I figured this'd be as good a place as any to rest my weary bones 'n make a few pence in the process." With that he stood up, raised his goblet in the air, and yelled, "This round's on me, lads." A mad rush ensued, nearly toppling Tilly as the thirsty gang charged to be first in line.

That overture made Malcolm everybody's new best friend. Anyone lavish with their money was never questioned, as long as the generosity kept coming! It was early morning before Malcolm dragged himself to his pallet over the stable, exhausted and carrying a head thrumming with the effects of too much friendliness. He collapsed into a heap on his bed, snoring loudly within minutes.

During the next two weeks, Malcolm was everywhere. Making horse shoes for Henry, the blacksmith, repairing buckets and barrels for the fishermen, and carousing every night in the pubs. He was above suspicion. He'd picked up the local accent and was never without a lewd remark to the men and an endearing pat for the women. Malcolm had never worked harder in his life. Growing up in the primitive and treacherous Highlands looked easy when compared to all his present activities in what was considered to be civilization. He longed for the sounds and smells of the mountains.

But Malcolm knew that sooner or later, he would hear from these working folks any plans the English had to attack the Scots. The gentry could try with diligence to keep their plans secret, but the fact was, the peasants visited among themselves and knew exactly what was happening. Blacksmiths, who performed the ironwork needed by an army, knew which landowners had ordered more shields. The smiths were also privy to which horses were the rankest and how many swords were broken during everyday practice. He heard other workers grumble about how impossible it was to have all the additional equipment and supplies ready by a proposed attack date.

"Ahh. Henry," Malcolm said to the smith. "Ye know ye're one of the best." Malcolm scanned a shield which needed new braces. "Ye can have these weapons ready in no time. How soon 're they plannin' this onslaught, anyway?" Malcolm asked nonchalantly, as he bent to pick his hammer up out of the dirt.

Henry spat on the floor, while assessing a horse with crooked front legs standing in front of him. "I'm runnin' short on nails. Fire me up some while I try to git the feet on this creature ready fer battle."

"Right, Henry. I'll do whatever it takes to help put them cowardly Scots in the ground," growled Malcolm, with a sincerity in his voice that belied the treachery in his heart. "How soon do we need to be ready?" he asked again, trying once more to extract the precious information without suspicion.

"Word from Lord Asheboro says they'll attack Friday, a fortnight hence. That means we'll be workin' over hot fires night 'n day," Henry answered.

"I'll finish these nails fer ye, then high tail it up to the kitchen 'n repair them pans of Tilly's. She'll be needin' 'em to fix the extra supplies fer men on campaign." Malcolm tried to be casual in his speech while his feet itched to get to Calvin and his Scottish dispatch riders to set their plans in motion.

Henry watched Malcolm's departing backside thoughtfully. He was grateful for the man who'd arrived at a time when the village was sorely in need of good workers. Everywhere Henry turned there were orders for supplies needed "immediately". His back ached. His hands were calloused and blackened from years of working in fire and smoke. Lately, he'd had trouble breathing.

Henry cleaned away manure and picked up iron and leather scraps from under his bench. The next two weeks would be easier with Malcolm's help.

Malcolm willed himself to walk slowly, nonchalantly chewing a sprig of hay. His stomach churned and his pulse raced. He entered the pub. "Tilly, give me them pans ye're needin' fixed. I'll repair 'em at my cart. Looks like we'll be runnin' headlong fer the next fortnight so I'd better git these done afore Henry needs me full time." He pinched her cheeks and brushed her lips with his own before leaving. She sighed and leaned her elbows on the bar as she watched him go. Tilly hoped Malcolm would stay in Lexington Cove long after this crisis was over.

Malcolm hastily repaired and returned the items Tilly had given him then hurried to his space over the stable. He hoped Henry believed him to be still occupied with kitchen utensils. As the sun slid into mid-afternoon he changed into his fisherman's attire, donning a rough shirt, a light sweater, and loose trousers – then he sat beside the tiny window to wait. He remained quietly in his cubicle until the laborers had finished mucking and Fred, the stable man, brushed an old cart horse. Malcolm chewed his lip and swore under his breath as the minutes slipped by. Finally, when he heard tools being stowed and goodbyes exchanged, he prepared to leave his lodgings. In a village preparing for war, no one noticed a humble fisherman going about his chores.

Even though a brisk wind swirled in from the sea, Malcolm was sweating. His face became reddened, his hands were clammy, and he could feel wetness in his scalp. Fighting the urge to run, he plodded down an alley behind the stable, hoping no one noticed him from behind closed windows. He clenched his jaw and ground his teeth. The pressure of living in disguise was taking its toll.

Malcolm forced his feet to walk slowly out of Lexington Cove to meet with Calvin and the others. They would set in motion a course of action that would jeopardize the lives of all of them. His heart was full of gratitude to these people who had agreed to put their welfare at risk for a group of rebels they didn't know, but with whom they shared a common bond.

# CHAPTER NINETEEN

Malcolm thought the lane to the Lucas farm would never materialize. He turned his head with every step to make sure no one was following him. His breath came in heavy gasps, dragging him down like a woolen cloak on this humid night. Like most conspirators working within the belly of the enemy, initiating rebellious action brought fear into the heart of the bravest of revolutionaries. He'd almost given up hope when the full moon illuminated the familiar worn-out gate ahead.

Malcolm ran to the cabin and pounded on the door, rousing the dog into full cry. *My God,* he thought, *they'll hear this all the way to Lexington Cove.* Within seconds, he heard footsteps and a muffled warning to the dog. The door squeaked on rusty hinges as Calvin pulled it open. "Come in," he said. "Figured it had to be ye this late at night."

Malcolm hurried into the cabin. He glanced quickly around the room, as if to be certain they were alone. "Calvin, they plan to attack Friday, September 13th, two weeks hence." He paused for breath. "Are yer men ready?"

"Aye," nodded Calvin.

Evelyn, who had become an ardent supporter of the effort, came into the room with night hood askew. "Is it time?" she asked her husband. He nodded. She sighed, resigned to the dangers that lay ahead.

The two men sat at the table, their voices low and urgent as they made ready to put the plan in motion. Evelyn brought out the ever-present ale and set it on the table. It seemed to her that in times of fighting all a woman could do was feed those about to take the risks.

Calvin sent Angus to their neighbor, Douglas MacClure, who would in turn inform the other Scots to begin gathering their forces. Theirs would not be sophisticated arms, like the weapons of the English, but rather the incidental traps long practiced by road bandits. Just enough distraction to give the Scots more time to prepare for the battle at Morris Glen.

Evelyn packed saddlebags with provisions to sustain Calvin on his trip into the Highlands. Being Scottish, Calvin had maintained communications with his family in the Highlands. He was familiar with Morris Glen and the trail leading into it. The clans would be waiting there to learn when the English would be on the march.

Malcolm headed back to Lexington Cove. Shortly thereafter, Calvin was on his way to Morris Glen. As she watched him go, Evelyn said a prayer. She hoped her children would not be fatherless when this was all over. It was a selfish thought, but she didn't care.

The barn rooster had just begun to crow when Malcolm clambered back into his room at the stable loft. Soon, Henry would be expecting him to help in the blacksmith shop, making more horse shoe nails as promised. As he stashed his fisherman clothes in a sack under his bed, Malcolm just couldn't resist lying down for a short rest.

He awoke three hours later, swatting at an oversized fly on his chin. He jumped out of his pallet, hitting the floor with a thump. In the stall below, a horse nickered, frightened at the sudden noise. As he yanked his tunic on he caught his finger in a hole, making it bigger. He hopped on one foot, pulled his hose over his long leg, then fell with a crash.

This time the horse below whirled in its stall, neighing frantically. He heard Fred running into the barn, yelling for his young assistant. "Albert! Git in here 'n see what's got into General. He's 'bout to tear hisself to pieces!"

Malcolm brushed the dust off his bottom and went down the ladder to the stable. "What's wrong with General, Fred? He threw such a fit he ruined my sleep. Twas a good dream, too. I was sleepin' with Tilly." He laughed, grabbing his chest to emphasize Tilly's luscious bosom then danced a jig out of the barn, heading toward Henry's shop. Fred shook his head in disgust at Malcolm's irresponsible attitude.

"Sorry I'm late, Henry. Just couldn't resist the women last night," Malcolm threw him a lascivious grin. "And since we're gonna be workin' 'round the clock, I figured to have me one last fling." Malcolm walked over to Henry's forge. "Point me to the iron 'n tools, 'n I'll git started on them nails."

Henry doused a hot shoe in a bucket of cold water. It sizzled like steaming coals exploding in the hearth. "Aye, Malcolm. But from now on, pubs is outta bounds. At least fer the next two weeks." He pointed toward a corner. "Over there's all ye'll need. Ye'll have to set yerself up. Got me hands full with them shoes here."

Malcolm turned to the second anvil and got started, thankful that everyone was too busy to notice how late he was.

For the next three days, the blacksmith shop bustled with horses to be shod and equipment to repair. Malcolm prayed that Calvin had made it to Morris Glen safely. Each night he fell onto his pallet exhausted, but too worried to sleep. Visions of Calvin lost or captured plagued his thoughts constantly. He wanted to see Morris Glen and Hamish for himself, to be certain the information had arrived according to plan. By Thursday, Malcolm had a legitimate reason to leave. He was nearly out of iron for nails.

"Whether ye like it or not Henry, I gotta go fer iron. Otherwise, we'll be puttin' them shoes on with our imagination."

Henry didn't look up. "I know, Malcolm. Abner, over at Litchfield is closest. But git yer arse there 'n back without wastin' time in pubs, hear?' He held a horse's foot at arm's length, squinting his eyes to see that the shoe was level. "While ye're at it, bring me some large iron fer shoes." He spat out of the side of his mouth as he took the foot once more on his knee and rasped the nails smooth with the hoof.

Malcolm saddled the horse Henry had loaned him, tied Loppy on a long tether to the back of the saddle, and rode out of the little settlement. The villagers resembled worker ants as each went about his or her assigned duties in order to have their troops ready to march. Fish was stored in salt and mead was carried in leather flasks. Tilly and the cook cut up smoked beef, pork, cheese, and bread to put into parcels for cool storage until time for packing into saddlebags. The children carried messages from place to place, while the elders rolled bandages. No one noticed Malcolm calmly walking away from all the activity. Or so he thought.

"Malcolm! Where're ye goin'? This is no time to be leavin.'" It was Robert, a fisherman he'd befriended.

Malcolm swore under his breath, then answered calmly. "Aye, Robert. But Henry's almost outta iron. Without nails fer horse shoes there won't be an English army goin' anywhere."

"Aye. Where 're ye gettin' it?"

"Abner, over at Litchfield is closest, so that's where I'm headed."

"Ye're goin' the wrong way then! Litchfield's west. Ye're headed north."

"First, I gotta go to Tysons 'n git saddlebags strong 'nough to carry the iron." He hoped Robert hadn't noticed his hesitation and confusion before coming up with an explanation.

Malcolm's clammy hands had difficulty holding onto the reins. *I'm getting good at telling lies on the spot,* he thought. *I pray Robert forgets about this meeting and doesn't say anything to Henry.*

Malcolm figured if he only stopped for short rest breaks, it would take him a day to get to Morris Glen. He needed assurance that Calvin had gotten word to the Highlanders and that Douglas had organized the Border Scots. He also had further information as to the number of English fighters the Scots would be facing. Though he was not a religious man, Malcolm prayed that Henry would allow him two days away before sending out a search party.

## *Morris Glen*

At Morris Glen, the Scots had gathered to prepare for this final fight against the English. Hopefully, they would achieve the freedom they had sought for so long. Nearly halfway between Clan MacDougal and Lexington Cove, Morris Glen was situated in terrain where the Highlanders were most successful with their fighting tactics. It was protected on three sides by a forest of large oak and pine trees that were surrounded by heavy underbrush. The front of the complex opened onto a small, flat meadow, which was perfect for keeping battle ready until the English were lured into the trap. The edge of the meadow dropped at a sharp angle for about ten feet then leveled out for fifty feet further.

The MacDougals had been joined by three neighboring clans - the Lowerys, Gordons, and Dunedins. It had been a test of Hamish's ability as a diplomat to convince them to join forces with the MacDougals. Scotland was a land of contentious families, fighting each other as well as the English to increase their holdings. He'd been working constantly to convince them to stand together for a common cause. The effort had brought him to a state of exhaustion.

Hamish's body refused to move with the speed he needed for the job at hand and his voice lacked its former ring of authority. Most discouraging, however, was that Hamish no longer wanted to face the inevitable bloodshed and death the coming days would bring.

At Lexington Estate, Edward sat astride Rory watching his men as they made ready for the conflict. It had been two weeks since

Colin had left, leaving a short note, with only a vague explanation as to why. It had something to do with an accident of Enid's, which had resulted in her death. Colin had written that he needed to find his relatives, who lived somewhere in the desolate Highlands. It made no sense to Edward. He was stunned that the man he'd regarded as his brother could so easily run off on a wild goose chase. He'd left the people who'd raised him leaderless! In one day, Edward had been left with the responsibility of continuing to train these men to fight in the new way. But Edward's own technique was sadly lacking. He feared his inadequate understanding and experience would mean the deaths of many of his companions.

Edward could not shake the feeling, that all the years he'd shared in close friendship with Colin had been a charade. That he'd never meant much to the Scotsman after all. Edward felt cheated. How could Colin leave the place where they'd grown up together without so much as a backward glance? Edward knew that his own regard for Colin would never have permitted such an action. *He doesn't know anyone in Scotland,* Edward worried. *Why would he want to leave Lexington Estate and go to a place where strangers are often treated very badly, especially when Colin's English accent is so noticeable?*

The enthusiasm he'd felt upon his return to England had withered in the face of Colin's departure. But in the tradition of all the Lexingtons who'd gone before, Edward took up the slack left by Colin's absence, accepting his role as Lord of Lexington and its inherent responsibilities with as much grace as he could muster.

He scowled and concentrated on the task at hand. The practice field was cut to ribbons by the rigorous drilling of attack and counter-attack Colin had put into place. Edward had observed the forces of other estates and knew the Lexington fighters were far superior. No longer were the men clumsy and cantankerous. They had become a fighting machine that worked as a team: quick and deadly, capable of inflicting great damage with the same speed and accuracy for which the Scots were noted. *Now, we have the advantage,* he thought with satisfaction.

As he watched the lethal warriors in front of him, Edward was haunted by the faces of those who'd been such an important part of his life. His father, Lord Neville, brave until the end. He'd fought valiantly for a way of life he believed to be right. Colin, who had apparently dealt with his childhood tragedy successfully, only to become confused as to whether or not he'd made a terrible mistake. Enid, poor wretch, unable to believe life could offer anything but sadness and anger, and unwilling to try to change her destiny. She was such a contrast to Lady Anne and Gwen, who had risen to the challenge of survival, whatever the cost.

Then there were the Scots: Kit, Malcolm, Hamish, and Oliver. People he respected for their courage and tenacity despite pathetic odds. He hated to admit it, but he'd feel no joy in waging war against them.

Edward looked out over the field at his men. They were willing to lay down their lives for Lexington Estate, even though they would gain nothing personally. He could not ask for more devotion. Edward rubbed at the dirt embedded in his face. That dirt had become a part of him, like the confusion which permeated his soul.

"Halt," he yelled. "In the morning, take any equipment needing repairs to Ned. Make certain your horses are sound and their shoes are tight. We must be ready when the order comes to attack."

The men nodded respectfully. Edward sighed, then slowly turned Rory around and headed for home.

The crisp September air in the Highlands had energized all the MacDougals, including Kit. Along with the men of the clan preparing at Morris Glen, back home Kit had spent night and day organizing the women and children for the upcoming battle. She worked long hours harvesting and packing food, as well as preparing nursing provisions for her father and the other fighters.

Occasionally she wondered, *Why did I ever hope that one Englishman might realize that Scots were not primitive?*

# CHAPTER TWENTY

With the fear of Robert alerting Henry and an ensuing group of horsemen chasing after his hide, Malcolm urged the borrowed horse, Ginger, and Loppy toward Morris Glen as fast as possible. Ginger was more than up for a run, but Loppy had a mind of her own and more than a slow trot took a great deal of goading. Even so, if he could keep moving and encounter no problems, he could make Morris Glen by dawn. Malcolm knew Hamish and the others would be glad to receive the information on the size of the English forces. It would help them plan how to entice the English into the forest to the greatest advantage for the Scots.

In the dimming light, Malcolm was watchful of stones lying in the trail. A lame horse would stop his journey in its tracks and put the entire undertaking in jeopardy. He couldn't let that happen. The forest deepened, blocking the moonlight. Malcolm's eyes ached as he strained to see even a few feet in front of him. The horses gladly obeyed his command to walk slowly.

He lost track of time. His eyelids drooped and his head bobbed against his chest. Years of riding and resting at the same time, made the jostling and the occasional stumble of his horse easy to ignore. From time to time, Malcolm stopped to refresh the horses, have a bite of cheese and bread, and relieve himself. Everything was quiet except for the frogs and night insects.

A sudden brightness in his eyes caused him to jerk his head up. The horses had stopped, heads down, too weary even to nibble at the tough late summer grass. The dawn light was warm on his face. They were standing at the edge of the forest, facing a steep uphill grade which led to Morris Glen.

Malcolm slapped Ginger on the flank, urging her to drag all three of them to the top of the hill. He could hear men yelling, horses neighing, and the blacksmith at his forge. The field bell clanged, announcing breakfast. Malcolm nudged Ginger forward and they stumbled into camp.

"Pa!" Malcolm yelled, when he spotted Hamish, who was chewing on a tough piece of smoked pork.

"Malcolm! Calvin left yesterday. How'd ye miss 'im? Have ye different word?"

"I took a different trail outta the village. Our paths wouldn't 've crossed," Malcolm replied.

Hamish set his trencher down and hurried toward Malcolm. "What news 've ye brought us?" he asked, leading Loppy to one side.

Malcolm slid off Ginger and leaned against the horse, both taking support from one another. Oliver ran to meet him and grabbed the reins.

Malcolm turned to Hamish. "As Calvin probably told ye, they'll attack Friday, September 13th. Since then, I've learned their total forces number a little more'n two hundred. The first contingent'll be led by Asheboro, followed by Lexington 'n two other groups. They plan to leave at one-hour intervals." Malcolm paused, out of breath. "Henry, the smithy, ran outta iron. I offered to fetch it as an excuse to git word to ye. God help me if MacKenzie hasn't got 'nough iron to let me take some back to Lexington Cove."

Malcolm sat down on an overturned bucket, pulled off his filthy tunic, and wiped his face with it. The smell and taste made him sputter to get the dirt out of his mouth. Hamish pointed him to the wash trough, throwing a clean cloth after him.

Within the hour, Hamish had met with the other clan leaders and informed them of the number of the English troops coming. All agreed that the best strategy for themselves would be to have the Border Scots start a rumor that the Highlanders were congregating at Morris Glen. They'd let the English advance without interference into Scottish territory. This would give the Scots the advantage of being fresh and close to their supplies. Word from Calvin was that Douglas had enlisted nearly fifty of the Border Scots into the cause, more than anyone had thought possible.

Malcolm rested for a few hours while MacKenzie loaded the iron on Loppy, who had not carried a load into Morris Glen as Ginger had. However, he would have to return riding a fresh horse, with the explanation that Ginger had become lame, making it necessary for her to be traded for a sound horse.

Shortly after noon, the sounds of shouting men and hammers clanging on iron followed Malcolm as he left Morris Glen and rode toward Lexington Cove. Because of Loppy's heavy load, Malcolm didn't arrive there until mid-morning the following day. When Henry got sight of the much-needed iron, Malcolm was relieved that no questions were asked about his delay because so many horses were badly in need of shoeing as soon as possible.

Malcolm felt like he was two people in one body—a man applauded by the English for helping to keep their horses and men battle-ready, and a man revered by the Scots for spying against the English. Sometimes he had to stop and think which role he was playing, so as to use the right accent. He'd made friends with the villagers in Lexington Cove and their lives were similar to his own. Like him, they were under the boot of the English landowners. He felt a twinge of guilt that undoubtedly some of them would die because of his deception.

On the other hand, without his direction and plans, the Scots could never have dealt the English so many devastating defeats. He shook his head in weariness and tried to forget what had to be done.

As soon as Malcolm left Morris Glen, Oliver was sent back to Clan MacDougal for more food and supplies for the camp. From her window, Kit saw his horse and a pack mule standing outside MacKenzie's shed. The pack mule was being loaded with iron and leather to replace what had been sent with Malcolm to the Borders. Oliver was nowhere to be seen.

Kit headed toward the shed. On the way, she stopped to see Brigit, who had just finished packing the last of the food parcels she'd been preparing.

"Brigit, where's Oliver?" Kit asked.

"Sleepin' in the blacksmith shed, poor child. He's near tuckered out, but he's gotta return to Morris Glen soon as I git these provisions ready."

"Have 'im stop by me, please," Kit said. "I've got warm quilts to send to Hamish 'n the men."

Brigit nodded without breaking stride. Kit turned back toward her home, thinking about the bandages and packing she needed to get ready for Oliver's next trip. She tried to forget that all these supplies were for use in the coming battle, where doubtless, many of her friends would be injured or killed.

She busied herself folding clothes into compact parcels, trying to ignore the feeling of dread that lay like a stone in her heart. Kit wondered, *What must it feel like to face death in battle, with each army believing right to be on its side. I don't understand why so many people have to die if both sides are right.* Her hands were still and her eyes fixed, pondering this dilemma that had no answer. *It's the women and children who have to clean up the mess and survive without husbands, fathers, and brothers. It's so pointless.* She jumped at the knock on her door.

"Come in," Kit said, as her hands returned to folding.

"Ye sent fer me, Kit?" Oliver asked, his young face haggard and his voice flat.

"Aye," she answered, placing the parcels in a leather pouch. She went to the exhausted boy and gave him a hug. Oliver stood woodenly, enduring this ritual that women seemed prone to do.

"When'll the battle take place?" she asked.

"Friday, September 13th," he replied, pulling himself out of her embrace. "Hamish says we stay put, 'n let 'em come to us. That way we'll be fresh 'n the English'll be tired, 'n maybe a little lost."

Listening to Oliver as he gave his matter-of-fact report of the upcoming carnage, Kit marveled at the maturity he'd achieved over the past few months. *How short childhood is,* she mused.

"I've gotta be goin', Kit. The men need them supplies." Oliver turned, and with dragging feet went to the mule and tied Kit's packets to those Brigit had placed there.

Kit watched him go. He would take his place beside the other men, fighting for the freedom of Scotland. He was still a child. She sighed with the futility of it all.

For the next five days, the camps of both Scots and English were in similar non-stop activity. The children ran errands, carried messages, and toted meals; the elders rolled bandages, organized the packing, and stored the food; the women cooked and cared for the livestock. All able-bodied men were preparing to fight or working to get the fighters, their horses, and equipment ready for the battle ahead. The only differences between the men at Lexington Cove and Morris Glen were the clothing they wore and their accents when they gave orders.

## The Borders, Asheboro Estate

With the death of Lord Neville, Lord Asheboro had taken over as leader of the English forces. He was a clever man, having served as a member of King Henry's army, until he'd been granted his own lands adjacent to Lexington Estate. He loathed this dirty business of bringing the Scots to their knees. Not because he had any sympathy for the rogue country, but because the time required to settle these matters lost him opportunities for his own money-making schemes. Additionally, he was bothered by a painful case of gout in his right knee, putting him in a foul humor whenever he had to ride. He would be glad to have the fighting done with, if for no other reason than his personal comfort.

Most of his waking hours were spent devising a plan to trip up the spy who had been the nemesis of the English for so long. He wanted to surprise the Scots in their own lair, with no time to prepare themselves or gather additional forces. He had ordered the English to leave on Thursday, the 12th, so they would be well situated at the battle site by Friday morning, the 13th. He kept in close contact with all the estates through the use of couriers.

On Monday morning, he sat in the pub with his painful leg propped up on a barrel and smiling as he emptied a tankard of stout ale.

"What's so funny to make ye laugh at a time like this, Lord Asheboro?" the barmaid inquired.

"You'll know soon enough, Clara," he chuckled. "Soon enough." With that Asheboro stood up and limped out, still smiling.

At Lexington Estate, Edward was making final improvements to his forces. They were no longer unhorsed by quick turns and few missed their mark with their lethal swords. This deadly efficiency would be a boon to the English. But it gave him little solace. Somewhere between Colin's departure and his own welcome back gala, Edward had lost his heart for the fight.

*Those foolhardy Scots,* he thought. *All heart and no reason. Why don't they accept the fact that the English will prevail in the end? Undoubtedly my men will cause many innocent people, perhaps Kit or Oliver, to lose their lives in this campaign. I cannot have that on my conscience.* Nothing made sense to him nowadays.

Edward signaled the men to quit for the day then rode toward home. Rory was a constant reminder of the people of Scotland, who occupied a larger part of Edward's heart than he was willing to admit. Rory had become the best mount Edward had ever ridden and would now carry him back to Scotland, to defeat the country where he'd been bred and raised. Edward sagged in his saddle as he rode toward an evening to be spent with morose companions and a dinner for which he had little appetite.


Five days had passed since Hamish had received word of the English attack date. He lacked the stomach for another battle. So much suffering. So many friends gone. After fighting for the same cause for more than thirty years, he'd accepted the fact that there would be no change in his lifetime. It saddened him that Malcolm, too, might fight all his life without making a difference. He massaged his sore chest and watched his men as they practiced defending their make-shift fortress. They had the upper hand. The exhausted English would have to battle uphill, after traveling over rough terrain for more than a day.

But the advantage ended there. The English had many more troops than the Scots. Their equipment was newer and made of higher quality materials. In addition, Malcolm had confirmed the fact that the English were now adept at fighting without armor while riding smaller, faster horses. Hamish sighed and wiped his sweaty brow with his sleeve. *Freedom for Scotland seems like an illusion. A fairy tale*, he thought sadly.

It was Tuesday morning, less than three days before the scheduled battle. Lord Asheboro sent for his fastest courier. "Adam, get this message to all the estates immediately. We leave tomorrow morning, before dawn. No exceptions."

"But sir, I thought we left on Thursday morning. Tomorrow's only Wednesday."

"You thought right, Adam. That's what I want the Scots to think as well. Their spies will have passed the word that we'll be at Morris Glen on Friday the 13th. I calculate we'll be there by dawn, on Thursday, the 12th. They won't be expecting us and morning will catch them unprepared."

Adam's eyes were big as saucers. His jaw hung open.

"Come, man! Get your arse moving. We've got much to do and very little time."

As Adam sped off, Asheboro congratulated himself that *this* time, the English will have the edge. He'd told no one of his change of the attack date, ensuring that the spy for the Scots would carry the wrong date into the Highlands. Even the English would be scrambling to be ready in time. Asheboro laughed out loud as he limped to the stables, palms sweating in anticipation of the coming victory.

Henry's shop was in chaos. News had been received from Lord Asheboro that the troops would be going into the Highlands on Wednesday morning, rather than Thursday, a full twenty-four hours sooner than expected. Henry had gone to the stable and yelled Malcolm into consciousness with the information, warning him that twenty-five horses were yet to be shod, not to mention countless shields and swords to be repaired. Every man could expect to work through the night and exhaustion was no excuse to be late. Back at his shed, Henry threw his hammer into the dirt and started the bellows to rekindle the fire.

Malcolm sat on his pallet, confused and unsure whether he'd heard Henry correctly. Had he said the English fighters would be leaving a day early? If so, the Scots at Morris Glen would be butchered in their beds, never knowing what had hit them. Maybe Henry was wrong. That hope was dashed when he heard Fred yelling at the slow-witted Albert to, "git them horses down to Henry's to be shod."

Malcolm's feet hit the floor solidly but the noise was lost in all the other sounds of haste and confusion. His throat constricted. For several minutes he just stood where he was, trying to decide what to do first. He'd never considered the possibility of a change in the battle date at the last minute. No alternate strategy was in place for this last minute change in the English plans.

The sounds of clanging anvils and neighing horses shocked him into action. Malcolm dragged his fishing clothes out from under his pallet and dressed. All was quiet down below, which meant that Fred and Albert were already down at the smith's shed holding horses for Henry. Malcolm crept down the ladder into the stable, checking every angle to be certain no one was around.

Henry's old mare, Stella, was closest. Malcolm grabbed a saddle and bridle, threw them on the startled horse, and led her from her stall. He watched for anyone who might become suspicious. He had to hurry because soon, Henry would send someone to look for him. He snatched some carrots from the stable supplies, mounted Stella, and left through the rear of the barn.

It was mayhem at the wharf. Men swore at one another to; "hurry up" or "git outta the way" or "go fetch this"; women ordered helpers to "pack this there" and "throw that into the bay" or "bring them parcels here"; children got in the way of everybody, unaware of the seriousness of the situation. Through it all, the gulls shrieked and swooped making the chaos sound more like a country fair than a prelude to war.

Malcolm's worry that he might be observed leaving the village was unnecessary. A contingent of the King's Guard would have gone unnoticed in Lexington Cove that day. He kicked Stella into a dead run and departed from the backside of the little village, hoping to get an hour head start before his absence was noticed.

It was perhaps forty-five minutes later that Henry finally realized he hadn't seen Malcolm working on any horses. He yelled at the top of his voice to anyone who would answer, "Anybody seen Malcolm?"

"Nossir," someone replied.

Henry's brow furrowed. It wasn't like the man to take so long, especially with such an emergency. He stopped his work and ran to the wharf. "Where's Malcolm?"

Nobody bothered to answer.

"Henry!" Robert yelled, as he was on his way for another load of supplies. "Maybe Malcolm's gone back up to Tysons fer more leather. I passed 'im a few days ago when ye sent 'im fer iron. Said he needed stronger saddle bags to carry it."

Henry ran toward Robert. "What'd ye say 'bout seein' Malcolm on 'is way to Tysons place?" He caught up with Robert and pulled him around by his shoulders.

"Damnation, Henry. What's got into ye?" answered Robert, as he looked at the sputtering man. He pushed Henry away, straightened his tunic, and continued. "I said I saw Malcolm headin' to Tysons, on 'is way to git the iron ye sent 'im fer last week. Claims old man Tyson makes the strongest leather pouches fer carryin' heavy loads. Talked like ye knew all 'bout it."

Henry took off running, leaving Robert staring into space. When he reached his shed, he called for Ben to saddle Stella up for him. "I've gotta git to young Edward right now," he said. "Don't ask questions. Just move!"

Ben headed for the stable while Henry banked the fires, stowed his tools, and left orders with his assistants. Then he headed to the stable. He'd barely gotten to the front of the building when he was nearly run over by Ben on his way back. Without Stella.

"Henry, she ain't here!" Ben shouted.

"Who's not here?" an outraged Henry yelled, grabbing the boy by his ears.

"Stella," answered a frightened Ben. "She's not 'n 'er stall."

Henry climbed the ladder to the loft where Malcolm had stayed. When he saw the room was empty, he shouted, cursed, and threw a chair across the room before leaping back down the ladder. He shouted at Ben, "Git me a horse. Any horse. Now!"

The befuddled Ben pulled out Goliath, who belonged to the tavern owner. Before he could fasten the throatlatch and put the saddle on, Henry was astride bareback and heading for Lexington Estate at a full gallop.

Fifteen minutes later Henry raced down the long circular drive, scattering geese and chickens in his wake. He passed the mansion and continued to the stable area where Edward and his men were making their final preparations. Everywhere, men were hurrying to make certain their horses and equipment were ready for battle.

"Sir! Edward!" Henry yelled at the top of his lungs, unsure how to address such a young landowner. But there was so much noise that no one noticed him until he rode Goliath into the middle of the paddock, causing several men to crash into one another.

"My God, Henry," Edward shouted. "You could get yourself killed doing a fool thing like that. Get out of there before you're skewered by one of those swords."

Henry hurried over to Edward. "Sir, the Scots know the new date fer the attack. Or at least they will, if we don't stop Malcolm."

"What are you talking about, Henry?"

"That new man in the village. Been helpin' me these past few weeks."

"Go on, Henry."

"Well, there's a good chance he's the spy. Soon as we all got the word today that the attack date's been set forward, I ran to 'is loft 'n told 'im to git down to the shop full-tilt. Never saw hide ner hair of 'im after that." Henry was out of breath and his two chins shook with all the words he'd just delivered. His round belly was close to breaking the seams of his shoeing apron. He presented an unlikely figure for one who had just unearthed the traitor who had eluded the gentry for so long.

"Slow down, man. What else makes you think he's the one?" Edward asked.

"Last week I sent Malcolm to Abner's place fer iron. That's west of here. But Robert met 'im on the road headin' north, toward the Highlands. Told Robert he was headed fer Tysons to git stronger leather pouches." Henry wiped the saliva from his mouth with the back of his hand. He didn't usually speak in such long spurts. "Then today, when Malcolm didn't come to work with the others, I sent Ben to saddle up my horse, Stella. She was gone, sir! And so's Malcolm!" Henry was looking left and right, as though he might find the culprit in their midst. "I figure he's run off to let them Scots know the new plan. That's what I think." Henry's breathing returned to normal now that he'd unburdened himself.

"How long ago do you think he left?"

Henry's eyes closed, as he recollected the morning work. "Reckon he's been gone more'n an hour now, sir."

"Well done, Henry. Go back to your shop. I'll take over from here." Edward wheeled Rory and faced his men, who were frozen in place, with swords and shields hanging limply at their sides. "Make ready to depart as soon as we hear from Asheboro." Then he dispatched his fastest rider to Lord Asheboro with the information and a request for the next action to be taken.

*I've done all I can,* Edward thought. *When the orders come, I'll follow them.* He turned toward home to tell Lady Anne and Gwen of this startling turn of events.

# CHAPTER TWENTY-ONE

Stella was tiring fast. She was old and not built for speed, even when she was young. She'd been bred to pull carts or plod about the countryside, leisurely carrying a rider. Malcolm wished he'd taken the time to nab Evan Bailey's racehorse. At the rate he was going, the English would overtake him long before he reached Morris Glen. Malcolm kicked harder but Stella refused to do more than grunt.

*The Williams farm is not far from here*, Malcolm thought. *I've seen a good horse or two there on my forays hereabouts. That could offer a solution, if there's no one around.* His legs beat a tattoo on Stella's side. She pinned her ears back and actually slowed her pace somewhat. Malcolm cursed into the wind that had begun to blow.

It was all he could do to coax Stella over the next rise, slight though it was. His eyes lit up when the Williams farm came into view on his right. He slowed the mare to a walk and carefully scanned the area for anyone who might be about. Malcolm reckoned the older Williams men would probably be in the village, ensuring that their horses and equipment would be battle-ready by dawn's light. However, since the Williams's had rarely passed a year without producing an offspring, Malcolm knew to be on the look-out for the young ones. They were known to be excellent archers and riders.

Malcolm stood quietly under a tree and watched the farm buildings, which were a quarter mile further on. No movement caught his eye. He decided to take the risk of exchanging Stella for the strong bay gelding grazing in the pasture adjacent to the road. He found a small gate, dismounted, and tied Stella to a post. After removing the saddle and the bags containing his small supply of carrots, he pulled one out, along with a length of rope for hobbling, and made his way into the field.

Keeping one eye on the horse and the other on the farm house, Malcolm slowly walked up to the big bay, who had a splash of white in his forehead. As he approached, the horse stopped grazing and looked at him curiously. He was just what Malcolm wanted—a mount that didn't excite easily and appeared to be strong enough to cover the remainder of the trip speedily.

He held out the carrot. The horse pricked up his ears and took a step forward. Malcolm talked soothingly and walked slowly toward him. The horse's head went up, he snorted, then took a step backward. Malcolm stopped and held the carrot in full view, groaning inwardly as precious minutes sped away. He fancied he could hear his pursuers in the distance. The horse stretched his neck forward trying to reach the tidbit, then one step at a time the big animal came toward him.

When the gelding was close enough to nibble the carrot, Malcolm stroked his nose and offered more. Within a few minutes, the horse lost all fear and was eating the carrot and looking for more. Malcolm slipped the rope over his head and led him to the gate. He forced himself to take care as he tacked up this unknown animal. The bay nuzzled old Stella, who barely blinked an eye. With little effort, Malcolm pulled down a section of the old, rotten fence, led Stella into the pasture and brought the gelding out onto the road. He replaced the timber as best he could, hoping he'd be well on his way before any of the Williams's noticed the strange mare now enjoying their pasture.

Never sure of what a strange horse will do, Malcolm decided to lead the animal until he was past the farmhouse before mounting up. He followed a small path that branched off the main road, opposite the farmhouse. *Probably leads down to their well,* he thought. He walked slowly, constantly looking toward the house for young archers aiming arrows at his heart.

All was quiet. Almost to a point where he felt safe to mount the big horse, Malcolm rounded a curve and walked right into the middle of a flock of guinea hens. In an instant, squawking foul and flying feathers resounded about the country side. The birds, furious at having their foraging interrupted, charged about the area with the ferocity of an enraged bull. Every dog on the farm was instantly barking and running pell-mell to see what had the hens in such an uproar. The big bay threw his head up, nearly getting away from Malcolm's grasp. The horse whirled around, kicking out at whatever might be behind him.

Before the horse had gone completely wild, Malcolm grabbed its mane, pulled himself into the saddle, and shot off down the road. Women and children ran from the house, yelling and brandishing their arms as though they were weapons. Malcolm outran the barking dogs, shouting people, and disgruntled guinea hens. However, he knew his advantage would be short-lived.

The Williams's would have a rider heading to Lexington Cove within minutes, to alert the English as to exactly when the debacle occurred and in which direction the thief had made his escape.

"Damn you," he shouted at the guineas, as he spurred the horse ever faster. The now empty saddle bags bounced on the bay's sides, causing a mighty leap now and then that challenged Malcolm's ability to remain aboard.

Douglas MacClure, who lived near the Williams farm, watched Malcolm's dust storm as it proceeded down the road and into the forest. He threw a bridle on his old draft horse and headed to the Lucas farm at a fast trot. When he arrived, Calvin had already saddled Ebenezer and was heading down the lane.

"What'd ye reckon's happened?" Douglas asked, as he fell into step beside Calvin.

"I figure somethin's gone wrong, 'n Malcolm's high-tailin' it to Morris Glen. I'd bet my old milk cow them English 're close behind." Douglas nodded as Calvin continued. "Let's round up our volunteers 'n follow Malcolm into the Highlands. He'll need all the help he can git."

"I'll take the west side, ye take the north," Douglas said, and the two men were off and running, putting into action the plan the Border Scots had prepared.

When Asheboro and his men reined up at the Williams farm, less than two hours later, Ida Williams was more than happy to relate what had occurred. She was incensed that the thief had left them with an old mare, a hole in their fence, and taken their best young gelding. Stopping only long enough to hear the story and find out which way Malcolm had gone, the men galloped away, scattering dogs and children in their wake.

Asheboro was furious that his plan had been thwarted yet again, but he was determined to do everything he could to catch the Scottish informer before the Highlanders at Morris Glen were warned. He'd left word for the other militias to follow without delay. Riding at a full gallop, he turned in his saddle and urged his men to ride faster, even though their horses were already blowing hard.

The fighters, riding four abreast, followed the narrow roadway around a sharp turn and ran full speed toward a herd of sheep slowly crossing the road. Asheboro threw his sword arm into the air, signaling his men to halt, then desperately pulled his horse into a sliding stop just before colliding with the sheep. Oncoming riders ran into the rear ends of the horses in front of them. By the time the entire company had stopped, warriors had been thrown, horses were loose, and wounds of varying degrees of seriousness had been sustained by both fighters and their mounts.

The shepherds angrily shook their staffs aloft, causing yet more horses to stampede into the forest, leaving a trail of broken weapons and scrambling riders. The morning air rang with cursing and name-calling from both sides, after which the shepards proceeded to take their good time about mollifying the easily frightened sheep. Lord Asheboro, too preoccupied with regrouping his troops to argue with the outraged farmers, quickly separated the horses and riders still sound enough to continue. He sent the others back to Lexington Cove, ordering them to acquire fresh horses and return with the next group of militias. Nearly an hour had elapsed before the road was cleared of sheep and Asheboro and his men were racing again toward Scotland.

As they disappeared from sight, Douglas removed his hat and fanned his sweaty face. "Well done, men. The others'll be 'long shortly. Let's git ready fer 'em."

Forty-five minutes later, Edward, who had been joined by the forces of Piedmont, Claridge, and Smithwicke rounded the same bend and found himself facing a disaster of a different kind. The road was blocked by a barrier of fallen trees, once again leaving riders unhorsed and their mounts running helter-skelter through the forest, entangling themselves in the dense underbrush. In all the uproar and his haste to get his troops on the road again, Edward had failed to notice that the axe marks on the trees were freshly made.

"Dismount," Edward ordered. "Half of you men hold the horses while the rest haul these trees out of the way."

It was heavy work, requiring at least eight men per tree to drag them out of the lane where the trees lay in muddy footing. Straining their backs and legs, the men swore mightily. In the melee, three additional horses pulled loose and had to be rounded up by soldiers on foot. After forty-five minutes of chaos, they remounted. Edward was so hoarse he could barely speak.

Malcolm stopped at a brook to let his weary horse drink and blow, amazed that he'd not heard the sounds of pursuing riders. He found three carrots in the bottom of his saddle bags, covered with all the dirt and grit that accumulates in tightly-sewn leather pouches. He washed them in the clear water, which also quenched his thirst, thankful for the nourishment they offered his empty stomach. Fifteen minutes later, he pulled his nearly spent body back into the saddle and continued toward Morris Glen.

Just before dawn, Malcolm galloped into the encampment, yelling at the top of his lungs. "Everybody up! The English 're on the way." He dismounted and ran through the camp slapping the sides of the buildings and pulling tartans off sleeping Scots. His horse stood rooted to the spot, head drooping and sides heaving. Men scrambled from their pallets, dressing as they ran for their horses. They were fighters who slept partially dressed. It was normal for them to be ready on short notice.

The clan leaders listened to Malcolm's information calmly, but the instant he'd finished, they began organizing their men and weapons with deadly efficiency. The Scots had been successful in the past with their surprise ambushes against the larger and better-equipped English. While the warriors prepared, the lairds discussed strategy. In the end, it was decided not to make a move until the English cavalry was well into the camp. While the English archers and foot soldiers milled about in the thick forest, the Scots would launch their attack, leaving the English mounted warriors without any back-up to support them.

Hamish explained the plan to the fighters. "Tis a small area, 'n we're situated 'bove 'em, so their archers 'n foot soldiers'll be useless in the beginnin'. The cavalry'll have to come first." The others nodded. "When they top the bank, we attack afore the others can come from behind to help."

Angus Dunedin agreed. "Aye. Tis the best plan to minimize our losses as well."

Scouts were sent into the forest while the others reported to their fighting positions. Within a couple of hours two outriders returned, informing Hamish that Lord Asheboro and a small group of riders were in the area.

"Don't make any sound or movement. Let 'em ride right into camp if they're that foolish," Hamish ordered. "We'll surround 'em, then hold 'em hostage til the others arrive. The English'll sorely miss the loss of Henry's men. That bunch was one of their best."

The Scots on foot scattered into the forest overlooking the path into the camp. Each man watched his leader for hand signals.

Malcolm's hands itched for the battle to begin.

Asheboro could barely see the trail through the swirling mists. As his company of men climbed the steep grade through the towering forest, horses grunted and occasionally stumbled. When they came into a clearing and the ground became almost level, he signaled a halt, giving them time to recuperate after the strenuous run from Lexington Cove. When the noise of chattering birds and scurrying wildlife overrode the sounds of blowing horses and men, Asheboro's order was whispered down the line. The more experienced of his fighters shook their heads in amazement and disbelief.

"Fan out. When I raise my arm—attack!"

It was a decision Asheboro would regret for whatever time he had left on earth. This was not the well-regulated and orderly battles he had commanded against the French. There the leaders often met in the middle of the battlefield, deciding in an unemotional way, when to begin the carnage. The age of chivalry had led them to believe this attempt at decency put them a rung above the barbarians

The English advanced into the clearing leading up to the battlefield. Leaves and moisture clung to their faces and scratched their eyes. The tired horses slipped and stumbled in the soggy footing. Even though Asheboro could not see what the terrain looked like, he raised his arm to lead the charge.

In the span of a heartbeat, a small band of Scots, wielding battle axes and claymores was upon them. Asheboro's men dropped like fleas from a dead dog. He was grabbed from behind and felt the cold blade of a dagger at his throat.

"What'll it be Asheboro? Death or surrender?" Malcolm snarled.

His face ashen, Asheboro raised his hand again and gave his sword to his conqueror. "Men! Lay down your weapons," he ordered.

There were six dead on the spot and many of the rest were wounded. The English had been so overwhelmed, they had not killed even one Scot nor inflicted any serious injuries.

The area was quickly cleared of most traces of the skirmish. The dead were carried to a shed behind the primitive fort, the wounded were taken to a lean-to, protected on one side by the stables, and the uninjured English were secured in an outbuilding at the edge of the tree line.

The Scottish forces entrenched themselves to await the main English contingent. Some were positioned behind small hillocks and large trees. Others were lodged in trees well above the floor of the forest and out of view of the oncoming English. Archers were concealed at the top of the steep incline behind the lip of the ledge. Behind the archers, Scots on horseback were ready to charge, after the arrows had made the first casualties in the English line.

On that same Thursday morning, Kit was riding through the thick fog, on her way to Morris Glen. She was bringing more supplies for the battle that was scheduled for the following day, Friday, the 13th. As she maneuvered her horse down a slight incline, she heard the sounds of horses thrashing, men shouting, and metal to metal clashing. Although muffled by the heavy air, the unmistakable noise of battle filtered through the woods around Morris Glen. She galloped forward, heedless of the treacherous footing.

She broke out of the forest just as her father's men were hiding the English horses. Their weapons were being passed out among the Highlanders. It gave the Scots a great incentive to fight the enemy with their own weapons.

"Kit! Git outta here!" Hamish yelled. He grabbed the horse's bridle and led it toward the shed where the wounded had been placed. "They've attacked a day early. More comin' behind this bunch." He helped her dismount and saw that she understood the situation. As he departed, he saw Kit walking among the enemy, to see who needed her attention first. Hamish shook his head in bewilderment as he watched her apply a tourniquet to the arm of an Englishman with a deep cut just above his wrist. It seemed so ironic that, once again, Kit's nursing skills were at the disposal of the enemy.

It was just past noon when Edward and his men entered the heavy woods which covered the climb to Morris Glen. Clearing the road of the fallen trees had taken its toll in time and exhausted men. As the climb steepened, his horsemen were slowed by the archers and foot soldiers who led the way. They were fighting their way through thick underbrush in a primordial forest. Low hanging branches slapped their faces, bringing blood. Horses and men slipped in the mud and stumbled over moss-covered stones. The uphill trek seemed to go on forever.

Edward was so engrossed in their progress that he was taken by surprise when the forest became quiet. The birds had ceased squabbling and no small creatures scavenged through rustling leaves. He raised his arm, signaling the entire company to halt, then rode forward alone to assess the situation. He came to the edge of a clearing where the land leveled out. The sod was deeply grooved by the hooves of many horses. Scattered bits of clothing and pieces of leather lay here and there in the grass. Over the brow of a bank, some fifty feet further on, he could see the roofs of buildings. The hairs on Edwards's arms prickled and he was assailed by a sense of urgency.

He turned slowly and motioned his men to retreat. They were at a serious disadvantage since they would have to fight uphill over rough terrain. Edward's fighters were limited by tight space, poor visibility, and terrible footing in the heavy underbrush. The English would have to attack in waves, trying to overcome the Scots with a never-ending stream of fighters. It was a difficult decision for Edward. It meant heavy losses, especially among the first to attack. He would ask no more of his men than of himself.

The lack of a level battlefield made it nearly impossible for Edward to place his fighters in an effective formation. The archers could not see above the steep bank to aim their arrows. Without cover from the archers, the foot soldiers would be at the mercy of the enemy. So, he would have to send the mounted warriors in first, hoping to drive a hole through the Scottish defenses by a full charge into the encampment.

The silence was more menacing than the sound of a hundred bugles. Edward could detect no movement from Morris Glen, nor could he spot even one warrior. His time of indecision was over - he must either attack or retreat.

He raised his sword and roared. "Attack!"

As the English raced their horses across the clearing toward the steep bank, the first volley of arrows from the Scots rained down on bodies no longer protected by armor. Many Englishmen were unhorsed, then trampled by the next wave of riders struggling to clear the overhanging bank. The English archers were rendered useless since their own men were in front of them, closing off any visibility of the enemy. There was nothing to do but continue charging full ahead.

Edward was at the head of the first wave. He rode recklessly, leaping up the embankment and clearing the first line of Scottish archers. On he raced. Battle was so much faster without armor. None of the other English riders were close to him. He was alone in the very heart of the Scottish fighting men.

Three horsemen were on him in an instant. Edward heard one of them yell. "Nay, this man's mine!"

Edward remembered that voice. He was looking squarely into the face of Malcolm MacDougal and knew that *this* time the Scot would not spare him.

# CHAPTER TWENTY-TWO

Hate rips through a soul with the ferocity and speed of a bolt of summer lightening. So it was with Malcolm and Edward. For an instant, the two combatants were etched, like a frieze from a Roman temple, amid the fury of battle that surrounded them. In that fraction of time, between life and death, all the injustices claimed by both sides came to rest in the hearts of Malcolm MacDougal and Edward, Lord of Lexington.

It was not a battle about Scotland's right to rule itself, nor England's desire to conquer and exploit the weaker country. The hatred each carried for the other went no further than their personal vendettas. It was Malcolm's dedication to avenging the deaths of his mother and brother and Edward's determination to protect his mother and sister from a rebellion led by the man who had killed his father, Lord Neville. Both men kicked their horses into a full charge and the struggle began. They fought alone, heedless of the maelstrom encircling them.

The force with which the two horses hit one another knocked both off-balance. But Edward's horse, Rory, was younger, smaller, and inexperienced. Magnet's strength and fearlessness had more than once saved Malcolm's life in battle and today was no exception. The collision knocked Rory to his knees and left Edward hanging off his side, clawing desperately to pull himself upright. In an instant, Malcolm was upon the compromised horse and rider. He drew his arm into the air and with a mighty heave, hit Edward in the middle of his back with the hilt of his sword. Edward's breath flew from his body, taking most of his life with it. He dropped his sword and kicked Rory forward to put some space between himself and Malcolm while he tried to regain his breath and balance.

Edward could feel the heat from Malcolm's horse. It was either turn and fight or get a sword in the back while retreating. Edward turned and faced Malcolm, protecting himself with his shield from the murderous blows that kept coming. Malcolm dropped his sword and pulled his battle axe from his belt. Edward saw the deadly weapon aimed at his head and made a desperate run toward Malcolm with his mace, knowing he had little chance against this seasoned fighter. Malcolm bore down on Edward, driven by hate and the hope that, finally, the MacDougal family would be avenged. Edward's instincts told him that changing tactics was better than a valiant death. He ducked to Rory's side and swerved away from Malcolm's horse just as the two animals came eye to eye. The lethal blow missed the intended mark, hitting Edward's thigh instead, nearly severing the leg just above the knee.

Edward fell to the ground, blood already staining his clothing. He lay still, arms and head akimbo like a rag doll, his life seeping from his body in a slow red ribbon into the tortured earth of a battlefield. Razors of light shot through his consciousness, sealing him in a cocoon of pain. His chest felt as if a band of metal was squeezing his ribs together, until finally all feeling and sound drifted away into a cold silence.

"Campbell," yelled Malcolm, pointing to Rory with his battle axe, "Grab that horse. He's one of ours anyway."

Malcolm spat on Edward's inert body, then rode back into battle.

Oliver had watched the battle from one of the stalls. He felt young and helpless. Hamish had ordered him to stay clear of any fighting since he would be needed to help Kit and Brigit drag the injured warriors into the shed for nursing. The fight between Malcolm and Edward had completely dominated the small area at the top of the steep bank. Oliver was amazed at the ferocity of Malcolm's brutal attack. He appeared to be possessed, as if killing this one Englishman was his only purpose in the battle.

When Edward's horse nearly went down and Edward was knocked to the ground, Oliver knew it was only a matter of minutes before he would be trampled into the mud. He was horrified, for he'd always liked Edward, even if he *had* embarrassed the Scots by escaping.

Oblivious to the uproar around him and unafraid of Hamish's wrath, Oliver ran from the stables, into the middle of the conflict toward Edward. He dodged countless men on horses, not to mention foot soldiers who were now topping the bank. Bodies of the dead and dying were strewn everywhere. Those still able to move grabbed at him as he scrambled past, begging to be dragged away from the deadly hooves. In the muck, it was difficult to distinguish Scot from English.

Edward was finally within Oliver's grasp. As he knelt over the body of his mud-splattered friend, Oliver could see that Edward was alive but losing blood fast. The Lexington shield with its proud emblem lay by his side, dented beyond use by the hooves that had trod upon it. He had to get Edward to the shed. There, Kit and Brigit would have to staunch the blood immediately if the young Englishman was to survive.

He grabbed Edward's collar and began dragging him to the nurses. Within a few feet of the shed, he was knocked into the slimy footing and pinned to the ground by a warrior thrown from his horse. When Oliver recovered from the sudden hit, he realized the man on top of him was either dead or unconscious. He heaved with all the strength in his scrawny body but he couldn't escape from the heavy weight. Then he saw Seth Cullen returning to the battlefield for more injured fighters to carry to the nurses.

"Seth! Help me."

Looking around to see where the call had come from, Seth saw Oliver struggling to get out from under the downed warrior. He scrambled to Oliver's side and pulled him and the injured man he was holding out from under the downed warrior. "Here, ye take 'is feet 'n I'll carry 'is shoulders," Seth ordered. Together, they dragged the unconscious Edward off the field.

"Why're ye wastin' time with this 'un? He's done fer, what with all that blood he's losin'." Then Seth took a closer look. "Damn, Oliver! He's English. Let 'im die." Seth's voice carried no concern for the life of an enemy.

"Twouldn't be right, Seth. Only barbarians leave injured fighters to die on the battlefield. And Scots aren't barbarians. We're civilized!"

Seth shook his head as he helped Oliver drag Edward's body the last few feet. He knew a little more fighting experience would teach the boy just how civilized war was.

Even though the day was wet and chilly, Kit and the other nurses were hot and red-faced from handling a constant stream of injured men. Bodies with broken bones, gaping holes, and severed limbs were arriving in the makeshift hospital. The space to lay them down and bedding to warm them, was fast disappearing. While in the process of bandaging a head wound, Kit tried desperately to remember how many nursing supplies remained at Clan MacDougal, and how long it would take to send a courier for them. From somewhere in the melee, she heard her name.

"Come quick, Kit," Oliver was pleading. "This man's dyin'!"

Brigit took over the head wound as Kit hurried through the maze of warriors to Oliver and the man he and Seth had pulled from the battlefield. He was lying unconscious on the ground with his head propped on a pile of straw and covered with so much grime that Kit could not identify if he was Scot or English. *Doesn't matter anyway*, she thought. *They'd all die if I take the time to distinguish between friend or foe.* Her breath quickened when she saw the ghastly leg wound, knowing this man had little chance of survival.

"Oliver, bring me a rolled bandage." Kit began the staccato orders which would continue throughout the day and into the night. Sometime during the ordeal, Brigit cleaned the man's upper body while Kit's attention was riveted on her patient's leg. She tied the bandage hard and fast just above the bloody hole in the warrior's thigh. "Oliver, while I clean this wound, ye loosen the tourniquet whenever I give the word." She looked him in the eye until his nod assured her that he understood. "Then it'll have to be cauterized. God knows what manner of filth's got into 'is leg."

Kit poured boiled water, which had cooled enough to touch, liberally over the wound. Oliver recalled watching Brigit cauterize MacKenzie's thigh when he'd been kicked by a big draft horse he was shoeing. He would never forget the agonized screams that had ceased only when MacKenzie lost consciousness. Oliver shivered in dread of what was in store for Edward.

With her patient unconscious, Kit took the opportunity to look into the exposed flesh and remove particles of dirt and tiny stones. She repeated this procedure over and over, each time using clean cloths to wash the wound and plenty of water to flush away the filth. This part of the nursing was critical. If even a tiny piece of debris was left in the leg, it could fester and cause an infection that could claim the man's life. Oliver wiped away the sweat running in rivulets down Kit's face. When the cleansing was finally done, the man's head had fallen to one side and only a faint chest movement indicated he was still breathing.

"'Tis time to burn 'is wound now, Oliver. He'll jerk hard so hold on tight!" She looked at Oliver's ashen face. "Let's git Seth to help."

Oliver nodded, then laid across Edward's legs while Seth sat on his chest, securing Edward's shoulders with his own muscular arms. Kit pulled the iron out of the fire and held the glowing cylinder close to Edward's leg. She took a deep breath, shook the wet hair from her forehead, and slowly lowered the red-hot sphere into the hideous wound.

An unearthly roar and a smell like chickens roasting, made

Oliver's eyes water so profusely that he appeared to be crying. But before Oliver could take a breath, the legs he was trying to hold kicked with the strength of a horse, throwing him into the air like a flimsy rag doll. Seth, too, found himself on top of a frenzied man who lurched with the strength of a wild boar, in an attempt to dislodge the body that held him captive to the unbearable pain.

Edward was fully awake now, in a world of agony that went beyond human tolerance. His torso roiled and his hips bucked. Kit laid over the lower half of his stomach and held on. Edward's eyes rolled up in his head, glazed with a film that obscured his sight. He wanted to die.

After several minutes of struggling, the body beneath the three exhausted workers quieted.

"Hold on tight," Kit ordered. "I've gotta do it once more." Oliver and Seth tensed for the struggle to come. Edward's flesh sizzled as the tube penetrated again. Oliver was thrown off, but Seth held firm while Kit completed the cauterizing. Edward's body stiffened, then went limp.

Kit exhaled slowly with the tiniest feeling of success, sat back, and wiped her face with her bloodstained apron. After a moment, she clambered to her feet and walked to the patient's head, which was covered with dirt from his fight to escape the pain. When she turned the man's head toward her to wash his face with a clean wet cloth, her own face froze as the black hair and arched eyebrows of Edward appeared in front of her eyes. Then, as though nothing out of the ordinary had turned her world upside down, Kit stood up and walked briskly to a nurse on the other side of the shed.

"Hilda! There's a patient over by the wall. See to 'im, please.

His leg needs dressin." With that, Kit retreated to the farthest corner of the shed where Ian MacGowan waited for a splint for his broken arm.

Outside, the battle raged on. The English were unable to capture the Scots stronghold and the Scots could not overcome the sheer number of English fighters.

Hamish and his men formed the right flank, defending the lean-to where the Scottish weapons were stockpiled, as well as the building which housed Lord Asheboro and his captured men. It was imperative not to let the English reach this area. Hamish was tiring fast. His voice weakened as he struggled to yell orders. His chest felt as if a large boulder lay on it, and the scene before him gradually became hazy images that moved in erratic paths. With the last of his ebbing strength, he shouted for MacKenzie to take over, then guided his horse toward a clearing where he slid to the ground. His old war horse stood protectively beside him.

Seth dodged between horses, fallen riders, and broken weapons to get to Hamish's side. He shouted at the nearest aide and the two men carried the old warrior to the nurse's shed. As they placed him on an empty pallet, his jaw fell slack.

"Kit!" Seth called. "Hurry. Tis yer pa."

Kit ran as fast as she could through the maze of wounded men lying on the floor of the crowded shed. Hamish was pale, disoriented, and his breathing barely discernible. She felt for his pulse. It was weak and erratic.

"He's gotta be kept warm," she said, as she covered him in wool blankets and began to spoon some strong ale into his mouth. Kit was now oblivious to all the other injured men. She was consumed with her father's survival. Whatever objectivity she'd maintained while attending to close friends and opposing warriors abandoned her at the sight of Hamish struggling to breathe. Her hands were clumsy and her orders unclear.

She beckoned for Brigit. The older woman took over Hamish's care while keeping Kit close by her side. Eventually, when Kit saw some color return to his cheeks and his head move, she was able to regain her composure and allow Brigit to return to the others. Hamish tried to speak.

She placed her fingers on his lips. "Hush, Pa. Rest. Fer once, don't be so stubborn." He nodded weakly, then turned his body and mind over to Kit for safekeeping. "I'll keep my eye on ye while I work," she promised. He closed his eyes and drifted to sleep.

She glanced at Edward's pallet as she left her father's side. His hair was matted with sweat. He groaned. She studied his face, contorted with heat and pain. With a sigh of resignation, she stooped and laid her hand on his forehead. His skin was hot and clammy—yet he shivered under the wool blankets. He was nearing death.

Even though Edward had hurt Kit more than she would admit, she couldn't ignore his dire situation. She examined his leg while Oliver placed cold cloths on his forehead. There seemed to be little hope. Once again, the battlefield was defeating her. For in the unlikely event he did survive, he would lose so much flesh that he'd be left with a limp, if he could walk at all.

She wasted little time lamenting, however. With the determination for which she was famous, Kit decided to fight with every ounce of knowledge she had to overcome the poison that threatened Edward's life. A schedule of cleansing the wound every two hours was set up. She hoped this would dislodge the filth and allow healing to begin. Then, when the torn flesh regained a healthy sheen, the two edges could be scraped to bring a good blood supply to the surface. This would prepare the entire wound to be closed. Strong stitches would be necessary to hold the sides tight enough to adhere to one another.

She sat quietly, watching the occasional twitch of an eyelid and considered what a profound change in Edward's future this day had wrought. At last, the contempt she'd had for him when he had departed the Highlands in such a cowardly way dissolved. In its place was a dispassionate sympathy for a strong young man in the prime of his life, who faced a future with a serious physical flaw. And in Edward's world, impairments of any kind were often looked upon with disdain. One so proud as Edward would find that hard to bear.

"Kit, why 're ye wastin' time on that piece of rubbish?" Malcolm demanded. His voice was filled with hate and disbelief. "I was sure I'd left 'im to die. Our own men need yer help."

She hadn't realized Malcolm had come to stand behind her. Her temper flared. "He's no different'n the other wounded men, enemy or not. That's what nurses 're expected to do, Malcolm!" She turned her attention once again to the terrible wound. "Brigit." Kit spoke without raising her head. "The water oughta be ready now."

Brigit brought one of the many pails of water, that had been boiled, then cooled, to ensure cleanliness. She helped Kit pour the water in a slow stream over the wound. "Looks bad, Kit," Brigit said, shaking her head.

"Aye. Hand me one of them rags over there," Kit replied,

nodding her head at the pouch lying on a stool.

Malcolm watched the two women, amazed at their ability to work so diligently on an enemy warrior. Even though Kit had made it clear that nurses were morally obligated to care for all, regardless of which side of the conflict they represented, Malcolm couldn't resist a parting shot. "He obviously didn't care whether he lived or died, the way he outran 'is own men. He endin' up in our midst, just askin' to be killed. Nay, a soldier he's not. He's a man too ready to die."

Both Kit and Brigit eyed Malcolm as though he were Satan incarnate. He threw up his arms in disgust and stomped off. He'd become head of the clan that day because of his courage, leadership, and ability to kill without question or remorse. He was in no mood to accept the idealism of nurses!

"How soon can I close the wound, Brigit?" Kit asked, wringing out the cloth she had used to dry the surrounding skin.

"When the brown flesh ye now see has sloughed 'n been replaced by healthy red flesh. Even then, tis gotta be done in stages." Brigit stooped and looked closely into the hole. "If ye close too soon it'll seep, 'n ye'll have to reopen. Then 'is chances of survival 're poorer 'n they 're now."

Kit nodded. She dressed the wound, covered Edward with warm blankets, and went to care for the newly wounded as they were brought to the shed.

Throughout the day, Edward wandered in and out of consciousness as his fever gradually dropped. His expression brightened when he was able to sip the broth and nibble the bread Brigit brought him. "Seems like we MacDougals 're destined to nurse ye after every fight ye're in, Edward," she said laughingly. "Ye've said we Scots 're primitive 'n uneducated, yet we've saved yer life more'n once." She took the sting out of her words with a wink of an eye. Brigit had always made Edward feel good.

Hamish had awakened from a sleep that had been forced on him by Kit's special herbs. *I feel stronger,* he thought. *Seems easier to breathe and turn my body.* He was surprised when he realized Edward was lying next to him. Hamish had no aversion to this—he even made an attempt to speak. But Edward was so consumed with pain that he was barely aware of his surroundings. Knowing how deeply Edward had hurt Kit, Hamish was still not surprised that she nursed him as she would a family member. When all was said and done, Kit was a care-giver, unable to withhold help from any injured creature.

Kit came to Hamish when she realized he was awake.

"Will he be alright?" Hamish asked, nodding toward Edward.

"He's doin' fine fer someone who nearly lost a leg. He's young 'n strong. I think he'll live if we can keep 'is leg from festerin'." She felt Hamish's forehead and checked his pulse.

"I'm almost ready to git back into battle," Hamish said, with a grin and the hint of a twinkle in his eye.

"Ye can ferget 'bout ever goin' into battle 'gain, Pa," Kit stated, with a finality that would not be challenged. "Yer heart's tellin' ye that its got no strength fer more fightin'. There's 'nough already dead, 'n ye don't have to add to that count by bein' foolish."

Hamish took her hand in his. "Never thought this time'd come fer me. Figured I'd always be a warrior—never condemned to live among the elders." He rested a bit before continuing. "I'm not sorry though. From this end of my life, plannin' strategy looks a lot better'n bein' the leader out in front of the fighters."

Kit squeezed his hand lightly then stood up. "I wish there was no need fer either of those skills." She wiped her hands on her apron and hurried to the next pallet, where the patient had an arrow protruding from his shoulder.

Throughout the day the fight continued. Neither group gained an advantage and casualties were high on both sides. While the English had more fighters, they were ineffective in the cramped space that led to a bottleneck where the Scots were in control. And the Scots could only hold the English warriors where they were, because there were too many English for them to overcome completely.

The sun dropped below the horizon and nightfall brought a heavy, cloying fog, chilling bodies that had hitherto been sweaty. Stiff fingers had trouble holding onto equipment, either to mend or clean. Feet grew numb inside wet boots. Despondency hung over both camps, like the cape of a dead soldier slung over his horse. No one looked forward to morning and the return to conflict.

Lord Asheboro and the survivors of his ill-fated charge had listened throughout the day to the sounds of battle. Some had stood on the shoulders of others and peered between the wall and roof, trying to observe first-hand which side was winning. But it was hard to tell since their view was obscured by other buildings and trees. When evening brought a lull in the fighting and it was clear that the battle would not be renewed until morning,

Asheboro decided to make some demands. He pounded on the flimsy door, nearly tearing it off its rusty hinges, in an attempt to get the attention of the guards.

"You out there! I insist on being taken to your clan leader. I am the commander of the English. Procedure dictates that I have an audience with whomever is in charge of the Scots."

The guards ignored the ultimatum. More pounding and yelling ensued. Finally, tired of the commotion and fearful for the security of the door, one of the guards shouted angrily. "Quiet! I'll see what I can do."

The noise ceased and Gordon went off to find Malcolm, who was walking slowly through his troops assessing the losses.

"Malcolm! Asheboro wants a word with ye. Otherwise, they'll smash the door 'n we'll have to round 'em up again."

Malcolm looked up, lines of grime and worry marred his youthful face. "Tell 'im I'll be there when my men 're taken care of 'n not afore. If he keeps on causin' a ruckus, tie 'im up so tight 'is hands go numb." Gordon nodded and returned to his watch.

Malcolm walked toward the stables to see how many horses had been lost and how many were wounded beyond use. He'd thought himself impervious to the casualties of war, able to withstand losses in a calm and sensible manner. But having just witnessed the dead and injured men of his own country and knowing how many wives and children were now without husbands and fathers, Malcolm rued his former heartlessness. So many faithful horses would have to be put out of their misery. Several of his men had been wounded and maimed so badly that they'd be unable to support their families. He was sick at heart. For the first time in his young life, Malcolm felt the responsibility and consequences of leading men and animals into battle. It was a burden nearly too heavy to bear. *How has Hamish dealt with such a heavy load for so many years?* Malcolm wondered.

Late that night, Malcolm arrived to see Asheboro. "What do ye wanna talk 'bout?"

Asheboro spoke imperiously, "At this rate, no one on either side will be standing when this is over."

"Aye," replied Malcolm. "What's yer point? I've little time."

Asheboro bristled at Malcolm's off-hand manner. "We should negotiate terms to end this battle. It looks like a stalemate."

"What'd ye mean, a stalemate?" Malcolm roared. "I don't see it that way. Yer men 're the ones in the woods who can't go forward or back. But we Scots can git outta the weather, 'n return to our camps fer supplies."

Malcolm hoped Asheboro believed the part about the English being trapped in the forest. He, too, wanted to stop the battle. But only with some concessions. And that meant money, rather than terms. Malcolm knew the English could not be trusted to live up to their treaties.

"MacDougal, be reasonable," Asheboro wheedled. "You don't have enough men to keep us trapped in the woods. It's just a matter of time before reinforcements come to our aid."

"That might be", Malcolm answered, "but ye'll be long dead by then."

Asheboro's face whitened. He knew Malcolm would kill them and leave their bodies to rot where they lay, rather than surrender to new English troops. The Scots would then melt into their infernal Highlands, like they always did, leaving no trace of their whereabouts. Asheboro tried again. "What would it take for you to discuss a truce?"

"Money," Malcolm replied, without hesitation.

"We don't carry money on a military campaign."

"Yer fastest courier could be to the estates 'n back 'n three days. Tis that or face the hangin' tree. And ye'll be the first to hang!"

"How much?"

"Five thousand pounds."

"Preposterous, MacDougal. And you know it."

Nodding his head, Malcolm continued. "Yer sorry hides aren't worth that much fer sure. But that's my offer. The money'll buy yer life. Take it or leave it."

"I must confer with the others," Asheboro said. "We'll decide if this is possible." Asheboro walked toward the back of their prison, pulling his sweaty tunic away from his back. "We'll have an answer by dawn."

Malcolm strode off, leaving Asheboro and his men with no doubt that the Scots would kill them without a second thought.

Before sun-up the next morning, Asheboro sent for Malcolm. "You have your deal. We're willing to send couriers to our estates for the money. I'll travel with the riders to make certain the landowners know the demand for money is authentic."

Malcolm's raucous laughter resounded through the camp. "I don't think so, Asheboro. In fact, if the money's not back by late afternoon on Sunday, ye'll be hanged in front of yer men. Give yer signet ring to yer best rider. That should be 'nough authenticity fer the families."

Asheboro hesitated no longer. He ordered two riders to travel as fast as the horses could go without collapsing. Along with his ring, they carried orders that each family was to immediately send its fair share of the money. Otherwise, the English community would be filled with widows and orphans.

The next two days dragged on with no improvement in weather or tempers. Both English and Scots prayed for the couriers to have a successful journey.

# CHAPTER TWENTY-THREE

First a shadow, then warm breath fell on Edward's face. His eyelids were crusty and sore. He forced them open, meeting a pair of green-flecked eyes that bridged the gap between death and the will to live. His hand was clasped and held to a cheek that was smooth and cool. A body lay so close to his that he thought he could feel a heartbeat. Edward fought to unite his soul to this other being - to save himself from returning to the dark chasm of pain. He gazed into those eyes without blinking.

Kit felt Edward's grasp strengthen as he gained energy from her. "Ye'll live, Edward," she whispered. There was recognition and trust in his eyes. "I gotta close the wound now. 'Twill be painful." He nodded, then turned his face away. She cupped his jaw and pulled him back around. "Tis the last of it, Edward." His body slumped as he surrendered to the suffering soon to come.

She knew it was deceitful to tell him this would be the end of his suffering. Assuming an infection did not set in on his trip back to Lexington Estate, this was just the beginning of a long recovery which would be fraught with agony. However, allowing the wound to remain open any longer brought with it the risk of further contamination from the filth that lived in every crevice of a battleground. She looked over her shoulder to where Brigit was standing.

"Brigit, bring me the needle 'n thread to close this wound, please." She turned back to Edward's ashen face.

He saw the compassion in her eyes. Edward realized how brave she was to work at putting back together the men that battles had torn asunder. It must seem futile to Kit and the others who attended wounded warriors. To them, healing meant that a man could fight again—until the unlucky time when a nurse could do no more.

Edward nodded for her to begin. She hoped her years of practice would steady her hands as she closed the wound on this man—an enemy, who lay close to her heart. She prayed that he would, indeed, recover as she had promised. Brigit knelt beside her with the thread and needle which had been cleaned in boiling water.

Kit studied the large hole in Edward's thigh. It was wide, deep, and nearly to the bone. Yet the flesh was healthy and red, with no sign of sloughing. A large part of muscle had been damaged and only time would tell how much the cavity could refill. It needed to be closed in stages, allowing the opening to become smaller. She could only stitch together about one-third of the injury now, because that would stretch the skin to its limit. Edward lay still, his eyes never leaving her face as she worked.

Within half an hour, her hand muscles cramped with the strain of the tedious work. Brigit wiped the sweat that covered Kit's brow and slid into her eyes. The sounds of suffering soldiers faded into the background as she threw all her strength and skill into the task of joining the edges of Edward's wound. When her fingers were only capable of jerky motions, she knotted the stitching off and laid her hands in her lap.

"If the flesh remains healthy, I can finish this in two days," she said to Brigit.

Edward closed his eyes, took one of her wrists, and pressed it to his lips. Kit made no move to pull from his grasp.

It had taken more concentration than Kit had believed she possessed, but her work that morning had just begun. The shed was filled with other patients needing her attention. She called Clare to clean Edward's wound and offer him some broth. Then she went to her father's side.

After a night of uninterrupted sleep, once again accomplished by Kit's herbs, Hamish's eyes were alert and his breathing almost normal. Even so, he was still very weak and had to be supported in order to stand up.

Hamish had watched Kit as she'd worked on Edward's leg. He'd had no idea his daughter was capable of rebuilding injuries of such severity. He wanted Edward to live, if only as a testament to her wondrous nursing abilities.

The time spent waiting for the couriers to return allowed healing and regrouping for both sides. Although no words were spoken, no one wanted to restart the battle. The men were weary of the fighting and longed to return to their families, taking their dead and injured with them.

It was well past noon on Sunday and the deadline was fast approaching. Henry Asheboro paced the floor in his cramped quarters, knowing Malcolm would be true to his word. *He* would be the first of the men to hang. The English had witnessed the hatred of the Scots. They feared the retaliation that would be exacted upon them in the event the deadline came and went.

*What's taking so long for the riders to get the money back to Morris Glen?* Asheboro wondered. *The women will pay dearly for the return of their husbands and sons. Perhaps the messengers have lost their way. Or worse, maybe they've been set upon by road bandits.* He ignored the dark looks of his companions and prayed they would soon hear the sound of galloping horses.


Malcolm stood in front of the stables, watching as the sun reached its zenith, then began its descent to the horizon. No sign of the couriers. He paced back and forth in front of the stables with hands clasped behind his back. *Now I must keep my word and kill those wretched men,* he thought. While Malcolm had no qualms about killing the English he so hated, he wanted the money more than any satisfaction gained by their deaths. He looked into the distant trees, hoping for the sight or sound of arriving horsemen. Hearing nothing, he proceeded to where the captives were held. The two guards stood aside for him to enter.

"Asheboro, it seems ye 'n yer men aren't held 'n very high esteem," Malcolm announced. "There's no sign of the men returnin' with the ransom, 'n the sun's gettin' low in the sky."

"See here, MacDougal! It was impossible to make that long journey, collect the money, and get back within three days. Surely you don't intend to murder us without giving us a bit of leeway."

"Leeway is it Asheboro? When did ye English ever give leeway to the Scots?" Malcolm snarled. At Asheboro's silence, Malcolm continued. "Aye, that's right. Never. And yet ye ask our favor." He let out a mirthless laugh. "However, I want the money more'n yer worthless hides. I'll wait 'nother hour, no longer." He turned on his heel and left without a backward glance.

Asheboro sat down heavily on the only bench in the room. His gout pained him mightily and, as he had since his capture, he pondered how an Englishman of his station had come to such a predicament. While he was confident that ultimately the English would prevail, Asheboro faced the probability that *he* would quite likely be dead at the hands of Malcolm MacDougal before any English assistance reached Morris Glen.

The others imprisoned with him stared dejectedly at the floor. Thomas Saunders wheezed in the corner, a condition that always beset him when he was under duress. Charles Caldwell had wet himself and Jerome Liddy tried unsuccessfully to keep from sniveling. All of them remained in a state of terror for the rest of the afternoon, praying that the riders would miraculously return with the money before the unreasonable Malcolm hung them all.

The sun's shadows played into the afternoon. As Malcolm walked to the building which housed the captives, it occurred to him that leaders should think through decrees very carefully. Otherwise one could be put in precarious positions. He had vowed to kill Asheboro and his men by sundown Sunday. But it was only three days after a battle in which both forces had suffered greatly. No one on either side wanted further killing. Only in the heat of battle or long *after* a fight, were executions a cause for celebration.

Unfortunately, Malcolm's reputation as a leader obligated him to follow through with his ultimatum. This would not be the last time a hasty decision would cause him to suffer through unpleasant consequences he had not considered. Practicing restraint in war can be made difficult by the hot fire of imprudent decisions, and Malcolm's period of apprenticeship as a leader had just begun. He unbolted the door and faced his hostages. His silhouette, illuminated by the muted sun behind him, gave the English prisoners the impression that the Devil himself had arrived to collect their worthless souls.

"All of ye, out!"

The prisoners stumbled outside and were led toward a large oak tree with many heavy ropes hanging from its sturdy limbs. Malcolm noticed his own men milling about, staring at their feet and loath to take part in any further bloodshed, even as spectators. Seth excused himself to go assist the women with the wounded. Oliver had returned to Clan MacDougal for more nursing supplies and food. Malcolm felt like a villain, not the hero, of a people maligned by the English.

Suddenly Donovan MacCorkle, an outrider posted to watch over the camp, came galloping through the underbrush. "Hold up, Malcolm," he yelled. "Rider comin' in without a weapon, 'n carryin' a white flag." Without exception, the entire group heaved a sigh of relief.

"Wait!" the courier shouted, as he burst from the trees and up the embankment. He threw a packet at Malcolm's feet. "Four thousand pounds! Daniel will bring the remainder within the hour."

Monday morning broke bright and crisp, with the promise of a soft sun to warm the warriors as they began the arduous trek back to their homes. The dead were swathed in tight bindings, to be transported to family plots for burial. The wounded were being situated on litters.

Kit sat beside Edward, waiting until his horse, Rory, was fitted with a stretcher. He held tightly to her hand. There were no secrets between them now. He pulled her close, not caring that they were surrounded by both English and Scottish survivors. She molded her body to his as her arms climbed up around his shoulders, mindful not to jar his bandaged leg. His beard scratched her cheek. Her breath tickled his ear. For this moment, both ignored any allegiance they felt toward their personal heritage.

It was an embrace that embodied a lifetime commitment, even though it was a union that could never be. Long past any bitterness, they faced the realities of their different worlds. Nothing could ever destroy the love and respect that had developed between them during their struggles together. In a few short months, Edward and Kit had weathered tribulations that normally took years of married life to negotiate. This precious time would be the intangible thread that would bind them together. Later in their lives, when distance and spouses strained the limits of daily coping, this thread would become a bright memory, which, regardless of any rejections each might suffer in the future, would remain the one splash of color, deep within their souls, that no one could touch.

Kit was drawn to Edward's lips as the moon draws the tide to shore. The fire in that touch released a passion that would last for her lifetime. Their lips parted and their breath traversed between them, leaving a part of each in the chest of the other. Edward refused to loosen his hold, unwilling to give up this woman he now loved more than his blood family. How could he possibly return to England to marry another?

"I cannot leave you, Kit. I will not cast aside this happiness."

She touched her fingers to his lips. "We must. Today, this love is our highest flame. But in the harsh light of tomorrow, I'd not fit into yer world any more'n ye'd fit into mine." Edward shook his head, but she interrupted before he could speak. "Our love's perfect now. Draggin' it through our judgmental families would only destroy its beauty, 'n leave us lookin' 'cross a void too wide to be bridged by passion. I couldn't bear fer that to happen." Edward could not argue with her wisdom.

Brigit took Kit by the elbow and lightly pulled her up. "The litter's ready fer Edward now," she whispered. "And Seth's here to help git 'im situated."

"Aye," Kit answered, holding her tears tightly beneath straining eyelids. As Edward was lifted onto the stretcher, she touched her mouth to his lips. "Git well, my love." He tried to hold on to her. "Please Kit, I love you so much." But she slipped from his grasp, turned, and walked away—unable to watch him leave.

As the sorry line of English fighters made their way down the steep hill toward home, Kit watched from behind a large oak tree that shaded the stables. Edward's recovery was still tenuous, but she was confident he would receive the best of care once back at Lexington Estate. His wound had begun to heal and she had closed all but a small opening to allow for drainage. "In time, he'll fergit the Highlands 'n me," she said softly. "Can I ever fergit him?"

Edward struggled for one last glimpse of her before the descent began. He spotted her under the tree, looking at him. *I shall remember her this way,* he thought. "Farewell, Kit," he whispered. "There will never be another like you."

# CHAPTER TWENTY-FOUR

*Six months after the battle at Morris Glen*

The wind gusting across the meadows and into the portico door of Lexington Estate, blew the words of the angry dissenters back into their faces.

"What do you mean you're going off to the Highlands again?" Lady Anne shouted. Something she rarely did. "What could possess you, Edward?"

"I've told you before, Mother. I must return and decide for myself what my true feelings are for Kit MacDougal."

Gwen chimed in. "What possible feelings would you have for an uneducated woman, living in a godforsaken place, who wormed her way into your heart simply by nursing you back to health." Lady Anne nodded in agreement.

Edward turned on them, his hands straight out in front as though to stop the two women from coming closer. For a moment, the only sound was the wind whistling through the oak trees that lined the carriage sweep.

"I thought you and Agatha Winslow were nearly ready to announce your engagement. Why would you want to spoil that by making a trip to Scotland?" Lady Anne continued, her composure reclaimed and her words quiet, in an effort not to give the staff any more to gossip about than they'd already heard. Gwen stood behind her mother, hands clasping and unclasping.

"I know it makes no sense to you," he said. "I only know that before any marriage to Agatha takes place, I must see Kit again to know where my heart truly is." With that, Edward limped toward the stable yard where Rory and a pack horse awaited.

Anne and Gwen watched, horrified, as Edward's familiar frame disappeared down the drive and into the land that had nearly cost him his life little more than six months earlier.

Kit watched the man coming up the path and marveled, as she always did, when Thad Tyler came into view. She chuckled as she remembered how he'd sauntered into her life.

*It had occurred just after the battle at Morris Glen and the Scottish clans were on their journey back to the Highlands. So many men on both sides had been wounded or killed. As Kit had watched Edward head toward his home at Lexington Estate, she'd wondered if in the end, he too, might succumb to his wounds. The heaviness in her heart had taken all the spring from her steps. She grieved for the loss of a love that could never bloom.*

*"Why such a face, lass. We won!"*

*Kit looked around to see who owned the taunting voice that had interrupted her misery. She was staring into a smile that blinded her with its mouthful of straight, white teeth. Blue eyes, dancing with an enthusiasm she normally considered belonged only to*

*Oliver, greeted her. His bright red hair, pulled back with a leather thong, matched the full eyebrows defining the border between his wide forehead above and high cheekbones below.*

*Fat lot of fighting he's done, she thought, what with his face not showing even a scratch.* She was put off by this obnoxious young man and his irresponsible attitude. As if he hadn't noticed the angry look on her face, the warrior, who towered a good six inches above her, fell into step beside her and went on talking.

"I'm Thad Tyler. What's yer name?"

Her quick intake of breath failed to alert Thad that she had no kindly thoughts toward him. There was little recourse but to answer. "I'm Kit MacDougal. And mind ye, nobody won! Everyone loses in a war."

"Aye. Old Hamish's daughter," he replied, overlooking her bad humor. "I've heard what a good nurse ye 're, but nobody told me ye were so bonny."

Kit blushed in spite of herself, making her even more determined to be rid of such a persistent fellow. "I'm exhausted 'n heartsick at the battle we've just been through. I've no reason to be so jubilant." Kit walked faster. Undaunted, Thad sped up to match her strides.

"Didn't mean to upset ye, lass. Just wanted to make yer acquaintance." His voice had lost some of its sparkle.

She felt guilty at having trod on his feelings. "Tisn't yer fault, Thad. I'm always discouraged after tryin' to repair all the wounds men acquire when they fight one 'nother." She looked up at him. It was Thad's turn to be dazzled by her smile. "Will ye be long travelin' home?" she asked, in an effort to be more pleasant.

He chuckled. "Tisn't so far, but with Balthazar lame, it'll take longer'n normal. My family has a small farm on Gordon land."

*Kit was familiar with the Gordon clan north of Berwick, which was not so far from the MacDougal holdings. "Then ye'll be passin' close by us. If Balthazar's none too good, stop 'n have a wee rest with us." With that, she nodded her head, gathered her skirts about her, and hurried to catch up with Brigit.*

*Throughout the winter Thad became a regular visitor to Clan MacDougal. Like an overgrown puppy, he quickly became a favorite of the children. With his spectacular good looks, he'd be an object of lust for the young girls of any clan. However, his eyes were only for Kit.*

On this evening of March 21, the celebration of spring would begin. The tables were set up, drums tightened, and mouth harps tuned. Kit ran toward Thad like a lamb just turned loose from shearing. He grabbed her and swung her high into the air as though she were weightless, making her feel as desirable as any mermaid ever seen off the North Sea shore. By now, she was used to his gusto and childlike manner. She enjoyed someone less serious than Malcolm and more talkative than Hamish.

The Scottish sky, streaked with red tendrils of the dying sun, provided the perfect setting for a Highland festival. Nippy evening air caused old bones to shiver and families to bring out the warmest comforters they had for just such an occasion.

Children chased puppies and threw sticks for them to fetch. The women had prepared fish, fowl, and venison dishes, accompanied by early greens, hot breads, and steaming pies. As twilight deepened, long tongues of fire leapt toward the heavens, adding more merriment to the fest. On the edges of it all, the men folk sat and talked of crops, families, and the coming planting season. Somewhere further away, was the sound of metal hitting metal and boisterous yells of young people as they cheered their favorite players in a game of horseshoes.

Thad stepped behind Kit and enclosed her shoulders within his powerful chest. "Come, lass. There's music 'n dancin' to be done and fun to be had." She turned to face him, squealing with mock indignation as he swept her into his arms and carried her to the meadow, joining a group of rowdy and enthusiastic revelers.

The dancers succumbed to the night. Everywhere, tiny flower buds had popped through the restraining earth, making young people anxious to escape their own constraints. It was a pagan ceremony that unleashed emotions held at bay throughout the cold winter months. A time when lust was blatantly celebrated, rather than hidden under the gentle restraints that were upheld throughout the rest of the year. Sounds of the festival reverberated through the valley, carried to the skies by the bonfires. Kit and Thad were among the most joyous of the celebrants. Her voice mingling with his in a shameless tribute to the season of renewal of life.

Edward's trek had not been easy. His lame leg still pained him greatly, especially when he rode for a long distance. As he got closer to the place where he'd been held prisoner for two months, his heart quickened. He wondered if Oliver would be glad to see him. He was afraid to let his thoughts center on Kit for fear it would put a bad 'spell' on their meeting—like when old Emiline had cast such catastrophe for the English at Potter's Crossing.

In the distance, the first cottages of Clan MacDougal came into view and the smell of the wood smoke prickled his nostrils. He'd forgotten how narrow and rocky the path was. Thinking it best to dismount, he led Rory the rest of the way. Edward saw no one. Even Timmy Campbell was absent from his tree limb where he normally perched, keeping an eye on the comings and goings of the clan.

He came to the Duplin cabin. He hadn't remembered it being so shabby. No flowers or herbs dressed up the sparse grass around what would be considered a hovel in England, and certainly no servants were ready to take care of a horse for a guest. He brushed his forehead to skim away the doubts. They would not be dispelled. Gwen's comments slid through his consciousness. Did he really want to deny his English heritage and allegiance to marry a Scots woman and settle near such poverty? He unsaddled and hobbled Rory, leaving him to graze while he walked slowly into the community.

Somewhere ahead, he heard shouting and saw fires reflecting in the night sky. He followed the sounds of mouth harps and the smell of meat roasting on spits. He topped the hill and stood, looking down at the green meadow he remembered so well. It looked like a velvet ballroom mirrored in the pristine lake below.

This was how Edward remembered Scotland. Old and young alike having a grand time with each other; singing, dancing, playing games, and visiting. All interspersed with ale and an array of food seen only a few times during the year. He scanned the group looking for Kit.

From above the din of it all, he recognized her laugh and followed the sound to its source. She was being flung about with total abandon by a strapping young man with bright red hair and a set of shoulders that could just as easily hoist a young calf.

Edward was engulfed in emotions that tore him to the core. He was filled with a rage so great, that all doubts of returning to 'primitive Scotland' were buried under his determination to repossess Kit from the arms of this giant. He started to run down the hill, immediately floundering in the stones and dirt—unable to do more than slowly bring himself to an upright position. In his haste to get to Kit, the wound he'd suffered at Morris Glen had thrown him to the ground.

He couldn't take his eyes off Kit and her partner. Someday, perhaps, he might run a bit. But he knew he would never be able to toss her into the air then restore her safely to the ground. And he would have to rely on a horse for moving fast. That might not be enough for a young woman with Kit's energy.

Edward turned back to where Rory waited. "These festivities are not for me. I should probably return to Lexington Estate at first light and no one here will be the wiser," he mumbled. *How ironic,* he thought as he limped off. *Lady Anne and Gwen may get their way—but not because it's my wish.*

The next morning, Kit hugged her memories tight to her chest. Life had never been so inviting. She'd wanted the celebration to go on forever. Toward midnight, before Thad had to return to his home, he'd taken her in his arms and for the first time since they'd met, he spoke seriously.

"I doubt it'll come as a surprise that I care fer ye a great deal, Kit." He rubbed her shoulders softly, fingering the weave in her shawl before letting his hands slide down her waist and over her hips. She caught her breath. No one had ever touched her so. He tilted her chin upward and met her lips with his, softly exploring their fullness. She trembled—then nibbled his mouth until it opened and he offered her his tongue. She sucked it gently until she was giddy, then pulled him to her with a naturalness that caught Thad off guard.

He stepped back. "Lass, I'd best take my leave afore things git outta hand."

Kit was inexperienced, but she was aware of finding a femininity she didn't know she possessed. It felt good. Her bosom expanded, outlining taut nipples which strained through her course linen tunic. It was a powerful feeling that was hard to give up. Her eyes glittered.

Thad held her again and buried his chin in her glorious hair. "Would ye think 'bout spendin' a lifetime with me?" She nodded.

"I'll be back Sunday next," he said, then turned on his heel before he lost all control of his aroused body.

"I'll think 'bout ye 'til then," she'd answered, in a breathy whisper.

Nell kicked the side of the barn. Kit let go of her memories and attacked the bright spring day with her usual vigor. She grabbed the pail and headed for the barn. Later, as she carried the pail full of milk back into the kitchen, she thought how her ideas about love and marriage had changed since the battle at Morris Glen. *Edward made me see how wonderful the relationship between a man and woman could be. True, early on I didn't feel the passion for Thad that I'd felt toward Edward. But after last night, perhaps I was wrong.*

While Edward's endearing face would remain with her until the end of her days, her memories of him were a poor substitute for the flesh and blood man who now pursued her heart. Through the winter, she had pushed her feelings for Edward to the back of her mind. Thad's jubilant nature had begun to erode the picture of him, making it fade until Edward was becoming just a pleasant recollection.

Kit was excited about Thad becoming her husband and father of her children. *Our offspring should be the handsomest and strongest of the clan,* she thought happily. Spring has a way of making the young forget a love that's absent. Spring makes all animals appreciate what's close, rather than pine for what's unattainable.

"So much to be done," she muttered. "This daydreamin'll git me behind in my chores." She bustled about, gathering the dirty clothes and collecting all the paraphernalia it took to wash them. A sprig of errant hair brought one hand to her forehead as the other pushed Stripes off the table.

The door scraped open, letting in a breeze that made her hair fall into her face again. She blew it back out of her eyes and leaned over to pick up a crock of breakfast porridge. A loud crash brought her head up with a jerk. The wind had toppled a stool, which hit an earthen pot on the hearth, shattering it into pieces. Stripes let out a screech and jumped under Hamish's old chair.

"Good grief, Malcolm! Why can't ye be more careful?" she yelled. Before more damage could be done, the door slammed shut. Kit looked in the direction of the noise, then fell into the nearest chair like a rock. It was more than the old piece of furniture could tolerate. The legs buckled and it slowly fell to the floor, enfolding Kit within its broken parts.

"Your disposition hasn't changed since my stay here last summer, Kit," Edward said solemnly. "Have you been nursing another wretched Englishman?"

Kit sat in the middle of the broken clay and destroyed chair, supporting herself on her arms, with legs straight out in front of her. Her face was splotched with porridge and her hair had fallen from its clasp, causing it to cling in sticky ringlets along her neck. She spit the porridge and hair out of her mouth while she struggled to her feet.

After looking around the kitchen, that had been spotless not two minutes earlier, she let out a yell that resounded through the settlement. "What're *ye* doin' here?" She stood in the middle of the mess, trembling with rage and wondering where to begin to put things right.

"Yes," Edward muttered, under his breath. "She's the same feisty woman who's trod through my mind and on my heart these many months."

"Why must ye always demolish anythin' ye come close to? God's truth Edward, ye could destroy Edinburgh Chapel with a wooden mallet!" She looked everywhere, except at Edward. Her fingers pushed at her hair, swiped at the porridge, and straightened her apron.

He couldn't take his eyes off her. She was never more beautiful than when chaos surrounded her. He didn't say a word, unless of course, one counted the occasional chortle.

It didn't take long for Kit to overcome her embarrassment and confusion. She was furious with this man, who had put both her kitchen and her heart in complete disarray. She grabbed the broom and attacked, bringing Edward to immediate attention.

He shielded his face with one arm, while deflecting blows aimed at his midsection with the other. He couldn't stop laughing as he stumbled through the rubble-filled kitchen. She ran him into a corner.

"Let's see how funny this is," she threatened, holding him at bay with the broom handle lodged in his stomach. Edward slid to the floor, wiping tears of laughter from his cheeks as he went. Kit went with him, keeping him eye to eye.

It was a standoff. They were face to face, noses nearly touching, eyes throwing sparks as bright as lightening at each other. Kit's jaw jutted forward in a valiant effort to maintain her haughty attitude. Finally, she demanded, "Why have ye come here?"

"To ask you to marry me," he replied loudly.

A silence, so profound that a rose petal could be heard falling, filled the little cottage. Kit tried to digest what she'd just heard. She shook her head, causing a few clumps of porridge to fall to the floor, and tried to explain. "Edward, things've changed."

"I know," he interrupted. "But before you say more, I want you to hear again, that I love you and want to marry you." She stared at him—speechless.

Taking full advantage of her closeness, Edward leaned toward her, took her face in his hands, and kissed her hard on the lips. This was not a shy, exploratory touch, but rather a passionate battling of wills, just as their relationship had always been. The kiss deepened, claiming her mouth, her breath, her very being. She dropped the broom.

"Could we stand up? My leg isn't right yet." Edward massaged his leg to emphasize the point, then pushed himself up by pressing his hands on his thighs. She watched him struggle, belatedly offering her hand.

"But what 'bout yer home, yer. . ."

"I've said my goodbyes. You've shattered any allegiance I have to Lexington Estate and England."

"Edward, will ye cease yer interruptions! I'm tryin' to tell ye, I've practically promised myself to 'nother."

"If that means you've not made a definite commitment, does it also mean I might have a chance?"

"Ye're incorrigible, Edward. Comin' here, confusin' me, 'n tearin' up my house."

Before she could say more, he pulled her into his chest so hard she could feel his heart beating. "Think on it, Kit. That's all I ask. I'll wait at MacKenzie's until you come with your answer."

Before Edward could turn to leave, the kitchen door opened with a bang, again filling the room with outside air. "Kit, when'll the bacon be ready? I can't smell. . ." Looking up, Hamish realized he'd walked into a personal moment that belonged only to Edward and Kit. He closed the door as quietly as he could on his way out.

Hamish met Malcolm on the path to the barn. "Pa, where in God's name's Kit? She milked Nell 'n hour ago. We oughta be smellin' breakfast by now!"

Hamish took Malcolm's arm, turned him around, and headed him back down the hill. "Kit's got a visitor, Malcolm. One I don't think ye'll approve of. Breakfast'll be a little late today. Why don't we go to Brigit's? She's always willin' to feed a couple of hungry, wifeless men."

All afternoon, Kit sat looking at the lake where she'd made all the most important decisions throughout her life. *Why does it all have to be so complicated,* she fretted silently. *Just when Thad made me forget what Edward looked or sounded like, he comes back up from Lexington Estate and turns my world upside down!* She stood up and paced back and forth, then sat down again beside Freckles, the old yellow dog who was always at her heels. She scratched between his ears and spoke softly into the breeze that ruffled the grass at her feet. "Life'd be easy with Thad," she said. "He's a Highlander, 'n hardy 'nough to care fer me 'n our bairns in whatever nature throws our way." Freckles grunted and settled closer to her foot. "He'd not be an embarrassment to family or clan. He's strong as an ox, easy to talk to, 'n willin' to eat whatever's put afore 'im."

Figuring she'd hit on all the high spots any Scots woman would consider important when choosing a mate, Kit let her thoughts dwell on Edward. "Can't think of many advantages to marryin' up with an Englishman, Freckles." The dog snored and his paws began to quiver. "Both our families'd disown us. We'd have to live by ourselves. And I don't think Edward can accomplish any manual labor without servants. Sooner or later, he'd wanna return to 'is life 'mong the gentry, where I'd never fit in."

Having thought it all through, she clambered to her feet and went to meet Edward in MacKenzie's shed.

"Ye must be outta yer mind!" Malcolm yelled, when Kit told him of her decision. "How I wish the man'd died of 'is wounds at Morris Glen." He strode out the door to wear off his rage and resentment with work. Kit bowed her head and stood by the window, watching her brother storm down the trail, realizing that by choosing Edward as a husband, she was losing her brother's love.

Hamish sat silently in his favorite chair, worried about the sadness that lay in Kit's future. "He doesn't mean 'is words, lass. Tis only the shock of it that brings such venom from 'is mouth."

"I wish that was so, Pa. But I fear the hate Malcolm harbors in 'is heart fer this match'll never leave." She gathered up her skirts, pulled the milk pail from its peg on the wall, and headed toward the barn to begin her morning chores.

"I refuse to attend such a travesty!" Lady Anne wept as she yelled at Edward, her face mottled with disbelief and fury. "Marry if you must, but you'll do it without my consent or presence." She turned and walked away, back stiff and expression unchanged.

"She'll come around, Edward," Gwen said, with a worried look, first at her departing mother, then into the distressed face of her brother. "I know she will. In any event, I'll be there to watch and represent the Lexingtons."

Edward hugged his sister with more emotion than a man should show and laid his chin on her shoulder for several minutes before letting go. "Gwen, I knew this would not be easy, but never did I think Mother would be so adamant. I love you for not condemning me for marrying the woman of my life, even though she is Scottish."

Brother and sister clasped hands and walked toward the stables together. They knew that this marriage would cause the couple to be ostracized in both the Scottish and English communities. Gwen also knew that Edward's decision to sacrifice his elite position in order to be with Kit would never change. For her, if it meant accepting a Scottish sister-in-law to keep the relationship with her brother, so be it.

# EPILOGUE

"Hurry Kit or ye'll be late fer yer own weddin'," admonished Brigit, as she looked in the bedroom where Kit was being assisted by Clare. It was a luxurious fall day at Morris Glen. The sour winter grass had not yet appeared, the apples and pears were at their juiciest, and the last of the summer flowers peeked around the edges of the meadow. A cacophony of frogs, birds, and bees performed their symphony in this outdoor cathedral.

Kit gazed through the window overlooking the new face of Morris Glen and remembered its transformation. Edward had agreed that somewhere between their respective homes would be the best place for them to live. That place was Morris Glen. Where once a battle raged, velvety grass now sprayed forth like a carpet for the gods.

As though it was yesterday, the memory of short tempers and terse words followed her as she began her descent to the ground floor, on the way to be with her groom.

*"Damn!" she'd yelled, when she mashed another finger with the mallet she was using to fix a shutter on the wattle and daub structure. "I hate these wretched pegs that don't fit the holes," she howled, and sucked the injured finger.*

*"Kit, if you didn't insist on hitting so hard you wouldn't get hurt so often. I have no trouble at all," came Edward's superior male voice, from somewhere on the other side of the house.*

Now, on her short walk to the spot where she and Edward would become husband and wife, Kit recalled the most difficult task she'd had to do. It was telling Thad that she intended to marry Edward. He'd ranted and raved, wondering why she wanted to attach herself to an Englishman. A crippled one at that! She'd remained quiet while he let his fury run its course. Then she'd embraced him in a sisterly way and promised he'd find a woman better suited to his nature than one known for her temper and lack of patience. In the end, he'd returned to his home, and while many a woman had hoped he'd find favor with another MacDougal lass, he stayed within the Gordon lands and wed one of their daughters.

The sun was warm enough that no one had to bundle up in heavy clothes. While Kit and Edward had been afraid this ceremony might never happen, some of the family members, on each side, had prayed for anything that would stop it. Thus, it was an odd and tense mixture of people milling about the old homestead.

When Lady Anne finally accepted the fact that there was no ultimatum she could threaten that would dissuade Edward from marrying Kit, she'd reluctantly agreed to make the trip. Gwen had been elated. She was amused when Mildred and her assistants began packing clothes, cutlery, and china, as well as foodstuffs that would not spoil during the journey into the mountains.

"Goodness, Mother," Gwen said, with a laugh, "we're not going to a place totally bereft of amenities."

"I'll believe that when we get there," came the brusque reply. "We'll be lucky if we're not all killed by thieves somewhere along the way. Why he wants to live in such an inaccessible area, among such primitive people, is beyond my comprehension." Anne then packed a silver candelabra carefully within a woolen bag.

When she was certain they had enough finery to properly represent the Lexington family, the impressive caravan set forth. Lady Anne, Gwen, and two maids were in the first carriage, followed by Mildred and Orville in a large wagon with all the provisions. Several landowners and friends, who wanted to honor the memory of Lord Neville, had added their crested carriages to the group traveling north. The last coach in line was driven by Ned, who would stand as attendant to Edward.


At the MacDougal household, it had taken all of Hamish's influence, plus some threats, to convince Malcolm to attend the wedding. Hamish wanted no rift in the family that could ever cause Kit and Edward to not allow their children to mingle with their MacDougal relatives. Malcolm growled at the thought of a niece or nephew who would be half English. Nevertheless, he promised not to cause dissension. But he vowed to be conveniently away during any other time he might have to come in contact with Edward. He hoped that, eventually, the union would dissolve and Kit would return to Clan MacDougal. This would allow Malcolm the opportunity to influence any children she and Edward might have had.

Hamish had watched Edward and Kit as the two had worked to make Morris Glen into their home. They were so absorbed with each other, that any disapproval around them went unnoticed. Few people Hamish knew were ever blessed with such a love. More often, couples compromised in order to have someone to grow old with. He prayed that someday Malcolm would find love like this and not a diluted substitute. Perhaps only that would wash the bitterness from his stone-cold heart.

It was a difficult time for everyone. Mildred and Orville sat quietly under a tree. She twisted her fingers while he kept wiping the sweat from around his neck. Both wondered if this Scottish woman would be a good wife for Edward. Mildred wished both Colin and Enid could be with them today. Maybe somehow, Edward's marrying a Scottish woman would have satisfied Enid's mind and given her some peace. She felt sad for Edward. He was heartsick that Colin was not there to share in his wedding ceremony. This was more important than all the games they'd ever played or battles they'd ever fought together.

Ned leaned against an outbuilding, absentmindedly chewing on a pine twig, wondering where Colin was and what he would think of this wedding. Ned had noticed Malcolm, the bride's brother, and realized that the hate in his heart would never abide this union. He was glad that a man such as Malcolm was not a factor in *his* life.

Brigit and Clare bustled about the kitchen and carried food to the long tables set up to serve the guests. The Lexington damasks and candelabra accentuated the wondrous array of food seldom seen in the Highlands: beef, pork, lamb, fish, and wild game.

Sweets of every description taunted the youngsters, so that Scots and English alike took turns sneaking goodies when the adults weren't looking.

Hamish studied Lady Anne and Gwen. Anne's gown was silk lavender brocade, while Gwen was breathtaking in a light blue silk. Both wore fashionable shoes with pointed toes that made Hamish uncomfortable just looking at them. Anne's headdress was an elaborate concoction, that made him wonder how it had been brought so far without damaging the fabric and frame. Anne and Gwen seemed ill-at-ease in this mountainous region. Looking neither left nor right, their feelings of distaste were mirrored in their eyes. It was clear to Hamish, that fear of losing Edward's love was the only thing that had dragged them into this wilderness.

Malcolm stood stoically by the fence, adamant in his desire to disassociate himself from this wedding. His fists clenched and unclenched until his fingernails made marks on his palms. With a face full of shadows and his mouth in a scowl, he refused to look at the bride and groom. In fact, only the frailty of his father's health had made him watch his beloved sister marry one of the hated English gentry.

The residents of the two communities sat in groups, opposite one another. Conversation was hushed - no laughter or joking. Only Oliver seemed happy for this day. He was devoted to both Edward and Kit and was never comfortable when they were at odds with one another. His body was scrubbed until it was nearly raw, and he'd cajoled Brigit into washing his best set of worn-out clothes.

As Hamish scrutinized the gathering, he realized that what should be a joyous celebration of love and hope, was fast becoming a sullen debacle. Acutely aware of his own loneliness and desire for a soul mate, he prayed for the wisdom to rescue them all from so much hatred, if only for this one day. With all the bravado he could muster, Hamish picked up his mug of ale and strode to the middle of the two camps.

"Let's toast Edward 'n Kit." His voice was strong, like the commander he was. "Not just fer their love, but fer their courage to defend this love. To face the animosity on many of the faces I see today, on both sides of the path."

All eyes were riveted on this normally taciturn man. Hamish paused, took a swig of ale, and continued. "How many of us'd give our lives to feel such love fer 'nother. And how many 'mong us'd guard that love against antagonisms put in place long afore they were ever born." Hamish scanned the group slowly, surprised and a bit embarrassed at his defense of this union. His eyes tore into their souls. . .making them feel naked and mean-spirited.

Few could hold his stare - looking at their feet instead. Ned squatted with his arms resting on his knees, crumbling a piece of sod between his fingers. Gwen coughed nervously and smoothed an imaginary wrinkle in her gown.

Lady Anne twisted her lace handkerchief. Then taking a breath so deep that it seemed to add several inches to her height, she walked resolutely to stand beside Hamish. She felt like a traitor to her people. But as the representative of Edward's family she must show as much grace as Hamish had. A few breathless moments passed. All eyes on both sides looked, first at each other, then at the two enemies now standing together in the center of this unlikely group. Quietly, Lady Anne raised her hand alongside Hamish's, faced him squarely, and nodded her head in approval of his words. The hard glint of revulsion in her eyes was visible only to Hamish.

Malcolm toyed with a pebble under his foot. In his mind, this marriage had taken the Highlanders' struggle for freedom out of the realm of possibility. Who, in the Lexington or MacDougal families, would now be willing to join a fight that would mean killing people who had relatives on both sides of the conflict? He scowled, straightened his shoulders, and tried to accept this preposterous situation as best he could.

The rest of the guests began to talk in low tones, as they watched Lady Anne accept Hamish's arm and walk among the visitors, greeting and welcoming all to this idyllic place. For this day, animosities were forgotten, and all thoughts dwelt on the couple who were about to join their lives forever.

Crashing sounds from a nearby barn turned all heads abruptly toward the stable. A colt, with its saddle halfway off and bridle reins flying in the wind, bolted down the hill into the throng of people. A frantic Oliver followed in hot pursuit. People scattered everywhere. Ladies grabbed their skirts and ran behind the nearest tree. The men waved their hats trying to slow the runaway colt, who was obviously having a good time eluding his captors and causing mayhem.

"Joker! Stop!" Oliver yelled, as he ran panting and stumbling after the colt. He was holding forth a carrot as an inducement to halt the frolicking youngster. Within minutes, the guests had mingled without a care as to who was English and who was Scottish. The biggest concern was to catch the pesky animal and get the ceremony back on track.

Some men fell in the now soft ground. Those standing helped those who had fallen get back on their feet. The onlookers were soon doubled over laughing at the absurd sight. Tiring of the game, Joker finally stopped under a tree to munch a clump of clover. Oliver sidled up beside him and grabbed the reins.

It was impossible to hold grudges under these circumstances. Soon ale was flowing like a spring flood and dispositions improving by the minute. Hamish actually had to bellow for quiet so the marriage could proceed. He nodded to Lady Anne in appreciation of her support. She acknowledged with a slight lowering of her eyes. It was a shaky truce, but served as the catalyst to knit the two sides together for this special occasion.

The sun sliced through the clouds and showered the bridal path with prisms of color, filtered through a canopy of branches. Edward and Kit walked arm in arm toward the priest, who stood under an enormous oak tree. The couple was flanked by Brigit and Ned, who tried hard to appear comfortable in their new clothes bought specially for the occasion. Ned was self-conscious in his tight brown hose, topped by a medium length gold tunic. Brigit had never worn a new frock in her life. She was so afraid of soiling the lovely yellow gown, that it took a nudge from Hamish to get her to walk forward.

Kit had captured her unruly hair in a braided crown woven with flowers. Her gown of silk was white, shot through with threads of green. The bodice was cut so low that she kept trying to cover her shoulders with a lace shawl, which Clare finally confiscated. The long sleeves came to a point over the top of her hands and the bouquet of fall flowers she carried was tied with gold lace. Unaccustomed to such finery, Kit was determined to walk with elegance, ignoring the stylish shoes that pinched her toes. She was a vision Edward could barely believe was the headstrong Scots woman who had captured his soul with her strength and humor.

Edward missed Colin. With so much happiness in his heart, he wanted to share it with the man who'd been at his side during that first battle, when this entire saga had begun. It was only fitting that Colin should have witnessed the wonderful conclusion now upon them. Perhaps somehow, Colin would hear of this wedding. He would know it could only have happened because the bride and groom were willing to overlook centuries of feuds between the Scots and English to fulfill their love.

It was time for the vows. Edward and Kit faced one another - their devotion reflected in each other's eyes. Edward knew, that for the remainder of his life, there would never be another decision as right as this one. Kit's eyes glistened with a love that no longer had to settle for practicality. She never expected such happiness. She had accepted the fact that people did their best to garner joy in the small pleasures life might occasionally offer. She was unsure why *she* had been singled out to be so special.

Edward walked with a limp, but no one noticed. He took Kit's hands in his and possessed her with his eyes as the sacred words were spoken. Their uncertain future was shrouded in mystery, as all tomorrows are. Today their hearts were bound together for all time. Nothing else mattered.

Ready for the adventure to continue? It is our pleasure to provide a preview of

# THE IN BETWEEN

Book II in the *Highlanders' Legacy* series.

Thought we might whet your appetite for this book which is ready for publication soon.

We hope you enjoy this excerpt and invite you to get this next book in the series!

# *The In Between*

## PROLOGUE

**1420, Near Berwick, The Borders between England and Scotland**

**Mid-July, Windcrest Home**

Colin MacDonnogh ran through the swirling mists following the sound of the dog's frantic barking. It had been a short but vicious squall, not unusual to whip out of the North Sea with little warning. Thunderbolts ripped through the sky making him shade his eyes from the brilliance. The tall wet grass grabbed at his bare feet and pulled him to the rocky ground. He fought to free his hands from the tough weeds, but his arms clutched empty space instead. Salty beads of moisture, part tears, part sweat, burned his eyes and his breath came in raspy spurts. He sat up only to realize he wasn't at the edge of the cliff overlooking the North Sea at all, but rather in his bed at Windcrest with Rex at his side whining.

As he emerged from the agonizing dream, the sharp edges of his memory brought into focus the terrible sight of his sister, Enid, lying broken and dead at the bottom of the cliff. Rex was licking her face, trying in vain to coax her to rise and scratch his itchy back. Colin had gathered her to his chest and rocked her back and forth, wishing it were within his power to restore life to her frail, limp body. Wishing he could undo the years of pain and her final decision to give up. Wishing none of the bloodshed had happened, trapping the two of them into a life of unending controversy with the only answer being yet another senseless tragedy.

He'd built a little pine coffin, and buried her next to their parents in the field close to the sea she had loved so much. Rex sat quietly by as Colin had mouthed words of praise for Enid's courage and prayed to whatever Almighty she believed in for the salvation of her immortal soul. He had honored Enid's rejection of the English by not informing the Kingsleys and Lexingtons of her death until after she was laid to rest. It was the least he could do for her. Somewhere deep within his own spirit, where one believes in the impossible, Colin hoped Enid knew he'd finally understood her point of view. But nothing could erase the reason why she had been the author of her own demise.

Colin forced his reluctant body to descend the steps to the kitchen where he prepared a breakfast of porridge, bread, and ale. He threw the scraps to Rex, packed his saddlebags with provisions for the long journey ahead, and went to the stables for the last time. He closed the barn door tight, crisscrossed it with wide oak strips, and fastened them with wooden pegs. As he stood back and studied this place that had been a part of him for all his twenty-two years, he could still remember the terror of that night ten years ago when his parents had been killed and his life was changed forever.

Now the barnyard was lifeless; empty of chickens scratching, geese squabbling, and Enid's pigeons swooping down from trees. Yesterday all the farm animals, the sheep, pigs, cow, and chickens had gone to Mildred and Orville Kingsley. Even Puss now lived in the Kingsley cottage. *How is it,* he mused, *that this place of such stability for so many years can lose its character in a few short days? Already I can imagine cobwebs and smell the decay. By tomorrow there will be little evidence left that Enid and I ever lived here, and most of the villagers will be glad to put the saga of the MacDonnoghs out of their minds as quickly as possible. We were a wound that Lexington Cove has endured too long.*

Ten years earlier their Scottish parents had been murdered by peasants from Lexington Cove. Margaret and Liam MacDonnogh had worked at the Lexington Estate alongside an old English couple, Mildred and Orville Kingsley. After the massacre of their parents, Colin and Enid had been raised by the Kingsleys and educated by the Lexington's, alongside their own children, Gwen and Edward. Enid had resented every minute she and Colin had spent in the presence of this English family in their misbegotten need to be charitable to the orphaned Scottish children. Colin, on the other hand, had taken advantage of the opportunity. He believed the education offered to him and his sister was the only way to avoid being put to work in the fields, like all the other youngsters born beneath the gentry, and losing their Windcrest home to the English overlords.

Through the years he'd tried, to no avail, to dislike and ignore Edward and Gwen, the Lexington children. Edward, future Lord of Lexington, had attached himself to Colin's side with the determination of a barnacle clinging to a ship's hull. And Gwen made it impossible not to laugh at her pranks and loving hugs Colin tried so hard to reject. As the years went by and his life centered around Lexington Estate and its engaging family, all his resistance had slipped away. While Enid remained aloof, Colin participated in all the Lexington gatherings as enthusiastically as Edward and Gwen. Eventually, he even rode beside Lord Neville and Edward at the head of the Lexington Estate militia.

How he regretted that now. Enid had always meant more to him than anyone else in the world, even though he'd never been able to convince her of that. All she'd ever believed was that, to her way of thinking, Colin had collaborated with the people responsible for the slaughter of her family and ruination of their lives. Over the years he'd given up trying to persuade her that if she could endure associating with the English long enough to acquire an education, they would be able to better themselves and perhaps travel to Scotland one day to find their relatives. Now he faced that journey alone.

Colin's shoulders sagged as the breath left his chest in one big sigh. As he approached the entrance to the little cottage known as Windcrest, he memorized its familiar lines. But it was more than just the house that aroused his recollections. He closed his eyes and let his childhood skitter through his memory one more time. *He smelled the aroma of the delicious soups and stews that his mother, Margaret, concocted with the simplest of ingredients. He saw the colorful bouquets of fresh or dried flowers that always brightened every nook and cranny of the humble dwelling. He heard the enthusiastic voice of his father, Liam, when he'd come into the shadowy little house after finishing the nightly chores. Liam's stories about the family of MacDonnoghs back in Scotland tantalized him still. He remembered his mother as she, too, reminisced about her homeland while she mended a frayed tunic. The children had tried to picture in their minds the wild Highlands and how hard it must have been for the newlyweds to leave kith and kin for a warmer climate in the south.*

Colin sighed, then walked into the house to pack for the journey that would leave these memories behind forever. Rex lay quietly under the table while Colin stocked the saddlebags with cheese, dried pork, bread, and ale.

Within an hour they were on their way and, even though Colin had promised himself not to look back, he couldn't resist one last glance at his childhood home. His massive stallion, Thor, whose fiery red coat matched Colin's own hair, stood patiently as if he knew what a solemn moment this was. Old Jeff, the pack horse, nibbled at the hedgerow which formed the barrier between the barnyard and house. Rex sat on his haunches looking into the mists and sniffing the air for a wayward rabbit.

Nostalgia bombarded Colin like a blowing rain in a summer storm. This small plot of ground, situated in the middle of the chaos that had existed for centuries between England and Scotland, held the most precious and most frightening experiences of his life. Beyond the happiness of his first twelve years nestled in the arms of a loving family, dwelt the awful sight of his parents' mutilated bodies. An act that Enid had witnessed while Colin was doing the nightly barn chores.

Now, Enid too, was gone. If there was to be any future for him, he must unearth the past and recover his soul that lay hidden somewhere in Scotland.

*The In Between*

*Kay Meredith*

# Author Bio

The roots of Kay Meredith's story telling can be found deep in the hills of West Virginia. She entertained both teachers and classmates with her tales of wild places, peopled by riveting characters.

In her first profession, Kay became a world-renowned competitor for the United States Dressage Team. She traveled the globe representing her country with her horses.

But throughout her riding career, Kay knew that upon retirement, she would write historical novels. Always fascinated by history, but disappointed with the way it was taught in school, Kay weaves history in, around, and through her characters, setting, and plot.

Ms. Meredith's first two novels, *Affair at Boreland Springs* and **A Distant Whistle**, relate to events that happened during her parents' lives.

Her **Highlanders' Legacy** trilogy focuses on the struggle in the early 1400s between Scotland and England along the Borders area between the two countries. Kay follows several families and examines how their personal relationships change over time as they interact with one another.

The **Highlanders' Legacy** includes *Shattered Allegiance*, *The In Between*, and *Nobody's Savior*.

Kay Meredith currently lives in Raleigh, North Carolina. Links to all her novels can be found on her website:

*KayMeredithAuthor.com*

# Other books by Kay Meredith

*Affair at Boreland Springs*
ISBN: 978-1-944662-36-3

Available on Amazon at
https://www.amazon.com/dp/1944662367

*A Distant Whistle*

ISBN: 978-1-944662-41-7
Available on Amazon at
https://www.amazon.com/dp/1944662413

Made in the USA
Monee, IL
09 April 2021

65311331R00225